Ant Middleton was the frontman for Channel 4's hit show, *SAS: Who Dares Wins*, among other major series, and a hugely bestselling non-fiction author. Born in Portsmouth and raised in rural France, Ant set his sights on a career in the armed forces and didn't stop striving until he achieved his goal. Over the course of his career he has served in the Special Boat Service, the Royal Marines and 9 Parachute Squadron Royal Engineers, achieving what is known as the 'Holy Trinity' of the UK's Elite Forces.

Also by Ant Middleton

First Man In
The Fear Bubble
Zero Negativity
Mental Fitness

ANT MIDDLETON

COLD JUSTICE

SPHERE

SPHERE

First published in Great Britain in 2021 by Sphere
This paperback edition published by Sphere in 2022

3 5 7 9 10 8 6 4

A CIP catalogue record for this book
is available from the British Library.

ISBN 978-0-7515-8041-9

Typeset in Sabon by M Rules
Printed and bound in Great Britain by Clays Ltd, Elcograf S.p.A.

Papers used by Sphere are from well-managed forests
and other responsible sources.

MIX
Paper from
responsible sources
FSC® C104740

Sphere
An imprint of
Little, Brown Book Group
Carmelite House
50 Victoria Embankment
London EC4Y 0DZ

An Hachette UK Company
www.hachette.co.uk

www.littlebrown.co.uk

To my father Peter, who left us way too soon! Thanks, Dad, for forcing me to self-reflect, to take charge of myself and my mind from such a young age. It's the greatest gift you ever gave me without even realising it. I promise to pass it on for future generations to come! I love you

FARYAB PROVINCE, AFGHANISTAN

SIX MONTHS AGO

It's called Hell Hour.

Every kill or capture mission is the culmination of days, months, sometimes years of careful planning. Intelligence gathering and data crunching and rehearsal exercises and contingency development. But when the clock ticks down to those final few seconds, when Hell Hour begins, only two kinds of soldier know what's going to happen next: fools and liars.

Mallory, who was neither, crawled to the top of the ridge and looked down on the compound, the closest wall barely a hundred metres away. Everything had gone to plan since the Chinook had dropped them ten kilometres south-east of here. It felt like his boots had hit the ground five minutes, rather than two hours ago. He had been the last one out, Westwick and Donno immediately ahead of him in the line. He remembered the whisper of Donno's short, nervous

1

breaths before stepping out into the night. He remembered the deafening chatter of the rotor blades, quickly dropping away until the desert was as quiet as a graveyard at midnight. He remembered the lingering dust kicked up by the rotor wash, that familiar taste and smell overwhelming him. To Mallory, the Afghan dust tasted like combat.

He heard Westwick's clipped voice in his ear, drawing him back to the present. 'How's it look?'

Mallory tapped the button on his radio and spoke at barely more than a whisper. The wind was in his direction, but he didn't want to risk the sentry catching the slightest hint that there was more out here in the dark than the odd wild dog.

'One bad guy, north-west corner.'

He watched as the sentry moved along the interior walkway that ran the length of the walls. He was moving, which meant he was awake and alert. That was the bad news. The good news was that it looked like there was only one of him. Mallory adjusted the focus on his night-vision goggles and studied the man.

From his size and body language it looked as though he was reasonably young, and in good shape. He handled his rifle with easy confidence. Something stuck out about the weapon. Mallory adjusted the magnification on his goggles to take a closer look. He was carrying a US military M4, not the usual antique AK-47. Which meant it had to have been taken in battle. A highly prized weapon, which was more confirmation that this was the right compound.

The sentry paused a few yards from the corner of the building and then started walking again. What had he been doing? Mallory didn't think he could have been communicating with anyone inside. He would have heard a voice at this distance.

He reached the edge of the wall and turned. At once, Mallory saw what he had been doing. He smiled as he spotted the soft red glow of a cigarette.

'Looking good,' Mallory whispered. 'We're unexpected guests.'

He widened the focus on his goggles and surveyed the area, clicking through the different settings.

The compound looked pretty much as it had on the diagrams back at base. Rough, ten-foot-high adobe exterior walls. One main entrance big enough to drive a vehicle through when the steel gate was open. One rear door, heavily reinforced. Inside was a wide courtyard and a nest of buildings. According to intelligence, their high-value target was in the largest of the buildings.

The target had crossed the border from Pakistan at 2.27 a.m. local time three nights before. A positive voice ID was made on a call from his cell two hours later. The next two days he had spent on the move, bouncing between safehouses, making sure he had shaken any surveillance. He would have been spending his time reorganising troops, reaching out to his lieutenants, delivering the next set of orders.

Drone footage confirmed him arriving at this compound eight hours ago. He had settled down, apparently comfortable that his whereabouts were unknown.

He was about to discover how wrong he was.

Mallory broke the silence on his radio again to open the communication wider. 'Everybody in position? Confirm.'

There were four teams of four ranged around the compound at a similar proximity. Each of the teams had a set objective, interlocking goals that would result in the successful completion of this mission.

If everything went to plan.

Mallory could quote dozens of aphorisms about plans going to shit. There was a reason why there were so many. Right at this moment, the one on his mind was from General Dwight D. Eisenhower: *When preparing for battle, plans are often useless. But planning is indispensable.*

He glanced behind him and saw Donno and Westwick had already crawled up to within a few feet of him. The rear man of the patrol, Yorkie, was hanging back, keeping his eyes on the ground behind them. Mallory was pleased. He had barely heard them move.

Donno reached him first. He was tall and wiry, just twenty-two years old, but with a maturity Mallory had found lacking in men twice his age. He caught a glimpse of Donno's eyes and saw fear in them. He could see sweat glistening on the younger man's forehead in the night vision. The night was warm, but not that warm.

'Mate,' Mallory whispered. 'You're good. This is just another one off the network. Be over before you know it.'

Donno swallowed and nodded.

Westwick made the crest of the hill next. He observed Donno, and then shot a concerned look at Mallory. 'Is he all right?'

'I'm fine,' Donno whispered, before Mallory could answer. His South African lilt seemed strangely out of place in the setting, even though Mallory knew his own and Westwick's accents weren't any more at home here.

Mallory took a deep breath in through his nose and out through his mouth. He raised his goggles for a moment and lifted his gaze to look at the jagged black line of the mountains against the northern sky. The stars seemed unnaturally

4

bright in the void – a billion pinpricks of light, each one of them utterly unconcerned with what was about to happen here on earth.

Donno tapped Westwick on the shoulder. 'Let's do this.'

Westwick lined up his rifle.

Mallory lowered his goggles again and waited until Westwick gave a thumbs up to say that he was all set. He sparked up comms again.

'Stand by,' Mallory said. 'Three, two . . . '

Westwick activated his laser sight and a second red dot appeared, a few inches higher and to the left of the red dot on the sentry's hand.

'One.'

Westwick squeezed the trigger.

And Hell Hour began.

NOW

1

BIRMINGHAM, UK

FRIDAY

Suddenly, everything seemed a lot louder. More noise, more flashing lights, more bodies.

Mallory leaned back in his chair and drank the last of his pint, watching the three men standing by the entrance. They were in their early twenties, their brash, overconfident voices occasionally rising above the hubbub. Friday evening, seven o'clock. The after-the-office crowd mingling with the early starters. Probably a hundred people in the pub. A couple of dozen spilling out on to the pavement, braving the February chill in shirtsleeves and skirts. If there was going to be any trouble, he knew it would be started by the three at the door.

An orange-haired glass collector in a black, short-sleeved shirt noticed Mallory's empty and adjusted his route to pass by his table. He picked up Mallory's glass and the one next to him, and glanced at the empty seats around him. The only table in the place with only one occupant.

'Celebrating?'

'Something like that,' Mallory said. 'Quit my job today.'

'Nice one.'

Mallory sat back in his seat and watched the people. A few drinks had dulled his senses a little, but this was hard-wired into him now. Getting the measure of any room he was in, looking for the unexpected. The group of young business suits by the bar. The hen party in the corner on their first stop of a long night. They sounded like they were Irish, going by the occasional exclamations rising above the rest of the voices raised in competition with the pop song that was playing too loud.

It had been quiet when Mallory had walked in here at four in the afternoon, fresh from telling Riccarton where to stick his job. He had sat in the same spot while the afternoon turned into evening and the character of the bar changed around him. It was like a different place now.

He thought about Riccarton again. He supposed the manner in which he had given his notice might cause him problems later on down the line, but it had been satisfying. 'Ever thought about anger management?' had been Riccarton's parting shot. He couldn't know it, but that was pretty much the same thing the military had said when they bid him farewell. Things had come to a head today, but he had known he wasn't a good fit for Riccarton's operation since day one. Which begged the question: what kind of operation *was* he a good fit for?

A roar erupted over by the door. Mallory tensed, straightened in his seat. But it was just the three loud boys greeting two more of their number as they arrived. The first in was tall, broad and fair-haired. Despite the temperature outside, he wore only jeans and a blue T-shirt that was a size too small, with BENIDORM – NORTHBANK LADS 2019 emblazoned on it. On his heels was a shorter, dark-haired guy with a pointed goatee. The plain white T-shirt he wore under his jacket gave no clue to his travel history.

Mallory had already stayed longer than he had intended to. But then, he had nothing else to do and nowhere else to be this evening, so inertia had won out.

One more for the road, he decided.

He got up and made his way to the bar, passing by the gaggle of men in suits and the hen party. He caught the eye of the barmaid.

'Same again?' she asked.

'Always.'

He dug in his pocket for a tenner as she moved away to get a clean glass. His hand came out with a handful of pound coins and some change. He may not have fitted in with Riccarton's business, but he would have to figure out somewhere else he could find gainful employment before the end of the month.

Someone brushed past his back roughly, almost knocking the coins out of his hand. He turned quickly, fists clenching. It was one of the girls from the hen party, tottering unsteadily on her heels. She looked about twenty, maybe even younger. Jet-black hair and purple lipstick. She flinched back and then smiled, 'It's all right, I'm not going to hurt you.' Her accent was well-to-do Dublin. What they call a D4 accent around there.

'Pleased to hear it,' Mallory said, lowering his hands. 'Sorry.' He was more pissed off than he had thought about what had happened earlier.

She waved away the apology. 'You having a good night?'

Mallory murmured something equivocal and turned back to the bar, watching as the barmaid poured his pint.

The Irish girl took the space at the bar next to him and started reading out a long order of different shots and cocktails written on the back of a crumpled receipt in her hand. She stopped and squinted her eyes at something on the list, and then turned quickly to yell a question back at her table. As she turned, the bag around her shoulder clipped a half-full bottle of Becks on the bar, knocking it off. Mallory bent and caught the bottle one-handed on the way down, placed it back on the bar.

'Nice catch,' the barmaid said, returning with his pint. 'And to think I was about to check if you had had too many.'

'It's either too many or nowhere near enough,' he said. He handed over the contents of his pocket and told her to keep the change. Definitely the last one.

He turned away from the bar and saw that his seat had been taken. A group of students had pounced while his back was turned. He shrugged and turned back to the bar, lifting his drink.

The fair-haired guy in the Benidorm T-shirt from the noisy group had squeezed in between him and the Irish girl, who was still waiting for her massive order. He was leaning over her, yelling something into her ear above the music. She looked uncomfortable. When she saw Mallory looking, she raised her eyebrows. A plea.

Mallory tapped the big guy on the shoulder. No reaction. He kept talking. The big guy put a hand up on the small of the girl's back, and Mallory saw her shiver. He put his hand back on the beefy shoulder and squeezed. That got a reaction.

Mr Benidorm turned around, squinting at Mallory. He might just have arrived in this pub, but he had been to a few others first, going by the way his pupils were dilated.

'Give her some space, mate?' Mallory said, making sure to say it with a good-natured tone. He thought about what Westwick would have said: if you can resolve a situation with a quiet word and a smile, that's always plan A. It was worth a try.

Benidorm took his hand from the girl's back and glanced at her, then looked back at Mallory.

'What's it to you?'

Mallory felt his teeth grit together. But he took a breath. 'No need for that. I'm not looking for trouble.'

As he spoke the words, a quiet voice inside his head questioned them. Was that really true?

'Good,' the big man said.

He turned back to the girl. This time, he put his hand on her back and ran it up her spine. A deliberate screw-you. Sorry, Westwick, he thought. Time to move to plan B.

Mallory reached out and grabbed Benidorm's wrist, his thumb and index finger digging into the pressure points on the underside. At the same time, he put his left hand on the Irish girl's shoulder and moved her firmly out of the way. She took a sharp breath and backed off further. She was one of the only three people in the pub who knew what was about to happen.

Maybe two. One of the three still seemed to be lagging a little behind. Benidorm was looking down in surprise at Mallory's hand around his wrist, as though confused about what was happening. Maybe he wasn't accustomed to this part.

13

'Does that hurt?' Mallory asked, barely resisting a grin. This was *his* kind of anger management. 'You going to do something about it? Or just run home and tell your mum?'

Benidorm wrenched his hand away and pulled it back, fist flying towards the side of Mallory's head.

Mallory was ready. He ducked and punched him hard in the stomach. He doubled over and staggered back. Again, more surprise than pain in his eyes.

'Speaking of your mum, you can tell her I was asking for her.'

Benidorm straightened up fast and launched himself forward, rage flashing in his eyes. Mallory sidestepped, caught him and helped him on his way. The big man's momentum did most of the work, sending him crashing into the table the three suits were sitting at. Pint glasses and pitchers overturned, messing up some nice business wear. Someone at the other end of the bar screamed.

Mallory heard a grunt from behind and turned in time to block a punch from one of Benidorm's friends. The one with the goatee. Mallory jabbed him hard in the middle of the face, feeling the nose break. He went down hard, almost taking a bystander down with him as he flailed. Mallory turned to see Benidorm scrambling up from the ruins of the table.

He needed to take this outside.

He moved quickly to the door, the crowd parting before him like the Red Sea. A third man from the group came running for him, brandishing a chair: one of the three who had been in the pub for a while. He was slower and clumsier than his two recently arrived mates. Mallory caught the leg of the chair as it swung towards his head, tightened his grip and used it to launch the surprised assailant gripping the other end towards the door. He crashed out on to the pavement. He was back on his feet to meet Mallory as he followed him outside. Mallory felt the sharp chill of the night air. It sharpened everything up, made everything suddenly feel more real than it had inside the bar.

Benidorm appeared from within a moment later. The broken nose had been enough for the third attacker, he guessed, and seemed to have dissuaded the others from getting involved.

These two would require more persuasion.

Mallory took a couple of steps back, placing himself at the top of a triangle. The two of them circled, fists clenched. Little clouds drifted from their mouths in the freezing air, telling Mallory they were both a little out of breath from the sudden exercise.

Benidorm lunged in first. He had boxing training, looked like he knew what he was doing. Which is fine, assuming everybody is fighting according to the rules. Mallory ducked again and hit him hard in the ribs. He turned in time to drive his elbow into the stomach of the other one who was coming from the opposite direction. As he was falling backwards, Mallory pressed forward, grabbed him around the neck and bounced his head off the guard rail separating the pavement from the busy road. The man yelled out in pain and put his hand up, yelling something that sounded like, 'Stop!'

Mallory smashed his head into the guard rail harder.

He turned again, too slow to stop the next punch from Benidorm, but it glanced off the side of his head instead of connecting fully. It hurt, but it didn't slow him down at all – the worst possible result for his opponent.

Blinking the stars out of his eyes, Mallory lunged forward.

And then everything started to move faster. Like time-lapsed freeze-frames and disconnected sounds. The first three blows connecting. Then Mallory's arm up, blocking a clumsy retaliatory swing. Then Benidorm on the ground, his head swaying. Then Mallory with the front of the blue T-shirt bunched in his left hand. Then someone screaming. Then nervous male voices, maybe speaking to him. He wasn't paying attention.

At some point, he heard sirens.

A voice in his head told him he needed to stop. He didn't listen to it.

2

SATURDAY

The first thing Mallory wondered was why the hell he had left the lights on when he had gone to bed. The next thing he wondered, on opening his eyes, was why there was a new east-facing window in his bedroom, and why it had bars on it.

He straightened up and examined his surroundings. A six-by-ten-foot room. Whitewashed breezeblock walls. A stainless-steel toilet in the corner with no seat. His bed was a rectangle of wood, bolted to the floor, topped with a foam mattress. He shrugged off the thin sheet and stood up.

The sudden change of position was accompanied by a sharp, stabbing pain in his head. He groaned and sat down, closing his eyes for a minute. When he opened them, he became aware of another, less intense ache from his hands. The knuckles on both were skinned and bruised.

Looking down, there was a large smear of dried blood on the front of his T-shirt. He lifted the shirt to confirm that it wasn't his own blood. It started coming back to him. One last beer. The big man with the fair hair. A chair swinging towards his head.

He heard a low electronic buzz followed by a click as a lock disengaged. He turned his head as the door opened. Mallory squinted at the tall, beefy police officer standing in the doorway.

'There's no place like home, eh?' Judy Garland's line didn't sound quite the same in a deep Brummie accent. He stepped inside the cell and took a pointed look at the blood on Mallory's shirt and his bruised knuckles.

'Hiya, Smitty,' Mallory said. 'What's the other guy look like?'

'I imagine he's in much the same state, or worse. I wouldn't know because he wasn't bloody stupid enough to stick around. Remember any of it?'

'I'm pretty sure the twat had it coming.'

'I'm sure,' Smitty said with a raised eyebrow. 'You never start it, and yet it always seems to find you, doesn't it? Why is that?'

'Just lucky, I guess. Wouldn't say no to a cup of tea if you're making, Smitty.'

'You're on your own, mate. Come on, it's checkout time.'

Smitty took him out to the front office and handed him his shoelaces and his belt and the contents of his pockets.

'Jacket?' Mallory asked.

Smitty shook his head, and Mallory remembered his jacket had been hung over the back of his seat in the pub the last time he saw it. He wondered how happy the establishment would be to see him again if he went back for it. Maybe it would be less hassle to buy a new one.

'Want me to sign anything?'

'Nah. Off the books. It won't be next time. You're lucky the guv isn't about.'

'Appreciate it.'

Mallory walked out of the station. It was a little milder this morning, well above freezing, so he only missed the jacket a little. He went into the coffee shop next door and ordered a tea and a cappuccino to go. Took the cappuccino back into the station and placed it on the counter for Smitty.

'This make us even?'

Smitty examined the takeaway cup. 'Double shot?'

'Of course.'

'Then we're evens,' he said, taking the cup and looking down at a stack of paper. 'Mallory,' he called as he was leaving. 'Count to ten next time. You need to be more careful.'

'Careful is my middle name, Smitty.'

The sky over Meriden Street was dishwater grey, but Mallory's headache felt a little better in the cold, fresh air. He had to admit, everything felt a little better. Last night had been a mistake, but it had also been a necessary release of tension that had been building for too long. The thought of getting on to a bus didn't appeal, so he opted to walk the three miles to the flat.

The flat. Calling it 'home' didn't feel quite right, even though the seventh-floor one-bedroom in Nechells had been his residence for five months now. He thought back to Smitty's little wake-up joke. *No place like home.* What did it say about him that a police cell felt as comfortable to him as his flat? Nothing good, about him or the flat.

The lift was out of order again. He breathed shallowly to avoid inhaling the piss stench as he climbed the seven flights of stairs. He heard lighter footsteps coming in the opposite direction and a moment later, Angelika, the Polish woman who had been his neighbour for the last month, rounded the corner carrying a basket of laundry. She jumped as she saw him, then smiled nervously and hurried past.

He felt his heart beating a little faster by the time he reached his floor. *Just the hangover*, he told himself. *You're not out of shape*.

The Ukrainian couple at the end of the corridor were having another row. He opened his door and closed it behind him, still able to hear the muffled yelling.

The flat was as neat and impersonal as a Travelodge room. Nothing but a couch and a TV in the living room. The office-style grey vertical blinds that had been there when he moved in blotted out the scenic view over the Costcutter car park across the road.

Stripping off his blood- and sweat-stained clothes, he dumped them into the laundry bag and stepped into the shower. A couple of minutes on scorching heat, then a plunge to the other side of the dial. He gritted his teeth against the cold as it cleared the haze from his brain. The long scar on his left shoulder ached a little bit at the abrupt temperature change. The pain brought back memories of other senses: the deafening roar of rotor blades, the coppery smell of blood. Back to hot for a final minute and then out. He towelled off quickly and changed into clean jeans and a shirt. There was a fresh hoodie in the cupboard that would be just about warm enough for outside.

Stepping back into the bathroom, he wiped away a patch of steam mist and examined his reflection in the small door of the medicine cabinet – the only mirror in the flat. There was a two-inch scratch on his cheek just above his beard, but it wasn't deep. It would heal in a couple of days. He could feel a good-sized lump on the side of his head where the big guy had caught him, but it wasn't obvious beneath his short, dark hair.

Presentable. It was good to make an effort when visiting a friend.

Even if that friend wouldn't notice.

3

The carriage was nearly full when Mallory stepped aboard the train at Aston. He found a window seat across from a teenager in a red puffer jacket who was sprawled halfway down his seat, knees taking up most of the space in front of him.

Mallory said, 'Excuse me,' and the kid looked up, the instinctive challenge in his eyes evaporating when he saw something he didn't like in Mallory's.

The kid mumbled something and straightened up in his seat, giving him space.

Mallory settled into the seat, put his head against the window and closed his eyes, feeling the motion of the train. It was a mistake. His destination meant that the past was on his mind more than it usually was. Almost as soon as he closed his eyes, the unwanted movie began to play. The last operation. Hell Hour.

He opened his eyes and straightened up. He gazed out of the window as the train rumbled through the Chinese Quarter. He was still getting to know the city, its intricacies and idiosyncrasies.

When he had arrived last year, fresh off the plane from Afghanistan via a US base in Frankfurt, the change of scene had been a shock to the system. Like turning the shower to the coldest setting. He had wanted that shock. He needed somewhere new, somewhere he would not fall into old habits. The last few months had shown him that old habits have a way of finding you wherever you go.

The train rumbled to a halt at University station and the doors opened as the electronic announcer called the stop and reminded passengers to make sure they had all their belongings.

Mallory waited for the other passengers to leave first. Where possible, he liked to be the last to exit. It was habit: easier to tell if you're being followed.

University station was undergoing heavy redevelopment. Every month, when he made this trip, the site had changed noticeably. A new structure had been assembled, or the configuration of the wooden hoardings had been altered. He moved through the crowds of students and people in business dress. The Queen Elizabeth was a short walk from the station. Half a mile. He noticed that since returning to the UK he had eased back into thinking of distance in miles rather than kilometres.

The long approach to the glass-fronted entrance, made on foot beneath a high-vaulted weather shelter, always reminded Mallory of arriving at an international airport rather than a hospital. So did the way the name of the hospital was proudly spelled out in six-foot-high letters on the side of the building. The Royal Centre for Defence Medicine was located on the south of the campus, but Donno's ward was in the main complex. The usual receptionist recognised him as the electronic doors parted before him. Her shift pattern seemed to align with Mallory's visits on the first of each month. She was Australian, with glasses and a crooked smile. Mallory might have asked her out for a drink by now if she worked anywhere but here.

Mallory tapped in his name to sign in on the tablet fixed to the desk.

'You know where you're going, right?' the receptionist asked.

'Yeah. Donovan Nel, ward five-eighteen.'

The receptionist squinted at the screen in front of her through her glasses. 'Oh, actually it says he's been moved.'

'Moved?'

'Ward six-two-four.'

'What does that mean?'

'You'll have to ask the doctor.' Then she smiled. 'But apart from that, it means another flight of stairs.'

'Cheers. I could do with the exercise.'

The wards were arranged into the three linked oval buildings at the heart of the complex. He took the stairs up to the top floor and crossed through to the next building. Barely five minutes out of the cold winter air, and the stuffy, overheated interior of the hospital already had him longing to be back outside again.

Ward 624 was bustling with medical staff. The visitors were different from the sample you would find in a normal hospital ward. Those tended to skew younger. Adult children and grandchildren visiting nan after a fall. Here, the visitors – the civilian ones, at least – were older. They weren't visiting a parent who was getting on a bit. In most cases they were visiting a son, or sometimes a daughter.

And sometimes, the patient had no one to visit them. No one but the man who had put them there.

Mallory stood at the doors. He dreaded this. Every month, taking that first step inside and seeing Donno. Seeing what he had caused. It seemed to become more difficult every time. Maybe that was why he did it.

One mistake. A split-second decision. And it had cost everyone around him dearly.

With an effort of will, he crossed the threshold and walked into the ward. There were two staff at the duty station. One of them, a woman, looked up as he approached, tapping a sheaf of paper square as she did so. The other one didn't look up. He was dressed in green scrubs and leaning on the desk, looking down at a form on a clipboard with a ballpoint pen clamped between his teeth.

'Can I ask who you're visiting?' the nurse asked.

'Nel, D,' Mallory said.

She studied the list in front of her. 'Ah, he's just been moved here.'

The guy in scrubs had turned around at the mention of the name, and Mallory saw from the name tag that he was a Dr H. Patel. He was on the young side for a doctor, but with a little premature grey hair at the sides. He examined Mallory for a moment over the top of his glasses, and then looked down at the list in front of the nurse.

'Any particular reason he's been moved?' Mallory asked the nurse.

The doctor answered before the nurse had a chance to. 'Are you immediate family?'

Mallory shook his head.

'Can I ask who you are?'

'Can I ask why you're asking?' Mallory asked. 'I don't usually get the third degree.'

Dr Patel held his gaze for a minute and then looked at his list again. The message was clear. He wasn't going to engage, but Mallory wasn't going anywhere until he had answered the question.

'My name is Mallory, they've seen me over at the other ward.'

'Give them a call,' Patel said, addressing the nurse without looking up.

Mallory sighed. He disliked jobsworths, but he knew it wouldn't be advisable to make an issue of it, if he wanted to continue to be welcome here.

The nurse tapped out an internal number on the phone in front of her and spoke to someone down at ward 518. She asked about patient Nel's visitors and said, 'All right,' a couple of times.

She thanked the person on the other end and hung up. 'Karen says he's a regular,' she said, addressing Dr Patel.

'Okay,' he said. He looked up from his papers. 'We need to make sure we know who's in and out.' He took a closer look at Mallory, seeming to size him up. 'You served with him?'

'Yes.'

'Well, we can't discuss treatment with a non-family member. You'll have to take that up with his next of kin.'

Difficult to do that when they're in another country and I've never met them, Mallory thought. 'It's all right. I'm just in to see how he's doing.'

Patel nodded and looked down again. Mallory suspected that, as far as the doctor was concerned, he might as well have ceased to exist.

The nurse stood and leaned over the desk to point all the way down to the other end of the ward. 'He's just over there.'

Mallory walked in the direction until he found the right bed. It didn't look like much had changed, other than the ward. Donno was still unconscious, still hooked up to a variety of wires and tubes and sensors. Mallory didn't know what most of them were for. His own medical knowledge was limited to the immediate aftermath of trauma. Staunching bleeding, stabilising, administering intramuscular morphine. Everything focused on getting an injured man off the battlefield.

The machine hummed away, the signals charting Donno's breathing and heart rate and who knew what else. Waves and bars rose and fell in regular patterns. He had had a haircut since last month. The red surgical scars on the left side of his head were more noticeable.

Mallory remembered the sound of gunfire. The darkness inside the building. A mocking smile. And he remembered a blinding flash of light and a concussion wave that seemed still to be hitting him. He gripped the steel rail along the top of the bed frame as he watched Donno lie motionless, as he had lain for the past six months. He closed his eyes and let the images come. Hell Hour.

'I'm sorry, mate.'

When Mallory opened his eyes, he became aware of a presence behind him. He turned quickly and saw a woman watching him. She was in her late forties or early fifties, wearing black trousers and a sky-blue blouse with the sleeves rolled up. The silver chain of a necklace dipped below the neck of the blouse. He didn't have to ask who she was. The greying hair that still had enough of the same blonde colour as Donno's, the same blue eyes, the same cheekbones.

'I'm sorry,' the woman said. 'I didn't mean to disturb you.'

The voice clinched it: the rising South African inflection.

'You're Donno's mum,' he said.

'Susan,' she said. She looked from Mallory to her sleeping son, then back to him again. 'How do you know Donovan?'

4

'I thought you had served together,' Susan Nel told Mallory. 'I didn't think a casual friend would visit so regularly.'

At Susan's suggestion, they had walked across the road to the small park between hospital buildings. The temperature had dropped, and spring seemed a long way over the horizon. The red winter sun was already touching the bare branches of the tops of the trees lining the edge of the park. Susan's comment about visiting regularly brought Mallory up short. He hadn't noticed her before, but she had clearly noticed him. That was unusual. It suggested she had deliberately kept out of his way, and had done so in a way that was not obvious.

'I didn't want to intrude,' she said, in answer to his unspoken question.

'Intrude?' Mallory repeated. 'You're his mother, I'm nobody.'

'Nobody is nobody. Do you have a first name, Mr Mallory?'

'People don't tend to be on a first-name basis with me,' he said.

'You're more comfortable with just Mr Mallory?'

'Forget about the "mister". And I don't give it much thought, to be honest. In the military, it's always nicknames or last names.'

She considered this for a moment. 'What was Donovan's nickname?'

'We all called him Donno.'

'Were you with him?' Susan asked. 'When he was injured?'

Mallory nodded slowly. How much did Susan know? Did she know she was speaking to the man responsible for the fact that her son was lying in a coma upstairs?

'I'm sorry. I'm sure it's difficult for you to talk about.'

'He's a good soldier,' Mallory said, being careful to use the present tense. 'One of the best I served with in my time.'

'You're not in the forces any more?'

He shook his head. 'I PVRd after ...' He caught himself quickly. 'After I decided I'd done long enough.'

'PVR?'

'Sorry, premature voluntary release.'

Mallory was glad that she didn't ask the follow-up question. Why had he left prematurely? He had tried to change the subject, but it kept circling back to him.

They moved to single file to let a sweaty jogger in luminous Lycra pass by them, his dead-eyed stare fixed on the horizon, and then Mallory quickened his pace to draw level with Susan again.

'Do you know why they've moved him?'

She smiled. 'It's good news. They think it's looking promising.'

Mallory was surprised. But it was a welcome surprise. 'Promising, as in ... ?'

'As in they think he might wake up soon.'

'Really? That's fantastic. The doctor wouldn't tell me anything. I was worried it would be . . . ' He trailed off, because how could he end that sentence? *Less promising?*

'It is fantastic, you're right.'

'Are you staying over here while Donno is in hospital?'

She laughed softly. 'Yes, the commute would be a little challenging otherwise, wouldn't it? I decided I had to be here early on. I'm renting a house in Selly Park. I'm very fortunate that we had the means, and I'm retired.'

Moving halfway across the world, and renting a place in Selly Park. She was definitely a woman of means.

'Donno didn't tell me much about his family,' Mallory said. 'I never really asked him about why he joined up. I wondered. You know, with him being . . . '

'A foreigner?'

'Well, I wouldn't put it like that.'

'It's all right. Donovan had always wanted to serve in the British armed forces. It was his dream. Ever since he was little. I don't know where it came from.'

'You're not a military family?'

'Oh, goodness, no. I was a nurse back in Johannesburg before I retired last year. My late husband was an academic.'

'So what went wrong with Donno, then?' Mallory asked, making sure to make eye contact so she could see the twinkle in his eye as he said it.

'Search me. A calling, I suppose. Like wanting to be a priest, or a teacher. Bartho and I tried to talk him out of it, but it was pretty clear we were on a hiding to nothing.'

'Did he have to surrender his South African citizenship?' Mallory asked. He knew other South African soldiers who had served four years in the British military. That was usually the limit, then they went back to the SA National Defence Force. The alternative was giving up their passport and becoming a British citizen.

'We didn't even try to talk him out of that,' Susan said. 'Some of our friends couldn't understand, but I was proud of him. To be so committed to something. It was how I felt about nursing, how my husband felt about his work. It told me that the apple hadn't fallen far from the tree. Well, *that* one hadn't.'

Mallory picked up on the aside. He wondered if it was related to why they were here, walking and talking. If Susan had seen him on his other visits, she could have approached him at any time for a chat about her son. He could tell she welcomed the opportunity to talk about him with someone who had known him, but there was more to it than that.

'You mind if I ask you something?'

'Of course not,' Susan said.

'You noticed me visiting before. You could have spoken to me any time, but you never did. Why today?'

Susan stopped in mid-stride and looked away from Mallory, across the park to the hospital buildings on the opposite side. An ambulance was arriving. No flashing lights, in no great hurry. She sighed, as though they had reached an inevitable part of the conversation, but one she wanted to delay for as long as possible.

'You think I must be talking to you because I want something.'

'I didn't say that, Mrs Nel.'

'Susan. And you're right. I do want something. I need help, and I just don't know where to turn.'

32

Mallory said nothing. He wanted to know more, before he explained that whatever kind of help Susan Nel was looking for, whether it was financial, practical or emotional, he was in a uniquely poor position to provide it.

Susan started walking again. 'Mallory, I'm worried about my son. I think he could be in danger.'

'I know. That's just natural. But you just said it looks promising. They're doing all they can. They have great people here, Susan, I know the work they do. They've worked miracles. There was one guy I knew ...'

He shut up as he realised Susan Nel had stopped walking and was looking at him. 'I'm not talking about Donovan. It's my other son I'm worried about. Donovan's brother.'

5

Donno had never mentioned a brother. Come to think of it, he hadn't talked much about his family at all. Or had he? Mallory searched his memory. Donno had mentioned his family back in Johannesburg a couple of times, said something about his dad being a scientist and that he had died recently, but a brother? That had never come up. Then again, that wasn't all that unusual. Not everyone wants to talk about themselves all the time. Mallory was one such person. Where you were at was always more important to him than where you had come from.

'His name is Scott,' Susan continued. 'He's had a rough time of it the last year. We all have.'

'Of course,' Mallory said.

'Not just Donovan's injury. My husband was killed last year.'

'Donno mentioned that. I'm sorry,' Mallory said. 'Was he sick?' As soon as he asked the question, he knew the answer. She had said 'killed', not 'died' or 'passed away'.

'It was an accident. It was a terrible shock to all of us.

34

Scott took it badly. I mean, we all did. And then what happened to Donovan made it worse. With Scott, it was more than shock, though. He was angry. He had never wanted Donovan to join the military. He couldn't understand it. The two of them were always so different.'

Mallory felt a raindrop impact on the back of his neck. He looked up at the sky above the treetops and the hospital building. It seemed to have darkened in the last couple of minutes. Susan Nel dug into her handbag and pulled out an umbrella. She put it up and tried to lift it to cover both of them. Mallory waved it off. 'I'm fine.'

'Scott's a good boy, but he always . . .' She considered her words. 'Lacked focus.'

Mallory could tell she was being as generous as she could be. A mother's indulgence. Just from those two words, *lacked focus*, he had an idea of the personality already. Black sheep. Tearaway.

Perhaps Susan saw the judgement in his eyes, because she quickly added, 'Really, he's a good boy. He's just . . . he's had a very tough year. We all have.'

'Of course.'

'This is going to sound awful, but Bartho's accident was even harder for me than what happened to Donovan. It was just so sudden.'

'I understand,' Mallory said. He didn't have the blessing – or burden – of close family, but any soldier knew how it affected a family when their husband or son was on deployment. It was a constant existence on the edge. Waiting for the phone to ring; the knock on the door. More than one fellow soldier had observed that their job was easier than the job their family had to do. The soldier had a measure of control over their fate, or at least the illusion of control. With the people back home, all they could do was wait and try not to think about the danger.

Usually, of course, the call or the knock never comes, and the husband or son returns home. But when it does come, it's never unexpected. It's a confirmation of worst fears rather than a bolt from the blue. From what Susan had said, her husband's passing had been unexpected.

'He was just here one day, gone the next.'

'What happened?'

Susan put a hand to the back of her neck, adjusted the chain of her necklace. 'Bartho loved climbing, it was how he unwound. He said he loved the beautiful simplicity of it. The way the world was reduced to looking for the next handhold. I remember him being so happy when he left for that trip. He had been so stressed with work lately, and putting in long hours. He was climbing at Waterval Boven, in the north-west. One of his favourite spots. The accident investigators found that something had gone wrong with his rope. He fell more than four hundred metres.'

She swallowed and Mallory recognised the look on her face. It was causing her pain to talk about it.

'And then later, after Donovan's injury, it felt like it was the last straw for Scott. He'd been just about holding it together. He started drinking more, staying out late. I had always worried about the kind of friends he seemed to attract.'

'Wrong 'uns?'

She smiled. 'I love the British vernacular. Yes, I suppose you could say that. "Wrong 'uns."' She spoke the phrase like someone attempting to order an unfamiliar item in a foreign language on the menu. 'Bartho called them *rampokkers*, which comes to the same thing.' She shrugged. 'I'm sure some of them weren't bad kids. But you know the type. Drugs, parties, cars. Scott had a couple of run-ins with the police. He just wasn't like . . . '

'Like his brother?'

'Donovan's friends were so different. He had a smaller social circle. He got on well with the quiet kids. The bookish ones. I often thought Scott would have been the one more likely to be a soldier.'

'Because he liked a scrap?'

'I didn't mean it that way. Just the way he was more confident, more physical.'

A picture was beginning to form in Mallory's mind. Two brothers: the good son and the party animal. Mallory had seen the dynamic a hundred times. Perhaps Scott was the little brother. Indulged too much from birth, and then growing resentful of his more responsible older sibling. All of which would serve to drive the wedge in harder.

'He tried really hard after Bartho's death, he really did. He came to visit me at the house more often. He seemed to really be making an effort. I remember thinking Bartho would have been proud. He would have seen that we'd raised two good kids, after all. But then after . . . after Donno was injured as well . . . '

'Scott went off the rails?'

'I came back home after the first time I visited Donovan, but I knew I had to come back to Britain. I felt so guilty, leaving Scott. It felt like I was choosing one son over the other. When I told Scott, it was like he couldn't care less. I made him promise we would talk once a week.'

'Did he keep it?'

'Yes, to my surprise. Every Thursday evening we used to have a video call. It was good to see him ... except when it wasn't. He wasn't taking care of himself. He looked really thin. He kept telling me everything was fine. Said he had got a new job in a bar.'

'That's good,' Mallory said, though he suspected Scott had been telling his mother what she wanted to hear.

Susan had started walking more slowly. He could sense she was getting to the nub. He prompted her, gently.

'When was the last time you spoke to him?'

'Seventeen days,' she said, her voice quivering a little.

'Any word at all?'

She shook her head. 'That last call, I remember feeling relieved. He seemed happier. He was on his way out to meet someone. I thought maybe it was a girl. He asked how Donovan was doing. He even remembered to tell me he loved me at the end of the call, and he said we'd talk next week.'

'Maybe he's been too busy to get in touch.'

'For over two weeks? No. Scott can be forgetful, but he wouldn't do that.'

'You've tried getting in touch by other means?'

'I tried everything. His phone, his apartment, the bar he was working at, his friends. No one had seen him in days. I didn't have numbers for a lot of his friends, but eventually I got lucky. One of the friends, Dante, had seen a shared Facebook post. He called me back and said he had seen Scott the day after I'd spoken to him.'

'That must have been reassuring.'

'No, that was when I really started to worry. Dante said he went over to Scott and he acted like he didn't know him.

He was with another friend, talking to two men. One of them had gang tattoos. He said Scott and the other boy he knew seemed different, somehow. And that was the last time anyone saw him.'

'You're worried that something bad has happened.'

'Yes.'

'Have you talked to the police over there?'

'For all the good it did.'

'What did they say?'

'They said it was probably nothing to worry about. They said unless there was any evidence something had happened to him, they couldn't do anything. He's an adult, so they said he has the right to disappear if he wants to.'

Mallory wasn't surprised. He wasn't familiar with policing in South Africa, but even in this country, he knew missing adult males didn't usually hit the priority list. 'Not helpful,' he said.

'No. And I didn't want to leave it like that. I have a friend on the Metropolitan Municipality. I spoke to him and he got in touch with the police. The division chief called me back – he didn't sound too happy about it, but he said they would look into it.'

'Do you think they will?'

'I think they'll pretend to. Mallory, I don't know what to do. I was all set to go back home, but then the doctor said that it was possible that Donovan might wake up. I don't want to miss that if there's a chance. And, like you say, it could be Scott is fine, that he's just dropped off the radar. But I just feel so helpless, thousands of kilometres away. And then I saw you again and I thought ...'

'That I could help?'

'Yes.'

'You don't know anything about me. Why would you think I can help?'

'Oh, but I do,' she said. Mallory felt a chill down his spine. Did she know? Did she know he was the one who had put her son in that hospital bed? Was she about to play that card?

'I know you served with my son, which means you were very good at what you did. I know you take the time to visit him every month, even though he doesn't know you're there. I know you're a good man.'

'You've got me wrong,' Mallory said. 'And I'm sorry, but I don't think I can help you.'

Susan bunched her hands in front of her. 'I don't have anywhere else to turn,' she said. 'If you could just go over there, ask around, see if you can find out what's happened to him. I'm happy to pay whatever your rate is.'

'I don't have a rate because this isn't my line of work. Right now, I don't have a line of work. Like I told you, I'm nobody.'

'I don't believe that.' She held his gaze, her eyes pleading.

'Believe it,' he snapped, irritated that she wouldn't stop pushing.

Susan Nel took a deep breath and put a hand to her chest. It was as though she had got too near a dog that had suddenly barked at her. Mallory felt a swell of self-loathing. There were probably a hundred ways to handle this kind of situation sensitively. Instead, he had practically yelled at a distraught mother.

He made an effort to soften his voice. 'Look, I would love to help you, but I'm not the guy you need.'

She bit her lip and lowered her eyes from his. 'I understand.'

Damn it.

'I've got a few contacts,' he said after a moment. 'I don't know if it'll help, but I might be able to talk to someone, get hold of someone on the ground who can make enquiries.'

She opened her mouth to say something, then changed her mind. The she said, 'Anything you can do would help. I'd be so grateful. And I'm sorry. Here you are, minding your own business. You don't need some hysterical mum pestering you.' She handed him a business card with her number and email address on it. 'You'll call, if you're able to talk to someone?'

'I'll see what I can do.'

'Thank you.' She wiped the corner of her eye and looked back up at the hospital. 'I'd better get back. Did you want to come in again?'

He shook his head. 'I have to get a move on. I'll make a couple of calls and let you know either way, okay?'

She nodded, but he could see the disappointment in her eyes. He felt an urge to say that he would go after all. It was clearly what she wanted him to say. Perhaps it would even make him feel better. But he had told the truth. He wasn't the guy she needed.

Mallory fought a daily struggle not to put himself into situations where things could kick off. As last night had demonstrated, he couldn't even go out for a quiet drink without waking up with blood on his shirt and a set of bruised knuckles. And the stakes were so much higher here. Susan Nel needed someone who could exercise self-control. That wasn't him. Perhaps it never had been, but it certainly wasn't now. Flying thousands of miles to an unfamiliar country, getting involved in a potentially dangerous situation he knew nothing about? It was a bad idea, end of story. He would just end up making things worse.

'Chances are he's sleeping off the mother of all hangovers somewhere,' Mallory said. 'He'll probably be in touch soon to apologise for putting his mum through this.'

She seemed unconvinced. He knew what she was thinking. Seventeen days. There was a long pause. She looked down at her feet.

Mallory cleared his throat and glanced over at the hospital building. 'Now, go back up there and tell Donno I said hello when he wakes up, all right?'

As Susan Nel walked away, back to her sleeping son, Mallory wondered if she'd have been so keen to ask for his help if she'd known he had been the man who'd put him in that hospital bed.

6

JOHANNESBURG, SOUTH AFRICA

Scott Nel opened his eyes, waking from fractured dreams. He was still in the nightmare.

A line of golden light along the plywood nailed over the window told him it was either dawn or sunset. He had no way to be certain which it was, because he didn't know if the window faced east or west. He could hear distant sounds of traffic outside, a main road perhaps a mile or two away. In a different direction, he could hear the sounds of a construction site. Thinking about it, that made it more likely it was morning than evening, didn't it?

His mouth was parched. He shuffled over to the empty water bottle in the corner and held it above his mouth, but it was as dry as a tinderbox. It had been hours since he had been given water. More than a day? It was hard to tell. With an effort, he climbed to his knees on the floorboards and stood up, the cuts and bruises aching as he changed position. A wave of dizziness hit him and he had to put a hand against the rough brick wall to steady himself. The dizziness abated and he walked unsteadily across the room to the bucket in the corner. He pissed, noting the dark yellow colour that suggested dehydration.

He was so thirsty. If no one came soon ... no, he wasn't that desperate yet.

Why the hell was this happening to him? He hadn't been a model citizen, sure, but what had he done to deserve this?

He thought about Mum. Had she even noticed he hadn't called? Probably not. She was used to him forgetting to check in. Most likely she would assume he was caught up in his own world. She probably wouldn't start to worry for weeks. He wished he had been a better son. Maybe he had lost the chance now, the chance to be that son.

How long had it been?

At first, he had been too terrified to think straight. When the men had dragged him into the back of the van, he had screamed himself hoarse against the duct tape across his mouth. The cable ties had cut into his wrists from his struggles.

Later, when they had pushed him into this room and slammed the door, he knew that they meant to hold him prisoner, which if nothing else was a step up from killing him.

He hoped that there would be a quick resolution to this situation. When the men brought him here, he assumed they wanted money, and he was more than happy to pay them whatever the hell they wanted to let him go. He had fifty thousand rand or so in his account. That would surely make it worth their while, wouldn't it? He didn't want to, but if they pushed for extra he supposed he could ask Mum for more. He could imagine the disappointed tone of voice when he called her. Perhaps he could say he needed it to invest in something.

But he had quickly been disabused of the notion that he could buy his way out of this locked room. The men just told him to shut up when he offered to pay them.

Mistaken identity. That had been his next thought. They believed he was someone else. Some kind of rich kid who they could ransom off, perhaps. The Nels were comfortable, but he wouldn't say they were wealthy. Not really. He could understand why people like these guys might think so, though. He was often teased by his friends for his well-spoken voice, his groomed appearance. He was from the right side of the tracks. It had always gone unsaid, but he knew some of his friends judged him for it, consciously or unconsciously. They looked at him as though he didn't quite deserve to be there. Like he had a safety net.

Jesus, what he wouldn't give for a safety net right now.

A more worrying thought. What if he was right that it was a case of mistaken identity, but it wasn't about money? What if they thought he was someone they had a grudge against? What if he happened to resemble someone who had wronged these people in some way?

Pointless questions. There was no one to answer them. So there had been nothing to do but wait and hope.

That period after he was first taken had been the longest. How long, he didn't know. More than a day. His relief almost overcame his fear when he heard footsteps outside the door. He could explain to them that they had got the wrong guy. Promise not to tell anyone. Hell, offer to pay his way out if he had to.

But the relief was short-lived.

He was visited twice a day. Once for a beating, once to have some cheap bread left on the floor, together with a small bottle of water, which he forced himself to eke out.

Now, as the sky brightened outside, he heard footsteps again.

Before he knew what he was doing, he was kicking at the floor with his legs, pushing himself back into the corner.

The footsteps got closer. Heavy shoes, boots, tapping rhythmically on uncarpeted floorboards. It sounded like the rest of the building wasn't any better furnished than this room. The footsteps stopped outside. Scott looked up at the viewing slot, knowing that whoever was out there was looking through it at him. The slot was homemade – a small, horizontal rectangle roughly cut through the door and covered with chicken wire on the outside – one of the reasons he knew his prison was a makeshift one. Was it the big man with the tattoos? Or the little one with the shaved head, the one who had done the talking?

'Hello?' he said after a minute.

There was no response.

'There's been a big mistake, I'm not the guy you want.'

Again, no response. He counted to ten.

'If you—'

There was a loud click as a lock disengaged. The door swung open. There was a figure filling the doorway, silhouetted in the daylight out in the hallway. Scott shielded his eyes from the sudden brightness. As his eyes adjusted, he could see that the motionless man in the doorway wasn't one of his usual visitors. He was taller, bigger. He stepped forward and Scott could see that he had close-cropped blond hair, almost white. There was a holster strapped to his chest. It was empty.

Scott's mouth was dry already, but somehow it got dryer looking at the man in the doorway. He wanted to get up and run. He couldn't, so he backed further into the corner.

The man just stood there, his broad arms at his sides. Someone spoke from out of Scott's line of sight.

'This is the kid?'

The blond man regarded Scott for a moment longer, making up his mind, and then nodded. 'Give me ten minutes.'

Not a local accent. It was kind of neutral, colourless, so it was hard to tell for sure from four words. But it sounded ... American? Could that be right?

The blond man stepped inside and the door slammed shut behind him. The lock snapped shut again.

'Sir, I don't know what this is about, but I think you have the wrong person. I'm just—'

'You're Scott Nel. Born February eighth, 1997. Father deceased, one brother, Donovan Nel. Correct?'

What the hell was this about?

The man stepped forward, crouched down so he was on the same level.

Then he hit Scott in the face, harder than he had ever been hit before.

7

BIRMINGHAM

Mallory ascended the stairs of his tower block, passing his floor and climbing another few flights, past the level where the illumination still worked. The lighting on the top two floors had been busted since he had moved in. He pushed open the door with the long-ago broken lock and walked out on to the roof, feeling the chill of the night air that reminded him a little of Afghanistan at high altitude.

Walking to the waist-high barrier at the edge of the roof, he looked out over the city. A couple of miles to the south-west he could see the lights of the BT Tower. From behind him, he could hear the steady purr of traffic on the M6. He closed his eyes and savoured the feeling of calm.

Mallory came out here whenever he needed to think, get some perspective. Usually, he had the rooftop to himself. The only other person he ever saw out here was Ricky, the occupant of one of the flats on the top floor, who liked to smoke potent skunk here in the warmer months. He didn't mind Ricky. The two of them had an unspoken pact to leave each other alone, but still, he was pleased to see that he was on his own tonight.

Brigance answered his call on the fourth ring. 'Mallory? This is a surprise. Where the hell have you been?' The opening words were warm, but Mallory thought he could detect an undercurrent of wariness in the Scot's voice. He knew Mallory wanted something.

'Enjoying retirement,' Mallory replied. He took two steps towards the parapet and looked at the lights of the city, twinkling in the night.

'Retirement? You're but an infant. What have you been doing for money?'

'This and that. Cash in hand stuff, mostly.' Mallory hoped Brigance couldn't hear the evasion in his voice. He really didn't want to get into why he had left the military, or what he had been doing since.

'I know where you're coming from,' Brigance said. 'A few months of doing something mindless. Clear the cobwebs. Decompress. Am I right?'

'Something like that.'

'But now you're ready for a real job?'

Mallory smiled. 'If that happens, you'll be at the top of my list, Eric.' It was a big if. 'Right now, I'm looking for some help. You were working in South Africa last I heard.'

'That's right. Cape Town, Joburg. A little time in Pretoria.'

'You still down there?'

'Finished up last year. I'm in Dubai now.'

'I hear it's nice.'

'I saw somebody talk about it on the internet a while ago, saying it's like the Trafford Centre if they banged up the heating. That's about right. Money's great, though. Why the interest in South Africa?' He slipped into a pitch perfect Afrikaans accent as he pronounced it. *Sarth Efrica*.

'Friend of a friend might be in a bit of trouble. I thought if you were still out there, you could take a look.'

He heard Brigance suck his teeth. 'Sorry. I left six months ago, but it feels like it's further back in the rear-view mirror, you know? Tell me more – maybe I can think of something.'

Mallory relayed Susan Nel's story, leaving out the details of his connection to her, and why there was a gnawing urge to help her. He said only that she was the mother of someone from his old unit. Brigance occasionally asked a clarifying question but otherwise let him tell the story without interruption.

'I'm afraid the mum's not overreacting,' Brigance said at last. 'I think your boy's in trouble.'

'What makes you say that?'

'Reading between the lines, I think he's involved with some shady people.'

'I've heard some of the gangs down there are a bit rough.'

'Some of those guys are extremely nasty bastards. Extortion, murder, drugs, torture. Fun for all the family. I take it no one has been in touch with the mother?'

Mallory got his drift. 'There's been no ransom demand, nothing like that.'

'No?' Brigance sounded surprised. 'Is she sure of that? You said she's in the UK. Could she have missed something?'

'I don't think so,' Mallory said. 'She's been turning over every stone. I don't think she's going to miss an email or a note through the door back home.'

Mallory could hear Brigance take a long inhalation through his teeth as he thought about it. 'All right. So he has some shady friends, but not getting in touch is out of character. That suggests someone else is involved. So either they've made a demand and it's slipped through the cracks, or the demand hasn't come through yet.'

Mallory could tell from his tone of voice that Brigance wasn't finished yet. There was a third possibility.

'Or?'

A heavy sigh. 'Or it's not about money. Maybe this kid pissed off the wrong guy. If that's the case, they'll find his body in a ditch. Or maybe they won't find him at all.'

'Not acceptable. She needs to know either way.'

Mallory put a hand on the parapet and looked over at the drop. Sixteen floors, straight down. He had hoped this call would help soothe his concerns, and those of Susan Nel.

'You know of anyone reliable out there? Anyone I could talk to?'

'Sorry. You know me, Mallory. I make best friends everywhere I go, but ...'

'But not in Joburg, I take it?'

'Oh, I made friends. But none that I would trust to watch my drink when I went for a piss, much less hire to do a difficult job.'

Mallory looked out at Birmingham's twinkling lights again. He had hoped Brigance would still be in South Africa, or at least able to recommend a good man in Johannesburg.

What now? He had no other contacts in the area.

'I'm sorry, mate. I wish I could be of more help.'

A notification pinged in Mallory's ear as Brigance was speaking. A text or an email.

'Thanks anyway,' he said. 'At least I know what the score is.'

'You're thinking about it, aren't you? Doing it yourself.' There was amusement in Brigance's voice, which dropped away for his next words. 'I would advise against it. But if you go down there, be careful.'

'I haven't decided yet. Besides, you know I can handle myself.'

'I know. But even so ...' Brigance trailed off and then cleared his throat. 'When you get back, give me a call. I mean it.'

'Thanks, mate. Talk to you soon.'

When Mallory took the phone from his ear, he saw that there was a new email.

Sender: Susan Nel
Subject: My boys

No message; just an attached picture. Mallory opened the attachment.

And took a sharp breath of surprise.

The picture showed the Nel brothers. They were standing at the side of a road, a ploughed field rolling into the distance behind them. The morning sun rose over a stand of trees on the horizon. Donno was on the left. At least, he thought it was Donno on the left.

Scott Nel, on the right, was a dead ringer for Donno. They weren't just brothers, they were identical twins.

Something gave way inside Mallory, like glass suddenly breaking.

My boys.

One in a coma. One who knew where? Maybe dead, definitely in deep shit. And Susan Nel was powerless to help either of them.

But was he in any more of a position to help? He had already nearly got Donno killed; what made him think he wouldn't make a bad situation worse? He didn't want this decision. He wished he hadn't gone to visit Donno today. No good could come of this – for him, for Susan or for Scott.

But underneath, he knew that was an excuse – an excuse to avoid testing himself again. A fear of failure that hadn't existed within him before last year. And perhaps a fear of something else.

Since the moment he had returned home, he had felt like an imposter. He could walk down a city street and look the same as everybody else, but inside he was nothing like them. Inside, he was still in the mountains over there, the taste of dust in his mouth. Every waking minute was a struggle to keep his natural impulses in check. He wasn't always successful, as last night had shown. But even last night he had been holding back.

If Brigance's first or second scenario was right, then Susan Nel would be receiving a ransom demand soon. It made sense to get the ball rolling on a rescue mission before that happened, so it could be as carefully planned and as coordinated as possible. If Brigance's third scenario was right, then perhaps this would be a recovery mission. Recovery, and retribution.

He dialled Susan's number.

She answered with his name. He felt his stomach dip at the hopeful tone in her voice. He knew he could only dash that hope.

'Do you still want me to look for him?'

'Yes, of course, I—'

'I'll do it,' he said, before he could change his mind.

53

8

SUNDAY

Susan Nel had put together a file on her son's disappearance. She sent it over by courier, and it arrived at Mallory's flat within two hours of their phone call. He got the feeling she had thought everything through a long time before he had said yes to the job.

Mallory read over the file before getting a couple of hours of sleep, and he and Susan spoke again in the early hours of the morning as he waited for his taxi to the airport. She told Mallory she would wire him some money for expenses. She offered to fly him business class, put him up in a nice hotel. Mallory didn't get the impression that she was stretching herself to make these offers, but he explained that he would rather fly economy, and a bog-standard hotel would suit him fine. He preferred keeping it simple, and he liked places where he wouldn't stand out.

'Are you sure? Money is really no object. With our savings, and Bartho's life insurance, we're comfortable.'

'Offer again and I'll take it as an insult. Donno would have done the same for me.' He had used past tense. Too late to go back and correct himself without making it any more awkward.

If Susan Nel noticed, she didn't let on. 'Well that's very kind of you. But you will tell me if there's anything you need.'

'Deal.'

Mallory was sitting on his living-room couch looking at the map of Johannesburg on his laptop. A series of hotels were pinned, radiating out from the last place Scott was seen. 'On second thoughts, you mentioned Scott had an apartment?'

'Yes, in Newtown, in the city centre. It was quite nice. I only visited once.'

He thought about it for a second. 'Would you mind if I stayed there?'

'No, not at all. I can call them and make sure the doorman gives you the spare key.'

Staying at Scott's place would both give him a base and let him get more of a feel for the man he was looking for. He might turn up some kind of clue to where he had gone, or exactly what kind of trouble he had got himself into. If, as all indications suggested, Scott had been taken against his will, then he wouldn't have had time to conceal anything he didn't want anyone to find.

'Great. But can you do me a favour? Don't give them a name.'

'Oh. I was going to say, they might want to see identification.'

'Hang on a second,' Mallory said.

This had been on his to-do list, anyway. He went to the

chest of drawers in his small bedroom, opened the bottom drawer and reached under the folded jeans. He took out a small bundle of laminated cards, bundled together with a rubber band. He had arranged these for the jobs he had been doing for Riccarton, for when it was prudent to leave a trail that would lead nowhere. He selected one of the driving licences and one of the debit cards with a matching name: John H. Dixon. He would transfer some cash into that account later, just in case.

'Tell them to expect a Mr Dixon.'

Susan sounded a little hesitant, but said she would do as he asked.

'I don't know how to thank you,' she added. 'Like I said, I had nowhere to turn.'

'Don't thank me yet. There's a good chance I'll go out there and come back empty-handed.'

'I know. But just knowing that someone is looking for him ... well, it means everything.'

'I'll give you a call when I get there. In the meantime, try not to think about it. Focus on Donno. He'll need you there when he wakes up.'

After the call, Mallory finished packing. In the old days, he would have had a standby bag by the door, ready to be picked up at a moment's notice. This time, he had a bit more time to prepare. Even so, he wanted to travel light, as always. Nothing extraneous: a couple of changes of clothes, chargers, adaptors, a toilet bag. He would grab some South African rand at the airport currency exchange. He added a second wallet: brown leather to make it easy to distinguish from his own black wallet. The brown wallet would contain the effects of Mr John Dixon. Everything fitted comfortably into a backpack. He might need a couple of other items that were not essentials to most tourists, but those would have to be sourced locally, after he had passed through immigration.

He zipped up the backpack and grabbed his door keys, catching a glimpse of his reflection in the living-room window. He stopped and took a closer look. He seemed ... different, somehow. Like something had changed.

Maybe something had. Yesterday he had felt as if he had nothing. Nothing but bad memories and guilt. Today, there was something new about him. He had a purpose. A goal. He had an opportunity to make amends, to save a life, or at least get some answers.

His phone buzzed with a text from the taxi company. It told him his vehicle was approaching. He picked up his case and locked the door of his flat. The Ukrainian couple were arguing again as he passed their door. Starting early or, more likely, finishing late.

The taxi was already there when he got outside. It had been drizzling on and off all night, and the wet road surface reflected the street lights back up at themselves. There were no other cars in sight, the windows of every house in the street dark.

The driver was a burly man wearing a white shirt and jeans. He had the boot open, expecting a big case, but closed it and stowed Mallory's pack on the back seat instead. He confirmed the airport was the destination and put the car into gear.

'Off somewhere nice?' the driver asked as they pulled out on to Aston Church Road.

Mallory considered the question before answering. 'I've heard mixed reports.'

AFGHANISTAN

SIX MONTHS AGO
SEVENTY-TWO HOURS TO HELL HOUR

The picture on the big screen on the wall of the briefing room showed a Middle Eastern male in his forties. It was a passport photo. The man was wearing a cream shirt. He had dark hair and bushy eyebrows. The expression on his face was neutral, as per the requirements of passport authorities, but Mallory could read danger in the dark brown eyes. Perhaps that was just projection.

Lieutenant McAffee was standing between the screen and the two rows of eight chairs, every one of them occupied. McAffee was built like a bin lorry. Six-four, with a fully shaved head that gleamed in the illumination from the recessed spotlights in the ceiling. On a chair to one side of the screen sat a skinny, bespectacled man who looked in his late twenties, dressed in suit trousers and a white shirt. He hadn't spoken yet, but Mallory knew he would be pitching in later. When he did, his accent would tell them whether he was MI6 or CIA. McAffee gestured at the face on the screen.

'Anwar Salim. One of the very highest of high-value targets. He's one of the most effective commanders the enemy has. Number three on the network, but responsible for most of the worst atrocities in the region you can think of over the past three years. His operations have been responsible for killing a dozen British soldiers, many more Americans, and for hundreds of civilian deaths. He's been a challenge to pin down.'

Westwick, sitting in the chair next to Mallory, cleared his throat. 'I take it that's changed?'

'That's what we're hoping,' McAffee replied. 'Otherwise you wouldn't be here.'

He stepped towards the screen and tapped on it. The screen divided into two and the picture of the HVT narrowed and moved to the left-hand side. On the right was a satellite image of mountainous terrain. There was no text labelling the map, but Mallory could trace the contours of that particular strip of land in his sleep. The mountains of Waziristan, on the Pakistan–Afghan border.

'We've been looking for this guy for a long time. He's wily. We've had unconfirmed sightings of him in Islamabad and Karachi, but nowhere we can move on him without causing a headache for the brass.'

The usual story. Once an enemy commander was in Afghanistan, and within a designated theatre of operation, he was fair game. But the challenge was finding him when he was in the right place. It was like a game of whack-a-mole, where the mole was armed with automatic weapons and IEDs.

'Three hours ago, his phone was picked up crossing the border here.' McAffee indicated a spot on the map between two mountains. Mallory knew the place. It wasn't one of the more common crossings. 'He made a call to one of his operatives from three miles inside the country. Voice ID confirms it's him.'

McAffee tapped on the screen again and the crackly sound of a cell phone call drifted out from the hidden speakers. Mallory could hear strong wind in the background. He could see Anwar Salim standing on a mountain pass, perhaps looking back the way he had come, across the border. There was no option out there but to travel on foot. The nearest dirt road was at least ten kilometres away. He would have been picked up north or north-west of the position the call had been made from.

The conversation began, starting with the person receiving the call. The translation appeared on the screen, synced to the speech. Mallory closed his eyes and focused on the voices. He knew enough Pashto to parse it without the translation.

A voice. Male, but a little high. A teenager, perhaps.

Who's there?

It's your Uncle Sam.

How was your trip?

Disguising names and places was tradecraft 101, of course, but Mallory didn't know why they bothered trying to make it sound like an innocent chat. Anyone listening in to a call made on a sat phone from those mountains at 2 a.m. knew the caller wasn't calling his wife from the supermarket to check they were okay for milk.

Perfect. I will be with you in two days, God willing.

We're all set for the funeral.

The funeral. In the old days, it was always a wedding: 9/11 had been a wedding, back in the days when communications like these were given a lot less attention.

The two voices on the call bid each other farewell and the sound cut off.

'Voice identification suggests that the person Salim called is this man.' Another picture appeared on the screen. He was older than Mallory had guessed from the soft voice. Twenty-seven years old according to the stats over the picture. 'Omar Massoud,' McAffee continued. 'One of Salim's top men. We don't have any way of knowing where he took the call, but we do have a better idea of his movements over the last six months.'

Mallory could see where this was going. 'So where are they doing the planning for this funeral?'

McAffee looked mildly irritated by the interjection, but he didn't voice his irritation. He knew very well it wouldn't be him in harm's way in the hours and days to come. It would be the sixteen men in front of him. He cleared his throat and looked over at the man in the chair, who raised his eyebrows, as if surprised that the attention had suddenly fallen on him. He stood up, clapping his hands together.

'Thank you, lieutenant.'

Lef-tenant, not *loo*-tenant. Hint of a Yorkshire accent, smoothed out by public school, Mallory guessed. So it was MI6, then.

The man took a deep breath and let his gaze roam across the expectant faces of the men seated in front of him.

'Good afternoon, gentlemen. My name is Cartigan. We've been working this subject as priority one for the past thirteen months. As to your question ...' He turned and tapped on the side of the screen. 'Our best guess is this compound.'

The pictures of the two men and the map disappeared from the screen, replaced by what looked like magnified drone footage. It was of a large, adobe-walled compound surrounded by desert. There was a single figure just outside the perimeter. Mallory estimated the walls were about ten feet high, using the figure in the shot and the shadows for scale.

'This is located around a hundred kilometres west of Mazar-i-Sharif. We know Salim's pattern. He spends five days max in-country. He moves around a lot. Given that he risked communicating with his man within an hour of crossing the border, we think it's something big, and we think he's going to end up here. We're going to be keeping tabs, and if anything changes, you'll know about it as soon as we do. But as of right now, we think this is the place.'

Mallory leaned back in his chair and scratched his chin. He looked around him, at the faces of the other men. Some were studying the image on the screen, some exchanging wordless glances with each other. Donno was looking at Mallory, as though waiting for a signal from him.

Westwick was staring up at the ceiling, his jaw set. An observer might have thought he had tuned out, or was bored, but Mallory knew he was thinking. He was already running the operation in his head. He would be for every waking minute between now and Hell Hour. Mallory knew he could count on him.

'You're one of the top units, as you know,' Cartigan continued. 'We requested you specifically, because of the Qara Bagh operation.'

Qara Bagh. July last year. There had been a treasure trove of information recovered. They had been told to make sure they retrieved all computers, physical storage, notebooks and so on as always, and they had done so, but even as Mallory had overseen the harvesting, he had known there was something different about that raid. The volume of material, and the meticulous way it had been stored. The fact that all of the laptops were new and top of the line.

'We think Salim could have information that will dwarf the haul from Qara Bagh. If you can capture Salim – preferably alive – and get us his computers ... well, this could be quite a disruption for the enemy.'

'Any questions for Mr Cartigan?' McAffee asked, after giving them a couple of minutes to absorb the information. Cartigan took a step back and folded his arms. McAffee's question had basically been rhetorical. In all his years, Mallory had never seen one of the British spooks give up one word of information more than they had walked into the room prepared to give.

Mallory waited for anyone else to speak, and when no one did, he smiled at McAffee.

'This guy's looking for a funeral. I think we can oblige him.'

9

JOHANNESBURG

MONDAY

Scott could identify the regular footsteps of the blond-haired American's boots approaching by now.

He stiffened and got to his feet. There had been morning light shining through the gap in the plywood for the last hour, and it seemed a little noisier outside than yesterday. Did that mean it was a weekday? He had lost count of the days.

The footsteps got closer, stopping at the door.

Scott was shrinking back into the corner. He forced himself to stop, stand in the middle of the room. There was nowhere to hide. Cowering in the corner would make no difference. It wouldn't make the American go easier on him. It wouldn't evoke a hint of sympathy in those blank grey eyes.

He flinched as the lock snapped back. He heard that sound in his dreams, so often that by rights he should be inured to it by now. But like the pain that was to follow as sure as night follows day, each time felt worse.

The door opened and the American stood there, as usual.

There was no one beside him this time. He entered the room and closed the door behind him. Scott resisted the urge to shrink back, to raise an arm in defence. But something was different this time. The American never usually paused when he entered the room. Every other time, he had gone straight for Scott, administering the introductory beating before moving on to the questions. Always the same questions. The questions that made no sense.

Scott had to fight down another urge. To speak first. To tell him once again that he had got the wrong guy, that he didn't know anything about 'Anambra'. He had learned that speaking out of turn would only result in an extra blow to one of the sensitive areas on his body which the blond man seemed able to find with such unerring ease. So he just stood there, not shrinking, not guarding his face, not speaking.

At last, his captor spoke. 'Do you have anything to say to me?'

Scott shook his head slowly. 'No, sir.'

There was no reaction on the American's face. There never was. His even features were like those of a facsimile of a person. This had been going on for days now, and the blond man's expression never changed, the eyes never betrayed a hint of emotion. He had been questioning and beating Scott to no avail for days, but he betrayed neither irritation nor enjoyment nor anger. He was a mechanic working on a difficult job. The subject in front of him was nothing more than a machine to be taken apart and reassembled in the required formation.

'We know where your mother is.'

Scott had been expecting a physical blow, but this was somehow worse. The American hadn't mentioned Mum before, other than on the first day when he reeled off the names of Scott's immediate family to show him they had the right person. He had thought that he was in hell, that his situation could not possibly get worse. Those six words were like a sharp blade running down his spine.

He tried to swallow but couldn't. His mouth was too dry.

'Do you have anything to say to me?' the American repeated.

'I don't know anything. She doesn't know anything, either.'

The blond man took a step closer. With an effort of will, Scott didn't flinch.

'I told you. I don't know anything about Anambra. I swear to God. I would tell you if I knew.'

'We know she's in the UK. Perhaps she'll be more cooperative.'

Scott hesitated. Something about the way the man had phrased that gave him pause. They knew she was in the UK, but did they know where?

'You told us your mother was in Botswana.'

'I thought she was,' Scott said quickly. Shit, he *had* told him that. He didn't think the American had picked up on it, because it was removed from the focus of what he'd been asking about at that time. 'I mean, she was as far as I know.' The pitch of his voice was all over the place. He wouldn't have believed himself, either.

The blond man slowly raised his hand and extended his index finger so that it was hovering an inch from Scott's nose. 'You see, that's interesting.'

Scott tried to swallow again, before remembering he couldn't.

'It is?'

'Very interesting. When you told us that, it sounded real.

66

It sounded like you weren't even thinking about what you were saying. You know what that tells me? It tells me you know how to lie.'

Scott opened his mouth to protest. Before he knew what was happening, the hand that was pointing at him closed into a fist and slammed hard into his face. The blow set off a white flash in Scott's eyes like sheet lightning. The force of the blow was unbelievable, given that the man hadn't pulled back for a longer swing. How had he put so much energy into that punch? Scott reeled back, bouncing off the wall and falling to one knee.

The American dusted off his hands as though he had touched something unclean, and walked unhurriedly across to where Scott crouched. He bent down, bringing his face down to Scott's level. Still, his eyes showed no emotion.

'Now,' he said. 'Let's get started.'

10

'Ladies and gentlemen, the captain has turned on the seat-belt sign, and the restrooms are now closed as we begin our final descent to O.R. Tambo International Airport.'

Mallory had been roused from his fitful sleep by the ping of the seatbelt sign going on. He straightened up, murmured an apology to the woman in the next seat who had hunched over to the side to avoid his arm, which had spilled over the armrest in his sleep. She frowned at him over the rims of her glasses and turned her head to look out of the window as the clouds started to thin.

A minute later, the city sprawled out in every direction below them. It was far bigger than Mallory had expected, inasmuch as he had given any thought to Johannesburg before yesterday afternoon. Ten million in the urban area, and he needed to find just one individual.

He looked away from the window and took the plastic document file out from the seat back, leafing through some of the information Susan Nel had couriered over to his flat. It was meticulously put together, separated into sections, all the background information she had been able to access on her son: scans of Scott Nel's South African passport and driving licence, a copy of his CV listing his past employers. Mostly bar work and a short spell ushering at a museum. The one that stuck out was a stint as an administrative worker at a place called MTC – some sort of tech company. According to Susan, her husband had been retained as a consultant by the company, and had pulled strings to get Scott an entry-level position there. Judging by the start and end dates on the CV, he hadn't been a good fit.

The key points of what Susan had managed to learn so far were filed chronologically in one section. A timeline. The dates and times of the last few calls to the second, annotated with Susan's recollections of what they had spoken about. All standard family conversations by the looks of it, but Susan had understood that it was important to capture everything, in case it might be important. There were four pages of printouts of emails to the unhelpful police contacts. Mallory had taken note of the names of the officers and the precinct addresses in the email footers.

He had a list of locations to check, starting with Scott's apartment. The last confirmed sighting had been in the Joubert Park area of the city, where he was seen by his friend Dante talking to three other men. Susan didn't have a last name for Dante, but had included his phone number and email address. During the ninety-minute stopover in Amsterdam, Mallory had tried calling the number. When it rang out, he left a short message explaining that he was a friend of Scott's mother and wanted to ask him a couple of questions.

He had more luck with the next call, to MTC. Scott's line manager no longer worked for the organisation, but

Mallory had been able to speak to an executive by the name of Luca Van Deventer. Van Deventer spoke warmly of Bartho Nel, expressed concern that his son was missing, and offered to meet with Mallory if he was coming to South Africa.

Even allowing for a stretch of sleep, Mallory had read through the file twice during the flight to Johannesburg, absorbing the information and getting to know his quarry as well as he could from this dossier. Susan had been thorough, but Mallory understood that there was a lot that a twenty-something young man would keep from his mother, a lot still to uncover.

Mallory leafed to the end of the file, where Susan had included a series of scanned photographs. There was the one of Scott and Donno that she had emailed him, and a few dozen candid shots of Scott in various bars and at beaches that looked as though they had been culled from social media. In one picture, Scott was in a bar or club, drinking from a long-necked bottle of beer, and had one arm around the waist of a bikini-clad girl. There was a green neon sign behind him that looked like a stylised palm tree.

Another picture showed the two brothers together. They were out in the country somewhere, on a dirt track with mountains on the horizon. By now it was easy for Mallory to tell the twins apart. It was in the eyes, the expressions. The body language, too, evident even in a still photograph. Scott, full of smirking bravado, wearing a vest and with one toned arm draped over his brother's shoulder. Donno with that pensive gaze that Mallory remembered so well. Donno was one of the most capable soldiers he had ever fought alongside, but he never lost that manner. The one that said he was waiting for the other shoe to drop.

'Business or pleasure, sir?'

The eyes of the immigration official lingered on Mallory's passport picture, then looked up, awaiting an answer.

'Just a holiday,' Mallory said, smiling.

She stamped the passport and handed it back to him. 'Enjoy your stay in Johannesburg.'

Mallory got into the first taxi in the row outside the terminal, a silver Volkswagen sedan. He sat in the passenger seat, and gave the driver the address of Scott Nel's apartment. The driver was tall and broad-shouldered. It was hard to judge with him sitting down, but he only barely fitted in the seat, even though it was jammed all the way back. Had to be six-six minimum. He wore a beige, short-sleeved shirt and a porkpie hat. The car radio displayed Rock FM 91.9. It was playing 'Enola Gay' by OMD.

'Where you coming from?' the driver asked as he pulled out into traffic, his voice deep and with a raspy quality.

'The UK. England.'

'I thought so. The Americans have tans.'

Mallory laughed despite himself. Usually he preferred not to engage in chit-chat with drivers, but it had been almost twenty-four hours since he had spoken to anyone other than the immigration official, and he immediately liked this guy. There was an ID tag hanging from the rear-view mirror showing the driver's photograph and details and appropriate licensing dates. His name was Bokamoso.

'Where in England? London?'

'Nowhere, really,' Mallory said. 'I move around a lot.'

Bokamoso negotiated a worryingly short ramp on to the motorway, tucking in between a semi and a VW van, seemingly with inches to spare between the bumpers. He checked his mirror and accelerated out into the fast lane.

'No hotel,' Bokamoso said. It took Mallory a second to realise he was referring to the address he had given.

'No hotel. I'm staying with a mate,' he said.

'Short trip?'

'What makes you say that?'

The driver glanced back at the single backpack. 'Either you lost your luggage, or you're not planning on staying long.'

Mallory let the pause draw out as he looked out of the window. In the distance, sun glinted from glass towers. 'Looks like a nice town.'

'Give it a while,' Bokamoso said. 'Some parts are very nice, some . . . ' He took a hand off the steering wheel to tilt his hand this way then the other. 'Your friend is British too?'

'Great weather, though,' Mallory said, ignoring the question. 'It's winter back home.'

'Give it a while,' Bokamoso said again. 'It's the rainy season. And it doesn't look like you brought an umbrella.'

Mallory smiled, and Bokamoso didn't press on with the questions. Mallory looked out of his window as the motorway curved between canyons of skyscrapers. A haze of smog hung over the city, giving everything a yellowish glow in the morning sun. Johannesburg was known as the city of gold, a reference to its origins. Gold had been discovered on a farm in the 1880s, in what was now Gauteng Province, and from there the city had boomed. Wilderness to mega city in a hundred years.

Bokamoso slowed for an exit and darted on to the off ramp. Tall office and apartment buildings lined either side of the road. Mallory looked at the pedestrians, dressed in summer clothes here in the southern hemisphere.

It felt strange being so far from home, in a different season, but with barely any time difference. He had rested enough on the flight to get straight to work.

The street they were on now was wide, with car dealerships and hotels on either side of the street.

Mallory asked if they could stop for a second. Bokamoso answered by pulling smoothly into a parking bay outside a Holiday Inn. 'I thought you said no hotel?' he asked as he pulled on the handbrake.

'You okay to wait five minutes?'

'Sure, if you're okay with what's on the meter.'

Mallory grabbed his bag and got out of the car. He glanced up and down the street. There were few pedestrians, none within a couple of hundred yards. He entered the foyer through the automatic doors. It looked like a Holiday Inn foyer anywhere in the world. Tiled floor, light, polished wood furnishings, beige walls, framed landscapes.

The woman at the desk straightened in her seat as he approached. He took the brown wallet out of his backpack and told her he needed a room for three nights. No, he didn't have a reservation.

She took his details. John Dixon, of 12 Tailor's Court, Bristol.

'That's perfect, Mr Dixon, I just need your payment card and your passport.'

He sighed. 'My travelling companion has the passports.

I'll need to tell him to come back, unless ... would my driving licence be okay?'

She looked uncertain for a moment and then said, 'That will be fine.' She checked the driving licence and the credit card, both carrying the name of John Dixon.

He took the key card, emblazoned with the hotel logo, and listened to the directions to his room on the fifth floor. He stepped away from the desk, waited for her to start serving the next customer, and then walked back out to the street, where Bokamoso was waiting at the kerb.

'Everything okay?'

'All good,' Mallory said.

They drove for another couple of minutes and the hotels and car dealerships gave way to boarded-up shops and groups of men hanging around on the street corners. A sketchy neighbourhood. At one point, Mallory noticed Bokamoso's eyes going to the mirror as they heard a motorcycle engine behind them. Simultaneously, his right hand reached for the button controlling the central locking and locked the doors. The motorcycle passed them a little slower than it needed to and kept going.

Bokamoso saw Mallory watching him. 'You can't be too careful.'

Mallory nodded approval. He had read the travel warnings. Don't get stuck at a red light in the wrong neighbourhood with the doors unlocked.

'Don't worry, your friend's part of town is nicer.'

Something had changed Mallory's mind about opening up a little. Perhaps it wouldn't hurt to be a little more like Brigance, try making some friends with local knowledge.

'Actually, the reason I'm here is to find him. My friend.

He's stopped calling his mother and she's worried. I said I would take a look.'

Bokamoso glanced over at him. 'Oh yeah? You think he's in trouble?'

Mallory related the broad details, not mentioning names or identifying details. Mother in the UK, in regular contact up to a couple of weeks ago, then radio silence. He told Bokamoso about Scott's mum contacting the police to no avail, raising a wry grin from the driver.

'She try paying them?'

'Who, the police?'

'Yeah.'

Mallory shrugged. 'I don't know, I didn't ask.'

'She should have tried paying them.'

When Mallory explained about the last sighting of Scott Nel, having to think to remember the name of the neighbourhood, the driver's grin disappeared.

'Joubert Park. Rough neighbourhood.'

'So I've heard.' Mallory was about to ask if it was rougher than the area they were driving through, but as he looked out of the window, he saw the surroundings had changed again. Clean pavements. Coffee shops and fashion stores. The city was like a patchwork quilt.

'You be careful if you go down there.'

'People keep telling me that.'

They pulled up outside a tall apartment building, each floor lined with balconies. Mallory paid the fare and added what he hoped was a decent tip. Bokamoso raised his eyebrows and thanked him.

'Hope the rest of your shift goes okay,' Mallory said, opening the door.

'Wait a second.'

Mallory paused as Bokamoso reached across and popped the glovebox. He reached in and found a receipt pad.

'It's okay, I don't need—'

Bokamoso scribbled a cell phone number on the back and handed it over. 'You need a ride, anything else, give me a call, okay? I hope you find your friend.'

Mallory got out and waved Bokamoso off as he peeled away from the pavement to beat an approaching bus. The bus driver leaned on the horn and shot Mallory an aggrieved look. He put the card in his pocket and looked up. Scott Nel's apartment was on the seventeenth floor.

11

The apartment building was a world away from Mallory's place back home, though they were both urban high-rise dwellings. He knew it would be a nice place before he saw the building itself, not just from the character of the surrounding neighbourhood, but because it had a name, The Springwood. Not Springwood Tower, or The Springwood Apartments, but just The Springwood. To tell the truth, it wasn't the kind of place Mallory would go for even if he had the resources. This kind of neighbourhood looked the same the world over. You might be standing on a street in Toronto or London or Hong Kong. It had no character of its own. Perhaps that was the point.

The entrance was a stone arch in the side of the building flanked by trellises covered in thick ivy. There was a doorman in a grey suit and a cap. He picked up Mallory's approach from twenty yards away and watched him carefully.

Mallory was half-expecting the third degree, but the doorman smiled in a way that almost convinced him he was pleased to see him. 'Good afternoon, sir.'

'Good afternoon,' Mallory said. It had been noon on the dot when he checked the time a moment ago. This guy was on the ball. 'I'm staying with a friend, Mr Nel. I believe his mother called ahead?'

'I see. Do you have an apartment number?'

'Seventeen oh-seven.'

The doorman nodded in a way that told Mallory he had known the correct answer to that question before he had asked it. 'Excellent,' he answered, reaching into a recessed shelf by the door and producing a white plastic card that looked like the key card he had just been given at the Holiday Inn. This one was emblazoned with a stylised gold letter S. He took a clipboard and pen from the same shelf. May I ask you to sign the visitor's log?'

'No problem.' Mallory filled in 'J. Dixon', followed by the apartment number, followed by an illegible squiggle in the signature box.

'Have you travelled far?' the doorman asked as he filled out the form.

'Far enough.'

He handed the clipboard back. The doorman examined Mallory's name and signature, gestured at the entrance. Mallory didn't see him touch anything, but the doors parted. 'May I assist you with your ... ?' The doorman paused as he noted the backpack.

'Thanks anyway,' Mallory said.

'Then have a pleasant day, and enjoy your visit.'

Mallory walked inside the foyer. It was narrow, with large black floor tiles, white walls and some framed art that looked a little more avant-garde than what they'd had in the Holiday Inn. There were two elevators at the far side, with a closed, unmarked door to one side. He tapped his key card against the sensor between the elevators. A green light lit up and a second later the doors on the right slid open. Floor 17 was already selected, no doubt from the information on his card.

He let the doors close and tried the unmarked door instead. He could use the elevator once he was satisfied with alternative routes in and out of the building. The door opened on a stairway that led down, presumably to a parking garage, and up, to the floors above. He climbed the stairs quickly, wondering if he was imagining the spring in his step compared to yesterday. It took him under five minutes to reach the seventeenth floor. He opened the door and stepped out into the corridor.

The apartments were all on one side, floor to ceiling windows on the other, providing a panoramic view east over the city. The glass was slightly tinted, so the sun wasn't dazzling. Mallory followed the corridor until he reached 1707. He stopped and listened for a moment, putting his ear to the door. He knocked twice, trying the handle as he did so. It was locked. He stood to one side and listened again. No sound at all from within.

There was a soft click as he touched the key card to the sensor. He turned the handle, staying in the corridor as he let the door swing open, then stepped inside and closed the door behind him.

The moment he did so, his first question was answered. There was no sign of a struggle or an invasive search.

He stood in the doorway and did a quick visual check of everything within view. It was a light, spacious studio apartment. In the corner opposite the entrance was a small bathroom. The door was open, so he could see that it was empty. He stepped inside the apartment. Aside from the bathroom, there were no interior walls, which meant no need to go room to room. Still . . .

The kitchen was four paces from the door. He plucked a paring knife from the wooden block on the counter and started to walk the floor. The living space was in the middle with a deep carpeted floor, a leather couch and a television, and at the far end was a raised dais with a double bed in the middle. Beyond the bed was a closet with twin louvred doors. The west-facing side of the apartment was the same slightly tinted floor to ceiling glass as in the corridor.

Mallory approached the bed, bending slightly so that he could see the space underneath, then moved to the closet. He turned the handle and stepped back as he pulled one door open, then the other. Nothing more threatening than some hanging T-shirts in slightly obnoxious colours.

Mallory put the paring knife down on the bedside table and turned around to survey the space.

The apartment was nice. Not huge, by any means, but it didn't feel cramped. It was tidy, but not too tidy. There were a couple of glasses on the drainer beside the sink, a pair of trainers discarded on the floor of the living space. The bed was unmade.

The first thing he wanted to take a look at was Scott's computer. There was a desk on the window side of the living area. There was a laptop power cable plugged in, but nothing attached to it. He checked the drawers in the desk, the space under the coffee table, the drawers in the bedside table, even the kitchen cupboards. After five minutes, he was confident he had searched everywhere in the apartment where a laptop could have been left and found nothing. Not necessarily suspicious. Scott might well have taken it out with him the last time he left.

But in the closet he found a backpack with a sleeve for a laptop. Maybe Scott had another bag, or maybe he had taken the laptop out without a bag. Or perhaps it was being repaired. All of these were possibilities. It was like Scott's case in microcosm. Lots of potential explanations for its absence, nothing to definitively suggest foul play ... but something about it made Mallory uneasy. He didn't like unanswered questions, and the whereabouts of Scott Nel's laptop was a big one.

He opened the fridge and immediately recoiled at the smell. There was a half-full carton of milk and a plastic bag full of some green mush that might have been salad at some point. Aside from six cans of Heineken and various condiments, there wasn't much else in there. The takeaway flyers held to the outside of the door by magnets told the story of Scott's culinary skills. Anyway, the spoiled milk showed Scott definitely hadn't planned to go away for an extended period.

He poured the solidified milk down the sink and binned the carton and the salad. There was only one other item in the trash – a pizza box from somewhere called Akhalwaya's, folded over so it would fit. He noticed there was a printed receipt attached to it with a name, address and phone number. The name was 'Adriaan', the address on 16th Street. Perhaps Scott had brought home leftovers from a friend's place. Mallory snapped a photo of the receipt on his phone, making sure the text was in focus.

He walked over to the couch and sat down, looking out at the view. Johannesburg stretched before him. He could see the early afternoon sun glinting off traffic on the motorway. The mountains on the horizon disappeared into the haze. Scott had to be somewhere out there, if he was still alive.

He called Susan Nel and told her he had got to his destination and was at Scott's place already. He heard an intake of breath.

'Is everything ... all right?'

He could hazard a guess at what she was imagining. Blood. Signs of a struggle. A suicide note.

'It's fine. No sign of any trouble here. You're right, though – he wasn't planning on going anywhere.'

She released the breath. 'Knowing Scott, he won't have much in the cupboards, so make sure you pick up everything you need. He keeps his spare sheets in the ottoman, we got that for him when he moved in. I don't know what the weather is like, but if you get cold—'

'Don't worry about all of that, this is a nice place. I just wanted to let you know I was here.'

'Of course. I should let you go, you must be exhausted.'

'I'm fine, slept on the plane. In fact I'm just about to get to work. I've got a meeting with Mr Van Deventer at MTC lined up this afternoon, but before that I thought I would have a chat with Scott's friend. The one who saw him last.'

'Dante? I got the feeling he thought I was this crazy over-protective mother.'

Mallory thought of something. He put the phone in the crook of his neck and dug the file folder out of his backpack. He leafed through to the page of narrative about Susan's response from calling around Scott's friends. The only name that had more than a line of text next to it was Dante's. The other name he was looking for didn't appear.

'Do you know if Scott has a friend called Adriaan?' he asked. 'Two As.'

'Adriaan. Yes, he's mentioned him a few times.'

'He's not on your list. Did you try to call him?'

'I did, but he never answered. Why do you ask?'

'Just checking. I found a receipt with his name on it. I'll keep you posted. You just sit tight and be there for Donno. You've got enough on your plate over there. Leave this to me.'

She thanked him again, said goodbye and hung up. Mallory stood in silence for a minute, holding the phone.

Despite his reassurances to Susan, something didn't feel right about the apartment. When he had opened the door, he had been prepared to find the place ransacked. Ripped upholstery, upturned drawers. But it hadn't taken him long to carry out a thorough search. It wouldn't take someone else long to do it, either. Someone else could have checked the place out without leaving evidence. The minimalist decor would help with that. There weren't that many nooks and crannies.

There were no books or magazines or DVDs. Just the basics. The wardrobe was fully stocked, mostly expensive-looking casual wear – designer jeans and hoodies and half a dozen or so pristine trainers in their boxes. It was functional, but barely lived in. The one concession to a personal life was the array of framed photographs on the chest of drawers in the bedroom.

Mallory walked over to give them a closer look. There were three of them. One was a copy of the photograph Susan had sent him the other night. Scott and Donno together. He smiled when he saw the second. It was a picture of Donno in the Baba Wali mountain range, west of Kandahar. He was standing with his rifle in front of a mountain pass, a cerulean blue sky overhead, a couple of other soldiers in the background. Mallory knew exactly when it had been taken. He knew because he was one of the two men in the background. The picture was from about three months before the operation that had put Donno in his coma and four other men in their graves.

The third picture showed a man climbing a sheer rock face. He looked in his sixties. He was bald, wearing mirrored sunglasses. This had to be the boys' father, Bartho Nel. Susan said he had been killed in a climbing accident.

Mallory knew exactly how people would have tried to comfort his wife and sons after the accident, reaching for that old platitude and telling them that he died doing what he loved. That was bullshit. Mallory had come closer to death than most people, and he knew life satisfaction would be the last thing on someone's mind as they plummeted hundreds of feet to certain death.

The smile of recognition at the Donno picture had faded from Mallory's face, and he felt a chill in the room. The three pictures were a triptych of tragedy. The father, killed while climbing. Donno, lying in a coma since a few months after this picture was taken. And now Scott, whereabouts unknown, but unlikely to be anywhere good.

None of the people in the photographs knew what the near future had in store for them. Suddenly, Mallory was keenly aware that at this moment, he didn't either.

12

Susan Nel had contacted several different departments of the
Johannesburg Metropolitan Police Department. The section
of her file with the printed-out emails told a story of dead
ends. Each time she tried to escalate the enquiry, she would
be politely and sometimes bluntly herded back towards the
same source: the division that covered the area where Scott
had last been seen.

From the tone of the emails, it sounded like standard
bureaucracy. *That's not on our area; you need to talk to the
people who cover this patch.* Which is fine, as long as the
people responsible for that patch do their job. Susan Nel's
communications had gone through an Officer Ferreira. His
emails had been humouring at first, quickly moving to irritated. She had tried to go over his head, which seemed to
have been a mistake, going by the single terse reply from his
senior, Lieutenant Theron.

*No evidence that anything untoward has happened to
your son, who is an adult. We wish you good luck in recon-
necting with him.*

After that, she had been stonewalled.

Mallory didn't doubt they had a lot on their plate, and he knew most police departments would take a similar view: Scott Nel was a grown-up. There was no evidence to suggest foul play, and no one else had raised any concerns. He knew that missing persons enquiries like these weren't a priority, particularly when the subject is a twenty-something male of sound mind and body. He suspected Susan Nel had been at a particular disadvantage, trying to make her enquiries all the way from the UK. It was much easier to give someone the brush-off if they couldn't show up at the station. That was where Mallory could make a difference right away.

The 5 division of the JMPD was at the corner of Village Main Road and Loveday Street, beneath a motorway flyover. Mallory circled the building a couple of times, getting a feel for the surroundings. He passed by the gated official vehicles entrance and then saw a sign in English and Afrikaans directing him to the public entrance, or *publieke ingang*. He stood across the street for a couple of minutes, pretending to look at his phone. Smart-looking officers entered and left the building, dressed in short-sleeved blue shirts with peaked caps. They wore guns, obviously. The crime rate in Johannesburg was high. He thought about Bokamoso instinctively locking the doors of his car earlier on.

He put his phone back in his pocket and approached the public entrance, giving way to a pair of officers leaving by the main door, nodding respectfully at them. A male and a female, both of them young. The man didn't acknowledge Mallory at all; the woman gave him a suspicious look before passing by.

He was used to getting that look from police officers. The good ones quickly learn to identify potential threats.

He stepped into the foyer before the automatic doors closed. The floor of the reception area was black and white chequerboard tiles. There was a short row of plastic-backed chairs and a long counter with glass partitioning with the duty officer behind it. He was black, in his fifties, with salt and pepper hair and glasses with thin frames. There was an embroidered name tag across his left shirt pocket that said *Myers*. He didn't look up as Mallory entered. Mallory waited a respectful distance from the counter until Officer Myers finished what he was doing and looked up.

'Can I help you?'

'Yes, I'm here to see Lieutenant Theron.'

'Do you have an appointment?'

'We've spoken via email,' Mallory said. Not exactly the truth, but he was the representative of someone who had spoken to Theron.

'He's not available right now.'

'Officer Ferreira, then.'

'May I ask what this is regarding?'

'I'm happy to discuss that with Officer Ferreira.'

The officer's eyes narrowed. 'Name?'

'John Dixon,' Mallory said.

'I'll see if he's available.'

Myers tapped a code into the lock of the door behind him and disappeared for a minute. Mallory looked around the reception area. The desk divided the space in two, extending to either wall. There was a door at the far end. The automatic doors opened again and a skinny young guy in a hoodie shuffled in and sat down in one of the chairs, resting one leg over his other knee. Mallory looked up as he heard the interior door open again and saw Myers had returned with another officer. He was white, about five-six, in his thirties or early forties. He had buzz-cut fair hair and was holding his hat in one hand. His name tag said *Ferreira*. He glanced at the two occupants of the chairs in the reception area. Myers pointed in Mallory's direction.

'Mr ... Dixon?'

'That's me. I'd like a few minutes of your time if possible. It's about Scott Nel.' He stood up, and immediately Ferreira stiffened.

'Step back, please sir.'

Mallory did as he was told.

'Can I ask you to put your hands against the wall?'

Mallory hesitated and then did as he was asked. He glanced at the guy in the hoodie, who didn't seem to be surprised by this request.

He felt Ferreira's hands on him, patting him down. Shoulders, sides, hips, ankles. He found Mallory's wallet and took it out. Mallory kept his eyes on the wall as Ferreira went through the brown leather wallet, wondering if this was routine or because of the person he was asking about. Either way, it vindicated his caution.

'John Dixon,' Ferreira read from the licence, as though surprised to confirm it matched the name he had been given. 'You're from Great Britain?'

'That's right.'

'All right, sir, you can turn around.' He handed Mallory back the wallet. 'You're a long way from home. Follow me.'

They went beyond the glass partition and into a small interview room.

'Sorry about that, but I'm sure you understand.'

'Can't be too careful,' Mallory said. 'It's a rough town.'

'Now, what was that name again?'

'Nel. Scott Nel.'

Ferreira frowned, affecting ignorance. Mallory could tell it was as fake as a three-pound coin. He shook his head slowly. 'I'm not sure I'm familiar with that name.'

'You and Lieutenant Theron were in contact with his mother, Susan Nel. He disappeared about three weeks ago, hasn't been seen since. She's concerned something has happened to him.'

Ferreira pretended to catch on. 'Ah, I do recall that. We investigated Ms Nel's enquiry and there's no reason for concern.' He smiled thinly. Conversation closed.

'You investigated,' Mallory repeated.

'That's what I said.'

'What avenues did you pursue, exactly?' Mallory asked. 'Did you check his apartment, speak to his friends?'

'I'm afraid I have an engagement elsewhere, Mr Dixon. If you leave your details with Officer Myers, we'll be happy to get in touch if we have anything more for you.'

Mallory considered his response, decided that now wasn't the moment to be difficult. There would be ample time for that later. He took out one of the blank business cards he had bought in the WHSmith at Birmingham airport. On the plane, he had filled out a dozen or so with his mobile number and the country code someone dialling from South Africa would require. He handed it to Ferreira.

'You'll call me, if you think of anything?'

Ferreira left a long pause before answering. 'Of course.'

'Thanks for your time,' Mallory said.

Ferreira took him back out to reception and then watched as he left via the sliding doors. It would be interesting to see if they used the number. When his phone buzzed in his pocket halfway along the street, he reached for it in surprise.

But it wasn't the police.

13

The incoming number was in an unfamiliar format, which suggested it was a local call. Mallory tapped to pick up and then held the phone to his ear, not saying anything.

There was a pause and then a voice. 'Hello? I had a call from this number, you asked me to call back.'

Male, young sounding. Suddenly, Mallory knew who it was.

'Is that Dante? Scott's friend?'

There was a long pause, as though the question required careful thought. 'You said you're looking for Scott?'

'I am indeed. I landed in Johannesburg a few hours ago. I'd really like to meet you if you—'

'No,' Dante said quickly. 'I can't do that.'

'If this afternoon isn't good for you, I'm going to be here for a few days.'

'Never is good for me. I'm not in town any more.'

Mallory was curious. The kid was scared. He sounded like he might hang up at any second. Up until this moment, Mallory had kept alive the possibility that the police might be right. There was no proof anything was wrong. But the fear in Dante's voice told him something was very wrong. Something that he hadn't shared with Susan Nel. But he had made the choice to call, which meant he wanted to help.

'Has someone threatened you, Dante?'

'You could say that.'

'I'm here to find Scott. To help him. If you know anything else, anything you didn't tell his mum, now's the time to tell me.'

'I told her everything I knew. I saw him and ... and another guy, talking to those men. Then I got a visit from somebody the next night saying I better shut up.'

'Okay,' Mallory said. Definitely scared, then. Whoever knew he had been the last person to see Scott Nel clearly didn't want him talking about it. But *had* he been the last person? According to Susan Nel's account, Dante had seen him talking to two sketchy-looking men and one other person. A mutual friend.

Mallory decided to try a bluff, with the only card he had. He remembered the name on the receipt on the pizza box.

'The other guy – it was Adriaan, right?'

There was a long silence. 'How did you know that?'

14

James Branagh took his suit jacket off and hung it carefully over the back of one of the chairs in the small office they had rented. Too late, they had discovered that the air conditioning wasn't working. Christ it was hot. He hated Joburg. It wasn't just the heat. It was the pollution, the traffic, the petty crime, the way the heavens opened without warning and if you were caught in the downpour you would be walking around smelling of damp until you could shower. He hoped that he wouldn't have to be in the city for much longer. He had already been here longer than he had intended.

He hadn't envisioned quite so much fieldwork when he had come up with the plan for Sentinel ten years before. The idea was to spend a few years recruiting and securing as many contracts as possible, then keep loose tabs on things from the comfort of semi-retirement. It had seemed as though it was working out perfectly at first. He had built a great team, and the contracts had been lucrative, even if there hadn't been as much interest from the bigger players as he had hoped. But he had made a classic mistake: overextending at the wrong moment and leaving the company vulnerable to a sudden reversal in fortune. The Ukraine contract last year had been a reversal and then some. If Sentinel couldn't find an eight-figure sum in a hurry, they would be over.

Then again, 'they' wouldn't be over on an individual level. The others would find work elsewhere. They didn't bear the same level of risk as Branagh did as the founder, which was reasonable since they hadn't been in line for the same reward.

That was why this contract was almost too good to be true, coming only weeks before the most crippling of the debts would come due. When Branagh looked into the detail, he understood why the client was offering to pay so much. Compared to the guaranteed return, it was chump change. It was a tricky assignment, too. Not especially dangerous, but complex. It required a degree of investigative skill and intelligence gathering that rival outfits simply weren't set up to carry out. They had to design their own way out of the problem. But now, it looked like they were most of the way there.

Branagh moved to the window and looked down on the narrow alley below. Where the hell was Foster? He had been gone longer than an hour. He glanced over at his two phones where he had left them on the table. The work phone had no messages. His personal phone had the opposite problem. Three unanswered check-in texts from Maddie at home, asking when she could book a day for them to visit Charleswood House with Olivia. His wife had no way of knowing it, but her blissfully oblivious calls and messages over the past few months were starting to make him feel as though someone was slowly tightening a rope around his throat.

'Any sign of him?'

Branagh was grateful to have his thoughts brought back to the current issue, which was for a change a low-stakes situation. He shook his head in answer to Willer's question from across the room.

Willer exhaled a pissed-off sigh. 'Probably got lost again. I'm starving. I bet he forgets to tell them no olives again.'

Branagh looked over at the other man. Willer was dressed in dark combat pants and a black T-shirt that stretched over his biceps. The American brought many important skills to their team, but at six-foot-two and sixteen stone, with striking blond hair, he was no good for blending in. He wasn't the guy you sent for pizza when you wanted to keep a low profile, in other words. Foster, on the other hand, was no good for the physical side but reliable when it came to anything involving a computer or junk food. Teamwork makes the dream work.

'You can always take it over to our guest, Simon,' Branagh said mildly.

He looked around at Willer, who gave him a sarcastic look. 'Not exactly out of the instruction book for this kind of guest, is it?'

'I wouldn't know, I've never seen the manual. Isn't there some sort of good cop, bad cop element?'

'The point is I'm starving.'

Branagh's phone buzzed on the long table below the window, rattling on the glass surface. He reached for it.

'That's probably him now,' Willer said. 'I swear, if he forgot to take cash again ...'

But it wasn't Foster. At least, if it was him, he wasn't calling from the number Branagh had assigned him at the start of this three-day cycle.

But it would be somebody he wanted to talk to. It had to be. Otherwise they wouldn't have this number.

He picked up the call and held the phone to his ear. 'Good afternoon.'

The caller hesitated. When he spoke, it was with a local accent. He sounded like he was lowering his voice, and wasn't used to having to do that.

'I'm calling about the Nel account.'

Now Branagh knew who was speaking.

'Developments?'

'Yes, within the last hour.'

'Has the mother called again?'

'No, this was a visit. A visit in person.'

'In person?' Branagh was confused. Their latest information said that Susan Nel was in the UK. He didn't think they would have to act on that knowledge, but if she had come home it would save some time if they did. 'What did she want?'

'It wasn't her. It was a man. He was asking questions about Scott Nel. I think he's here on behalf of the family'

Interesting. Perhaps Susan Nel had decided that the local police were unlikely to make the sort of progress she was hoping for.

'Private investigator?'

'I don't think so. No licence or anything like that. He was a Brit, like you.'

'No licence,' Branagh repeated. 'You asked for identification?'

'His name is John Dixon, he's staying at the Holiday Inn in Rosebank.'

Branagh took out a pen and jotted down the details on the back of the pizza menu.

'And what did you tell him?'

'What we agreed, of course.' A hint of irritation. 'Nothing.'

'Excellent. You will tell us if he appears again?'

'Sure.'

'Your efforts are very much appreciated, thank you.'

Willer was watching him as he hung up, a bemused look on his face. 'I don't know why you bother.'

'Bother?'

'Being nice to these flatfoots. You know they despise us.'

'Manners cost nothing, and it's important to keep them onside.'

Branagh saw movement at the end of the alley and moved closer to the window. A figure emerged from the far end.

'What is it?'

'Looks like you won't starve to death after all,' he said. 'It's Foster.'

15

Mallory checked Adriaan's number on the fast-food receipt he had found in Scott's apartment and called it. He told him he was looking for Scott Nel, and had heard that he was one of his friends. To Mallory's surprise, Adriaan agreed to meet with him. He suggested a sandwich place in the Braamfontein district of the city, saying he would be there at four o'clock.

Mallory made sure to be twenty minutes early. The area was marked out by a cluster of tall office buildings, a mix of architectural styles from Brutalist hulks to gleaming modern towers that looked as though they might have been erected last week. The sandwich shop was on one of the older blocks, overlooking the wide train-marshalling yard that cut through the south of the city. He completed a circuit of the block, surveilling the nearby buildings, taking note of people sitting in parked cars, anyone loitering in doorways. It looked innocent enough. Traffic was flowing quickly from the Nelson Mandela Bridge that spanned the train yard. He entered the sandwich shop and paused at the entrance long enough to get the lay of the land.

There were half a dozen customers in there, none of whom looked up as he entered. It had a hipster vibe, the kind of place that would be popular with students and backpackers. Terracotta tiled floor, stucco walls with faux tribal art, a blackboard showing the specialities of the house, and another listing all of the different blends of coffee that they offered. A waiter approached, wearing black trousers and a short-sleeved shirt buttoned up to the collar. His head was shaved on one side, with a long wave of black hair banking over the opposite side. It looked like it would be a challenge to maintain. Mallory could understand the decision to have long hair and the decision to have no hair, but he couldn't understand doing both.

Mallory took a table at the back. He ordered a black coffee, selecting a blend at random from the blackboard when the waiter asked for specifics. He watched the street outside. The coffee arrived. It was all right. Strong, with a faint spice aftertaste.

He put the cup down as he saw a guy in his early twenties push the door open. He wore a T-shirt over a long-sleeved top, board shorts and blue Chuck Taylors. He had dark, shoulder-length hair and a deep tan. His eyes were searching the room, looking for someone. Mallory held his hand up. The kid hesitated for a moment and then walked over to the table.

'Hi, are you here for ... ?'

Mallory nodded. 'You're Adriaan?'

'Yeah, and you're ... ?'

'A friend of the family. Thanks for coming. Take a seat.'

Again, Adriaan hesitated, casting a furtive glance back at the door. He didn't want to be here.

Mallory offered to get him a drink. Adriaan declined. He didn't seem to be the sort who wanted to make a lot of small talk before getting down to business, which suited Mallory just fine.

'So as I said on the phone, I'm over here to find Scott. His mum is very worried about him. Any help you can give me will be appreciated.'

Adriaan pushed a lock of his hair behind his ear and avoided Mallory's eyes. 'Sure. I mean, I don't know what help I'll be. I haven't seen him in a few days.'

'I understand that, mate, but you know how it is. Sometimes you remember stuff later.'

'So you think he's missing?'

Mallory nodded again. He wasn't going to give any more information than he had to.

'What do you want to know?'

'Anything you can tell me. According to my information, you were the last person to see him.'

'Okay. I mean, I guess. Did Dante tell you that?'

'We've talked to a number of sources,' Mallory said, looking down at his notebook, where he had built up a timeline of Scott's last movements, as far as his mother had been able to establish.

'You and Scott were seen talking to a couple of guys with gang tattoos. This would have been about three weeks ago. Friday the third.'

'I wasn't talking to them. I remember Scott was, though.'

'What were they saying?'

Adriaan shrugged. 'I think Scott knew them.'

'But you didn't?'

Headshake.

'You must have been there for a while, though, if people remember seeing you.'

'I was going to the store, and I saw Scott,' Adriaan said.

'This was outside a convenience store in Joubert Park?' Mallory had the store on his list to check later.

'Yeah, the JB3 on Tower Hill.'

'What did you go in for?'

Adriaan's brow furrowed. 'I don't remember. Water, maybe something to eat. Does it matter?'

'And you saw Scott inside the shop.'

He shook his head. 'No, he was coming out.'

'You said hello to him?'

'Yes.'

'What was he wearing?'

An uneasy smile crossed Adriaan's face.

'What's the matter, Adriaan?'

'Nothing, it's just ... man, you ask questions like a cop.'

Something about the kid pissed Mallory off. He was treating this whole thing like it was a big hassle, like he couldn't wait to get out of there. It begged a question: why had he agreed to the meeting?

'I'm not the police, Adriaan. Scott's mum can't be here just now, but she's worried sick. I need you to help me, okay?'

Adriaan composed his face and had the sense to look a little contrite. 'Sorry, I just ... so many questions. It's hard to remember everything.'

'Did the police talk to you?'

'No.'

Mallory wasn't surprised.

'Are the police looking for him?' Adriaan asked.

'It doesn't appear that way. You were telling me about Scott's clothes. What he had on that day.'

Adriaan was concentrating. 'Clothes. Okay. He was wearing shorts, I guess, and a T-shirt. It was black, I think. We just talked for a minute. How you doing, that kind of thing. I told him about a party that night. He said he was on his way to meet a guy who had some good stuff.'

'Drugs?'

Adriaan looked embarrassed. He opened his mouth, changed his mind, started to say something else.

'Not a cop, remember, Adriaan. Was it coke?'

He hesitated, then nodded.

'Did he mention this guy's name?'

'No, sorry.'

'And then what did you talk about?'

'That was it. I went inside the store, bought a drink and a bag of Doritos . . .'

'There you go, you're remembering now,' Mallory said. 'You're doing fine.'

'I came out, and I saw Scott a bit down the street. He was talking to the two men. I think they had come out of a van that was parked nearby.'

'What made you think that?'

'I think the door was open? Or maybe I saw one of the men get out, I can't remember exactly.'

'What kind of van?'

'A Volkswagen, I think? Maybe? It was black or blue, I think.'

'Old, new? Anything stick out about it?'

'No, and before you ask, I didn't look at the plate.'

'No reason you would have,' Mallory said. 'Describe the men.'

Adriaan thought about it. 'I don't know. Average.'

'White? Black?'

'White.'

'How old?'

'I don't know, kind of old. Thirties? I really didn't see them for that long.'

'Thirties. Old,' Mallory repeated drily, jotting that down. 'What were they wearing?'

Adriaan scrunched up his features, clearly wanting to tele-graph that he was thinking about this really, really hard. 'I'm sorry. Just, casual clothes. I don't remember.'

'So, not business suits, not swimming costumes. Nothing that stuck to you.'

'No, sorry.'

'You said Scott was looking to buy some coke. You think it could have been from these men?'

'Maybe.'

'What happened next?'

'I'd forgotten to pick up my ouma's newspaper, so I went back in the shop and bought it.'

'Ouma?'

'My grandma. I must have been in there less than a minute. When I came back out, they were gone.'

'The two men and Scott?'

'Yeah. The van was gone, too. I didn't think anything of it at the time. I just thought he had caught up with a couple of friends and then headed off.'

'"At the time,"' Mallory repeated. 'So when did you start to worry about it?'

Adriaan looked taken aback, like he had never considered that until this moment. 'I didn't, really. I didn't see Scott every day or anything, so it wasn't like I noticed he hadn't shown up to something.'

'His mum says she tried to call you. She called around all of his friends.'

'I didn't get any call. I mean, the first I knew there was a problem was when you called me. I don't even know how you got my number.'

'Speaking of phones,' Mallory said, 'Scott's phone stopped working around the last time you saw him.'

'How do you know that?'

'His mum used the Find My Phone app. Last known location was right outside that shop, right at the time Dante saw you and him.'

'Shit, for real? I mean, maybe it could have run out of charge ...'

Adriaan's eyes found Mallory's. The kid seemed guilty about being the last person to see his friend. Maybe he knew he should have paid more attention to the unfamiliar men and the van, or that he should have raised the alarm when the three of them had disappeared together. Adriaan let his suggestion about running out of charge hang in the air, waiting for Mallory to come up with a more plausible suggestion. He seemed to be willing Mallory to give him something to hope for.

Mallory couldn't oblige. 'No,' he said finally, shaking his head. 'It didn't run out of charge. Somebody switched the phone off, and I don't think it was Scott.'

'The guys he was talking to,' Adriaan continued. 'They looked like bad news, you know? They looked like the people you wouldn't mess with in a bar. Or maybe some-body you would buy drugs off, like you said.'

'Did they look like gangsters?'

'Yeah, I suppose. I don't know anything about that.'

Mallory held eye contact with him for a long time, but Adriaan said nothing more. He was a frustrating inter-viewee. Difficult to read. Mallory couldn't tell if he knew more than he was letting on, or if he was just one of those people with a permanent guilty conscience.

He took out one of the cards he had written his number on and handed it to Adriaan. Reluctantly, the kid took it, examining the number. It was the only thing on the card. 'Do you have a name?'

'Yes,' Mallory said.

Adriaan looked up at him expectantly, and then realised that was the only answer he was going to get. 'Fine.'

'If you think of anything else, Adriaan . . .'

'I'll call you. Got it.'

Mallory thanked him again and got up to leave.

'Mister?'

He turned back to Adriaan. 'Yes?'

'I hope you find Scott.'

16

What goes through a man's mind when he falls four hundred and fifty metres?

After meeting Adriaan, Mallory had gone back to Scott Nel's apartment to kill time before his meeting at MTC. He was reading a short news article on his phone about the climbing death of Scott and Donno's father, Bartho Nel. The headline was to the point: CLIMBER KILLED IN WATERVAL BOVEN.

The article provided some of the details of the fall, as far as they could be established by accident investigators. It looked like a freak occurrence rather than human error. A ledge had given way, severing Nel's rope as he was nearing the top of a vertical cliff. A climber in another group had heard him cry out and seen him fall. Climbers from the group rappelled down and tried to administer CPR, but he was dead when first responders finally arrived ninety minutes later. Bartho was described as an experienced climber, having taken up the sport in his twenties and kept it up all his life.

Mallory finished the article and searched for pictures of the wall Bartho Nel had been climbing when he fell. It towered high above the surrounding landscape, and Mallory knew a drop from there would kill anyone. He understood the attraction of carefully calculated risk. Nel would have been well aware of the consequences of a mistake, but he had decided it was worth the risk. Mallory understood and respected that. But still. Four hundred and fifty metres. Fifteen hundred feet, give or take. How long would it take to fall that far? Ten seconds, maybe? A lot of time to think about what was happening to you. When Mallory's time came, he didn't want that long to contemplate his fate. A bullet to the head, quick and clean. That was the way to go, if you absolutely had to.

It just went to show, you never knew what life had in store for you. Donno's family would have spent those last few months anxious about his safety. On tenterhooks, waiting for his safe return from Afghanistan. And then, of course, less than a week after Bartho had been killed, Donno had been critically injured. Mallory couldn't imagine how those two blows would have affected the remaining members of the family, coming in such quick succession. Adversity has a way of revealing character. Susan Nel had rallied, moved her life thousands of miles north to support her son. Scott, by the sound of things, had retreated into himself. Got himself into trouble.

A reminder popped up for Mallory's meeting with the executive at MTC in one hour. He called up the MTC website. It was one of the region's dominant tech companies, many of which had sprouted up over the past couple of decades in a second gold rush. Joburg had found a way to be the city of gold in the twenty-first century as well as the nineteenth.

The company website was slick, with information on their initiatives in a range of different fields. Mallory had already checked it out back at his stopover in Amsterdam at Schiphol. He had gone looking as background, trying to get a feel for how the lives of the four family members fitted together, but had been unable to find any mention of Bartho Nel on the website, let alone his son.

Luca Van Deventer, the man he was meeting with this afternoon, had explained over the phone that Nel was not an employee of MTC, but an independent contractor, helping on a number of their projects.

Mallory put the phone down on the coffee table, feeling a little frustrated despite himself. He had been in the city only a few hours, and had already made progress, but he didn't feel like he was getting anywhere fast. He hadn't even been able to establish that the men Adriaan had seen talking to Scott were actually members of a gang, although it sounded likely. If he could narrow down the list of suspects who could have abducted him, he thought it would get him a lot closer to finding Scott Nel.

But in the meantime, he had an appointment in an altogether more salubrious part of town.

The MTC building rose forty-three storeys from the corner of Jellicoe Avenue and Sturdee Avenue in Rosebank, north of central Johannesburg. Mallory stood on the pavement outside the building and looked up, thinking about how Bartho Nel had fallen twice the height of this edifice.

The foyer was a wide, austere space with a marble floor and pristine white walls. There was a bank of desks in front of a row of turnstiles guarding the approach to the elevators.

A security guard took the name Mallory had given to Van Deventer – Greg Owen this time, to give John Dixon a rest – and checked it on some kind of app on his phone. When that checked out, he held his hand out to the nearest turnstile and a green light lit up.

'Elevator is straight ahead, Mr Owen.'

'Thank you. Wait, which floor?'

The security guard gave him a wide grin, as though he would have been disappointed not to be asked.

'The elevator will take you to the correct floor, sir.'

The correct floor turned out to be thirty-seven. A tall, skinny guy in a white tennis shirt and shorts who looked as though he was just out of uni greeted Mallory as the doors opened.

'This way, Mr Owen. Mr Van Deventer is waiting for you. My name is Trevor, and I'll be delighted to take you the rest of the way.'

Mallory didn't think he had ever met a Trevor born after 1960 back home, but evidently different names were in vogue down here. Trevor led Mallory along a corridor with floor to ceiling glass partitions on either side. Mallory could see people working at stations with double and triple screens. Most of them were dressed casually: board shorts and T-shirts. In his jeans and black T-shirt, Mallory blended in a lot more than he usually did in a corporate setting. The only necktie he had seen since entering the building had been on the person who had greeted him at reception.

As opposed as the two ways of life were, Mallory found himself wondering if there was a similar dynamic at play in the dress codes of the tech sector and special forces. Both set themselves apart by forsaking the rigid dress and grooming of the rest of the business world and the military.

'Have you come far today?' Trevor asked as they walked, after offering tea, coffee, water or fruit juice, all declined by Mallory.

'Pretty far,' Mallory said.

'Your accent sounds English.'

'Does it?' Mallory hoped that Trevor would move past the pleasantries soon.

'I'd love to visit the UK,' he continued. 'All that history. The architecture.'

'We definitely have history.'

Trevor slowed and stopped outside an office. The door was opaque glass, the words on the glass said LUCA VAN DEVENTER, CHIEF OPERATING OFFICER, MTC FOUNDATION. Trevor knocked and opened the door. Mallory looked past him to a spacious office with floor to ceiling windows looking out at the city stretching to the hazy horizon. There was a wide desk with a man in his early sixties seated behind it and a younger woman with blond hair standing in front of it. The two of them looked over as the door opened.

'Mr Van Deventer?' Trevor said. 'Your four-thirty is here.'

17

Van Deventer stood up and beckoned the two of them in. He had a deep tan and silvery grey hair. His age manifested itself in slightly more old-school attire than the other staff Mallory had seen: a white open-necked shirt, but paired with expensive-looking jeans.

'Mr Owen, I'm delighted you could visit us.'

The blond woman standing to one side of Van Deventer's desk, who looked in her early twenties, smiled at Mallory and Trevor and held the tablet she was carrying close to her chest. The pose made her look like a character from an American high-school movie carrying her books after class. She had a slight build and was wearing glasses with thin, burgundy-coloured rims. She looked back at Van Deventer. 'Shall we finish up after your meeting?'

He waved a dismissive hand. 'No need, Ivy, you know what you're doing better than I do.' He looked beyond her to Mallory and Trevor. 'Thank you, Trevor. Have you offered Mr Owen a drink?'

'He did and I'm fine, thank you,' Mallory said, hoping to head off further pleasantries. Trevor smiled and left them.

'Pull up a pew.'

Mallory took one of the two upholstered armchairs in front of the desk and smiled in acknowledgement at the young woman as she left the office. Van Deventer stayed on his feet, leaning on the edge of the desk in front of Mallory. He wondered if it was a conscious move, some kind of executive power strategy to position yourself above the visitor. Mallory responded by relaxing back into the chair.

'I appreciate you taking the time for this,' he said.

'Bartho was a dear friend to all of us at MTC,' Van Deventer said.

Mallory was positioned so that the door was reflected in the window in his line of sight. As Van Deventer said Bartho's name, he noticed the woman – Ivy – pause as she was opening the door and glance back into the room. She only hesitated for a second, and then stepped out into the corridor, closing the door behind her.

Van Deventer sat down behind the desk again, folding his arms. 'I understand you're here on important business.'

'That's correct. Susan Nel asked me to come to South Africa on her behalf. She's very concerned about her son. He hasn't been seen in almost three weeks.'

Van Deventer unfolded his arms. 'It is most concerning. Have the police looked into this?'

'They've been made aware of it. They don't seem to have made much progress.'

'You shock me.' Van Deventer kept his face entirely straight, and then broke into a rueful smile. 'I hope it goes without saying that any assistance we can offer, we'll be glad to.'

'I appreciate that, though I'm not sure how much you'll

112

be able to help. The reason I asked to meet you was because Scott worked here for a short time last year.'

'I believe so, although I'm afraid I wasn't aware of that until you got in touch. We have eight hundred staff in the non-profit division alone, and, with the best will in the world ...'

'I get it. So you didn't know Scott personally?'

'I don't believe our paths crossed, though of course it's impossible to be sure about that. I had HR send me through the details.' He waved a hand at his computer. 'He joined us in January of last year as a B2 coder. He ... appears to have decided to move on in April.'

Mallory leaned forward in his chair. 'Mr Van Deventer, you don't need to be diplomatic with me.'

'I see. All right, it appears he was terminated.'

'On what grounds?'

'Extremely patchy attendance, for one thing. We paid him for seventy-four days in all. The system says he worked eight of those.'

Mallory raised his eyebrows. 'You said attendance "for one thing". What was the other thing?'

'According to the record, he showed up intoxicated on his last day.'

'Model employee, then.'

Van Deventer gave a pained look in response.

Mallory decided to move back to more comfortable ground for a moment. 'Tell me about Bartho.'

'Oh, Bartho was a real asset. He wasn't on our payroll, he was an independent contractor.'

'His wife told me a little about him. He was some kind of scientist, right? Not a computer guy.'

'Bartho was something of a renaissance man. He gave us

a shot in the arm when we needed it. If you repeat this, I'll deny it, but the company as a whole is sometimes in danger of becoming a little complacent, a little reactionary in its thinking. You go from nothing to a multi-billion-dollar corporation in the space of less than two decades, and I guess that's going to happen. But here in the Foundation, we pride ourselves on staying true to the founding ideals of constant innovation and creativity. It's why I'm doing this job, even though my other half would probably be happier if I took the big pay cheque and less hassle of working in the main org.'

Mallory didn't doubt his pay cheque was probably still considerable. 'MTC Foundation is separate from MTC the company, then?'

'Yes, it's the non-profit arm. Two per cent of profits from MTC are invested in MTC Foundation, always have been since day one. Everything we do is for the greater good, and I like to think that benefits the parent organisation, too, and not just in the usual greenwashing, CSR ways. The Foundation is where we innovate, really think out of the box. That's why Bartho was such an asset.'

'What was he involved in?'

'Humanitarian relief, largely. He lent his expertise to a few different programmes. We're involved in work across the whole continent.'

'So famine relief? That kind of thing?'

'Yes. Drought and famine, but also people fleeing conflict and exploitation. And we do a lot for underprivileged young people right here in Johannesburg, too.'

That caught Mallory's attention. 'What sort of underprivileged young people?'

The question seemed to catch Van Deventer out. 'Oh, well, you know ... not every part of the city is as nice as this. There's real poverty out there. Kids who don't have much of a chance.'

'Gangs?' Mallory suggested. 'You do work on that? Outreach or something like that?'

'I don't think so. I mean, not directly. We put a lot into education, scholarships. Funding devices for schools in poorer areas. I would like to think that gives young people who might otherwise become involved in that kind of thing another option. A chance to better themselves.'

Mallory nodded. 'This is kind of a long shot, but do you think Bartho's son could have been involved with one of the gangs in the city? Could that have been anything to do with why he was fired?'

Van Deventer looked confused. 'There's certainly nothing in his record to suggest that. You think that's what explains his disappearance?'

'It's a possibility. The information I have about the last time he was seen seems to fit with some sort of gang involvement.'

Van Deventer's expression changed from confusion to concern. He slid off the edge of the desk and circled around to sit down in his chair.

'The police – what do they think about this theory?'

'They haven't got that far, from what I can see. They don't think there's a problem. I'm starting to think there's a big one. Scott hasn't been seen or heard from in nineteen days. The last people he was seen with looked like they were from a gang. I'm told this city has a problem with kidnappings.'

Van Deventer swallowed, and suddenly Mallory realised

that the concern on his face wasn't just for Scott. The dynamic of the meeting had changed.

'Are you saying that you are expecting a ransom demand?'

'Relax. This isn't a begging visit. I don't want money, and there's no sign of a demand.'

Van Deventer's brow relaxed with relief, and then creased again in confusion. 'But surely if your theory is right, if Scott has been abducted, there would be a ransom demand.'

'That's the part I haven't worked out yet.'

'This raises all sorts of questions.' Van Deventer's brow furrowed. 'Have you considered ... ?'

'That whoever took Scott might have killed him already? Yes, I have. But I don't think so. If they wanted to kill him, he wouldn't have disappeared. If you kill someone and it's not about money, then you generally want people to know about it.'

'What if ransom was the initial motive, but something went wrong?'

'A possibility,' Mallory agreed. 'But again, there's no evidence he's dead, and no demands. It wouldn't be the first time someone had successfully ransomed a dead man. But we keep coming back to that. Everything tells me he was taken against his will, but there's no ransom demand.'

Van Deventer straightened in his chair. 'I'll make some calls. If nothing else, I think I might be able to persuade the police to take this a little more seriously. It might help grease the wheels.'

'I appreciate that. And I know you're a busy man, so I'll be on my way.'

Van Deventer tapped a button on his desk and asked

someone to come to escort Mallory. He walked him to the door and they exchanged goodbyes.

Another young man who looked a lot like Trevor and was dressed like Trevor, but who was not Trevor, appeared at the door. He was less chatty than Trevor. As they made their way back along the corridor, Mallory thought over his conversation with Van Deventer.

He had come here for a couple of reasons: general background on Scott and his father, but also because he wondered about the timing. The father dying violently a few months before the son was kidnapped. It could be coincidence, but it was worth checking. But from what Van Deventer was saying, he couldn't think of any reason why there would be gang involvement. He knew tech companies could be involved in all sorts of fields, but this one didn't seem to be involved in anything that would be of interest to criminals, organised or otherwise.

Scott's job at MTC had been very low level, by the sound of it. Nothing to do with any of the usual areas of gang interest: drugs, prostitution, extortion, illegal gambling. Even thinking about his father's role, it didn't sound as if they were doing anything that could be harnessed by a more advanced gang for cybercrime. No easy profit in humanitarian aid, and therefore it would be of no interest to an urban street gang.

The outreach programme interested Mallory, though. Just because Van Deventer didn't think there was a link didn't mean there wasn't one. If Scott had had any involvement with that side of things, it could have brought him into contact with the people who had made him disappear.

Not-Trevor reached the elevators and gestured to one as the doors smoothly slid open at their approach.

'Psychic elevators,' Mallory said. 'I like that.'

'Your route's programmed from the moment you leave the room,' Not-Trevor said. 'Saves a lot of time.'

Mallory stepped inside and gave Not-Trevor a wave as the doors started to close. Just before the doors met, a hand reached in and triggered the sensors, making them slide open again. A young woman stepped in. The blonde who had been in Van Deventer's office.

'Excuse me,' she said, shooting Mallory an apologetic glance. 'Just made it.'

'The psychic elevator didn't anticipate you,' Mallory said. 'Ivy, wasn't it?'

The elevator started descending at speed. Mallory didn't believe Ivy rushing for this particular elevator had been a coincidence, and she had forty floors and dropping to get to the point.

She turned to him and said, 'You were here about Bartho Nel.'

18

Ivy suggested walking down to the coffee place on the corner of Baker Street. It was in a red-brick building with faded lettering that showed it had once been a fire station. They stood outside on the street with takeaway cups while Ivy spoke.

'I loved working with Bartho. We all did. He just had this ... energy. It was such a shock what happened to him. I guess I've never had that before. Someone I worked with just dying suddenly like that. It knocks you off your feet, you know?'

'I know,' Mallory said quietly. He had experienced what she was talking about more often than most.

'I overheard Mr Van Deventer say that you were here to talk about Bartho and I was curious. Were you a friend of his?'

Mallory shook his head and took a sip of his coffee. They only had three blends at this place, but he liked the taste better than the coffee at the hipster joint where he had met Adriaan earlier. 'I never met Bartho,' he said.

'Then what's your interest?'

'His wife hired me. Their son went missing a couple of

weeks ago and I'm trying to find out if he's okay. As a matter of fact, I was just going to ask you—'

'Wait a second, are you talking about Scott?'

'That's right, Scott Nel.'

Ivy suddenly looked concerned. She put her cup down on one of the outside tables. 'Scott is missing? What happened?'

'I take it you knew him?'

'Yes, I mean, not like *knew* him, knew him, but we met. He actually worked for MTC for a few months.'

'I know. That's what I wanted to speak to Van Deventer about. Did you work with him?'

'A bit. He was on our team for a few weeks.'

'What was he like?'

'Nice. I mean, work-wise he was a disaster. I think poor Bartho was embarrassed he had got him the job. He barely showed up until they fired him, but ... I mean as a person he was okay. He came out for drinks with the team a couple of times. You couldn't help but like him.' She seemed to snap out of the memory, and her eyes focused on Mallory. 'What happened?' she asked again.

Mallory told her what he knew. How he'd been in regular contact with his mother until a couple of weeks ago. The last sighting. His phone becoming inactive around the same time he was last seen.

'Oh my goodness.'

Ivy asked if they had spoken to the police, and responded with the same sardonic look others had given when Mallory told her how much help they had been.

'Your boss is going to try to put a good word in. Maybe that will do some good.'

'You think so?' she asked.

'Not really, no,' Mallory admitted. 'I don't think the police believe there's a problem. They won't until there's a ransom demand, or something else to go on. Meantime, I'm looking into a few things. Did you get the feeling Scott was mixed up in anything serious? I'm not talking petty stuff, maybe something to do with the gangs.'

'I didn't know him that well,' Ivy said. 'I know his dad was really worried about him, though. Like I said, he was a little embarrassed when Scott didn't work out at MTC. We all liked Bartho, so we tried not to talk about it in front of him. One night it was just three of us working late in the lab, and he was talking about his kids. He said he had two boys – I didn't know that until then – and he was so proud of the other one. He's in the army or something.'

'Donno,' Mallory said. 'His name ... is Donovan.' He had almost said *was* and caught himself. The guilt at what had befallen Donno was so great that it felt like he had been responsible for his death. He felt his nails digging into the palm of his free hand and glanced down, noticing that he had made a fist subconsciously.

'You know his brother,' Ivy said. 'You're in the army too?' How had she guessed that? Perhaps the look on his face had given him away. He didn't respond, just motioned for her to go on.

'Anyway,' she continued, 'Bartho said he wished Scott could be as together as his brother. He said Scott had always been kind of a party guy. Wasn't good with responsibility. I kind of felt sorry for him, though. You could tell he wanted to live up to people's expectations, but ...'

'He was a screw-up,' Mallory finished.

She shrugged. 'Doesn't always make you a bad person.'

'How did he take it? When his old man died, I mean.'

'I don't know, he was gone by then.'

'When was the last time you saw Scott?'

'It was a couple of days after he had been fired. He came into the office to get his stuff from his desk drawer and they wouldn't let him in. I took his things out to him in a box. He was full of bravado, boasting about how he still got paid for his notice. I asked him if he had anything lined up and he said he had a bartender gig over in Hillbrow. He said I should come by sometime.'

'Was he hitting on you?'

'Oh no, not really,' she said quickly. But the way her cheeks coloured a little made Mallory suspect she was being modest.

'What was the name of the bar?'

She thought about it for a second. 'Twenty-nine Palms, I think it was called. It's in kind of a rough part of town. Not the sort of place I would really go.'

Mallory looked down the street towards the towering MTC building. 'Sounds like he gave up a pretty nice gig.'

'Office life isn't for everyone, I guess.'

'Fair point,' Mallory said. 'I don't think I could do it.'

'So you do this full-time? Track down missing people?'

'No, this is the first time.' Thinking about it, maybe that wasn't quite accurate. His old job had involved quite a bit of tracking people down, although not to make sure they were all right.

Ivy looked at her phone and put her hand to her mouth. 'I have to be getting back.'

'I'm sorry I kept you.'

'Not at all. I hope you find Scott. That family has been

through enough after losing Bartho. Give me a shout if you think of anything else you need to ask – I'm on the website.'

Mallory thanked her and watched as Ivy walked hurriedly back towards the MTC building. As she disappeared in the crowd, he felt his phone buzz in his pocket. It was a text message from someone he hadn't expected to hear from again. He found a doorway to stand in to dull the traffic noise. A moment later, he was speaking to Adriaan.

'Listen, I know you said to give you a call if I thought of anything else, and I just wanted to let you know I remembered something about one of those men.'

'The men who were talking to Scott?'

'Yeah. After talking to you I started thinking more about it. It was like you said, talking about it kind of jogged my memory. I remembered that one of them had a scorpion tattoo on his arm.'

'Left or right?'

'Left I think, on the bicep. I got to thinking maybe I had seen one of the guys before, but I couldn't think where. Then I remembered: I had seen him in the bar where Scott worked. I went back through my Instagram and I had a pic of me and Scott from that night. The guy with the tattoo was in the background.'

Mallory asked him to message him the picture.

'Will do. I mean, I don't know if he was a regular or anything, but I thought I should let you know.'

'I appreciate it, Adriaan, thanks for this.'

'No problem. The name of the bar is—'

'Twenty-nine Palms,' Mallory finished.

'How did you know that?'

19

Darkness was falling as Mallory stepped off the bus at the stop on Kapteijn Street. The heavens had opened right after he had boarded the bus, and for a while it had been like they were driving underwater. The downpour had ceased just as suddenly a few minutes before Mallory's stop. He knew that Susan Nel's budget would cover taxis to anywhere he wanted to go, but he liked to take public transport. It gave him space to think, and to absorb the feel of the different neighbourhoods without being distracted by conversation. The bus had been almost empty. Most of the citizens seemed to drive, and going by the fact this bus only seemed to operate every two hours, he thought he understood why. Johannesburg's public transport provision reminded him of Los Angeles's. It existed, but it kept a low profile.

On his way, he had visited the convenience store in Joubert Park where Scott Nel had last been seen. The clerk didn't remember seeing anyone, or even if he had been on duty on the day in question. Mallory wasn't surprised. There were no CCTV cameras on the street outside. Nothing to see but an empty street.

Looking at the map on his phone as the bus pulled away, Mallory saw that 29 Palms was a five-minute walk. He found the bar along a narrow side street leading off the main drag. The street surface was uneven and potholed, and puddles had formed from the rain, reflecting the red neon palm trees on the sign. Below the trees was the name of the bar. Its main attractions were listed in smaller type beneath.

29 Palms
Liquor * DJ * Late Nite

There was no bouncer on the door, but it was a Monday night, and still early. Mallory heard loud rock music filtering out from inside. Something with a familiar rhythm. He pushed through the doors and the tune revealed itself as 'Because the Night' by Patti Smith. He stood in the doorway to get the lie of the land.

There was already a modest crowd inside. Mostly male, grouped around in small knots at the tables and at the bar. The walls were exposed brick and the flooring was scuffed linoleum. It reminded Mallory of some of the dodgier pubs you find near military bases. There was a pool table in the corner. Two men were facing off across the baize: one noticeably tall, one noticeably short. The tall one, the older of the two, had dirty blond hair that was long at the back, receding in front, with a handlebar moustache. The other one was skinny as well as short. He had red hair on the top of his scalp, and rusty five o'clock shadow that ran from his chin all the way up the shaved sides of his head.

The bar ran the length of the far wall, with a long mirror behind it with the name of the bar etched out. Mallory spotted the neon palms from the photograph of Scott. Beside them, a glowing sign advertised Castle Lager. He guessed that was the local tipple. There was only one barmaid on duty, and she was currently serving a tipsy couple seated at the bar. Aside from the barmaid, the woman was the only one in the joint.

Mallory felt eyes on him as he stepped inside. Definitely a regulars pub. He was a long way from the tourist trail. A bald man scanning the song list on the jukebox glanced over at him as he entered. The two pool players looked over at him before turning their attention back to the table. The barmaid was taking cash from her customer. Mallory reached the bar and waited his turn. She left the change on a plastic tray between the couple and moved up to Mallory.

She had a low-key goth look, although maybe it was just the combination of her black blouse, dark hair and pale skin. She had a lip piercing, though, and Mallory supposed you would have to work at it to maintain pale skin in this part of the world. Probably an intentional look, he decided.

'What can I getcha?'

'Evening. I'll have a pint of Castle,' he said, pointing at the sign.

She asked if a bottle was okay. 'Not from around here?' she said, reaching into the fridge behind her for a brown glass bottle with a red and white label.

'Pint gave me away, huh?'

'You're on vacation?'

'Business,' Mallory said. He glanced around him. After the initial curiosity, no one seemed to be paying too much attention to him. He took out his phone and found the picture of Scott. 'I'm trying to get hold of a former employee.'

The barmaid leaned over to inspect the photo. 'Scott?'

'You know him?'

'For about five minutes. I came in for cover and ended up replacing him.'

'He got fired?'

'I don't think he gave them the option, he just stopped showing up.'

'When was this?'

'Couple of weeks ago? Maybe three.'

That checked out.

A high, insistent voice called out as Mallory opened his mouth to ask a follow-up question.

'Hey, do you sell peanuts? Bacon ones. Bacon flavour.'

Mallory and the barmaid both turned to look at the source of the voice. It was the woman at the other end of the bar. She had raised her voice a lot more than she needed to for it to carry over the music. From that and the slurring of her words, Mallory decided the couple had been in here for a while.

The barmaid raised her eyebrows at Mallory and moved down to see if she could accommodate the request.

Mallory turned and looked around the bar. He couldn't see anyone who matched the description of the people Adriaan had seen Scott with. But the bald man at the jukebox caught his eye as he looked around and looked away quickly.

Mallory turned back to the bar and sipped from the bottle. It was so chilled he could barely taste it, but it hit the spot.

Mallory liked a drink from time to time, but he had never been one of those people who *needed* it. One of the men in his old unit, Hawkins, had been a functional alcoholic, although he would never have described himself as such. He talked often about the buzz of that first drink. The way he made it sound, it was like a religious experience. Mallory almost envied that feeling. To want something that much, to savour the anticipation a moment before that first sip.

He used the mirror behind the bar to keep his eyes on the man at the jukebox. He was relatively young, though the complete lack of hair made it difficult to judge. He was dressed in khaki shorts and an olive-green T-shirt. He glanced around again, and the way his shirt tightened as he moved told Mallory that there was a gun tucked into the back of his waistband.

His eyes stayed on Mallory for a second, and then he looked across at one of the men at the pool table. The shorter one with the red hair. He paused in the middle of lining up a bank shot and then he followed the bald man's gaze in Mallory's direction. His long-haired partner didn't react. No one else in the place had changed their behaviour at all, but these two were practically flashing warning lights.

Mallory took his phone out and lowered his head so from behind it would look as though he was scrolling a social media feed, but he kept his eyes up and on the reflection of the bar. He had identified the two people he needed to keep an eye on.

The bald one looked over at him again and then approached, taking the stool two along from him. As he sat down, Mallory looked up as though he had just noticed him and nodded acknowledgement. His first thought was that he had come to accost him, but he said nothing, averted his eyes quickly.

Okay. Not someone who wanted to challenge him, at least not in here, but clearly someone who was interested in the stranger asking questions about a former employee. Mallory had some more questions he wanted to ask, but it would be difficult to do that without his new neighbour overhearing, which meant waiting until baldie got bored and went away, or giving up and coming back later.

Or perhaps, a third option. The third option might involve getting physical.

Mallory felt a tingle at the base of his neck. His sinuses cleared and everything around him seemed to change subtly. The music from the jukebox was clearer. The red of the neon seemed more vivid. Everything was sharpening up, reality becoming more heightened. He thought about Hawkins again. The anticipation of that first sip. Perhaps they weren't so different after all.

Mallory put the beer down and waved the barmaid over again. She put the schooner glass she had been polishing beneath the bar and sauntered over.

'Everything okay?'

'Everything's great. How you finding the job?'

She shrugged, as though she hadn't given the matter much thought. 'It's money.'

'Tips good?' He glanced at a jar that was way too big for the pitiful heap of coins at the bottom of it.

She looked around the bar as if to say, 'In this place?' and then looked back at Mallory.

'Scott Nel,' he said, making sure to say the name slowly and clearly.

The bald man two seats along from him stopped with his beer halfway to his mouth, and then took a drink without looking over at Mallory.

'Help me find him and I'll make that tip jar look a little healthier.'

'Sorry. I'd love to help you, but I really didn't know him. What did he do to you?'

'Nothing, he's a mate and I'm a bit worried I haven't heard from him in a couple of weeks. I know he worked here, so I thought I would swing by.'

The bald man wasn't looking at him. In the mirror, Mallory could see that his posture had stiffened and he seemed to be listening intently. Mallory kept talking to the barmaid, but with one eye on the bald man's reflection. He cast another glance over in the direction of the pool table. The guy with long hair was lining up to pot the black. The player with the red hair couldn't have looked less interested in his impending defeat. His eyes were on Mallory's back.

'We might have a number for him.' she said.

'I have his number already. There's another guy I've been trying to trace. I think he's one of Scott's friends. He drinks in here. Tall bloke with a scorpion tattoo here.' Mallory tapped his right hand against his left bicep.

The barmaid scrunched her face up. 'I don't know, I mean, the customers all kind of merge into one ... no offence. Maybe I would remember a scorpion tattoo, I guess.'

Mallory picked up his phone again. He scrolled away from the picture of Scott and found the one Adriaan had sent him earlier, showing the man with the tattoo in this bar. He looked about forty, with close-cropped dark hair and a look in his eyes like a challenge, or a warning.

He put the phone down on the bar for her to look at. Out of the corner of his eye, he saw the bald man trying to angle his body so he could see the picture.

'Sorry, haven't seen him,' the barmaid said after a moment.

'No problem,' Mallory said. 'Do me a favour though – look out for him. I'll come back tomorrow, okay?'

'Sure.'

Mallory slid a two hundred rand note across the bar. 'Thanks.'

He took his time finishing his beer. The bald man stuck around for another few minutes, then slid off his stool. He patted the back of his waistband and headed for the exit. Mallory gave it another five minutes. He drank the last of the beer and when the barmaid wasn't watching, he slipped the bottle into the pocket of his hoodie. Then he got up and headed for the door, watching the red-haired guy at the pool table out of the corner of his eye.

20

It was fully dark outside the bar, the sky a featureless black against the street lights. The traffic noise had died away a little, though Mallory could hear that it was still busy on the main road a couple of blocks south.

Mallory started walking back in the direction of the main road, weaving to avoid the puddles of rainwater. He made a turn into one of the alleys leading off between two rows of buildings. He slowed his pace as he heard the first footsteps.

'Excuse me,' a voice called from behind him.

Mallory turned to see a figure about thirty yards from him, just inside the alley. Difficult to tell for sure in the darkness, but he was pretty certain it was the short, red-headed guy from the pool table. His bald friend would be circling the block to close off the other end of the alley. Mallory put his hands in his pockets, curling the fingers of his right hand around the neck of the empty bottle.

'Can I help you?'

The pool player walked towards him. A little hesitantly, his eyes focused beyond Mallory at the end of the alley. He clearly wasn't confident he could take Mallory all on his lonesome. He was right not to be.

'You got a light?' No slurring of his words, his eyes were alert. Mallory didn't know how long he had been waiting inside 29 Palms, but he hadn't been drinking.

Mallory shook his head. 'I don't smoke. It's bad for your health.'

Finally, a voice from behind him. 'So is sticking your nose in where it doesn't belong.'

Mallory didn't turn around. He didn't make any sudden moves. The red-haired guy was close enough to rush him now. As he watched, he took something from the pocket of his jeans. He heard a click and sodium street light glinted off a blade.

Mallory stepped back, standing against the wall of the alley, so he could see both the men without having to turn fully to face either one of them.

The bald one in the olive-green shirt was at the mouth of the alley on the other side. His hands were empty for the moment, but Mallory remembered the way he had patted the small of his back as he left.

'Where you from, my *boet*?'

'Why do you ask?'

'You're not from anywhere round here with that accent.'

Mallory kept his eyes on the one with the knife, who was approaching with some trepidation while his compatriot hung back at the end of the alley.

'I'm looking for a friend. Perhaps you know him? His name is Scott.'

The short, red-haired guy was almost within arm's reach now. His eyes wide. Ready for it to begin. Mallory kept him hanging on, even though he was more ready.

'How about you? Do you know my friend?'

The redhead stopped, his eyes looking past Mallory to his friend for instruction.

'Who the hell are you?' The bald one was speaking again; his voice had lost the playful edge. Mallory could tell both of them were unnerved by the fact he seemed so relaxed. They were right to be. He let go of the bottle inside his pocket. He didn't need it. He was going to take the knife from the first guy instead, so he needed both hands free.

'I'm nobody,' Mallory said, stepping out from the wall and raising his hands. 'I'm just a guy who spends a lot of time trying to be on his best behaviour at home. But I'm a long way from home right now.' He turned full square to the man with the knife. 'You going to use that thing, or manicure your fucking nails with it?'

The redhead blinked in surprise and then launched himself at Mallory, yelling out as he did so.

Mallory set his feet, kept his eyes on the blade. At the last second, he reached out, grabbed the wrist holding the knife, and sidestepped the path of the blade. He kept hold of the wrist while smashing his elbow into the bridge of his attacker's nose. He didn't hold back, gave it all he had. The knifeman crumpled and dropped to the cracked concrete of the alleyway. He rolled on to his side, dazed, one arm beneath him, the other flat on the ground. He tried to get up, scrambling to his knees, bracing his weight on one hand.

Mallory crouched and slammed the knife down through the back of the hand. The blade penetrated all the way and the tip snapped on the concrete.

The guy screamed in surprise and pain. Mallory took a

step backwards and kicked him under the jaw, cutting the scream off dead.

He turned to see the other one had already moved closer. He had made a big mistake, though. He hadn't foreseen the speed with which Mallory would dispatch his friend and was still reacting. He was reaching back, behind his waistband. Mallory knew what that meant: gun, not knife. And in this environment, that meant closing the distance.

Mallory wasn't consciously thinking about his next move, just acting. His body knew what to do, how to anticipate and counter every action from his attacker. It was almost as though he was watching from a distance.

He was almost on top of the bald guy as he drew the gun.

As Mallory had planned, the unexpected charge spooked his opponent. He fumbled the gun, and had nothing like a good fix on Mallory as he brought it up. Mallory slammed into him, going low and throwing his shoulder into the centre of the chest. The gun went off, the sound echoing off the walls of the alley.

The bald guy staggered back but stayed on his feet. Mallory caught the desperate look in his eyes and knew he was way past threats and questions; he understood he was fighting for his life. He tried to raise the gun again. Close range, easy to hit the target. But close range worked well for Mallory, too.

Anticipating the move, he brought his right arm up horizontally, knocking the gun hand up so sharply that the muzzle was pointing at the night sky as the second shot rang out.

There wouldn't be a third shot.

Instinctively, the gunman reached out with his left hand to try to ward off a grab, while raising the gun further out of reach while he tried to step back, pre-empting an attempt to take the weapon.

Mallory didn't try to grab for it. Instead, he set his feet and went for the wide-open target. Baldie's face. Purely on the offensive. He hit him as hard as he could on the bridge of the nose, trying to punch straight through the target. Once. Twice. He was already toppling backwards on the third impact. Mallory's fist sent him all the way down.

Mallory launched himself forward and came down on top of him, wrestling the gun out of his hand now that his attention was focused on the damage to his face. He shifted position and planted his knee hard in his opponent's sternum. Blood was flowing fast from Baldie's shattered nose and his eyes rolled dazedly in their sockets.

The muzzle of the gun was already pressed against the centre of the forehead, Mallory's finger already tightening on the trigger. Mallory had to stop himself from executing the next natural move. He couldn't be an observer to his own actions any more. It was as though he had to step in and tell himself to ease off.

He gritted his teeth and forced his trigger finger to stop travelling the rest of the distance.

The bald man blinked. Bare seconds ago, he had been taking his time approaching an outnumbered victim, waiting for his friend to cut him, or just intimidate him into submission. Now his friend was out for the count and he was on his back, bleeding all over the dirty concrete.

Classic mistake: underestimating your target.

Mallory now understood that he could have taken care of these two with less force. But, on balance, he was happy with his decision. Nothing left to chance.

He pushed the sleeve of the T-shirt up – left first, then right. No tattoo. Keeping the pressure on his knee, he pushed the muzzle of the gun into the bald guy's forehead.

The bald guy blinked and tried to shake his head. Mallory pushed the gun against his head harder to keep it still. He spoke slowly. 'If I see you moving anything except your lips, I will blow your fucking brains out. Do you understand me?'

The man's eyes focused and Mallory could see he was about to instinctively nod understanding, before catching himself.

'Yes.'

'Where is Scott Nel?'

'I don't know who you're—'

Mallory raised the gun and brought the butt down on the side of the bald head. Not hard enough to knock him out, but enough to add to the pain he was already in. Having to hold back was frustrating, but he needed him conscious. The bald guy grunted loudly in pain.

'Shut up.'

Mallory could hear a siren in the distance. Was it approaching? How long had it been since the two gunshots?

'Don't mess me about. I get the information from you or I get it from the next guy. All the same to me.'

The bald guy blinked. Thinking about it. 'Just . . . just give me a second.'

Playing for time. He could hear the siren, too.

Mallory moved the muzzle a couple of inches to the side and pulled the trigger.

It was deafening at close range for Mallory, so he could only imagine how it must have sounded from less than an inch away from this prick's right ear. He screamed out. His forehead was bleeding from where a splinter of concrete from the ground had nicked him. He managed to get one hand free to jam his hand against his ear.

Mallory stood up and shot him in the left kneecap.

The bald guy jerked up and gripped the injured leg under his thigh. Mallory kicked him in the chest and aimed the gun at the right kneecap.

'CBD! He's in CBD!' he screamed.

'What is CBD?'

And then Mallory realised he was out of time. A wash of blue lights passed by the alley at speed, followed by a screech of brakes and the low whine of a vehicle reversing.

Mallory stood up and started to run back in the opposite direction, stepping over the motionless body of the knifeman.

By the time the cops got out of their car and entered the alley, he had reached the opposite end and disappeared into the shadows.

AFGHANISTAN

SIX MONTHS AGO
TEN HOURS TO HELL HOUR

Confirmation came in at 06:00. Anwar Salim had reached the compound. They had picked up a communication that suggested he was going to be meeting with one of his lieutenants the next day. Unless anything changed, they had him nailed down to a location for the next forty-eight hours.

In the changing room, the men were suiting up for the operation. Mallory checked his kit out: rations, water, medical kit, knife, sidearm, AR-15.

'Thank fuck, I was going out of my mind the last few days,' Yorkie said, lacing up his boots. 'About time for a bit of excitement.'

'Be careful what you wish for, Yorkie,' Westwick said.

'I know, I know. You don't like having to work for a living, do you?' Yorkie smirked and finished towelling his upper body, before balling up the towel and tossing it across the room at the laundry bin. It hit the edge and landed on the floor.

Mallory gave him a critical look. 'I told you you'd never make the NBA.'

A softer voice spoke from behind them. 'How soon do we go out?'

Mallory turned to see Donno emerging from the showers, his towel wrapped around his waist. He had a nervous look on his face. Mallory knew his question needed a straight answer rather than another joke or more pre-action bravado.

'Next couple of hours. We'll get a definite soon.'

Yorkie bent down and picked up the towel, depositing it in the bin from close range, and looked across the room at Donno. 'You look like you want to call in sick, mate. Casper the Friendly Ghost has a better tan.'

'What the fuck is that supposed to mean?' Donno snapped, his whole body tensing for a fight.

The smirk vanished from Yorkie's face and he stepped forward. 'What?'

Mallory was in between them. He stood up and put a gentle hand on Yorkie's shoulder. 'Easy. Let's keep our energy for the bad guys, okay?'

Donno and Yorkie stared each other out for a long moment. Yorkie opened his mouth to say something, and then noticed Mallory staring at him. He gave a slight head-shake and Yorkie sat down. 'Just saying,' he muttered.

Yorkie finished dressing and left the changing room.

'That man likes a confrontation,' Westwick said after the door had closed.

Mallory shrugged. 'He's probably in the right place, then.'

'You really think so?'

Mallory thought about Westwick's question before shaking his head. It takes all sorts to make a team, but he was less and less sure that they needed Yorkie's sort. Unlike the others, Yorkie didn't see killing as a necessary part of the job. He enjoyed it. The man was a bully with a weapon, and Mallory had no time for soldiers like that.

He looked over at Donno, who was bent over, lacing up his boots. 'You okay, mate? Yorkie's a wanker, but he had a point about you looking pale. You coming down with something?'

Donno didn't look up. 'I'm fine.'

Mallory noticed that there was a pendant hung around his neck, swaying as he pulled the laces tight. It looked like some sort of polished stone. Flint or something. It hung between his dog tags.

'What's that?' he asked, pointing at it.

Donno looked down at his chest, as though he had forgotten he was wearing it. He took the pendant between his thumb and forefinger and looked down at it. 'Oh, it's just a keepsake. From home.'

'All the way from Australia, huh?' Westwick said.

Donno looked up at him and opened his mouth to correct Westwick before he saw the glint in the other man's eye.

'Sorry kid, I'll stop it soon, I promise.'

Westwick had genuinely thought Donno hailed from the Antipodes the first time he met him. He made a point of repeating the mistake now and then. It was good-natured. He was much better at interpersonal skills than Yorkie, though that wasn't saying much.

'Don't believe it,' Mallory said. 'When he gets hold of a

joke, he'll stick with it for at least a couple of years. Some people don't have the smarts to come up with new material.'

'I play the hits,' Westwick said. He squinted at the pendant. 'From your girlfriend?'

'No. Actually my uh ... my father gave it to me before I came out.'

Donno hadn't mentioned family members before, and Mallory was suddenly curious. He had meant to ask how a kid from South Africa had ended up in the British armed forces, but he had never had a chance to ask.

'Your folks okay with it?'

'With what?'

Mallory turned his eyes to the ceiling and gestured around him. 'With this. Being out on the front line. It's tough for some people.'

Donno said. 'I guess. I mean my mum worries about me.'

'But not your dad?'

Donno hesitated, his eyes turned downwards. Mallory realised he had hit a nerve. Perhaps the father wasn't okay at all with this. Perhaps it had caused some kind of rift in the family. It wouldn't be the first time. Generally, those rifts can be overcome, as long as you go home at the end of deployment.

'No, actually, my father ... well, he's dead.'

Westwick shot Mallory a look that said, 'Put your foot in it there.'

'I'm sorry,' Mallory said. Donno said that his dad had given him the pendant before he came out here, which meant that this was a recent development. No wonder Donno looked out of sorts. 'What happened?'

'An accident back home. Last Friday.'

'Last Friday? When did you find out?'

'This morning. There was some kind of problem getting a message through to me.'

'Jesus,' Westwick said. 'I'm sorry, mate.'

Donno didn't look up. He was still absently holding the pendant. 'He said it was for luck. Told me to keep it on.'

Mallory moved over to Donno and put a hand on his shoulder. 'Look, we can manage this one without you. You need to take some time.'

Donno looked up and shook his head vociferously. 'No. I'm coming with you.'

Mallory glanced back at Westwick. He looked sceptical, but didn't say anything. Both of them understood why Donno wanted to be out there. To throw himself into the job. But that didn't mean it was a good idea.

'When we're out there, you need your head in the game. No distractions.'

'I know,' Donno said. 'That's why I need this.'

Mallory opened his mouth to ask if he was sure, but before he could speak, the call alarm sounded from one of the recessed speakers in the ceiling. All three of them knew exactly what it meant.

Game time.

21

JOHANNESBURG

CBD.

Was that some kind of company? Another bar?

Mallory worked through the possibilities while he focused on the immediate priority: putting as much distance as possible between himself and the bloody mess in the alley beside 29 Palms. He kept to the backstreets and walked as fast as he could without breaking into a run. Without slowing, he examined himself for evidence of the fight in the snatches of light between dark alleys. There was a big smear of blood on his right forearm from the bald guy's nose. He rolled his sleeves down to cover it, thankful that he wasn't wearing a white shirt. He slowed his pace and considered what to do with the gun. Big problems if he was caught with it, but the risk was justified by the fact it could very well come in handy. He snagged the safety on and tucked it into his belt at the back as he approached the light and traffic of a main road. He could hear another set of sirens approaching in the distance. He hoped they would confine their search to the immediate locale of 29 Palms.

He stepped out on to the street and merged into the stream of pedestrians. A police car drove past him slowly, the cop in the passenger seat scanning the pavements for trouble. Mallory kept his eyes straight ahead and matched his pace to the other people on the street.

A bus pulled into a stop ahead of him. The destination display said it was bound for Orange Grove. He had no idea where Orange Grove was, but going anywhere that wasn't around here seemed like a wise decision.

He settled into one of the rear seats and took a moment to scan the other passengers. This bus was busier than the last one, but there were still only five of them. A mum and her kid, two young girls on a night out, and an old man with a dirty canvas coat who looked as though he might live on the bus. They pulled away from the stop and to Mallory's relief they didn't pass any more police cars over the next few minutes. He had the feeling that gunshots and assaults weren't all that rare an occurrence in the neighbourhood he had just left.

He took out his phone and looked up the three letters the bald guy had blurted out before Mallory's interrogation time had run out.

It turned out CBD stood for Central Business District. From a brief scan of the information, it sounded as though the name was out of date. It had been a whites-only district under apartheid, and the main business hub. After the early 1990s it had become one of the no-go areas of town. It looked like it was still a pretty rough neighbourhood. The only problem was, it was a big area to search. If he'd only had fifteen more seconds, he might have got an address out of the bastard.

But if Mallory was right about his other conclusion from his trip to the 29 Palms bar, there might be someone else he could get the address out of.

22

Adriaan was drunk, from the sound of his breathing and the clumsy way he stumbled through the door and dropped his keys.

Mallory settled back into the armchair and waited. A light went on in the hallway, and a moment later there was the sound of urine hitting the toilet bowl, intermittently finding the water. Adriaan blew his nose loudly and spat, and then the toilet flushed. The light went out and another light came on from a different source. A cupboard door opened and closed. Something fell out. There was a muffled curse. Water running, a glass clinking off the tap.

The door of the living room opened and Adriaan fumbled for the light switch. He was holding a glass of water in one hand and what looked like a packet of painkillers. Treating the hangover early. It showed more foresight than Mallory would have credited him with. Adriaan looked straight at Mallory sitting in his armchair and then did a double take.

'Evening, Adriaan.'

Adriaan screamed. The full glass of water dropped to the carpet and water splashed everywhere.

'What are you ... why are you ... ?'

'Have a seat.'

Adriaan sat down hard on the couch. He made a furtive glance back at the doorway, then calculated that he had no chance of making it there and unlocking the door before Mallory reached him.

'So you weren't expecting me?'

Adriaan's voice was shaking. 'How do you know where I live?'

Mallory smiled. Telling him how easy it had been – that he had got his address from the same discarded takeaway receipt that showed his phone number – would spoil the mystery a little.

'That's what I thought. You weren't expecting me. Which makes a difference from the two gentlemen who just tried to ambush me outside Twenty-nine Palms.'

'What are you talking about?' Adriaan said, struggling to hold eye contact with Mallory. The tone of his voice and body language was about as natural as Donald Trump's tan.

'You told them I was coming. They were watching me from the moment I walked through the door, from before I asked any questions about Scott. How much did they pay you to sell out your friend?'

'I ... I would never ...'

Mallory leaned forward in his chair and sighed. 'Adriaan, I just came from beating the shit out of two big lads who were a hell of a lot handier than you. One had a knife, one had a gun. You have a packet of paracetamol.'

Adriaan started to say something and then buttoned it.

'I want to know everything. No bullshit. Who's got him and why?'

'I don't know—'

'I said no bullshit.'

'I was going to say I don't know *exactly*. We got into a little trouble with a guy who used to be our regular source.'

'A dealer?'

'Yeah. I mean, it was nothing, just a misunderstanding, but he really had it in for us. We were really worried about it. But then one day he got me on my own and told me he would clear the debt if I just did what he said.'

'What did he want?'

'He said he had some friends who wanted to talk to Scott. He said no one was going to get hurt, they just wanted to scare him to send a message to other people.'

'And you believed him?'

'I ... I didn't have any choice.'

'So you didn't just happen to run into Scott that day. You arranged to meet him.'

Adriaan nodded sheepishly.

'And no one would ever have known about it if Dante hadn't seen the both of you. So you knew you had to come up with a story about seeing him. Was there a van? A man with a scorpion tattoo?'

'That was all true. They took him into the back of the van and they drove him away. An hour later I got a text saying if I told anyone ...'

'You still have the text?'

Adriaan reached for his phone. He scrolled through to the message and handed it to Mallory.

The text had been sent at 2.37 p.m. on the date Scott had been abducted. It said simply:

Tell no one or we take you next

'I just hoped they would let Scott go, you know, after they had scared us.'

'No one knows who took him,' Mallory said. 'There's no ransom. What does that tell you?'

'I don't know.'

'It tells you they weren't trying to send a message. They wanted Scott, specifically. And you better hope he's still alive.'

Adriaan shuffled in his seat. 'So, what now?'

'Now, you do exactly what I tell you.'

23

TUESDAY

Branagh's alarm sounded at 7 a.m. He hit snooze. At 7.01, his phone buzzed. Not the work phone, his personal phone. He felt the usual sinking feeling when he saw *Video call from Madeleine Branagh*. He rubbed his eyes and forced his expression into a smile before answering.

The screen blanked and then he saw his wife and daughter looking back at him. In the background, Maddie looked tired, wearing a white robe and sipping from one of the blue china cups. Olivia was in the centre of the picture, and looked as awake as she always did at ungodly hours of the morning. On the shirt of her *Moana* pyjamas, she was wearing an oversize pink badge with the number 7 in sparkles. They were in the dining room, in front of the patio doors. It was still dark outside, of course. Branagh could see the vertical pillars of light from the spotlights in the courtyard shining in the cold air.

'Daddy.'

'Happy birthday, Liv,' he said. 'Isn't this a bit early?'

'Mummy says it's daytime where you are. Do you know when you're coming home?'

'I think it should be soon. I can't wait to see you in real life again.'

He could see Maddie in the background, not saying anything, sipping from her cup.

He cleared his throat. 'Have you opened any presents yet?'

Olivia started happily listing the bounty of presents she had already opened. Most of them Branagh was hearing about for the first time, and he had no idea what many of them were.

As she was speaking, his work phone pinged softly with a message. Without making it obvious on the video call, he reached for it and glanced at the screen. One message. It had been routed through the burner number, which meant it could only have come from one person.

'I'm so happy you're having a good day,' he cut in as Olivia was displaying something called a Squishmallow. 'I actually have a meeting really soon, so can I call you back later on and see how you're getting on?'

Maddie reached in from behind and ruffled Olivia's golden-brown hair. 'Daddy has to go now.'

Olivia blew a kiss at the screen and then she was gone. Maddie leaned in closer, her expression unimpressed.

'I signed the admission papers, Jim. She enrols next month.'

It took him a second to realise what she was talking about. 'For Charleswood?'

'Yes. Olivia didn't want to wait.'

'We haven't even *visited* yet. It's eight thousand a term, we—'

Maddie cut him off. 'She can't stay in that school. And we're doing fine, aren't we?'

He opened his mouth to answer that, and then realised he couldn't. Not right now.

'She's miserable,' Maddie continued, he voice cracking a little. 'Those little witches are making her life hell.'

Branagh cleared his throat and tried to keep his voice even. 'Okay, it's fine, just . . .' *Just don't go making any other extravagant purchases. Like food, or the electricity bill.* 'It's fine. I'll call you later, okay?'

Maddie's expression didn't change. The picture turned black as she ended the call.

Branagh grunted a curse and got out of bed. He made himself a coffee in the galley kitchen of his rented apartment before he went out on the balcony and called the number on the work phone. He looked out across the rooftops as he waited for the call to be answered. Whatever this was about, he suspected it would be less anxiety-inducing than his promised call to Maddie later on.

'Hi, it's Devos.'

'I know who it is.'

'Listen, I thought you should know, there's a guy who's been sniffing around, looking for the kid.'

'We know. Name's John Dixon, a Brit, we think, although nothing's coming up under that name. He talked to the police yesterday. He won't get anywhere.'

'That's what we thought . . .'

Branagh put his coffee down. 'But?'

'But he seems to be making a little more progress than we had anticipated.'

'Go on.'

153

'He managed to speak to Nel's friend. The friend gave us a heads-up that he was going to be at the Twenty-nine Palms last night.'

'No one there can tell him anything.'

There was an inhalation of breath and all of a sudden, Branagh knew why the caller sounded nervous.

'Ah ... actually there was a little problem there. We made sure two of our guys were down there to keep an eye on things. He was asking around. He showed a picture, asked some questions. My people confronted him outside.'

'Christ. If you're calling to say you need someone bailed out—'

'No, they didn't ... that is ...'

'What? He got the better of your guys?'

'I'm afraid so.'

Branagh let out a surprised laugh. 'I thought you had the toughest outfit in town, Devos.'

'We do,' he replied quickly, a stab of irritation in his voice. Then, more quietly, 'They're both in the hospital.'

Branagh considered this information for a moment. 'Well, that is worrying. Did either of them know the location?'

'Not specifically. And they assure me that they didn't give him any information before the police arrived.'

Branagh took that with a pinch of salt, but Devos was right – they didn't know the exact location they were holding Scott Nel. But they knew enough to let someone start to look in the right place.

'Nel's friend gave me a call a couple of hours ago. The one who set things up for us to take him. He says the Brit showed up at his place last night after he was at the Twenty-nine Palms. He knows he set him up. He scared the shit out of him.'

'I'm beginning to like the sound of this guy,' Branagh said. 'So what did he do?'

'He told the kid to set up a meeting today. He's going to follow him. He gave me a call to tell me all about it so we can be on the lookout for him.'

'How do you know he's not just telling you what Dixon wanted him to?'

'He says as scared as he is of the Brit, he's more scared of us.'

Branagh thought it over.

Devos started talking again. 'We reckon he'll be watching the meeting for sure. We're going to put two people at each corner. When they ID him, we'll follow him someplace quiet and take care of him.'

'No,' Branagh said immediately.

'No?'

'I don't want him dead. Maybe he knows something. Or maybe we can use him.'

'You want me to cancel the meet?'

'Go ahead with it. Try to flush him out. If you can take him alive there's a bonus in it. You can put it towards hospital bills.'

'I guess you know what you're doing.'

'Never doubt that, my friend. Never doubt that.'

24

Adriaan was late.

Mallory didn't trust the kid as far as he could throw him, but this was his best shot at finding Scott. The rendezvous was set up outside a café called Arcadia at 3 p.m. Mallory checked out the address online to get the lie of the land. The address was on the edge of a part of town that looked rough even from the satellite view on Google. Lots of waste ground and dilapidated buildings. The Arcadia café was also a laundromat, which was an interesting combination.

Mallory had identified a bar across the road with clear line of sight to the café, and told Adriaan he would be watching from there. It was a good position for a stake-out. There were tables outside, so someone could sit there undisturbed and leave quickly. This afternoon, there were a dozen or so customers enjoying happy hour in the sun.

It was hot today. It had rained only half an hour ago, but the evidence had already evaporated away in the heat. Mallory took a moment to look north along the street, then looked back at the tables outside the Arcadia café. A man was taking a seat at one of the tables, and even with the naked eye, he looked like a promising candidate for the man Adriaan was here to meet.

Mallory lifted the binoculars he had bought from a pawn shop earlier to take a closer look at the man. Early forties, short dark hair and pockmarked cheeks, wearing sunglasses, a black T-shirt and black shorts. There would be a scorpion tattoo under the sleeve of the T-shirt. It was him. His body language was right, too. Mallory could tell the man was very aware of his surroundings. Other customers seemed to avoid walking too close to his table.

It was 3.04 when Mallory spotted Adriaan appearing from the corner three streets north. He stopped before he came within sight of the café and took his phone out. Good. He was obeying instructions. Mallory already had his number on the screen of his phone. He hit the call button and waited for Adriaan to pick up.

'I'm here.'

'Good job, Adriaan. Put it on speaker and just make sure to keep the phone in your pocket. Forget it's there.'

'Are you sure about this?'

'You'll be fine. I do this all the time.'

Mallory hit mute on his end of the call. He watched as Adriaan pushed the phone into his hip pocket and then looked around the street. He paused fifty yards from the Arcadia café and his gaze lingered on the bar across the road where Mallory had told him he would be.

With their low-budget wiretap, Mallory should be able to hear the whole conversation. In any other situation, he would be concerned about the safety of the man he was sending into danger. In this case, he was willing to break a few eggs to make the omelette.

Adriaan came into line of sight of the tables outside the café and the man in the black T-shirt looked up. He didn't raise a hand or call out, just waited for Adriaan to approach.

Adriaan's voice sounded in Mallory's ear as he sat down. 'Hi.'

There was some traffic noise, and the sound was muffled by being in Adriaan's pocket, but Mallory could just about make out the man in the black T-shirt's answer. His accent sounded like Adriaan's – another local.

'What did you say to this guy?'

'I did what you told me, Mr Devos. I sent him to Twenty-nine Palms.'

Devos. Mallory took a mental note of the name.

'Yeah, well you didn't say he was dangerous,' Devos said. 'I've got two men in the hospital.'

Mallory saw Adriaan hold his hands up. 'Look man, I didn't know.'

'Tell me everything about him.'

Adriaan started to describe Mallory. He wasn't bothered about that. He supposed the two men he'd beaten the shit out of last night would have passed on a detailed up-close description anyway.

'He says Scott's mum hired him. She's worried. Maybe if you let him go . . .'

The other man – Devos – leaned over the table and, even from a block away, Mallory could see Adriaan flinch. 'Did I ask you for suggestions, kid?'

'I'm sorry.'

'Is that it?'

'Uh ... yes.'

'Good. Now beat it.'

Adriaan started to get up and then hesitated.

'What are you waiting for, sonny?'

'It's just, you said I could have more ...'

'More ... ?'

'You know, some more money.'

The two of them stared at each other for a long moment until Adriaan backed down.

'You know what, it's fine.'

'Wise decision, kid. You've cost me already. Don't push your luck. We'll be in touch if we need you.'

Adriaan turned and started to walk hurriedly back the way he had come. Mallory followed his progress along the street and then looked back at Devos. He hoped Devos would be leaving on foot. If all went well, there was a good chance he would lead him straight to Scott.

As Mallory watched, he saw Devos turn to look directly at the bar across from where he sat, at the pavement tables that made it a good stakeout position. Two men sitting there immediately got up and started leaning on tables, talking to the other customers. They weren't going to find what they were looking for.

Mallory took the binoculars from his eyes and smiled. The fact that the bar across the street was an obvious stakeout location was the reason Mallory hadn't settled on it. Instead, he had positioned himself about half a block away, on a fire escape attached to a derelict building he had scouted out first thing in the morning. It was concealed, provided an unobstructed view over the whole area, and would enable him to get to street level quickly.

That was where he was as he watched Devos's heavies scrutinise the other customers, and as he heard Adriaan's voice again.

'Can you hear me?'

Mallory glanced back at Adriaan and saw him with his phone to his ear.

'I'm here.'

'You get all that?'

'Yeah, good job.'

As he spoke, he saw Devos get up and leave cash on the table. He saw he had his own phone out. He was talking to someone, his eyes on Adriaan's back as he walked away. That wasn't good.

'Adriaan?'

There was no answer. Adriaan was walking along the pavement, glancing back the way he had come.

Mallory lifted the binoculars again and found Devos. He was putting the phone in his pocket. As Mallory watched, he turned and started walking quickly in the opposite direction from Adriaan.

Mallory was getting up to follow when he heard the gun-shot from two directions – from fifty feet down the street, and from close up in his ear.

25

Adriaan had advanced twenty yards from where Mallory had last seen him, abreast of the mouth of an alley. He wouldn't be going any further.

The kid was face down on the pavement, a dark stain spreading out from his head. Two female passers-by on the opposite side of the road were screaming. Mallory could see no sign of the shooter, and knew he would have vanished into the alley. He heard the retreating whine of a scooter.

Ahead, the man in the black T-shirt – the man Adriaan had called Devos – continued north, not breaking stride, not looking back, although the crowds were starting to flow in the other direction.

Mallory descended the stairs of the fire escape quickly. As he passed by on the opposite side of the street, he could see there was a knot of onlookers already gathered around Adriaan's motionless form. Phones in every hand. Some calling for help, some videoing the aftermath of the shooting. Adriaan wasn't getting up again.

Mallory quickened his pace and crossed over the road as

Devos rounded the corner. All of the other pedestrians were moving in the direction of the crowd or standing and looking in that direction. Devos was the only one who wasn't interested.

Mallory quickened his pace. Following someone who wanted to get out of the area in a hurry had its advantages. He wasn't pausing to look back.

Mallory followed him through a tight alley, past a row of restaurant kitchens with the doors wide open. The smell of spices and hot fat mingled in the air. A young, dark-skinned woman in kitchen whites smoked a cigarette in a doorway and watched Mallory with disinterest as he passed. The alley led out on a street that was much quieter. Barely any people or cars. In the space of a block, the city had changed again. It was like he had moved to the next square of patchwork. There was a line of boarded-up and shuttered stores. Many of the second-floor windows were smashed. It was quieter, more shaded, even the air seemed different, cooler.

It was much more difficult to follow someone on a street like this, compared to the main drag. Mallory hung back in a doorway and watched Devos make his way down the street. Even though there was less urgency now, he still didn't look back.

In the distance, Mallory could hear the siren of the ambulance that had been summoned for Adriaan. He suspected that Adriaan's killing had been set up from the moment he had made the rendezvous. Too bad. But then, it was too bad for Scott that he had got involved with Adriaan in the first place.

Devos turned into a covered passageway, even narrower than the previous alley. It was unlit. Mallory hung back and watched as he disappeared into the darkness, giving him time to cover the length of the passageway. Devos's pace had slowed a little, and he didn't want him to notice he was being tailed.

When Mallory passed through to the other side, he could see no sign of his quarry.

He was in a small open square, about twenty yards on a side. The surrounding buildings were decayed and shuttered. The only person in sight was a homeless man lying in a doorway with a ripped sleeping bag pulled over him. There were three alleys leading off, as well as the one he had just emerged from. He could hear no movement. He moved to the centre of the square and turned around so he could see along each of the passageways leading off. No sign of Devos.

All of a sudden, it didn't seem like a coincidence that this was where he had lost the man he was tailing. A quiet place away from crowds.

And then he heard footsteps.

Someone appeared at the mouth of the alley he had just come through. It wasn't Devos. This man was tall, about six-three. He stood in the entrance to the alleyway, blocking it, staring straight at Mallory. He was wearing jeans and a red jacket. As he evaluated the looming figure, Mallory heard more footsteps approaching from multiple directions. Another two men appeared at the other two openings, both big men.

Finally, Devos appeared in the mouth of the fourth alley, and Mallory realised why he hadn't looked back once. He had been leading Mallory to this place. A sealed box.

That was all right, though, because they still had no idea who they had in the box.

'Can we help you, sir?' he asked Mallory. His tone and the look in his eyes was mocking. 'You appear to be lost.'

'Just looking for a friend,' Mallory said. 'Maybe you've seen him.'

Devos took two steps forward. His three friends mirrored the action, closing the perimeter around Mallory.

'I don't think we can help you,' he said.

Mallory glanced up. Three-storey walls on all sides. Every way out blocked. All of these guys looked tougher than the two men who had come for him last night. This was going to be extremely difficult to fight his way out of.

But perhaps he didn't want to.

These guys were holding Scott somewhere in this area. If Mallory became another prisoner, it was logical that they might put him in the same place.

'I'll be on my way, then,' Mallory said, making to walk past him. Devos put a hand out and contacted Mallory's shoulder, pushing him back roughly, keeping him in the centre of the square.

'Not so fast. You hurt a couple of my friends last night.'

Mallory nodded. Pleasantries over.

'Perhaps they shouldn't have tried to hurt me first, Devos. And it was two against one.'

Devos looked surprised for a moment when Mallory used his name. 'Better odds for the home team this time,' he said, glancing at his friends. 'We can show Dixon here a good time, can't we, boys?'

Dixon. He was using the name to show that Mallory didn't have him at a disadvantage. Mallory hadn't given Adriaan any name at all, so he had to have heard it from elsewhere. But that was not a puzzle he had time to think about right now.

Mallory made to turn around and look at the other three,

giving the first guy an opening that he knew he would take. As soon as he saw him pull back for a punch, he ducked out of the path of the swing and hit him hard in the solar plexus. He crumpled but grabbed hold of Mallory's arm, stopping him from moving to the unguarded alleyway. It slowed him down enough that the one in the red jacket was on top of them before he could move away.

He ducked another swing and planted both hands on Devos's chest, pushing him back hard. He was untangled from both now, but backed into a corner.

The other two men were closing in. He pivoted towards the closest and blocked one blow with his left forearm, and then another with his right, before ducking under a third wild swing and making for the nearest alleyway. The fourth man got the first connecting blow, his fist glancing off the side of Mallory's head. He turned and kicked the guy in the stomach as he was still following through, sensing one of the others behind him before it was too late.

He felt something jab into the small of his back and immediately his body spasmed and white light exploded into his eyes.

Mallory's legs gave out and he crashed to the ground. With an effort of will he rolled on to his back, getting his arms up to protect his midsection. The one in the red jacket was holding a long stick with a fork on the end. A bloody cattle prod? What the hell?

Mallory couldn't help but grin at the craziness of it. He clenched his fists and started to get to one knee.

'Come on then!'

The guy with the cattle prod moved in again, stabbing

at Mallory's chest. He blocked the strike with his forearm but immediately electricity coursed through him again. He yelled out and then felt a kick to his side as he was trying to regain control of his limbs. A moment later, he saw one of the heavy boots Devos was wearing swinging towards his head. He tried to get an arm up to block it, but his limbs weren't doing what he told them to do.

The boot connected with an explosion and darkness seeped into the edge of his vision.

He didn't pass out completely. His senses dulled. The ache in his limbs seemed to get fuzzier, the blow to his head didn't feel as sharp as it ought to have. Reality seemed to become a series of snatched freeze-frames.

He heard broken fragments of speech.

Tough skelmpie …

Still conscious, I think …

Watch him …

He felt strong fingers digging into his wrists, his shoulders taking his weight as he was dragged. He thought he was passing out, then realised it was just the darkness of the closed passageway. He heard the heels of his boots scuffing against concrete.

And then he did black out for a minute, or maybe more. The next thing he knew, the dragging had been interrupted and he was being carried. Arms under his arms, hands clasped on his chest. Somebody else carrying his feet, peering into his eyes with curiosity.

Who the hell is he?

Not a problem any more …

He heard grunts and was aware of being carried up steep stairs. The stairs seemed to go on for ever. The darkness closed in again. And then he was somewhere bright, like somebody had turned a floodlight full on his face.

In fragmented thoughts, he started to wonder if they had done more damage than he realised.

He thought he could see Donno in the blinding light, reaching out a hand to him.

'Donno,' he murmured. 'Where is this?'

26

Scott looked up as he heard footsteps approaching. This time, something was different. This was not the usual confident, unhurried rhythm. There were two or three of them out there, and from the scuffing noises and grunts, they were carrying something. Something heavy.

There was a muffled curse and something heavy banged against the door, like somebody had swung a full sack of grain against it. And then there was an exhalation and a rattle of the key in the lock, and the viewing slot opened.

'Against the wall,' the guard called out. Not the American. The one he had heard the others call Ruan.

Scott knew the drill. He shuffled back and sat on his hands. He had forgotten the hands part the first couple of times and had earned an extra punch.

The viewing slot snapped closed again and the door swung open. Scott saw that it wasn't a grain sack, it was a man. He didn't recognise him. He had dark hair and a beard. He was in good shape, looked in his thirties. He was wearing a canvas jacket and a white T-shirt, and he was barely conscious. The right side of his face was covered with blood from a nasty gash at the edge of his forehead. He stumbled forward and was helped on his way with a kick.

The man with the black T-shirt, the one Scott thought was called Devos, dusted his hands and looked at Scott. He had a bloody nose. The man in front of him clearly hadn't gone down easy.

'Your lucky day, kid, you got a cellmate. For the time being.'

The door slammed shut. The dark-haired man had landed on his back. He raised an arm weakly, trying to block out the glare from the overhead light.

He mumbled something Scott couldn't quite catch. It sounded like 'Dunno'. As though he had been asked a question.

'Are you okay, man?' he asked. A stupid question. The guy looked as though he had been on the wrong end of an argument with a bus.

The man murmured something else incomprehensible and then his head tilted back, and his eyes closed.

Scott took a sharp breath and felt his neck for a pulse. It was strong, and the man seemed to be breathing regularly. He carefully pulled the man's jacket off and balled it up, putting it under his head.

Scott had no idea who the beaten and bloody stranger was, and he didn't care. Right now, he needed every friend he could get.

27

Mallory awoke in darkness with a dull pain on the right side of his head, worse than any hangover.

He touched a hand to the place where it hurt and winced as the pain changed from dull to stabbing. He rubbed his fingertips together and felt the tacky smear of partly dried blood.

His short-term memory started to return; slowly at first, like a tap turned slightly on.

Adriaan being shot, following the man in the black shirt. What had happened then? Painstakingly, he started to fit together the pieces until the picture revealed itself. Four attackers. A man with a cattle prod. The kick to his head.

And then some kind of hallucination, or near-death vision. Seeing Donno and a bright light.

He blinked a few times and turned his attention to his immediate surroundings, to the here and now.

All around was darkness. There was a musty, decayed smell, like rotten wood and damp. He could hear traffic noise from somewhere distant. He was lying down on a hard surface. He reached out and felt the ground beneath him. Uncovered floorboards, dusty and rough. His head was resting on something. Bundled-up cloth. His jacket. His attackers must have propped up his head while he was unconscious. Unusually considerate of them.

What was in store for him when they inevitably came back? Probably another beating, as well as some questions about who he was and why he was here. Mallory had undergone some pretty intensive resistance to interrogation training in Brunei. After that, he doubted if these cowboys could dish out anything he couldn't handle.

He cleared his throat and the sound told him the room was small and empty. A cell. The only source of light was a fine line of yellow artificial light, maybe five feet away and three feet above where he was lying on the floor. A boarded-up window, with just a crack where the street light could shine through. Not an official cell then, but a makeshift one. And the traffic noise suggested he was still in the city.

Carefully, he started to move his limbs, braced for the stabbing pain of a broken bone. But his arms and legs seemed to be okay. There was another, duller pain in his ribs where he must have taken a blow, but they felt bruised rather than broken.

He took a deep breath in and out, and it didn't hurt any worse. He braced himself on the floor and started to get on to his knees, wincing at the cramp in his left thigh where he had lain awkwardly. It took him a minute to get to his feet, but he was able to do so without feeling too dizzy. He was grateful for the darkness. He got the feeling bright light would increase the pain in his head a hundredfold.

He patted his pockets. They had taken his phone and the

John Dixon wallet, but they had missed the key card for Scott's apartment. It was still in his back pocket. A lot of good that would do him right now.

He took a step towards the line of yellow light, wondering if there would be enough of a gap to see anything if he got up close to it. He held his hands out in front of him like a blind man feeling for obstructions. One step. Two steps.

His right foot came down on something and he stopped. He knelt and felt in the darkness. A bundle of something. The bundle moved and cried out.

Mallory stood back, raising his hands.

'Who's there?'

'Sorry, you scared the shit out of me.' The voice was familiar somehow. Like someone he knew, but not quite.

And then suddenly Mallory knew where he was, who the person on the floor was.

'Scott?'

There was a shuffling as the man on the floor got to his feet. Mallory's eyes were adjusting to the dark, now. In the sliver of light from the crack at the bottom of the boarded-up window, he could make out a familiar form, even though he had never been in the same room as this person before.

'Who are you?' Scott said.

'My name's Mallory. I've been looking for you.'

'What?'

'I served with your brother in Afghanistan. Your mum hired me to find you.'

'You knew Donovan?'

'Yes. He's a good friend.'

'What ... how did you know where I was? *I* don't even know where I am.'

172

Mallory smiled ruefully in the darkness. 'Well, that's the bad news, Scott. I don't know exactly where we are, either.'

He explained how he had come to South Africa and started to make enquiries. Scott sounded almost surprised when he learned how worried his mum had been.

'I wasn't sure she would have noticed, to be honest. She's all about Donovan.'

'She noticed, Scott,' Mallory said sharply. 'She has two sons, and she can't be in two places at once.'

Scott sounded contrite at the rebuke. 'Sorry, I should have known. It's just . . . my parents have always kind of just left me to it. The worst thing about this is feeling I was all alone.'

'Well, you're not alone now. We're both in deep shit. What's the story, anyway? Why did they take you?'

'I don't know. At first I thought they were going to ask for money, but they haven't said anything about it. I even offered to pay them to let me go.'

It confirmed what Mallory had uncovered so far. It didn't appear that this was about money, at least not directly.

'What did you do to annoy them? Adriaan said there was some drugs thing. The two of you had got in trouble somehow.'

'What?' Scott sounded genuinely surprised. 'No. Nothing like that. Wait, you talked to Adriaan?'

'Yes. Your mum spoke to someone who saw you together before you disappeared and I tracked him down.'

'That's funny, Adriaan is into some pretty dodgy shit. At first I thought they meant to grab him, not me. You think they could have mistaken me for him?'

'No. It's not about him. Adriaan is the one who sold you out. He set me up for a beating, too.'

Scott paused for a second to take this in. 'That little bastard. I wondered ... it was like those guys knew exactly where I would be. That's why I wondered if they meant to grab him, but all along he had set me up. When I see him, I'm going to wring his neck.'

'No need. The people providing our hospitality have already seen to that.'

It took a second for the meaning of Mallory's words to sink in. 'You mean ... ?'

'Yeah. I used him to get close to the gang. It worked, but I have to admit it didn't go as smoothly as I had planned. I got a kick to the head, he got a bullet in his.'

'Jesus.'

'I don't think he's a great loss to the world. But it tells me these bastards are serious, and they're not messing around. So I need to know why you're here and why you're still alive.'

Scott's voice was shaking. 'Jesus, they *killed* him?'

Mallory put his hands on Scott's shoulders, hoping to make him focus on the matter at hand.

'You're telling me you have no idea why they took you?'

'I ... I don't know. They ask me questions, but they don't make sense. That's how I know they've got the wrong guy.'

'What kind of questions?'

'Just stuff about a code.'

'They grabbed you in Joubert Park, right?'

'Yeah. They brought me here with a bag over my head. It took maybe half an hour to get here, so I think I'm still in the city.'

'Probably somewhere in the CBD,' Mallory said. 'One of the men who attacked me last night said that was where you were, and it's close to where I got jumped.'

'How long has it been? It feels like a month. It's difficult to tell in here.'

'They took you on the third; it's the twenty-third today.'

'They beat me most days. They bring bread and water, I think in the mornings. The first few days, it was afternoon or evenings they would beat me. There's this one guy who's really bad.'

'What does he do?'

'The others, they just hit me. This guy is different.'

'Different how?'

'Totally different. I think he's American.'

Mallory frowned. That wasn't what he was expecting at all. 'American?'

'That's what he sounds like. He's the one who asks the questions. He gets the others to strap me to a chair and he puts a bag over my head so I can't breathe, then he asks me about the code. About something called Anambra. I don't know what the hell he's talking about.'

The technique sounded familiar to Mallory. This wasn't the action of some street gang. This was someone who had training. Someone versed in the skills of what is euphemistically called 'enhanced interrogation'. A more accurate description would be torture.

'The American, what does he look like?'

'He's over six feet, big guy. He has blond hair. He dresses differently from the others. His clothes look expensive. He wears a shoulder holster, but he always leaves the gun outside the room.'

'Did he seem like he could have been in the military?'

'I don't know. Maybe. Everything he does seems kind of ... deliberate, you know? Like he has a job to do. He's not just screwing around. I tried to tell him I don't know anything.'

'You said he doesn't come every day.'

'It's hard to tell, but maybe every couple of days or so. I don't know why he keeps it up, I don't know anything.'

'He doesn't believe you,' Mallory said. 'He thinks you're holding out, wants to break you.'

Scott laughed in the darkness. 'I'm broken already. I would tell this guy anything he wanted to know, if I knew what the hell he was talking about. I just ... I don't know who he thinks I am.'

There was a long silence.

What Scott had said in the last few minutes changed everything. This wasn't some small-time gang ransom thing they were talking about. This was something else. But it didn't change the first order of business: getting the hell out of here.

Mallory went to the window and crouched so his eyes were next to the gap between the board and the sill. He could see enough to confirm what he had been worried about. The window was barred behind the board. Even if they could find some way of levering the board off, they would be no closer to getting out that way.

Mallory straightened up and started to pace out the dimensions of the room, putting a hand to the rough brick wall as he walked around it. The smell of urine meant it was easy to tell where their toilet was: a bucket in the corner.

'So what do you think? Have they got the wrong guy?'

'Quiet, I'm thinking.'

The room was about ten feet by fifteen. Mallory repeated

the circuit of the room, knocking gently on the wall every couple of paces.

He turned back in what he knew was Scott's direction. 'What time is it?'

'I have no clue, they took my phone when they grabbed me.' He paused. 'Night-time,' he added, unhelpfully.

Mallory sighed. 'How long since they brought me in?'

'I don't know. A few hours?'

Adriaan's meeting with Devos had been at three o'clock, so it would have been three-thirty, four when Mallory had been knocked out. Sunset was around eight this time of year.

'You said they bring you bread and water every day. When?'

'Morning time. The sun's up when they come.'

'How many of them?'

'I don't know. There are always at least two of them. Except when the blond man comes. Then it's just the boss who lets him in.'

'When they bring you food and water, what do they bring?'

He looked confused. 'I told you, just bread and water.'

'What do they bring the water in? A mug? A bowl?'

'A bottle. Plastic.'

'Room temperature or cold?'

Scott hesitated, confused. 'Cold, usually. It's just a little bottle, it isn't glass or anything you could use for a weapon.'

'Okay.'

Mallory sat down and massaged the pain in his head. It still hurt to touch it, but he didn't think there was any permanent damage.

He felt around on the floor for the jacket and bundled it up again to use as a pillow.

'What are you doing?' Scott asked.

'I'm getting some shut-eye.'

'What?'

'You should do the same. Get some rest. I need you to be alert in the morning.'

28

WEDNESDAY

The thin line of light had changed when Mallory opened his eyes again. It was now a bright blade of real sunlight. So bright that he knew the room had to be east-facing. He could make out more of the space now, though it was still dim. It clearly wasn't a purpose-built cell. It looked like part of a flat. He wondered if their captors were elsewhere in the same flat.

Scott Nel lay curled in the corner, his eyes closed. His hair, features and body shape were a match for his brother. Ironically, the last couple of weeks of trauma had made him resemble his brother the last time Mallory had seen him in the hospital bed. Skinny, dishevelled and bruised.

He was snoring lightly. Mallory closed his eyes, blocked out the snoring and listened for other sounds.

Traffic. Regular, moving quickly. A motorway, perhaps. He tried to remember the layout of the CBD area from looking at the map the day before. There was a bypass road about a mile east of the street where Adriaan had met Devos. The same one? Impossible to tell.

Mallory put his ear to the door and listened, hearing nothing.

He had a kink in his neck and his body still ached from the beating. Quietly, he lowered himself to the ground and started doing push-ups. The first few hurt like a bastard, but in time, the exercise had the intended effect, and he felt his muscles start to loosen up. He got to his feet again, his arms aching, but not feeling as stiff.

He listened at the door again. This time, from somewhere beyond, he heard the low murmur of conversation. Not too close, maybe in another room along a corridor – as though a door had been opened that had been closed before. He couldn't make out any words, but the tone seemed to be conversational. There was a snort of laughter. He heard the creak as another door opened.

A voice, loud enough to make out the words. 'You want anything?'

Then a slightly quieter voice, from further away. 'Get me some cigarettes.'

'Sure, Ruan, just as soon as you pay me for the last pack.'

Mallory moved over to Scott and nudged him gently awake as the voices bickered.

He woke up with a start and shrank back instinctively from Mallory before remembering who he was.

Mallory kept his voice low. 'This is the time of day they bring food and water?'

Scott rubbed his eyes and looked around, judging the light. 'Yes. About this time.'

'One of them's going out,' Mallory whispered. 'This place

is falling apart. I don't think the water is on in the building. That's why someone goes out to get the food and water.'

'That's why you were asking about the water?'

'Yeah. It seemed considerate of them to chill your beverage, don't you think?'

'Ah,' Scott said.

The light from the gap in the board had dulled a little, and Mallory heard the sound of raindrops hitting the glass pane beyond. Intermittent at first, and quickly increasing in regularity until it was a constant rattle, like someone shaking a jar of pins. He could hear it from above, too, which meant they were probably on the top floor of the building.

'I think this is our opportunity. I'm going to try something in a minute.'

'Wait a second, they'll kill us if we—'

'Shut up.'

Mallory moved back to the door and listened. The two men had finished their negotiation and the first one was saying he would be back in five. The door creaked shut. Mallory counted forty-eight seconds until he heard a dim clatter of a heavy exterior door slamming shut below. They weren't too high up. They were probably in one of the abandoned apartment buildings he had seen the previous afternoon. Scott was already on his feet. Mallory told him what he wanted him to do. Scott's part was straightforward.

A minute later, Mallory lay face down on the floor and closed his eyes as Scott moved to the door.

'You sure about this?'

'Do it.'

Scott started banging on the door. 'Hello? Is anyone out

181

there? I think this guy is dead!'

He kept banging for more than two minutes before Mallory heard footsteps outside. He assumed this must be the 'Ruan' the other one had addressed.

'What is it?'

'The man you put in here with me – I just woke up and I think he's dead. His face is blue. He's not breathing.'

There was a muttered curse. The viewing slot snapped open. 'Stand back from the door.'

There was a pause and Mallory knew Ruan would be trying to see him through the slot. He had positioned himself so only the bottom half of his body would be visible.

Ruan addressed Scott again. 'Back in the corner, sit on your hands.'

Mallory listened as Scott did what he was told.

There was a rattle of the key, the lock disengaged and the door opened.

Mallory felt hands on his back, shaking him. Then a hand underneath him, trying to roll him over. Only one hand, which meant he was probably holding a gun on him while he did it. He let himself be rolled. As he turned over he opened his eyes and reached out and grabbed the guard's gun hand.

Ruan turned out to be the tall one in the red jacket from yesterday. He yelped in surprise. Mallory had hoped he could yank the gun free in one move, but Ruan recovered in time to hold on to it, though his finger had slipped out of the trigger guard. Mallory gripped the gun with both hands and started to pull towards him, angling the business end away from his face. Ruan kicked and tried to brace his feet to pull away.

'Scott ...' he started to say from between gritted teeth, but Scott was already on his feet. Moving towards Ruan. He grabbed him from behind, trying to pull him off Mallory. Bad move, he just helped the guy pull the gun away from Mallory.

But as he pulled back, Ruan's heel twisted on Scott's foot and the pair of them fell back against the wall. Mallory leapt to his feet and slammed his fist into the inside of Ruan's wrist as he tried to get his gun under control again. It clattered to the floor. Mallory liked the odds better now.

Ruan roared as he slammed Scott against the wall and then swung for Mallory. Mallory blocked the strike, and the follow-up attempt, and then headbutted him. He fell backwards and tried to stumble towards the gun. Mallory had been hoping he would do that. He let Ruan get his hand on the gun and then stamped down on top of it. He heard a couple of fingers break as Ruan yelled out in pain. Mallory bent and swung his fist at his head, going for a knockout blow, but Ruan moved at the last second and rolled. He got to his feet and charged, slamming Mallory against the wall. He had a weight advantage, but with one hand out of action, he knew he was losing the fight.

Mallory took two hits to the torso, both of them hurting more than he expected because of the bruising from yesterday. He didn't care. It gave him an open shot at his assailant's face. Three quick punches in succession. Ruan staggered backwards and Mallory moved in again. This time, he slipped an arm around his neck, moving around so he was behind him. As the fingers of Ruan's good hand scratched wildly at his arm, Mallory braced his feet, tightened the grip of his arm, put his palm flat against the side of the Ruan's head and pushed – hard.

The neck snapped and his body went limp, like his strings had been cut. Mallory released him and he dropped to the floor.

Scott was still getting to his feet. From the moment Ruan had rolled him until now had taken less than fifteen seconds.

'Holy shit. Is he dead? Did you kill him?'

'Of course I bloody killed him.' Mallory opened the door and looked down the corridor. There was nobody in sight. 'Now let's get the hell out of here.'

Scott blinked, still looking down at the dead man on the floor. He looked like he needed a sit down and a cup of hot sweet tea. Mallory was the opposite. The adrenaline was pumping. He couldn't slow down now if he wanted to.

Mallory bent down to pick up the dropped gun. He grabbed Scott's arm and pulled him outside the room and into the hallway. In the kitchen of the apartment there were a couple of chairs and a table. On the table were some empty beer cans, half-full packs of chips, a deck of playing cards, plus Mallory's wallet and his phone. Scott had picked up a light leather jacket that had been thrown in the corner along with a canvas bag.

'That yours?' Mallory asked when he saw Scott rummage inside the bag.

'Yeah. They've taken everything.'

'Forget it,' Mallory said, putting his wallet and the phone back in his pocket. He wasn't surprised to find the cash was gone, but they hadn't taken the ID that said he was John Dixon. Carrying the false ID was an easy, sensible precaution, but he was very glad he had done it. It would make life easier once they got out of here. *If* they got out of here.

He stepped back out of the kitchen and opened the front door of the apartment. The corridor outside was strewn with trash and the walls were coated with graffiti. It looked like nobody had lived here for a long time. The door to the stair-well was about thirty feet from their door. At the other end of the corridor was another door marked ROOF – AUTHORISED ACCESS ONLY.

Mallory stepped back inside the apartment and saw Scott hovering at the edge of the room that had been his cell for the last two weeks, staring at the body of Ruan.

'Get it together,' Mallory said. 'We got lucky that they left him on his own, the other one will be back in no—'

As though to prove his point, Mallory heard the sound of the stairwell door opening, outside in the corridor.

The voice he had heard earlier called out, 'Ruan – everything okay?'

The returning guard had already spotted that the door was open. Mallory cocked the gun and stepped out into the corridor.

29

A man wearing canvas shorts and a white T-shirt was standing by the open door to the stairwell, a bag of groceries with the red and blue Pick n Pay logo on it cradled in one arm. His hair and T-shirt were wet from the rain. He dropped the bag and reached behind him for his gun.

Mallory shot him twice in the chest. Blood blossomed on the T-shirt and he fell back. The bag landed on the floor, a milk carton bursting and splashing white over the wall.

Mallory heard a yell from beyond the door at the end of the hall. Somebody else was coming up the stairwell. He grabbed Scott's arm and pulled him out into the corridor, pointing in the opposite direction, towards the roof door. 'That way, go!'

Scott reached the door first and flung it open as Mallory backed along the corridor, hearing multiple sets of running footsteps ascending the stairs. The morning shift had evidently arrived.

He followed as Scott took the stairs. They headed up one flight to another door.

'It's locked,' Scott said, his eyes panicked as he rattled the handle. For a brief second Mallory wanted to slap the pathetic look off his face. He thought about how much he wished it was Donno who was by his side in this situation, rather than his brother. They would have nothing to worry about.

He pushed Scott aside and shot the lock off. He kicked the door open and they were on the rooftop. The rain was coming down hard, bouncing off the bitumen surface. He slammed the door behind them and surveyed the surroundings. It looked like they were about five storeys up. Too high to jump. The next building looked like it might be reachable, though. It was a little lower than the other buildings, and there was a billboard on top of it, the faded and tattered remains of an ad for the Carlton Hotel still clinging to it.

He heard the sound of voices, footsteps climbing the last set of stairs. Scott was eyeing up the gap between this rooftop and the next one.

'Should we—'

'Wait a second.'

Mallory stood to the side of the door and waited. A second later, it burst open and a man ran out, his head jerking from side to side, scanning the roof for the prisoners. The analytical part of Mallory's brain couldn't help but be dismayed at the guard's terrible awareness of his environment. He was utterly heedless of the way the heavy rain was masking sounds. Mallory pointed the gun at the back of his head and pulled the trigger. His brains exited his head from the front.

Mallory dragged his body and jammed it against the roof door, so he was blocking it from opening. It would take his compatriots another minute or so to get the door open with two hundred pounds of dead weight jamming it shut.

He tucked the gun into the back of his waistband and looked up, opening his mouth to tell Scott to run, but he was already sprinting for the edge of the roof. As Mallory watched, he seemed to hesitate at the last second before committing, and then jumped out into the void.

He wasn't going to make it.

Helpless, Mallory froze as Scott sailed out into the air and yelped as he realised he was coming up short. But then he managed to land half on the edge of the opposite roof.

He started to slip down, his elbows and forearms still gripping the parapet.

'Help!'

Mallory didn't waste another second thinking about it. He followed Scott's path, turning on the speed, the ache in his limbs totally forgotten, and launched himself across the space, passing over Scott's head and coming down on the opposite roof. He rolled and got back up on his feet to run back to the parapet. He was already drenched to the skin.

Scott was breathing fast, losing his grip. He had already slipped down so that only his hands were gripping the edge now. Mallory reached out and grabbed one of his wrists with both hands, just as Scott's other hand slipped off the wet surface. Mallory braced his feet on the rough surface of the roof and took Scott's whole weight as he dangled over the drop.

'I've got you, mate,' he said as Scott cried out.

Dimly, under the din of the rain, he could hear the noise of the other guards kicking on the door on the opposite roof and slowly shifting the weight of their dead friend. If he didn't haul Scott up soon, the drop would be the least of their worries.

Scott was panicking, grasping at Mallory's arm, and unwittingly making it tougher to pull him up. Mallory felt his fingers slip and regain purchase on the wet skin.

'Calm down, I've got you, it's okay.'

'I'm falling.'

The downpour seemed to increase in intensity. He could see the individual drops falling, bouncing off Scott's face on the way down.

'Scott, put your feet against the wall. I've got you. Just put your feet on the wall and walk up.'

Scott swayed and then managed to get one foot on the wall and then the other, taking some of his own weight. It was a relief to Mallory's arms.

'That's it, now just walk.'

Mallory risked looking up. The door on the opposite building was part way open now, and a long-haired man was squeezing out through the gap.

He looked back down. Scott was moving up. Mallory waited until he was close enough and then pulled, using his own weight as a fulcrum to haul Scott up and over. The two of them fell back on the rooftop.

'Thanks, I thought I was—'

Mallory pulled him to his feet. 'Save it.'

He heard a yell and then two bullets smacked into the surface of the roof a few inches from them. They ran towards the opposite side of the roof. There was another big drop, but on this side there was a balcony two floors down. Mallory waited for Scott to dangle over the edge and drop down while he turned to see how their pursuers were getting on.

He took cover behind a vent as they fired again, then vaulted over the parapet and dropped to the balcony.

He landed on a patio table that collapsed under his weight and deposited him on the floor of the balcony, knocking the wind out of him. Before he could get to his feet, he heard a shriek and saw an old woman standing in the room that looked out on them, holding her hands to her face in horror.

The door was partly open, so he pulled it the rest of the way and stepped inside, holding his hands up in apology.

'How do we get out?'

The woman pointed at the door. 'Take anything you want. Just please get out.'

'Sorry,' Scott said as he followed Mallory out. They exited the apartment into a long corridor and quickly descended three flights to the ground floor. Mallory made it out on the street first, looking both ways. A teenage boy wearing a backwards baseball cap and a white T-shirt under a translucent poncho was mounting his scooter at the side of the road.

Mallory looked back at the closest corner. Their pursuers knew they would be coming this way, and would be here soon. He approached the scooter rider, holding the gun behind him.

'You okay, man?' the boy asked Mallory, looking back at him nervously.

Mallory raised the gun and pointed at him. 'Give me the keys.'

'Wait, we can't just ... ' Scott started.

The boy put his hands up and stepped back from the scooter. The keys were in the ignition.

'Get on the back,' Mallory said, swinging his leg over the saddle and turning the key. The engine whined to life. He heard shouts and running footsteps from behind them. 'Get on!'

As soon as he felt Scott's weight settle on to the pillion, he revved the engine and tore away from the kerb, sending a shower of puddle water up as the wheels spun and gripped the road.

Mallory turned at the first cross street and steered into traffic. He had no idea where he was going, which was probably an advantage. It was impossible for their pursuers to predict which way they would be heading. He rode as fast as the scooter would let him, which wasn't as fast as he would have liked.

They passed a huge stretch of waste ground, fenced off with chain-link, then shot beneath a motorway flyover and out into a down-at-heel residential area. There were bungalows with wide, scruffy yards. A group of kids loitering on a street corner splashed in the puddles and yelled out insults as they passed. Mallory turned on to a wider road and followed it until the houses yielded to another patch of waste ground. Beyond that, the city started to encroach again: taller buildings. Pawn shops and cheap hotels and gun shops.

Another motorway flyover cut across the street ahead of them. Mallory pulled to a stop, keeping the motor running. As though in synchronisation, the downpour abruptly stopped. The sense-consuming sound and feel of the hammering rain gave way to a cold silence and the smell of ozone. It seemed warmer already. Scott shuffled off the back and looked back the way they had come with trepidation.

'I think we lost them.'

Mallory regarded the empty street. 'For now.'

30

The rain was coming down in sheets, making it difficult to see much of anything, but Branagh knew something was wrong from the moment Willer steered around the corner and he saw the apartment building ahead of them.

'Where's the sentry?'

Willer slowed as they approached the building. This was the first time they had arrived here and seen no sign of a man outside. Even in weather like this. Devos had been at pains to demonstrate how secure their makeshift holding facility was.

Willer pulled the black SUV up twenty yards from the door and waited with the engine running.

The two of them exchanged a glance.

'What's up?' Foster had leaned forward from the back seat, placing his elbows on the front headrests.

'No one's watching the store,' Willer said, rubbing his chin and eyeing the unguarded door.

Now that they were close enough for the entrance to be more than an indistinct blur in the rain, Branagh could see that the door was not just unguarded, it was ajar. He took out his phone and called Devos. He picked up promptly.

'Devos, where are you?'

'I'm at home. Why?'

'We're at the building.'

'Okay, I'll call Ruan to let you in.'

'We're outside the building. We're the *only* people outside the building. Where's your guard?'

Devos grunted. 'That fuckin' . . . Give me a second.'

Branagh waited patiently, tapping his fingers on the dashboard and keeping his eyes on the open, unguarded door through the rain. Willer tapped in the code to pop open the compartment between the seats. He took out the two Glocks, handed one to Branagh, checked the load in his own.

Meanwhile, Branagh could hear Devos on the end of the line, muttering under his breath. Dully, he could hear the ringing of another phone.

'He's not answering,' Devos said.

'Who isn't?'

'Ruan. He's on duty.'

'I see.'

'I'll be down there in ten minutes.'

Branagh hung up without an acknowledgement. He exchanged another glance with Willer. Willer looked back at the door, his nostrils flaring.

'What's happening?' Foster asked.

'Stay here, watch that door,' Branagh said. 'Anybody comes out of it you don't like the look of, kill them.'

They got out of the car and hurried to the building. Willer led the way, approaching the door with his gun drawn, pointed down but ready to raise the moment he saw movement. Branagh followed.

Five paces from the car, they were already soaked. The rain was warm. It was like standing under a shower that wasn't quite hot enough. Christ, he hated this city.

Willer reached the door, nudged it all the way open with his foot and waited until he had checked line of sight, then gave Branagh a thumbs up.

They stepped inside. The key was still in the lock on the inside, as though somebody had been about to secure the door, but had got distracted.

They heard raised voices from above. At least two male voices, raised in anger. Branagh couldn't make out individual words. He let Willer take the lead again. They moved quickly up the stairwell with a minimum of noise, covering all the corners as they advanced to each floor.

The apartment building looked like it had been abandoned for years. The only evidence of human habitation was broken bottles, discarded needles and graffiti.

The voices grew louder as they approached the top floor.

'—the hell did he get a gun anyway?'

'I don't know but he obviously did.'

A pause.

Willer slowed ahead of him, and a moment later Branagh saw why. A motionless hand was sticking out over the top of the stairs. As they climbed higher, they saw it was attached to a dead man. He wore a white T-shirt stained with blood. Blood was pooled beneath him, too, mingling with milk from a burst carton. His eyes were open, staring at the ceiling. Beyond the body blocking the stairwell, they could see two of the gang members having the argument at the far end of the corridor. One was in jeans and a hockey jersey, the other shorts and a grey T-shirt. They were so engrossed that they had yet to notice Willer and Branagh.

'What do we tell Devos?'

Branagh stepped over the body. 'Maybe you should worry about what you tell me.'

Only now did the two guys notice they had company. As one, they started and fumbled for their guns. Willer and Branagh had their guns on them already.

'Jesus,' Willer said. 'I thought Devos said he put his best people on this.'

'Best is relative,' Branagh said. 'Okay, guys, where the hell is my prisoner?'

As he spoke, he heard footsteps on the stairs below them, ascending rapidly. He turned to Willer, who was already on it. A moment later, Devos turned the corner, holding his gun. Immediately he put his hands up. 'It's me. Jesus.'

'Get up here,' Branagh said. When Devos reached the top step, Branagh waved his hand, encompassing the body on the floor and Dumb and Dumber in the motion. 'What the hell is this?'

Devos's eyes looked like they were going to pop out of his head. He looked from the body, to the other two, to the open door of the apartment. 'I ... I ... '

Branagh didn't wait for him to finish. Willer was already headed for the open door, gun trained on it. They moved quickly through the apartment. The door of the makeshift cell was open. Branagh could already see it was undamaged, which meant that brute force hadn't been used. Scott Nel and the other man had fooled their captors into opening the door somehow.

The cell wasn't empty.

A body was lying face down on the floorboards, the neck at an unnatural angle. Branagh knelt beside the body and turned the head around. He recognised the dead man. It was Ruan. Branagh had met him briefly when they came to speak to Scott Nel the first time. Willer stayed upright, inspecting the corpse with a professional eye.

'Somebody did this with his bare hands.'

Branagh straightened up and dusted himself off. 'Judging by the guy outside, he wasn't working with his bare hands after this.'

He looked around. The board was still secure on the window. The only evidence the prisoners had ever been in here was the half-full piss bucket and a couple of empty plastic bottles.

From outside the room, they heard a new voice calling Devos's name, betraying an unmistakable tone of panic.

Branagh stepped outside and saw another man standing at the doorway of the apartment, his face red. He wore a black T-shirt emblazoned with the skull and crossbones logo of the Orlando Pirates soccer team. It was soaked through with rain.

He started when he saw Branagh. 'Who are you?'

'I'm the guy who's paying you for this, and I'm not happy,' Branagh said.

Devos stepped outside and saw the man in the Pirates T-shirt. 'Jake. What happened?'

'Mikel is on the roof, he's dead,' Jake replied, looking relieved to see Devos.

'Where the hell are the prisoners?' Branagh asked.

'They got away over the roof,' Jake said. 'They can't have got far.'

'How long ago?'

'Not long. Ten minutes.'

'Then they can have got far. And they will have done,' Branagh said.

Devos shook his head and rubbed the back of his neck. 'I don't know what the hell happened here. Ruan must have gone into the cell alone and ...'

'Yeah, I think we get the picture,' Willer said, barely keeping the anger out of his voice.

'Nice of them to leave a trail of bodies for us,' Branagh said.

'Look, we can fix this,' Devos said.

'Bring all your men down here.' Branagh glanced at the body on the floor. 'All the ones who are still breathing, anyway.'

Devos said okay and went outside to summon his other men.

Branagh turned to Willer. 'Get our people together. I'm assuming Devos's punks would have taken their wallets, so they don't have any money. Put someone on Scott Nel's apartment. Get the list of his friends, employers. Check it all again.'

Willer turned to go. Branagh put a hand on his shoulder.

'Stay here for a minute. I'll need you to help me clean up.'

31

Mallory and Scott had dismounted the scooter and were standing beneath the motorway flyover. Above them was the rumble of cars soaring each way, thumping off the expansion joints.

'My place is about five kilometres from here,' Scott said. 'It's in—'

'I know where it is,' Mallory said. 'We're not going to your place.'

'But—'

'No, Scott.'

Scott looked as though he was about to burst into tears. 'I have to go home. I have to go to my place and—'

'Listen to me. These people didn't pick you at random. They had a reason to take you, and if we go back to your apartment, we'll be walking right back into their arms.'

'Then where do we go?'

Mallory waved a hand at Scott's stained clothes. He looked as though he had been through a tumble dryer. Mallory suspected he probably didn't look a whole lot better, though he imagined he smelled better.

'We need somewhere to get cleaned up. Somewhere to hide out until we can work out what's going on. Have you got any cash?'

Scott patted the pockets of his jacket and shook his head. 'They took everything. My phone, my wallet, my Apple watch . . .'

Mallory thought for a second. They needed money, and they also needed to get rid of the scooter somewhere that wouldn't lead back to them.

'All right, I've got an idea. Get back on.'

Mallory started up the scooter again and circled around to go back the way they had come. He retraced the last half mile until they came to a group of teenage boys standing outside a vape shop. They were all talking and looking at videos on their phones.

Mallory cruised to a stop alongside the group of teens. 'Morning, fellas.'

The biggest one looked contemptuously at the two dishevelled men on the scooter. His upper lip wrinkled in distaste.

'What do you want, perv?'

Mallory restrained himself from retaliating, verbally or otherwise. He didn't think this kid would be quite so brave if he was on his own.

'You like the scooter?'

'It's a piece of shit.'

'Right. It's yours for two thousand rand.'

The kid looked incredulous. If Mallory had the conversion right, that was about a hundred quid.

They negotiated and three of the boys clubbed together, digging out notes and coins, and they eventually agreed on fifteen hundred rand. Enough for a cheap hotel room,

Mallory hoped. Two birds with one stone: get rid of the bike, get some cash. He felt a little bad about the previous owner, but hopefully he was insured.

Five minutes later, they stopped outside a scuzzy-looking hotel that didn't appear to have a name, unless it was called 'rooms by the hour'. It was on one side of a small city square that looked as though it would have been a nice spot in years gone by, but had spent a long time going downhill. There were another two hotels on the square that looked even less inviting. The line of store fronts on the western side of the square were mostly shuttered, aside from a sex shop with a purple neon sign advertising its wares in explicit detail.

Mallory stepped inside, Scott following hesitantly in his footsteps. The small reception area was floored in ripped linoleum and it smelled of damp and stale cigarette smoke. The staff member at the desk was an overweight man with a receding hairline and a paunch that peeked out from under his grubby light grey T-shirt. It turned out the place did have a name. A brass plate on the desk said WELCOME TO THE HAUER HOTEL, with three stars underneath. Mallory guessed it was either a very old sign, or South Africa's star ratings worked on a scale of one to a million.

The receptionist looked at Mallory and Scott with distaste and handed over a brass key in exchange for the notes Mallory put on the desk.

They made their way up to the third floor, where half of the proceeds from the sale of the scooter had bought them a small room for the night.

There was a double bed and a television that looked like it might have been the cheapest model somebody could find in 1993. Mallory walked across the threadbare carpet and nudged the Venetian blinds to one side to look out at the street. It was quiet. A couple of parked cars, but no one passing on foot. They were way off any of the main routes through the city.

Now that the exhilaration of the chase had subsided, he felt tired. He knew he would sleep tonight. It was always the same after he had let himself off the leash, and the outburst of violence back at the apartment block had gone a long way beyond a fight in a pub.

He turned back to Scott. Scott looked the opposite of tired. He looked wired to the moon. Beads of sweat stood out on his forehead and he was shaking like a junkie three days from his last fix.

'There you go, we're safe here,' Mallory said. 'That wasn't so difficult, was it?'

Scott turned from surveying the tiny room with distaste to look at Mallory. 'Are you kidding me? You nearly got me killed. Several times. It's just blind luck that we—'

'*I* nearly got you killed?'

'It was your idea to run!'

'You're welcome. What do you think those guys would have done to you if I had left you there? Sooner or later they would have worked out that you really didn't know anything, and they would have taken care of you.'

Scott's gaze lowered to floor level and he shrugged a concession. 'Maybe.'

'How the hell did you get yourself into this situation anyway?' Mallory asked. 'Your mother said you had got in with a bad crowd.'

Scott rolled his eyes. 'Jesus, she's always saying that. I mean I can't do one damn thing right. *Why can't you be like Donovan? Why can't you be the perfect golden boy, the good son?* I've been dealing with this crap all my life.'

'Listen to me,' Mallory said, suddenly feeling a flush of anger. He wanted to hit Scott. The only thing holding him back was the knowledge of how much physical punishment the kid had taken over the last couple of weeks. 'I knew Donno. I fought alongside Donno, and he was – is – one of the best men we had. I've known you for a few hours and I already know he's worth ten of you, so if you can't tell me anything useful, at least quit whining.'

Scott looked chastened. He lay on top of the covers on the bed and started rubbing at one of the yellowed bruises on his forearm.

Mallory went to the window again. The square outside was still quiet. The centre of the square looked like it might once have been an urban garden; now it was just a patch of rough ground with patches of yellow grass here and there. The window was positioned well to see anyone loitering.

He needed some time to think. The people who had taken Scott hadn't done it for any of the reasons he had expected. They had wanted information of some kind. What did that mean?

His train of thought was broken when Scott spoke quietly. 'What was he like?'

Mallory looked back at Scott. He had his eyes closed, was still rubbing the bruise.

'Who?'

'My brother. You seem to know Donovan pretty well.'

'He's your brother, mate.'

'Exactly. Do you have any brothers?'

Mallory didn't answer.

Scott opened his eyes and sat up on the bed. 'Fine. Stay mysterious. Sometimes you know your own family less well than anyone else. I just wanted to know what he was like.'

'What he *is* like. He's not dead.' Mallory sighed and reminded himself of what Scott had been through. He softened his voice. 'He's a good soldier, like I said. You can count on him.'

'What kind of ... work did you do? Raids and stuff?'

'Something like that.'

'Must be scary.'

'I don't really think about it that way.'

There was another long silence.

'How long have you known him?'

Mallory hadn't thought about it in a while. 'I met him in Brunei, on jungle selection.'

'Jungle selection?'

'The tough part,' Mallory said. 'You get assigned to a team of six to eight men, they whittle each of those teams down to two or three. If you don't make the cut, that's it. I remember thinking Donno would be first out. He was skinny, a lot younger than the other guys. But he kept up. End of the first exercise, he beat a couple of the other guys back to the final rendezvous point.' Mallory was still looking out at the empty square, but in his mind he was in the jungle of Brunei. Feeling the humidity, the ache in his limbs, the taste of blood from pushing himself to the limit and beyond. 'We had six on the team. That day, everyone made it back except one. This big Welsh guy named Danny. He was built like a tank, but he could move. I would have put money on him making it through, but he was nowhere to be seen. We had fifteen minutes to spare before the headcount, so I decided I was going to go back and see if I could find him. I thought maybe he had broken a leg or got stuck somewhere. The others told me to sit tight, let him get RTUd. All of them except Donno.'

'He went with you?'

Mallory nodded. 'I mean, I could understand where the others were coming from. If we didn't make it back in time, we would be gone, too. But Donno wanted us all to make it. Even though he knew it was an elimination exercise. It didn't make sense, but ... I liked that he was thinking about his teammate more than himself. It was a good sign. Anyway, we found Danny a couple of hundred yards from the FRV. He was unconscious. Turns out he had some undiagnosed condition. He had pushed himself too far, had some kind of seizure. We got him stable and got him back to the FRV. It was touch and go, but he pulled through. Later on, the docs told us Danny would have been a goner if we hadn't got to him when we did.'

'You saved his life.'

'Perhaps. The thing is, if Donno hadn't been there, it would have been four against one. Maybe I would have just listened to the other guys and waited the fifteen minutes.'

Scott was quiet for another minute before he spoke again. 'You killed those men back there. Three people.'

'Yes.'

'What does it feel like?'

'It feels like doing what has to be done. If I could have got us out of there without killing them, I would have.'

'You don't feel guilty or anything? That you killed someone?'

Mallory turned from the window and looked at Scott. He had stopped rubbing his bruises and seemed to have calmed down a little. He was no longer shaking visibly.

'The guys that did this to you. Do you think they would have felt guilty if they had killed you or me?'

Scott thought about it for a moment. 'No.'

Mallory looked at the bruises on Scott's arms. There were scratches on his face too. Ligature marks around his neck. Nothing that indicated a serious attempt to cause permanent damage, but he hadn't been treated well.

'What did they want? They had to want something to do this to you.'

'I don't know. They beat me most days, usually two of them at a time. The worst days were the days they put the bag over my head.'

That reminded Mallory. The blond man. The American.

'The Yank who did that, what did he ask you?'

'I told you. He wanted to know about "the code". He said I knew where it was. I had no clue what he was talking about. Once he mentioned something that sounded like a name – Anambra.'

Mallory remembered him saying that before. 'Anambra?' he repeated. 'Who is that?'

Scott shrugged. 'Beats me. I don't know what any of this is about.'

Neither of them spoke for a while. The distant sounds of the busier parts of the city filtered softly through the open window.

'What do we do now?' Scott asked.

Mallory considered the question that had been on his own mind for the last half-hour.

'I'm still working that out. But right now, I think we should let your mum know you're in the land of the living.

AFGHANISTAN

SIX MONTHS AGO
FOUR HOURS TO HELL HOUR

'NO SLEEP TILL BROOKLYN!'

The yelled chorus and the crunching guitars through his headphones almost drowned out the din of the rotors of the Chinook. Mallory closed his eyes and nodded along with the beat. He felt completely calm. He enjoyed this part. It was like standing on the edge of the diving board before you committed to the jump.

He opened his eyes and took a look around the interior of the aircraft. The other men were doing the same as him in their own ways; enjoying the last few minutes of downtime before it was time to clock in.

Westwick was writing in his notepad, wearing headphones too. Mallory wondered what he was listening to. Probably a Radio 4 podcast about deforestation in the Amazon basin, or a biography of Miles Davis or something. Donno was checking his pack. Mallory had seen him go through his checks at least three times so far.

The red light went on for a pilot announcement. Mallory lifted the left side of his headphones away from his ear to hear it.

'Ten minutes to LZ.'

Mallory left the earphones on as he pulled out his own pack and started going through the final checks. The Beastie Boys track finished and the next one on his shuffled playlist started. 'Gasoline', by Audioslave. He always had two playlists on the go. Loud, aggressive rock, metal and rap for the way out, something more chilled for the return trip: blues and soul mostly.

He looked up and saw the other men were carrying out their checks. Donno had finished and started all over again. He looked completely absorbed in his task. Mallory called out his name, but his voice was carried away by the din. He reached for the whiteboard beside him and jotted down his message.

All good?

He turned it around and reached across to tap Donno on the knee. Donno looked up, saw the message, and gave a thumbs up before looking back down again.

Mallory watched him for another moment before reaching for his rifle. He hoped the kid would be okay. Grief hits different people in different ways. He knew some would argue that he shouldn't have to be on this mission, but if Donno had felt that way, he could have put in a request to sit it out on compassionate grounds. Perhaps this would be good for him. Mallory knew it would be his choice too, in that situation. Sometimes the best thing to do to deal with a loss is to throw yourself into a difficult and demanding job. And they don't come much more demanding than a night-time assault on an insurgent compound.

A boot softly kicked his and he looked up to see Yorkie holding his own whiteboard. He had drawn a crude caricature of Mallory with headphones on, DJing.

Mallory rolled his eyes, wiped his own board, and added a four-letter response. Holding it up without even looking back at Yorkie.

He finished checking his rifle and laid it beside his pack. He checked his night-vision goggles – full working order, fully charged. Finally, he hit stop on the playlist and took his headphones off. He ran his fingers through his hair and put on his helmet, strapping it underneath his chin.

Most of the others had done the same. Good to go.

Donno caught his eye again and nodded. He looked focused, determined. Game face on. Exactly what he needed to be.

The cockpit light went on again.

'Five minutes.'

Mallory leaned over to look out of the nearest window. The sky was dark. He could just make out the snow-dusted peaks of the mountains as they started the final descent. He kept his eye on the ground as it got closer.

The other men started to stand up, grip the canvas straps, get into position. Mallory took his place, second from the end, just behind Donno.

He patted him on the shoulder hard. Donno didn't react.

Yorkie was three men ahead in the line. He punched his palm and yelled, 'Let's fucking do this.' Mallory was pleased when no one else joined in with a whoop or a fist bump.

After this raid, he would have a talk to the higher-ups about team chemistry.

Mallory bent his head to look out of the window again and saw that they were a hundred feet or so above the ground. The man at the back pulled the lever and the tailgate of the Chinook dropped. The rotor noise became deafening. The cool night air flooded the cabin. It cleared his head.

He gripped the strap as the wheels thumped down.

Time to go to work.

32

JOHANNESBURG

Mallory put Susan Nel on speaker and told her he was with someone who wanted to talk to her.

'Mum,' Scott said. 'I'm okay.'

'Oh, thank God.' She sounded like she wanted to cry with relief. 'What happened to you?'

'I don't know,' Scott said. 'They kept me in a room. I don't know what they wanted.'

'Did they hurt you?'

Scott opened his mouth to reply and then saw the look in Mallory's eye. Mallory gave him a soft headshake.

'No, Mum, they just wouldn't let me out.'

Mallory gave him a brief approving smile. There was no point further traumatising his mother. She had enough to worry about.

'Well, thank goodness they didn't hurt you. I was so worried.'

'Mrs Nel, it's Mallory here.'

She laughed. 'I told you, it's Susan. You just saved my son's life, we can be on a first-name basis.'

'Susan, I'm still trying to work out why these men kidnapped your son. Up until a few hours ago, I thought it was a simple gang thing. Either they had a grudge against Scott specifically, or they could get some money out of him. It's not that. They wanted information, and I think they were working for someone else. I don't think it's mistaken identity. They knew who he was. Scott said they mentioned something about "Anambra" – does that ring a bell with you?'

'Anambra,' she repeated, and thought for a second. 'I know it's a state in Nigeria, but other than that, no.'

'No connection to you at all? What about your husband?'

'We were married for twenty-six years. As far as I know he's never been there.'

'Okay,' he said, thinking it over. Perhaps Anambra wasn't relevant. Or perhaps Scott misheard the word his captor used.

'I'm so glad you're safe, Scott,' Susan said, after no one had spoken for a minute.

'Me too, Mum.'

'I think it would be best if you came over here. To be with me and Donovan.'

Mallory put his hand up to silence Scott before he could reply. 'I don't think we should do that right away, Susan. Those men are still out there. They got to Scott easily the first time, and if we take things for granted, there's a danger they could get him again.'

'Oh, I see.' Susan's voice sounded deflated as she realised they weren't out of the woods yet. 'Then what would you advise?'

'Right now there's too much we don't know. But the one

thing I do know is this problem won't go away until we work out what those men want and find a way to deal with it. I'm going to find somewhere safe over here for Scott to hide out while I look into this further.'

There was a long silence. Mallory wondered if she was going to resist, insist that Scott come to the UK. Tough. He wasn't going to let that happen. As soon as Scott was on the move, he would be findable.

'I can't ask you to put yourself at more risk, Mallory, you've already done enough.'

'You hired me to do a job. The job isn't over yet.'

Susan took a deep breath. 'If you're sure, then I suppose you're right. You are the expert, after all.'

'That's right,' Mallory said, although he wasn't sure about that. There were too many unknown quantities here. How can you be an expert on the unknown?

'If you need more money—' she started.

'We're fine for now, but we'll work out a way for you to get Scott money if he needs it. Don't worry about us, we'll get to the bottom of it.'

Susan's voice hardened. 'Scott, you do whatever Mallory tells you, all right?'

'Mum, I'm not a little kid.'

'Scott, I mean it.'

Mallory stifled a laugh at the mum voice, and the way Scott visibly shrank. Mallory hadn't managed to achieve that reaction when he had been two feet away and on the verge of slapping him.

'Yes, Mum.'

'When it's safe to do so, I want you over here with me, and we're going to start again, all right?'

'Yeah.'

'I was so worried. I can't lose you.'

She had caught herself before she'd said anything else. Mallory was pretty sure it would have been ... *as well*.

'I know. And I'll be careful, I promise.'

'Good. I love you.'

'I love you too, Mum.'

When he hung up, he gave Mallory a sheepish look.

'She's one of the good ones, mate,' Mallory said. 'You're lucky you had her looking out for you.'

'I know. And thank you. I'm sorry I was a dick earlier.'

'Forget about it. Last couple of weeks haven't been a picnic for you.'

'You can say that again. Anyone else miss me?'

'Ivy from your old work helped me out a little.'

He frowned. 'Ivy Maritz? I always thought she hated me.'

'She seemed to have a soft spot for you,' Mallory said. 'No accounting for taste. What's that?'

Scott had taken what looked like a small stone from his jacket pocket. It looked familiar to Mallory, somehow. He saw that there was a black cord attached to it. Some kind of necklace.

'Looks like this is the only thing they left me with,' Scott said. He was looking at it unhappily, like he wished it would transform into an Apple watch.

Then Mallory remembered why it looked familiar. He remembered that Donno had a similar pendant. One of the few things the brothers had in common.

'Your dad gave you that, right?'

Scott looked surprised. 'How did you know that?'

'Donno had one, too.'

Scott hung the pendant around his neck and looked over at the window again. 'How long do we need to stay here?'

'I don't know. The main thing is we keep you safe until I can deal with these bastards.'

'What will you do?'

'Persuade them of the error of their ways.'

As he said that, a siren echoed from somewhere out in the city. Scott looked at him and he knew they were both thinking about the same thing. They had left quite a trail in their escape. Scott's captors probably wouldn't be the only people looking for them.

'Tell me about the people who were holding you again. Were there any others who didn't fit in? Like the guy with the American accent.'

'Not really. All of the others seemed local. The American ... it wasn't just his accent. You could tell he wasn't with them.'

'How do you mean? Like he was working for them, or they were working for him?'

'Like they were working for him.'

Mallory nodded. He had a hunch Scott would say that. All of a sudden, this was looking like it went beyond Johannesburg. It sounded like the gang were merely hired local muscle.

'Did he say anything else that sounded weird to you? Any military terms, anything like that?'

Scott thought about it. 'I don't think so. He didn't really say much apart from the questions. You think he's military?'

'Ex-military, maybe. Or CIA. His techniques sound like he knew what he was doing.'

'You can say that again. I would have told him whatever the hell he wanted to know ... if I knew what that was.'

'I believe you. I wonder why he didn't.' Mallory got up and took the remainder of the cash from the drawer in the bedside table where he had left it.

'Where are you going?' Scott said, obviously trying to hide the anxiety in his voice.

'Relax. I won't be long. We need some supplies, and I need to make a call.'

33

Mallory wasn't sure what the next step was, but he knew Scott would need to lie low for a while. They would need clothing, food and a pair of new phones in case they got separated. He told Scott to get cleaned up while he went out for supplies. Before leaving the hotel, he sent a short email to an acquaintance on the east coast of the United States. He knew Jake 'Mac' McIlroy was a night owl, so he hoped that he would be awake to see the message.

Mac replied almost immediately with a phone number. The email came through when Mallory had walked less than five minutes from the Hauer Hotel. He took a look around for somewhere quiet to talk. There was an old church just down the street. Its windows were boarded up, but there was a set of wide steps leading up to the front door. He sat down on the top step and dialled the number. The position gave him a clear view of the street in both directions.

Rather than the usual pleasantries, Mac answered the phone with, 'What the hell are you doing in Johannesburg?'

'I keep asking myself the same question.'

He explained the situation quickly, confident that he didn't have to go slowly or explain too much in order for Mac to keep up. As soon as he told him about Scott's blond American captor, he knew why Mallory had got in touch.

'It's not outside the bounds of possibility that he could be one of ours. Then again, he could be a lot of things. Russian maybe?'

'A Russian accent's difficult to mistake for an American one,' Mallory pointed out.

'I wouldn't say that. I've met Russians who sound more like an authentic New Yorker than I do.'

'Nobody immediately jumps to mind, though?'

'No, but I can make some calls. Somebody will know who this guy is.'

'That's perfect, thank you. Can I give you a call back in a few hours? It'll be from a different number, I'm going to pick up a burner.'

'Sure thing, Mallory.'

'Thanks, Mac.'

Mallory hung up the call and thought for a minute. He had met Mac in Iraq almost a decade before, and the two had kept in touch ever since. He was one of the few contacts Mallory had in American intelligence who hadn't retired or moved on to the private sector. It was a long shot, but if anyone knew why an American with training was working with a Johannesburg gang, he thought Mac might be able to find them.

The beginnings of a plan were forming in Mallory's mind. They could hole up in three-star splendour at the Hauer for a couple of days. He could leave Scott there relatively safely while he ventured out. With any luck, Mac would come back with some information he could use to get close to whoever had hired the gang to kidnap Scott. Failing that, he might be able to draw them out himself.

Either way, he needed to find out exactly who they were up against. Depending on what he found out, he would have to decide what to do next. Either go up against them, or make a plan to get himself and Scott out of the country safely. Before he could do that, there were too many unanswered questions to make a move.

There was a thrift store half a mile from the hotel. Mallory picked up a couple of pairs of shorts and some T-shirts he thought would fit Scott, as well as a baseball cap and a pair of sunglasses for himself. He was confident they had put enough distance between themselves and the apartment building, and a city of millions was a great place to hide oneself, but Mallory was a strong believer in the principle that you can never be too careful. Mallory paid with the last of the proceeds from selling the scooter.

Another five minutes' walk away, he found a newsagent with an ATM built into the wall outside. His online bank app gave him a code that allowed him to withdraw cash without a card. He drew the maximum and went inside the shop.

Mallory bought some snacks and bottled water, a preloaded payment card and two pre-pay phones. He kept his hood up, but the clerk barely glanced up from his magazine to scan the items.

The phone buzzed as he was putting the change in his pocket. His own phone. It was a withheld number. Perhaps he should have got rid of the phone.

He picked the bag up and turned away from the cashier, picking up the call on his way to the door.

'Mallory?' The voice was female, American, and immediately familiar. 'Mallory, it's Evangeline Graves speaking.'

'Graves?' Mallory replied. He looked around for somewhere to stop and talk and spotted an unoccupied bench. He put the bag down on it and sat down.

'You don't sound pleased to hear from me,' she said, sounding a little amused.

'No, it's not that. It's just a surprise. How long has it been?'

'Three years. But who's counting?'

Evangeline Graves was a name that conjured conflicting feelings. He thought back to earlier, how most of his contacts on that side of the pond had retired or gone private. He wasn't sure which one of those options Graves had taken. The two of them had crossed paths a few times over the years. Mallory had never met anyone quite like her: she was fiercely intelligent, a creative thinker, and always got the job done. But why was she contacting him out of the blue like this? And then the penny dropped.

'Jake McIlroy got in touch, I take it?' Mallory was impressed. Mac had been as good as his word, must have got to work on the calls straight away.

'Right first time. He says it sounded like you might be in trouble down there.'

'Nothing I can't handle. I just thought I would put my ear to the ground and see what I can hear. What did he tell you?'

'That you were in Johannesburg on some ransom thing, and you think you might have run into some other foreigners.'

'Just one, so far. And I haven't actually run into him yet. My client says one of the men who took him had an American accent. I never thought to call you, but maybe I should have. This might be right up your street.'

Graves affected a wounded tone. 'Because he's American? We're not all the same, you know.'

'Because he's had training. Enhanced interrogation stuff. The kind of things your agency unofficially gets up to.'

'You know as well as I do that's somewhat exaggerated.'

'Only somewhat.'

'And I'm not with the Company any more. I went freelance. Like you, by the sound of things.'

Mallory narrowed his eyes. 'How do you know that?'

'You're in South Africa tangling with gangsters and suspicious Americans. Unless the SBS has been deployed in Johannesburg, I can't think of any other reason you're down there. Who's the client?'

'Friend of a friend. His name's Scott. Some of the local boys snatched him a couple of weeks ago and his mum was worried. Turned out she was right to be.'

'She didn't want to pay the ransom?'

'There was no ransom. They just wanted to ask him questions.'

Graves sounded intrigued. 'Really? Who is this guy Scott?'

'He's nobody, and he had no idea what they were asking him about. But it's not mistaken identity, either.'

There was a long pause while Graves thought about it. Mallory saw a police car turning the corner. He turned away from it and started to walk unhurriedly in the opposite direction.

'So you think the American knows something about Scott, that Scott doesn't know himself?' Graves asked. 'And it's something worth kidnap and torture.'

'Something worth everything up to murder, by the sound of it. I think they were losing patience with him. From what

Scott told me, I think the gangsters were working for the American. There were at least half a dozen of them involved, round-the-clock guards. Probably didn't come cheap.'

'So whatever it is, is pretty important,' Graves said.

'Important to someone, that's for sure. Do you know if your people have anything going on in this neck of the woods?'

'They're not my people any more, Mallory.'

'You know what I mean.'

'Nothing official, as far as I know. But then, it's been a while. I'm not as connected as I used to be.'

Mallory let out an involuntary laugh. 'I don't believe that for a second.'

She sighed. 'Listen, I'll make some calls.'

'It's okay, Mac's already on that.'

'Mac doesn't know everyone, even though he likes to pretend he does. Tell me everything you know.'

Mallory went through it all from the first meeting with Susan Nel, through travelling to Johannesburg and making enquiries, right up to getting Scott out of the building where he had been held for weeks.

'Where are you keeping him?'

'Some shitty hotel. I'm keeping him away from his apartment and everything else until we sort this out.'

'Good. You should keep him away from the tourist parts. Away from cameras, familiar faces.'

'I know, we're in one of the rough parts. Somewhere in the north.'

'Smart,' Graves said, and waited a moment before speaking again. 'Okay, tell me about this American.'

'Like I said, I didn't see him personally, but Scott

described him for me. He's six feet, decent build, fortyish. He has blond hair. Scott said he reminded him of the actor from *Cobra Kai*, but younger.'

'What's *Cobra Kai*?'

'It's a TV show. I thought you were connected, Graves.'

'I don't watch television.'

'What do you think? Does it ring a bell?'

'Nothing comes to mind. But it sounds like you're right to be careful.'

'I think so too.'

'All right. I'll ask around quietly. Keep your phone on and I'll call you when I know anything.'

'I'll call you,' Mallory said. 'I'm dumping this one right after we get off the line. I don't think those boys this morning were savvy enough to bug it when they had it, but you can't be too careful.'

'Good to know you're learning.'

'Always learning.'

'I'll talk to you soon, Mallory.' She paused and then her voice sounded dead serious again. 'Be careful.'

34

When Mallory opened the door of the hotel room, Scott was sitting on the edge of the bed, a thin, cheap towel wrapped around his waist. His eyes were fixed on the television.

'What's happening?'

'We made the news,' Scott said, without taking his eyes from the screen.

'What?'

Mallory put the bag from the shop on top of the bed and looked at the screen. It was tuned to SABC News. The screen showed a building with boarded-up windows that Mallory didn't recognise until he noticed the familiar billboard on the neighbouring building. The place where Scott had been held.

White metro police cars lined the street. Crime-scene tape was visible in the background, sealing the entire street off.

Mallory shook his head. 'Wait a minute, this doesn't make sense. You're telling me *those* guys called the cops?'

'It's worse than that, they—'

Mallory shushed him irritably. He was reading the ticker

along the bottom now: *Mass shooting in cbd. eight con-firmed dead. police seeking armed suspect.*

'Mass shooting? There was no mass shooting. I only killed three men. I didn't even shoot all of them.'

Scott started to speak again, but Mallory silenced him by holding up a hand as the news cut back to the studio. He fumbled with the remote and turned the volume higher.

A young female newsreader was standing in front of a big screen depicting the same reel of images showing the apartment building: 'Once again, there is a heavy police presence in CBD in the aftermath of a mass shooting earlier today. Eight people are confirmed to have been killed. Authorities are searching for this man in connection with the killings.'

The display changed to an enhanced screen grab from CCTV. It was security footage from the 29 Palms bar the other night, and it showed Mallory himself.

'Police have identified the suspect they are seeking: John Dixon, a British national.'

Mallory's jaw dropped. 'What the hell?'

'That was what I was trying to tell you,' Scott said, gesturing at the screen as though Mallory hadn't noticed his own face on it. 'Why do they think your name is John Dixon, though?'

The picture changed to footage of a police officer being interviewed outside the building. 'This man is to be considered armed and dangerous. We do not want anyone to approach him, but instead contact the police immediately.'

Mallory thought back over his trip to the shops. He had already been alert for people paying too much attention to him, but he had been worried about Devos's men, not the police.

The screen showed a stretcher carrying a body covered by a sheet being loaded into an ambulance.

'What do you think happened?' Scott asked, as bemused as Mallory.

'Well, we can rule out mass suicide,' Mallory said. 'Somebody killed all of those men. Well, the other five of them. And then they somehow got this description to the police to pin it on me.'

'I don't understand.'

'It's your friend who was asking you the questions,' Mallory said. 'The American with blond hair. He did this.'

'But why?'

'A clean-up operation, so they couldn't run their mouths off about what happened. Or perhaps whoever paid them to kidnap you got pissed off that they let you escape.'

'So they killed *all* of them?' Scott was still staring at the screen in shock.

'I wouldn't lose any sleep over it, Scott. They had it coming.'

'What do we do?'

Mallory considered. The plans he had been working on were dead in the water. *Plans are often useless; planning is indispensable.* This required a rethink from the ground up. In yesterday's excitement, he had forgotten that Devos, the gang leader, had addressed him as Dixon. Now, he realised the name had to have come from the cop who frisked him the other day. Officer Ferreira. That meant that whoever was behind this had the police onside, and that was very bad news.

'I think I need to get out of the country. I can't do anything while there's this much heat on. They don't have my real name, that's about the only good thing.'

225

'But what about me? You said I can't go back home.'

'That's right. And you can't come with me, either. They're counting on us sticking together and doing something stupid to get caught. Best-case scenario, I'll be banged up in a cell for a few days. Worst case, they've got somebody in the police who'll just hand us right back to these bastards.'

Mallory went to the window and looked out on the square. It was quiet. He glanced around the room. It wasn't much, but it had a bathroom and a lock on the door, and nobody knew where they were. Moving Scott somewhere else would be a risk that wasn't worth the benefit. His time in the military had taught him a lot of skills, but the most important was one he'd had all along: the ability to think on his feet. If you can keep a cool head, adapt to circumstances that look impossible, you're halfway there.

'What are we going to do?' Scott asked.

'I'm afraid you're going to be banged up a while longer. You're going to stay here. I'll see if I can get out of here and get to the bottom of this.'

'But—'

'You've got food, water, television and a bed. This is a big upgrade on your previous accommodation, right?' He handed Scott some of the cash he had withdrawn. 'This'll keep you going for a few days. If it has to be longer, we'll work something out. Stay inside, order all your food as take-away and get them to leave it outside the door. Say you've got chicken pox or something. Meantime, I'll get the hell out of town and work out what's going on.'

'How long are you going to be gone?'

'I'll keep you posted.'

35

'There's no sign of either of them. We'll keep you posted.'

Branagh didn't reply to Ferreira. He just hung up and contemplated throwing the phone at the wall. It was over twelve hours since Scott Nel had escaped and they were no further forward. What was the use of paying police officers if they couldn't provide a simple service?

He got up from his chair and went to the window, looking out at the darkness. Every hour that Scott Nel had been gone made it more likely that he was staying gone. Whoever this 'John Dixon' really was, he seemed to know what he was doing. The three dead men at Devos's building, and the fact he had managed to stay under the radar in a strange city, demonstrated that.

Willer and the others were out there checking on the key areas where it was most likely Scott Nel could be lying low, but so far they had found nothing. The police had drawn a blank too, though he wasn't convinced that they were fully invested in the search. Obstructing some civilian enquiries was one thing, but the stakes had gotten higher since this morning. Branagh suspected Ferreira and his boss were regretting going along with the story that Dixon had killed Devos and his men.

Three messages had come in while he had been speaking to Ferreira. One from Maddie, one from an out-of-country contractor who was assisting with Sentinel's current job and one from Donald Ashcroft. The final message was the one that demanded his immediate attention.

There was a Zoom link and a terse message that said, 'Please get in touch at your earliest convenience.'

Branagh took a second to check his reflection in the window. He smoothed his hair back and straightened his collar. It had been a long and frustrating day, but it didn't pay to project that image to a client. Particularly a client who was starting to become impatient.

A moment later, Ashcroft appeared on the screen. He wasn't in the office, and he wasn't wearing his usual suit and tie. He appeared to be in his kitchen, wearing a robe. He didn't look pleased.

'It's good to see you, Don,' Branagh said, smiling. 'I was meaning to—'

'You told me you were a day or two from getting the code.'

Branagh winced inwardly. Ashcroft usually made at least an attempt at pleasantries before getting down to brass tacks.

'And we will have it soon.'

'The incident this morning, the shootings. What happened?'

Branagh sighed. 'I'm afraid something went wrong with our local contractors. Scott Nel was able to temporarily ...' He searched for a good way to say this. There wasn't one.

'Escape? Is that what you were going to say?'

'We have everyone on it. The local police have some leads and, as you know, they're extremely cooperative. We anticipate having him back by tomorrow at the latest.'

'And what makes you think that will get you any closer? From what you've said, it doesn't sound like he has the code.'

'We'll get it, sir. I won't let you down.'

Ashcroft stared back at him for a long moment, and then said: 'I'll be in touch tomorrow. Have some good news for me.'

The call ended, leaving Branagh staring at his own image in an empty Zoom room.

He put the phone down and rubbed an ache in his temple, deciding which of the other two calls to return first. He decided against calling Maddie. If he was lucky, she would be asleep by the time he got around to calling. Instead, he returned the second call.

The voice on the other end sounded amused. He was glad someone found this funny. 'Something tells me you're not having the best day.'

Branagh closed his eyes and massaged his eyelids. At least this American had a sense of humour, unlike Willer. 'Hilarious. Do you have something that can improve it?'

'I think I can. From what you've told me, I think I have a pretty good idea where your two fugitives went.'

Branagh opened his eyes and leaned forward in the chair. 'What do you mean?'

36

GABORONE, BOTSWANA

The creaking of the pickup truck's suspension changed subtly and Mallory opened his eyes to see that they were in a line of traffic. A billboard twenty yards along the road was welcoming the vehicles to Sir Seretse Khama Airport. He could see the terminal building beyond: glass-fronted with a jagged white roof shaped like a row of flattened diamonds. It glittered against the night sky.

Mallory rubbed his eyes and reached down into the footwell for his backpack. He had made better time than he had expected when he left the Hauer Hotel at dusk. From there he had walked across the city to Scott's apartment building. The man watching the place from a car parked out front had been easy to spot, and easy to avoid by entering via the basement car park. After retrieving his passport and bank cards, Mallory had called Bokamoso, the taxi driver who had given him his card on the first day, and asked if he knew of any airfields where someone who didn't want to go through normal channels could pay cash for a flight out of the country. A short hop across the border and a long drive later, he had reached his first destination without any extra drama.

Mallory thanked his driver, Tumelo, as they reached the drop-off lane and got out of the car.

Inside, he found a departure board and scanned the destinations. He hadn't entirely made his mind up about where he wanted to go, but the board made his decision for him. Although this was the major airport for Botswana, it was small by international standards. There were no direct flights to the northern hemisphere, so he would have to prioritise how quickly he could leave this airport and get on his way.

He went to the ticket desk, taking out his wallet. He didn't have any way of accessing cash, and knew a lot of airlines no longer accepted it, for pretty much the reason he would want to use it. The woman on the desk was in her early twenties and wore an orange hairband to match her tunic. She smiled as he approached.

'I'm trying to get to London,' Mallory said. 'Or anywhere in Europe, what have you got coming up soon?'

'London or Europe,' she repeated, tapping the keyboard in front of her and examining the screen. 'Good news, sir, we have an Air Botswana flight leaving for Johannesburg in just eighty minutes, and you can transfer there to BA 0056 direct to Heathrow.'

Straight back into the lion's den.

'Anything that doesn't go via Johannesburg?'

She looked disappointed that what she had thought was a perfect suggestion had not been acceptable, but turned back to the screen.

'Certainly, I'll have a look.'

Her brow furrowed and she ran her finger down the screen and started to shake her head. 'I'm sorry, but the only alternative we have today is via Dubai and then Washington Dulles. Very long way around, it would take you—'

'I'll take that one.'

'But sir, this will take you thirty-two hours in total rather than only twenty-one.'

'It's fine,' Mallory said. He couldn't go back to Johannesburg, so it was a moot point. But besides that, it felt like an opportunity. Some time to think, and perhaps an opportunity to catch up with someone who might be able to help.

'In fact, just give me the ticket to Dulles. I have a friend in the United States I'd like to catch up with.'

37

THURSDAY

Passport control and security at Gaborone were a breeze. The South African news sites said police were still looking for John Dixon in Johannesburg, which suited Mallory fine. Even if they had his real name, they weren't searching for him hundreds of miles across the border in another country. More importantly, the story had dropped down the news agenda.

As the attendants on the Boeing 737 sealed the doors, he settled back in his seat, allowing himself to fully relax for the first time in more than twenty-four hours.

Mallory managed to get some more sleep on the first leg to Dubai, and then it was a quick change for the long stretch across North Africa and the Atlantic before he landed at Dulles fourteen hours later. He had already bought his onward ticket online, and after passing through US immigration, he called Graves. It went to voicemail, so he left a message saying that he was in the States and planning to drop by. He boarded the United flight that would take him to his destination.

Two more uneventful hours in the air later, he landed in New Orleans. When he switched off flight mode, his phone told him that it was just gone four o'clock in the afternoon, local time. His body had no idea what time it was supposed to be. He thought about checking into a hotel and getting some sleep before calling on Graves, but decided against it. He was a little surprised he didn't have any messages from her. He would have thought she would have been in touch with some information by now, or even just to acknowledge his voicemail.

Through the glass ceiling of the terminal he could see a beautiful clear blue sky, and the display board told him it was sixty-five degrees outside. Quite a bit cooler than Joburg, but a hell of a lot more welcoming than Birmingham. In the airport, it was the same controlled temperature and canned air he had been experiencing since Gaborone. It would be good to venture outside into the world, rather than the weird, in-between space of airports and planes.

Before he went outside, Mallory called Scott. His sleepy voice answered with a hello.

'Everything all right?' Mallory asked.

'Yeah. We seem to have dropped off the news.'

'Not quite, but we're not in the top items any more. That's positive. Maybe they don't want too much attention.' Mallory could detect that Scott seemed to want to say something. 'How you getting on?'

'Okay. I just … I have trouble sleeping. I keep falling asleep and thinking they're at the door.'

Mallory softened his voice. 'That's natural, mate. Give it a few days and you'll be okay.'

'I was thinking I might go out for some fresh air ... ?' he began. It sounded like a question. He was asking for Mallory's permission. That was good, because it meant he could refuse it.

'No. Leave it a bit longer. Those guys are still out there looking for us.'

There was a pause. Mallory waited for Scott to agree with him. But instead, he pushed back again. 'It's just ... I can't just stay in here for ever. And the local takeout places are shitty.'

Mallory gripped the phone and wondered if it was just his imagination that his long-haul headache had worsened noticeably in the last two minutes. 'Well, thanks for the TripAdvisor review. Can I ask you something, Scott?'

Scott cleared his throat and had the grace to sound a little nervous. 'What?'

'Is it preferable to bread, water and fucking daily beatings?'

'Well ...'

'Exactly. Suck it up. If you get careless, you're dead.'

Mallory hung up, shaking his head. He had to take a moment to calm down before he called Susan Nel to tell her where he was.

'New Orleans? What on earth are you doing there?'

'Leaving from Johannesburg was looking a little dicey, so I'm taking the long way home,' Mallory said. 'Aiming to be on a flight back tomorrow, but there's someone I want to catch up with here first. Scott's fine, I just checked in with him. How's Donno?'

'I'm going to see him tomorrow. I don't dare hope. The doctors seemed so positive last week, but ...'

'Give it time. You just focus on being there for him, leave this other stuff to me.'

'All right,' Susan said, her voice suddenly hesitant again. 'I keep feeling so guilty that I've put you in this position.'

'I'm a big boy, I knew what I was getting into,' Mallory said. As he hung up, he wondered just how far from the truth that was. Not only had he not known what he was getting into, he still didn't.

38

LOUISIANA

Outside the terminal it was much cooler than it had been in Johannesburg, but also more humid. Mallory had a sheen of sweat on the back of his neck by the time he reached the Hertz pickup place. On the desk was a tanned man in his fifties. He had fine dark hair with streaks of grey that made it look like a paintbrush. He gave Mallory a welcoming smile.

'Long flight?'

'Three straight,' Mallory said.

Hertz rented him a black Chevy Suburban. Graves's place was an hour's drive at least, and besides, he didn't think she would appreciate Mallory giving her address to a taxi driver. This was the third time he had visited Graves, and he was using the same method she had told him to use the first time. He opened maps on his phone, found the nearest town – a place called Bohemia, in Plaquemines Parish – then looked for the long, dead-end road peeling off Highway 39 a couple of miles south. Down there on either side of the Mississippi, the map looked like a fractal pattern of blues and greens, showing a landscape that wasn't consistently land or water. Graystone Ranch didn't have a number or a street name, because it was the only home on that particular stretch of road. He found the spot he was looking for and tapped the coordinates into the GPS on the dash of the Suburban.

Mallory hadn't driven a vehicle since he had left the military, so it took him a few minutes to get used to being behind a wheel again. Like most American rentals, it was an automatic, so he didn't have to think about gear changes as he focused on keeping on the right side of the road on the way to the interstate.

The GPS guided him on to I-10, heading east and then turning south. The highway curled lazily around the Mississippi. He stopped at a gas station outside a small town named Caernarvon to buy a Coke and a sandwich, and tried calling Graves again. Still no answer. He hoped she hadn't decided to take a last-minute vacation. He got in the Chevy again and joined Highway 39 headed south for the final leg.

He recognised the turn to Graves's place as it appeared a mile ahead on the road. It wasn't signposted, but there was a tall cypress tree at the edge of the narrow road leading off the highway. He slowed and made the turn. About a hundred yards from there, the asphalt ran out and the road turned into dirt. He had asked Graves why she liked living out in the middle of nowhere once, and she had told him it just felt more comfortable.

He reached the end of the road, where it terminated in a patch of gravel. There was no vehicle there. As Mallory parked, he could see the tyre indents where a car had been. He got out of the Chevy and shut the door. The humidity was more intense here than it had been at the airport; it felt a little hotter, too. February in Louisiana was its own thing.

He looked around and listened. He could hear the cries of birds, the occasional splash of something moving through the swamp, but no human signs of life.

He took a deep breath, enjoying the sudden calm now he had reached his destination. The past day and a half had been spent on planes, in airports and on the road, and the sudden absence of artificial noise felt like a weight off.

He looked back along the road. He was far enough away that he could only barely hear the traffic on the highway. Perhaps it had been a mistake to call on Graves unannounced. She was retired from the Company, but Mallory knew that was a long way from being *retired*. She might be on the other side of the world right now.

The path that led to the cabin wasn't immediately obvious from the gravel lot. It was just a gap between the trees that someone happening on this road might assume was a trail that led to the edge of the swamp. He understood why Graves had bought this place. Maybe he had an even better understanding after the last few days. It was unlikely somebody would stumble upon her home by accident. He was thousands of miles away from the people who were looking for him, but he already felt safer just being so far away from any other humans.

Mallory followed the trail for a couple of hundred yards until it came out in the clearing. He was twenty feet away from the house before it became distinguishable from the woods.

The cabin wasn't particularly large, but it was no dilapidated shack. It was one storey, with dark wood siding and a

239

corrugated steel roof painted a dark red. From his angle of approach, Mallory could see the edge of the deck out back that extended into the swamp. The storm shutters weren't on the windows, which was a good sign. Perhaps Graves had only gone out to run an errand. He remembered her telling him that since the nearest town had been destroyed by Hurricane Katrina, the closest store was a round trip of almost an hour.

'What happens if you forget to buy milk?' Mallory remembered asking.

'You don't,' Graves had replied.

He paused at the edge of the clearing and looked around. Again, he heard the distant movements of flora and fauna and the chirrup of insects, but nothing else.

He was approaching the door when he heard the unmistakable sound of a gun being cocked. He stopped in his tracks.

Mallory froze. 'Can I turn around?'

The husky female voice was familiar.

'I thought that was you. What the hell are you doing here, Mallory?'

39

Mallory sat on the wooden easy chair out on the deck looking out at the evening sun glowing through the branches of the trees in the swamp as Graves changed inside. The cabin was right on the edge of the wetlands. There was a wooden jetty extending from the deck, and a small kayak tied up at the far end. A few yards beyond the jetty, tall trees jutted up from the shallow water, covered thickly in Spanish moss. Mallory liked the feeling on being on the edge of the unknown. Even in a country as vast as America, there were few places as untouched by civilisation as what lay just in front of him.

Graves appeared after a few minutes at the French doors. She was wearing jeans and a loose white blouse. Her dark, curly hair flowed around her shoulders. In her left hand, she carried two open bottles of Czech beer, her fingers cradled around the long necks.

Mallory took one of the beers. His hand brushed Graves's as he took the bottle, and they made eye contact for a second. The touch of her skin awakened a long-dormant memory. A sweltering night in Kabul, years ago. Nothing had happened between them since then, and he wasn't expecting anything to happen on this trip. Was he wrong?

But then Graves looked away and the moment was broken. They clinked bottles.

'Sorry for the surprise visit,' Mallory said. 'I tried to call ahead.'

'I've been out since last night. You don't even get much of a cell signal in here with the booster, so anything more than twenty yards away from the house? Forget about it.'

Graves sat down in the chair next to him. Mallory took a drink of the beer. It was cold and exactly what he needed.

'When you said you would get back to me, I didn't expect it to be in person.'

'I had a little trouble down in Johannesburg. I was going to have to take a few different flights to get home anyway, so I thought, why not?'

'That's stretching "I was in the neighbourhood" a little further than I've heard it before.'

Mallory smiled. 'I'll head back to the airport in a bit.'

She shook her head. 'Don't be ridiculous. I told you my door is always open, and I meant it. Stay as long as you want.'

'I appreciate it, but I need to stay on the move. I just needed some space to think. Someone to bounce some ideas off.'

Graves took her first sip of her beer. '"A little trouble" is stretching it a bit, too, from what I heard.'

'What did you hear?'

'After you called, I had a look at the South African news. Eight gangsters taken out.' She paused to give him a closer look over. 'And not a scratch on you. Good to see you haven't lost a step.'

Mallory touched a finger to the abrasion on his head

where he had been kicked, just above the hairline. 'Not quite without a scratch,' he said. 'And I can't take credit for five of them.'

'No?' Graves's tone was neutral. Not surprised, or disbelieving. It was the tone she always had. It was what made it so difficult to get a read on her. Most people couldn't do it. She had, predictably as a woman high up in the Company, developed an ice queen reputation. Mallory didn't buy that. She was merely too controlled to give any hint of her internal thoughts.

'Three of them were on me. The other five? I think they're down to our American friend.'

'I made some calls after we talked,' Graves said. 'I'm actually waiting on someone getting back to me on this.'

'I appreciate it.'

'Why don't you go through it all from the start? Starting with: who is this kid to you?'

Mallory puffed his cheeks out and thought about where to begin. Where did it begin, really? At Donno's hospital bedside, a little under a week ago? Or back in the mountains of northern Afghanistan, with a catastrophic decision that cost some of his men their lives. As he looked out at the swamp, he knew he didn't want to revisit that moment again, as the sun was going down and the shadows were lengthening.

'He's the brother of a guy from my unit.'

'But he's South African.'

Mallory nodded. 'He was serving with us. You can do that for four years. If you stay in after that point, they make you surrender your South African passport.'

'He must have really liked the military. Or your country. What happened to him?'

Mallory glanced across at her, about to ask how she knew that anything had happened to him. But then he remembered she was good at that. Intuiting things. It was one of the reasons she had been so good at her job. She could look at a person and know within two minutes what made them tick. Mallory wished he had the same gift.

'IED went off during a raid. We lost four guys. It put Donno in a coma.'

Graves simply waited for him to continue, not bothering with platitudes.

'His mother approached me,' he continued. 'She had seen me around at the hospital. She told me she had a problem, and she didn't know where to turn.'

Mallory went through the whole story from there. Travelling to Johannesburg. Speaking to the police. The friend who had guided him into a trap and then paid for his betrayal with his life. Mallory tailing the gang member and getting knocked out and tased for his trouble. Waking up in the locked room next to the very person he had been looking for.

'You have an unorthodox style, man, but you can't say it isn't effective,' Graves said wryly. The first time she had spoken in ten minutes.

Mallory laughed. It was the first time he had genuinely laughed in months. It felt good.

As though reading his mind, Graves said, 'You know, that's the first time you've cracked a smile since you showed up.' She leaned forward, her brown eyes searching his. 'Are you okay, Mallory?'

He looked away instinctively. Graves didn't push him. He thought about it as he looked out at the glow of the sun between the trees. 'I'm getting there.'

She looked at him with curiosity. 'You want to talk about where you're getting there from?'

'Not really.'

'Fair enough,' Graves said, and sat back in her chair. 'Continue.'

Mallory went through the rest of it, right up until the point where he had arrived at the airport in Gaborone and decided to drop in on her.

'I thought I would kill two birds with one stone. It always helps to talk this kind of stuff over with somebody who knows where I'm coming from.'

'Well, I'm flattered you picked me to catch up with.'

'It's a short list.'

Graves was quiet for a long moment. 'I told you I was waiting to hear back from somebody, but I already heard a few things.'

'Like what?'

'I think you might have stuck your nose into something that could cause you a lot of trouble, my friend.'

'What kind of trouble?'

'Well, the kind of trouble that makes your week so far look like a picnic.'

Mallory looked across at Graves in disbelief. 'Were you listening to that story? Since Tuesday I've been held at knife-point, gunpoint and fucking cattle prod-point, I've been beaten up, I've been knocked out, and I've been framed for killing five men.'

Graves nodded along with the list. 'And those were all just minor-league bad guys. You're about to step up to the majors, if you keep going down this road.'

'What do you mean?'

245

'Well, you called me because you knew I was connected, right? You thought I would know some people I could talk to.'

'Actually, you called me, remember? After Mac told you I had reached out.'

She paused for a moment and looked at him. 'Does the name Sentinel mean anything to you?'

Mallory thought about it. It didn't ring any bells. 'Should it?'

'It's a group of people in my line of work. Or who used to be in my line of work, to be exact. Private security consultancy with an intelligence bent.'

'Ex-CIA?'

'Ex-a lot of things. The Company, MI6, Mossad. They work for hire. I've been tracking them for a while. They've been linked to jobs all over. The usual hotspots we're both familiar with, of course, but in places you might not expect.'

'Like Johannesburg?'

'They hadn't popped up on that side of the planet so far, but maybe it was just a matter of time. This American with the blond hair, I have a feeling I know who he is. If I'm right, his name is Simon Willer. Fifteen years CIA before quitting two years ago. He's not somebody you want to cross.'

Mallory thought about the bruises on Scott's neck. The covered body being taken out of the building on the news. 'Sometimes wanting doesn't come into it.'

'Perhaps, but I don't think he's the only one you have to worry about. Could be this is some kind of solo operation, but I don't think so. I think he's part of this little group of entrepreneurs at Sentinel.'

'"Entrepreneurs." That's a new way of saying "mercenary".'

'Mercenary isn't quite the right word for it,' Graves said.

'Oh, I guess it's accurate when it comes down to it, but these aren't your standard Blackwater assholes. They don't get involved in petty shit. Small footprint, but effective. Sentinel is more like an expensive consultancy operation, only their specialty is jobs that require the judicious application of force.'

'They're definitely not averse to that. I'm surprised they haven't proposed you for membership.'

She shrugged. 'I never was a team player, Mallory. I'm enjoying my retirement.'

'Sure,' Mallory said. 'But it's semi-retirement, right?'

She didn't respond to that. 'I think somebody hired this team to pick up your boy. And if they could afford this service, they're either very rich or very powerful.'

'Which really comes to the same thing.'

'True. So that's the question. What does Scott have that they want?'

Mallory sighed. 'That's what I can't get my head around. He's nobody.'

'What about the family? This brother, could he have been involved with something shady?'

'Donno? No way. He was straight as they come. And he had been away from home for years. I know what you're thinking – that they could have mistaken one twin for the other – but that's not it. They knew who Scott was.'

'What do the parents do?'

'Mum's retired, which is why she's able to be over in the UK. The father is dead.'

'Oh yes?' Graves sounded curious at that.

'Climbing accident. Last year.'

'Accident?'

247

Mallory thought again about that before answering. 'I'm starting to wonder.'

'It's kind of a coincidence, isn't it? The father dies suddenly last year, then this.'

'I don't know. There was no sign of foul play. Some families just have bad luck. I don't see Donno's dad being involved with these kinds of people either, before you ask. I went to the company he worked for. He was doing humanitarian aid, for Christ's sake.'

Graves looked intrigued. 'What did he do?'

'He was freelancing for a non-profit. The philanthropic arm of one of those big tech companies. Johannesburg is like the Seattle of Africa; they have a ton of stuff going on down there.'

'Could it be some kind of tech espionage thing?' she suggested. 'Maybe a competitor?'

'I thought about that, but it doesn't fit. He wasn't working on anything commercial. I talked to a girl he worked with. She was all in on the idealism, it's not the kind of thing rich bad guys would be interested in. Nothing that would make them spend money hiring the kind of people you're talking about.'

Graves thought about it for a second. 'It would probably surprise you, the things rich bad guys can be interested in.'

Just then, there was a soft buzz from inside. Graves got up and went through the French doors into the living room. She answered the call and then moved further inside the house. Mallory sat back in the chair and finished the beer.

The setting sun was casting the gnarled cypress trees in a golden glow. At the end of the jetty, the swamp quickly became impenetrable. It wouldn't take a man long to get lost out there. The thought held an attraction. Mallory always felt a pull in places like this. Disappearing from the modern world for a few days, doing some hunting. Clearing his head. It would be good for him, if only he had the time.

Talking to Graves had helped already, just as he hoped it would. The change of scene was helping too. He was sure there was something he was missing; a puzzle piece that would slot in and everything would make sense. If Graves was right, and the blond man was part of this 'Sentinel' operation, it immediately begged another question. Who had hired this expensive group of ex-intelligence operatives, and why?

Graves appeared at the door. She had been barefoot before, but was now wearing boots.

'Was that your contact?'

'Not yet, I'm afraid. I have to go out for a couple of hours.'

'Anything wrong?'

She paused before answering. 'No. It was my dad's home, he's acting up again. Will you be okay here?'

Mallory looked around at the comfortably appointed cabin, mentally comparing it to the places he had been staying recently. 'I think I'll survive. Listen, you really don't mind me staying here? I know you weren't expecting a guest. I can head back to New Orleans tonight.'

Graves waved her hand. 'Don't be silly. You're the good kind of unexpected guest.'

She crossed the open-plan living room to the kitchen and took her car keys out of a drawer.

'There are steaks in the freezer, more beer in the fridge. Make yourself at home. I'll be back in no time.'

Mallory walked with her to the front door.

As she opened the door, she paused and said, 'Oh, and sheets for the guest bedroom are in the closet.'

'Got it, thanks.'

'That's if you think you'll need them.'

Without another word, she left. Mallory grinned as he watched her walk away. A minute after she disappeared into the dusk, he heard an engine growl to life and saw the headlights cutting through the thick woods. As the sound of the engine faded into the sounds of the swamp, he realised he was utterly alone for the first time in days.

He was looking forward to Graves's return, given what she had just said, but for now, solitude was just what he needed. Some time to think.

40

He's nobody.

That was what Mallory had told Graves. Maybe that was true, but Scott Nel was somebody in one sense: he was important enough for someone to spend a lot of money and break a lot of laws to try to get information from.

Graves's questions had helped him to think about it from a different angle. He had wondered about Bartho Nel's accident before. The accident report said that there were no suspicious circumstances, but was that really surprising? As far as the authorities were concerned, no one else had been there, so the natural conclusion was that the death was just what it appeared to be: a tragic accident. Hardly uncommon in the course of a risky pursuit like rock climbing. But Mallory knew it wouldn't be difficult to kill a man and leave no trace in a scenario like that. The inherent danger in climbing would provide an easy way to kill and would supply an explanation that no one would question. The absence of witnesses had only made that more straightforward.

Had the people Scott had got involved with killed Bartho?

He didn't think that was it. As far as Scott was concerned, the two things were entirely unrelated.

But what if they weren't?

It was dark outside now. He turned a lamp on and walked around the interior of Graves's cabin as he thought. The place was nice. Polished wood floor, framed photographs of Graves meeting foreign dignitaries and a couple of presidents. A big satellite photograph that showed her house at the centre of it. He could see the line of the highway and the dry land giving way to the swamp. On the opposite side of the space from the French doors was a breakfast bar separating a fully outfitted kitchen. There were two bedrooms, both with their own bathrooms. For a moment, Mallory remembered Graves's parting comment. Then he put sleeping arrangements out of his mind, forced himself to focus on the question at hand.

He went out on the deck again and looked at the blackness of the swamp. The twisted trees had become a wall of darkness, giving no hint of what lay beyond. A bird called out from somewhere close. It had a weird, trumpeting call that was nothing like Mallory had heard back home.

His stomach rumbled and he remembered he had eaten nothing since the sandwich he'd bought when he stopped for fuel earlier in the day. He walked back through the living room to the kitchen and opened the refrigerator. It was fully stocked. A round trip of an hour to the nearest store – it had to be. He wondered how Graves was getting on with her dad. Then he wondered what it would be like to have family who depended on you.

There was a cast-iron skillet in the cupboard. He took one of the thick rib-eye steaks out of the freezer. As he slapped it into the skillet with a sizzle, he thought suddenly of Westwick, sitting on the other side of the campfire, criticising Mallory's technique of heating his field rations. Conversation had turned to the more appetising food they could eat when they returned home. Westwick mentioned that his old man had been a chef, and told Mallory that not only could you cook steaks from frozen, they tasted better that way. It retained the moisture. Mallory had been sceptical, but he would try anything once.

He cooked the steak rare and took some green beans and leftover potato salad out of the fridge to go with it. He decided against another beer and took out a bottle of water instead. He needed to let his mind work clearly.

He deliberately didn't dwell on the problem as he ate, just blanked his mind and let his subconscious work away. It was like putting something in the microwave and setting the timer. Let it do its thing and wait until the ping went off to alert you that the job was finished.

The steak was excellent. Westwick had been right. It made Mallory wish he was here now. He would be able to offer support way beyond culinary advice. Hell, Mallory would even be grudgingly pleased to have that trigger-happy half-wit Yorkie with him. He finished eating and looked at the clock. Graves had been gone for longer than two hours now. He wasn't worried. New Orleans was over an hour's drive away, and he knew that remoteness was why Graves liked it here. 'A couple of hours' was probably just a figure of speech, rather than a firm estimate of the time it would take.

Mallory hunted through the cupboards until he found what he was looking for: an electric kettle. Graves was one of the few Americans he knew who appreciated a proper cup of tea. There was a caddy of loose-leaf Darjeeling in the cupboard, too.

He went over the known details again as he plugged the kettle in. Scott's abduction. Sentinel. Some kind of code. Bartho Nell falling from that sheer rock wall.

The water was coming to the boil when the ping went off in his head.

He put the tea caddy down.

What if he was coming at this from the wrong angle? He believed Scott when he said he didn't know what his abduction was about, but all this time he had been assuming that Scott, consciously or unconsciously, had done something that had put him in this position. Even when he started to wonder about how accidental Bartho Nel's death had been, he had been working on the assumption that if someone had killed him, it was blowback from something his son had been involved in. But what if that wasn't it? What if it was the other way around? What if something Bartho Nel was involved in had got him killed, and got his son kidnapped?

At that moment, he heard his phone buzz on the chair outside. He walked back out to the deck, expecting to see a message from Graves or Scott, but instead the message was from Susan Nel. Just two words.

Call me

The phone had adjusted to local time, telling him it was just before ten o'clock. That meant it was four in the morning for Susan. A 4 a.m. call is almost never good news. Mallory called her back, gripping the wooden rail on the edge of the deck as he waited for Susan to pick up.

'What is it?' he asked as soon as it was picked up, not waiting for her to say hello.

There was a pause and he could hear Susan take a breath. There was a catch in it, like she was about to start crying. Shit. Something bad had happened. Donno was dead, or—

'Mallory. He's awake. Donovan is awake.'

AFGHANISTAN

SIX MONTHS AGO
HELL HOUR

'Stand by,' Mallory said. 'Three, two ...'

Westwick lined up his laser sight and a second red dot appeared, a few inches higher and to the left of the red dot in the sentry's hand.

'One.'

Westwick squeezed the trigger.

And Hell Hour began.

The sentry went down. At the same moment, two shaped charges went off at opposite ends of the compound. One blew the steel gate in the west wall off its hinges, the other punched a hole through the middle of the east wall. Mallory, Donno and Yorkie were already moving. Westwick hung back and followed at a distance, covering the visible exits from the three buildings within the walls.

They ran towards the burning hole in the gate. Mallory's senses adjusted to the sudden bright light and noise after two hours of silence and darkness. It was like moving from a world of black and white to a world of bright, vibrant colour, like a messed-up version of *The Wizard of Oz*. It felt good to be able to move, to make some noise.

There still hadn't been any return fire from within the compound. That wasn't unusual. It usually took a few seconds to get over the shock, reach for a weapon and go on the defensive. Put that together with the fact that most of the people within would have been soundly asleep until twenty seconds ago, and the delay was understandable.

The lull couldn't last for ever, and it didn't. As Mallory and Donno made it to the gaping hole where the gate had once been, the shutters of one of the windows on the first floor of the nearest building burst open. The muzzle of an automatic rifle appeared, jutting out from the darkness within. Before the gunman had time to fire, Mallory and Donno concentrated a short burst of fire on the window. There was a muffled cry and the weapon jerked back inside.

Two men appeared on the wooden walkway that ran along the top of the north wall. Mallory swung his gun around to fire on them, but he was beaten to the punch. Within the same second, both figures jerked and dropped. One fell where he stood, the other toppled over the guard rail and fell ten feet to the rough dirt of the compound floor head first. One of their shooters had obviously drawn a bead on them from the moment they stepped outside. From the position, Mallory guessed it had been Gilmartin, in Bravo.

Mallory, Donno, Westwick and Yorkie made for the largest building at the centre of the compound. The buildings had been named alphabetically for their size: the smallest was Aberdeen, the mid-sized one was Bristol. Teams Bravo and Delta would take those two. Mallory wanted the biggest one: Cardiff. It was the one where their target was most likely to be.

As they approached the main building, the door on the ground floor burst open. A young guy, stripped to the waist, ran out, yelling, firing indiscriminately, not even taking time to find his targets. Before the others could react, Yorkie gave him what he was looking for, sending him out in a blaze of glory. Yorkie looked like a kid walking into Hamleys on Christmas Eve. He lived for this part of it. Mallory banished his usual misgivings about Yorkie's glee for combat. In this case, his quick trigger finger had been the right call.

In towards the doorway, moving fast. No lights on inside. The doorway was a black void in the adobe wall that was lit up red from the blaze behind them. Yorkie fired another burst inside the door as they approached. Mallory moved his goggles down. The world turned into a wash of shades of green. He heard the sharp bang of a charge going off and looked back to see the door had been blown off its hinges on the next building, the flaming debris raining down like bottle-green fireworks. There was more gunfire from elsewhere in the compound. The shock was lifting, their opposition had caught up with the situation.

They passed through the doorway and Mallory saw that the walls were maybe a foot thick. The gunfire and yells from outside were immediately muffled, as though under a blanket. They entered a short corridor with doors leading off, two on each side. The floor was tile. The sounds from outside were so dampened that he could hear every sound they made as they advanced, from the tap of their footsteps echoing off the stone walls to the individual breathing of each man.

There was a flight of stairs at the far end of the corridor. The building had three levels, the third one truncated for a roof terrace. Along with a rough idea of square footage, that was as much as they knew about the interior. These weren't kit houses – Mallory had never seen two with the same layout.

Mallory was in first, then Donno, then Yorkie. Mallory glanced back and saw Westwick at the door. Not for the first time, he was reassured to have him at his back. Donno wasn't himself tonight; Yorkie, as usual, was way too much himself. But Westwick he never had to worry about. He was always careful, always seemed to have everything planned out three moves ahead. In some ways, he was the most dangerous of any of them.

They didn't have to exchange a single word. Every man knew their play. Clear the ground floor first. Make sure there were no unsecured exits, no tunnels. Make sure no reinforcements could follow them in. They could take their time, relatively speaking, after that. One of their snipers could easily pick off anyone attempting to escape from the upper floors.

Mallory took the first door on the left. It was ajar so he kicked it all the way open and went straight in. For some men, this was the part of the job they most feared: going through a door. It had never bothered Mallory. The way he saw it, the odds were very much on his side. Entering a dark room, ready to fire at a moment's notice.

It was clear, though. Just a TV room. A couch, a big-screen TV, an Xbox. All the home comforts.

He opened his mouth to shout that the room was clear. Before he could speak, he heard two cracks from one of the other rooms. Pistol fire. It was immediately followed by a burst of automatic fire. He moved back to the door.

'Clear!'

Westwick backed out of the room. 'He's down.'

'Clear in here,' Mallory said.

There was another quick burst of fire from the third room. Yorkie yelled out, 'Down.'

Donno cleared the fourth room as Mallory approached the doorway Yorkie had taken. It was small and windowless. A dead man was lying slumped in the corner. He was wearing only boxers and a white vest. Yorkie's bullets had hit him in the chest and head and blood was soaking into the rug on the floor. There was no weapon in sight.

Mallory shot Yorkie a hard look. 'He wasn't armed.'

Yorkie shrugged. 'Better safe than sorry.'

Mallory muttered a curse under his breath and moved back into the corridor. It wasn't the time or place to get into a debate, but he would be talking to Yorkie later. He didn't believe there had been any uncertainty there. Yorkie had walked in there intending to kill anything that moved. Apart from any moral considerations, they could have taken that guy prisoner. Perhaps he would have had valuable information. Too late now.

'He's right, boss,' Donno said. 'Put them down fast, you can worry about it later.'

Mallory glanced in surprise at the younger soldier. He had moved into the doorway and was staring at the body on the ground. Mallory didn't like what he saw in Donno's eyes. He realised he had been wrong not to keep him off the mission.

This wasn't the place for him in his current mindset. Mallory glared again at Yorkie, who responded with a smirk.

'The kid's learning.'

A bully with a weapon. Mallory turned away from Yorkie. If he had anything to do with it, this would be the last time he went into battle with this arsehole.

The gunman Westwick had shot had been the only other man downstairs. The four of them did a quick scan of the rooms. No sign of any escape tunnels. If there had been one, more likely than not it would have been obvious. They had been inside the building within two minutes of the charges going off. Not a lot of time to carefully replace the door on a secret tunnel. That was good. It meant there was a strong chance the HVT was somewhere above them.

From outside, a voice called out. Mallory responded with the countersign. McKenzie, Khan and Drummon appeared at the door.

'Bristol is clear,' Khan said, his voice low.

'Nice work,' Mallory said. 'Let's go do the hard part.'

41

LOUISIANA

Donovan is awake.

Mallory had been so busy for the last few days that he had barely had time to think about Donno. Susan was in a taxi on her way to the hospital when they spoke, so he didn't press her for details. She told him the most important things. Donno had woken up just after midnight and he seemed to be able to communicate with the medical staff.

After Mallory had hung up, he dropped the phone and collapsed on Graves's couch for a minute, basking in the relief. It felt like setting down a twenty-pound pack after an endurance march.

Donno was awake.

He allowed himself a moment or two, and then wiped the smile off his face. It was fantastic news, but he had other pressing issues to worry about.

It took him a little while to remember what he had been thinking about before Susan had messaged him, but then he had it: the father. Perhaps what had gone down in Johannesburg was nothing to do with Scott or with Donno. Perhaps it all started with Bartho Nel's work at MTC. If so, he knew someone who might be able to tell him more.

A couple of minutes later, he was listening to another voice on the other end of another intercontinental phone call.

'Hello?' The voice was slightly muted, a little glitchy. He remembered what Graves had said about barely getting a signal out here.

'Hi, is that Ivy?'

Hesitation. 'Who's calling, please?'

'We spoke the other day. My name's Mallory, I was visiting your—'

'Oh, of course. The man who was looking for Scott.'

'That's right.'

'You got my number off the website?'

'That's right. I hope you don't mind me calling like this,' he continued. Suddenly, a thought occurred to him. He had no idea what time of the day or night it was there. Quickly he calculated. Tomorrow morning, he thought. Ahead of GMT. 'I didn't wake you up, did I?'

'No, I've been up for a bit,' she said. 'Just started on my emails. You're not still in Johannesburg, then? Did you go back to the UK? The line isn't great.'

'I'm en route. I thought you might be able to help me with a question.'

'No problem. I've been so worried about Scott since we spoke.'

'Well, actually, I have some good news on that score.'

'You've found him? He's okay?'

'Yes, I found him. But I don't know about okay. Some

bad people are looking for him, and he's still in danger. I've got him somewhere safe while I try to work out why he was taken in the first place. That's why I'm calling you, in fact.'

Ivy sounded surprised. 'I don't understand.'

'I wanted to ask you a few questions, if it's okay.'

'Of course, anything, but ... I told you, I really didn't know Scott all that well.'

'Not about Scott, about Bartho. What exactly were you working on together? Your boss just said it was humanitarian relief.'

'That's right. It was one of the long-running projects of the foundation. Technological solutions for making sure drought relief efforts are directed effectively in some of the worst-hit regions of Africa. The foundation brought him in to consult on some of the initiatives that weren't firing on all cylinders. He identified this particular project on day one. Threw all his energy into it.'

'What exactly did it involve? The project?'

She laughed. 'How long have you got?'

'Give me the Dummy's Guide.'

'Okay. You've actually come to the right person, because I used to give presentations on this to our funders. Bartho used to say that was my job, translating tech into human.'

'Sounds good. What was the project?'

'So we were developing new geophysics technology. You know when you put your baggage through the X-ray at the airport? Like that. Except this would be like using satellites to X-ray the ground itself. We were using the technology to identify fluctuations in the subsurface composition. You see, fluid has a different signature to solids. The idea was it could allow us to find large fluid deposits up to one thousand metres below the surface.'

'Which would allow you to identify a large water deposit in a drought zone, is that it?'

'Exactly. Drought relief operations are always complex and expensive because they focus on bringing the water in from elsewhere. This way, we can find water that's hidden under the bedrock, bring it to the surface and create reservoirs at source, with no need for them to be replenished.'

'But you'd need to hope that there was water down there.'

'That's the thing – many of these places have the water, if only we knew where to drill. It would have been a gamechanger in some areas. In another few weeks, I think we would have seen real results. But after Bartho died, they reviewed the work to date and decided they couldn't make progress anytime soon, so we were all reassigned to other projects.'

Mallory was quiet for a minute. A picture was beginning to emerge. Something that could hint at the reason behind all this.

'Where were you testing this thing?'

'All over the continent. That's the beauty of it: we didn't need to go anywhere. We could use the satellites to test everything from the office.'

'What about Anambra?'

'Where's that?'

'It's a state in Nigeria. I had never heard of it before a couple of days ago. At first I thought it was somebody's name. Was that one of the regions?'

'Nigeria ... we have some AZs out there, but Anambra doesn't ring a bell. Hang on a second.'

Mallory could hear Ivy moving about. A couple of seconds later he heard keys tapping.

'Nope. We had four amber zones set up in Nigeria, and none of them were in Anambra.'

'What's an amber zone?'

'It's just what we call the test areas. We used areas where we already knew there were water deposits at deep levels to calibrate the tech. Anambra's in the south of Nigeria. The nearest amber zone we were running was in Taraba. That's like six hundred kilometres away.'

'Do you know much about Anambra? Is it a drought region?'

'I know everything, Mallory,' Ivy said, a smile audible in her voice. 'Or at least, I will in a minute.'

There was another rapid clattering of keys, so fast it sounded like the beating of an insect's wings.

'No. The technology wouldn't have been needed there.'

Mallory considered this for a moment. 'How exactly does this thing work?'

'It detects variations in subterranean material. It differentiates solid from fluid. They each have different signatures. In fact, different kinds of bedrock have different signatures.'

'What about different types of fluid? Could it tell the difference between those?'

'Different types of fluids?'

'Yeah. This is turning out to be a family affair, and they always say blood is thicker than water, right? There's something thicker than blood. Something you also find underground.'

'Oil,' Ivy said, catching up quickly. 'But no, that wouldn't work. Water has a particular signature, you would have to ... '

There was a long silence. Mallory knew that kind of silence well. The wheels were turning. Ivy was working through the problem. He knew better than to interrupt.

'Unless ... if you recalibrated the depth slice, and if you adjusted to account for soil layering. But then you would have to ...' She started mumbling to herself. In the background, Mallory heard more keystrokes. Tentative at first and then becoming more rapid. And then they stopped.

There was silence again for a minute. Two.

'Ivy?' he prompted.

'Yes. I think you could do it. I mean, it's not as simple as the standard water program. You would need to know roughly where to look and it would take a lot of time to find anything unless you got very lucky. And even with that, it would take us weeks – months maybe – to reconfigure the code to give a snowball's chance in hell. I'm not even sure we have anyone who can do it, but I think it's possible, in theory.'

'Did you have someone who could do it in practice?'

'Yes. I think Bartho could have done it.'

Mallory nodded to himself. If Bartho had stumbled on a hidden deep oil field in Anambra, that would be something that was worth going to a lot of trouble for.

'I think Bartho did do it,' he said. 'And I think the men who kidnapped Scott killed him.'

Ivy took a sharp breath. 'But he was killed in an accident.'

'An accident with no witnesses.'

Ivy took a moment to let it sink in. 'But if that's what happened, why would they kill him? He was the only one who could complete the project. Without him, we're spinning our wheels.'

'I don't know. Maybe it really was an accident, as in they didn't mean him to die. Or maybe they thought they had everything they needed. Or maybe ...' He trailed off as something occurred to him.

'What?'

'The code. The people who kidnapped Scott kept asking him about a code. Could that be what it's about? Some kind of password?'

Ivy was quiet for a moment. 'We had five phases for development and we were stalled in the final phase. We went through Bartho's working after he died, but there was a whole section of code he hadn't completed yet.'

Mallory snapped his fingers. 'That must be it. Not a password; a section of computer code. This unfinished section: could someone else take it from there?'

'No. We tried, for weeks, but there were some problems we couldn't overcome. We decided Bartho had hit those same problems. We couldn't find anything in his files to indicate that he'd cracked the problem, but ...'

'But?'

'It looked like there was a gap in his files.'

'Ivy ...'

'I know. You think he did it?'

This was it. This was the missing puzzle piece. 'I think he cracked it; and I think the men who killed him thought they had everything they needed, only to discover they didn't after the fact. Maybe they threatened him and he junked the code so that they couldn't use it. Maybe they didn't realise until after they killed him.'

'No,' Ivy said immediately. 'I don't believe he would do that.'

'Why not?'

'He wouldn't just destroy months of work like that. And he knew how important it was, how many people it would help. He wouldn't just throw all that away, no matter what.'

'Then he must have given it to someone for safekeeping. And the men who took Scott think it was him.'

'But that doesn't make any sense. Scott wasn't involved in the project at all. As far as I know, he didn't have the skills to be involved.'

Mallory frowned. 'He doesn't have any idea why they were asking him, either. It's got to be this, though. Can you think of anywhere else Bartho might have stashed the missing section of code? He wouldn't keep it online, I'm guessing. Physical media, maybe a flash drive.'

'They cleared out his office. If there was anything there it would have been ...' She paused and considered. 'Actually, I know where his stuff will be stored. I'll have to go into the office, though, I'm working from home today. Can I call you back in a couple of hours?'

'Of course,' Mallory said. He was smiling. For the first time since Afghanistan it felt like he was working as part of a team. 'I really appreciate this, Ivy. I'll call you back in a couple of hours, okay?'

Mallory ended the call and looked at the screen. It had been ten hours since the last time he had called Scott, and he didn't know the good news about his brother yet. His phone went straight to voicemail. Mallory wasn't too concerned. Still early in Joburg, he was probably asleep. He would try again in an hour.

He glanced at the clock as he slipped the phone into his hip pocket. Graves had been gone almost three hours now.

Walking out to the deck again, he leaned on the rail,

looking out into the blackness. The sounds of the swamp had changed since the sun had gone down. Different birds crying out, larger splashes out there in the warm stillness of the night as the nocturnal shift took over.

The code. Anambra. It had to be the answer. And if Ivy was right, Bartho Nel would have taken steps to ensure the code was kept somewhere for safekeeping. Perhaps Ivy would find it at the office, now that she knew what to look for, but he didn't think so. He put himself in Bartho's shoes. He would have wanted to entrust it to someone who could keep it safe. The men who wanted it must have come to the same conclusion after his death, which was why they had kidnapped Scott. But Scott didn't have it. He didn't think Susan Nel would know either, otherwise she would have mentioned something about it before now.

And then another possibility occurred. What if the person Bartho gave the code to didn't know it?

It was perfectly quiet, other than the soft sounds of the swamp, so he heard the noise of the approaching engine thirty seconds before he saw the headlights. He went back through the house to the window at the front as he heard the sound of an SUV pulling to a stop on the gravel lot beyond the stand of trees.

He saw the headlights wink out and then opened the front door as he heard the driver's door open and close.

42

JOHANNESBURG

FRIDAY

Later, when he thought back, Scott realised that the decision to disobey Mallory to go out to buy painkillers may well have saved his life.

He had been careful to follow Mallory's instructions for the most part. He hadn't left the small hotel room since he and Mallory had arrived. He didn't want to risk ending up back in that room with the boarded-up window and the lock on the door. He wondered if a part of him had been resigned to his captors killing him sooner or later, until Mallory had somehow got them out of there.

In truth, it was the opposite of what he needed psychologically after the days of captivity. Too much was similar about the small, damp room. The walls seemed to be closing in on him. Both nights he had slept here, he had awoken multiple times, expecting the door to open and the blond American to come in. He had woken in the middle of the night in the grip of a panic attack that hadn't properly subsided.

So when he had woken again a few hours later to a headache that threatened to make his skull explode, Scott decided to take the risk of going to get some painkillers. Besides, a little fresh air to clear his head wouldn't be the worst thing in the world. The prepay phone Mallory had left showed him that there was a drug store only seven minutes' walk from the hotel. He could even plot out a route that avoided the main roads. He didn't think there was anything to worry about. They were miles away from the place those men had been holding him, and there hadn't been any new developments on the news after the initial flurry of coverage.

Before leaving, he looked out of the window and checked that the street outside was quiet. Mallory's words were on his mind.

If you get careless, you're dead.

Pulling on his hoodie and his sunglasses, he locked the door and went downstairs. The guy at reception glanced up at him and then looked back down at his magazine without commenting. Outside, the morning was relatively cool, and the streets were all but deserted. It was still early, and this wasn't the kind of neighbourhood where the pavements were packed with commuters at any time. He walked quickly to the drug store, reaching it in five minutes rather than seven. He picked up two packs of Adco-Dol and took them to the counter, keeping his head down.

When he got back outside, he looked around again and saw that the street was still deserted. By luck or by instinct, Mallory had found them a good part of the city in which to lie low. It wasn't a part of Joburg Scott had ever visited, or even passed through. But that very unfamiliarity made him feel better in a strange way. Surely, the people who were looking for him would focus on his usual haunts. His head was feeling clearer as he navigated the back alleys back towards the hotel. As he approached the final corner, something made him hesitate.

If you get careless, you're dead.

Scott stopped and listened. He couldn't hear anything other than the usual background city noise. The low murmur of traffic on the main road, car horns and construction noise in the distance, the cries of seagulls. Nothing from up close.

The three- and four-storey buildings all around crowded out the morning sunlight, creating a kind of twilight in these narrow streets. Lots of shadows.

Look at yourself, he thought with disgust. He was scared to walk around a corner. If his brother could see him now he would think he was pathetic. No, that probably wasn't true. Donovan would understand, tell him to follow his gut.

Scott stepped back from the corner. He went around the opposite way, approaching the little square the hotel was situated in from the other direction. Coming from this angle would allow him to see the hotel entrance without walking out into the open.

The moment it came into view, he knew he had made the right decision.

There was a black SUV parked outside the entrance to the hotel. A bulky, six-foot-tall man was standing next to the car, right beside the corner he had been about to round. He wasn't the blond man, but he was dressed similarly: a black T-shirt under a light jacket. He didn't recognise the man, but he didn't look like he was a lost tourist. And Scott didn't think he was imagining that there was something underneath the left side of the man's jacket.

Scott shrank back into cover and let his gaze travel up the side of the building to the window of his room. There was a light on in there. He had left the light off. His head had been pounding too hard for the too-bright bulb in the room.

He took a sharp breath and felt his head swim. They had found him. Somehow they had found him.

At that moment, the door banged open and he saw the fat guy from reception pushed rudely out. Another man followed him, dressed similarly to the one standing by the car. The receptionist shrank back from them and pointed in the direction of the alleyway Scott had used on his way out.

Scott could hear his voice from here, speaking rapidly and louder than his inquisitors. 'I think he went that way. He stays in his room all the time, he'll be back soon.'

Scott shrank back into the alley. He turned and started walking in the opposite direction as fast as he dared. He didn't want to move so quickly that the sounds of his footsteps would echo off the walls. He stole a glance behind him as he reached the end of the alleyway. It was still empty. As he got out into the open, he quickened his pace.

Then he started to run.

43

LOUISIANA

Mallory stood in the doorway, watching the gap in the trees at the head of the path as he heard footsteps approaching in the darkness. Graves appeared from the darkness a moment later. She was stuffing her keys in her pocket.

'Hey, any progress?' she asked.

'A little,' Mallory said. 'How's your dad?'

Graves seemed to think about that for a minute. 'Let's talk about something else.'

They went out on the deck at the back again. It was cooler than it had been in the evening, but it was still pleasantly warm. Too early in the year for the mosquitos to be much of a problem.

Mallory filled Graves in; first the great news that Donno was conscious, and then the call with Ivy. He told her that what she had said about the father being involved somehow had got him wondering, and now it looked like that was the key to the whole thing.

'That would make sense,' Graves said, when she had

listened to everything. 'For starters, this tech sounds like the kind of thing worth killing for. An unexploited oil field or a diamond mine could be worth billions. That would explain why someone is so keen to get this code.'

'Right,' Mallory said. 'But it sounds like they thought they had all they needed and they killed the father. But according to the girl at MTC, there's a big hole in the code on the program they need to make it work.'

'And they have reason to believe that he gave Scott the missing section of code. But why?'

'I don't know.'

Graves shook her head. 'Mallory, you have a talent for getting in over your head, you know that?'

'I used to have a talent for getting out of it, too,' Mallory said wryly. Since last year, he wasn't sure if he still had it.

Graves stood up and leaned on the rail for a minute, looking out at the night.

'What are you thinking?' he prompted after a minute.

'Honestly? I'm thinking you should cut your losses.'

'Are you kidding me?' That was the last thing Mallory had been expecting her to say.

'Look,' Graves said, turning back to face him. 'You got the kid back. He's safe. His brother is out of the coma now. Happy endings all round, right? Who cares if these assholes get the oil or the pot of gold at the end of the rainbow, or whatever the hell it is? Chances are they'll find some other way of getting to it. You got what you wanted – the kid is safe. It's time to move on.'

'No,' Mallory said. 'They won't stop. And they'll want to take care of him, anyway, like they did with the men they hired to kidnap him.'

There was a long silence and Graves sighed. She sat back down. 'Okay. You've got me curious now. Let's think about it. Who else could have this code? A co-worker? You said his wife didn't know anything about it.'

'No. The only other person I can think of is Donno.'

'The boy in the coma?' Graves said.

'The boy in the coma,' he repeated. For a second he wondered if she was referencing the Smiths song, but then he remembered that Graves cared even less about music than she did about television.

He considered it for a second. It had occurred to him earlier, but he had been distracted by Graves's return. The more he thought about it now, the more it made sense. Donno was the one person nobody could have asked about this, up until now.

'Of course,' Mallory said. 'I mean, he was the responsible son. If the dad was going to entrust something this import-ant to anyone, it would be ...'

Mallory stopped, noticing that Graves was staring right at him. She was leaning forward, almost on the edge of her chair. It wasn't like her.

'It would be Donno?' she prompted.

He shrugged. 'I was just thinking we can ask him. Once he's properly recovered.'

'You said he was responsive. That means talking, right? We could call him, see if they'll put him on the phone. I take it he's in a military hospital over there?'

Mallory swallowed. His throat had gone dry. 'Yeah. I mean, we don't have military hospitals any more. He's in the MDHU at Portsmouth.'

'Portsmouth,' she repeated. Her eyes betrayed nothing. Did she know he was lying?

They sat in silence for a while. There was the sound of another engine in the distance and Graves stiffened.

'I thought there was no one else out here?' Mallory said.

'Poachers. They always come out this time of the year, because that's the only direct road to the swamp. So, the girl you talked to at the company ... MTT?'

'MTC.'

'Right. What did you say her name was, again?'

'I didn't,' Mallory said. 'Why do you ask?'

Graves's eyes met his, giving nothing away. 'No reason.'

And then it was like a switch was flipped, and Mallory knew there was definitely something wrong. As impossible as it was, this was all very wrong.

In the next second, he was on his feet and moving inside. He ran over to the window at the front. He could see lights from the direction of the gravel turning spot. A lot of light, far more than from just a single vehicle. They weren't being careful not to announce their arrival. They didn't need to be. There was nowhere to go.

He turned to see Graves standing in the doorway. Her face was composed, showing no emotion. In her hand was a SIG Sauer P228, pointed straight at him.

44

'Jesus, I should have known.'

Graves kept her eyes, and the muzzle of the gun, fixed straight on him. 'Are you going to get all self-righteous on me, Mallory?'

Despite himself, he laughed, shaking his head at the fact that this hadn't occurred to him until it was too late. 'When you called me out of the blue, I thought – great, if there's one person who'll know who these bastards are, it'll be Graves. Turns out I was a lot closer to the mark than I thought.' He nodded his head back towards the door and the lights outside. 'I presume that's the Sentinel guys out there? I hope they're paying you well.'

She sighed. 'Of course they're paying me well. They were paying me a long time before you blundered into this situation. Keep your hands where I can see them.'

'They got here fast.'

'Not that fast. You gave me a heads-up when you called from Dulles.'

Mallory kept his hands by his sides. 'So this is how it is? You're going to hand me over to them?'

Graves shook her head. 'Don't even. You're screwing this up for me, Mallory, not the other way around.'

'Really? Because it looks like only one of us is on the wrong end of a gun.'

'I'm doing you a favour, you asshole.'

Mallory didn't respond verbally to that, but he trusted the look on his face would do it for him.

'I mean it,' Graves continued. 'They wanted to come in here and take you. I persuaded them that I could get the information out of you more effectively.'

'What information?'

'They want Scott Nel, and I think they'll also be interested in your thoughts on the Anambra code, and the fact his brother is back in play.'

'You think I'm going to turn him over to those bastards?'

'You don't have any choice. We are where we are. I told them you would cooperate. If you don't, I can't help you.'

He could hear car doors slamming. Voices. Boots on the gravel.

'How much are they paying you?'

'God *damn* it, are you listening to a single thing I'm saying? The world doesn't revolve around you, Mallory. I was here first. Cut your losses and you can walk out of here. Go home and forget about all of it.'

'No. It's not that simple. I already told you that Scott doesn't know anything. If they get him back, they'll kill him.'

'I told them to give me ten minutes. I haven't looked at a clock in a little while, but I think that time is just about up.'

Mallory could hear the footsteps getting closer. They were within a few yards of the front door, now. He remembered Graves locking it after she came in. She would have to let them in, if she didn't want them to kick it down. He narrowed his eyes and looked beyond Graves.

'I thought you said it was just us?'

She didn't look all the way round. She was too good for that. But for a split second, her gaze shifted. It was enough. Mallory ducked and rolled. He came up on his feet in the kitchen area and grabbed the skillet from the stove. In the same motion he swung and threw it at Graves. As it left his hand he ducked, expecting her to fire instinctively.

She either didn't have a chance or chose not to. The skillet hit her in the arm and smashed to the floor, denting the polished floorboards. The gun clattered across the floor, making a smaller, insubstantial noise.

By the time Graves had started moving to pick up the gun, Mallory had got to it and was holding it on her. She froze. He was getting sentimental. Anyone else would have had two bullets in their chest already.

'I think you broke my arm, you stupid son of a bitch.'

'I'm walking out of here.'

'There's nowhere to go. That's the only road.'

'Then I guess I'm going to have to go the hard way.'

Her brow furrowed. 'Are you insane? There's ten miles of swamp in that direction. Gators.'

'And there are some gentlemen out there who want to torture me before putting a bullet in the back of my head. I'll take my chances with the wildlife.'

He could hear the noise of boots on the wooden steps out front. Flashlight beams were streaming through the windows, reflecting in the picture frames on the wall. Time was up.

'When this is over, you and I are going to have a chat,' Mallory said.

Graves said nothing, just stared back with fury in her eyes as she rubbed her upper arm.

And then he ran out to the deck, vaulted over the railing and landed on the jetty. He was up to a full sprint as he heard the yells from behind as the men burst into the house. Powerful flashlight beams lit up the trees and the jetty, trying to find a target. And then he had reached the end of the jetty and launched himself out into the darkness.

45

JOHANNESBURG

Scott had his phone and what was left of the cash Mallory had given him, and the clothes on his back, but nothing else. He had tried calling Mallory a dozen times, but his phone seemed to be switched off.

He hunched down, keeping the hood over his face at the back of the bus. He knew he had to get as far away from the hotel as possible. They would be looking for him all over the area. But where could he go? Not back to his apartment, that was for sure. He was worried about trying to check in anywhere else. They had found him there; what would prevent them from finding him at the next place? It was blind luck that he hadn't been in the hotel room when they came. At any other time in the last two days, they would have kicked the door down and found him cowering on the bed. Cornered.

Scott felt a cold sweat break out on the back of his neck as he thought about it, how close he had come to being taken back. No. He couldn't let himself be captured again. He would stay out, somehow. He would shelter under a bridge if need be, as long as there was an escape route.

He risked raising his head enough to look out of the window as the bus passed through a neighbourhood that looked a little more familiar. Houghton. He had been to a pool party here last year. Thinking about that carefree, drunken afternoon, he wanted to cry.

For the first time since Mallory had found him, he thought about how utterly alone he was. He couldn't go to his friends. If Mallory was right, Adriaan had sold him out, and he trusted the other people he had been hanging out with even less, if anything. Mallory was uncontactable, and on the other side of the world, in any case. His mother just as far away. He had less than a thousand rand in his pocket, no friends and nowhere to go.

The bus slowed and stopped behind a tail of traffic under the M1 flyover. Scott looked out of the window at the pedestrians and cyclists passing by on the walkway, envious of how carefree their existences were, even if they couldn't fully appreciate it.

Looking south, he could see the towers of the financial district. One of those buildings belonged to MTC. He remembered how pleased his father had been when he got the job there. It was just a lowly coder position, but he had been so proud that The Difficult Son was finally on the right track. And then came the equal strength of his father's disappointment when he had inevitably been asked to leave. He had screwed that opportunity up, just like he had screwed everything else up.

Reaching under his collar, he clasped the flint pendant in his hand.

'I'm sorry, Dad,' he said under his breath.

Things would have been so different if he had just pulled it together for once and taken that opportunity. He would never have met Adriaan, never got involved with the gang. The bus started to move off again and the buildings seemed to shift configuration as his point of view changed. The MTC tower itself came into view.

Mallory had said he had spoken to Ivy, that she remembered him. He was surprised that she had been so keen to help. He had always had the impression she didn't like him. But Dad's team had been good people, so he had said.

He wondered ... maybe Ivy could help, somehow? Maybe she would have some other way to contact Mallory, let him know that Scott was in deep trouble, worse trouble than he had been a day ago.

Yes, it was worth a try. He could go to the office and pretend he had a meeting with Ivy. Hopefully she would see him, or they would put him in touch if she wasn't there. Downtown was a long way from the Hauer Hotel, so it would be as safe as going anywhere else. And he had to go somewhere.

When the bus reached the stop at the Rosebank Mall he would get off. MTC was just about within walking distance from there. As the bus pulled into another stop, he sat back, adjusting the hood to shade his face. It wasn't much, but it felt good to have a goal for the moment, a destination in mind. Ivy would help him get in touch with Mallory. If he could just get hold of Mallory, *he* would know what to do.

46

LOUISIANA

Mallory had no clue what to do next.

He moved out into the swamp. Its heady, decayed scent was all around him. The water came up almost to his waist. He quickly moved beyond the end of the jetty and changed his direction so that he couldn't easily be seen by the men who were on the back deck of the cabin already. He could hear their voices as they coordinated the search. The beams of flashlights stabbed through the trees, sometimes getting close to him. He stopped and plunged his hand into the slimy water, reaching down until he found soft mud at the bottom. He closed his eyes and smeared it across his face, the back of his neck, his hands.

He decided against a straight move through the swamp the moment he hit the water. It wasn't completely silent out here, with the sounds of things moving, but it was quiet enough that a man wading through water would be enough to betray his position from a fair distance, particularly to trained men who knew what they were doing. And he had every reason to suppose the Sentinel men knew what they were doing, both from what Graves had implied about them and from the evidence of his own eyes.

Fifty yards or so from the end of the jetty, there was a thick tree that grew at a forty-five degree angle out of an outcrop of solid ground. Mallory manoeuvred himself behind the tree and looked back at the cabin. It had been a split-second decision: whether to put as much distance between himself and Graves's cabin as quickly as he could, or stick around and take a closer look.

Most people would instinctively do the former. That was why he picked the latter.

There's ten miles of swamp in that direction. Graves had been bluffing; banking on the probability that Mallory wouldn't have looked at a map of the area. In fact, he hadn't, but he had taken a good look at the framed aerial photograph showing a two-mile radius around Graves's house. That was how he knew there was another dirt road a little north of here, leading through the ruins of a small town that had been wiped out by Katrina. All he had to do was get to that dirt road in one piece. A task that would be difficult enough in the dark, without a group of trained men ready to kill him.

The gun he had taken from Graves felt unnaturally light. As soon as he had picked it up, he had known there was something wrong. Now he checked, and his suspicion was confirmed. It wasn't loaded. He supposed he ought to take that as a compliment. Graves had never intended to shoot him. An empty gun wasn't going to do him a hell of a lot of good now, though. He tucked the useless weapon into his waistband and looked across at the men who had come for him.

There were six of them. They were all men. All in their thirties and forties, all in good shape. They were exactly the kind of men Graves had spoken about. Mallory knew the type. They looked like they had already served their time in branches of the military or intelligence, and had moved on to parallel work. They had kept in shape. They would have kept abreast of changes in tactics and technology.

Three were at the foot of the jetty. All were armed with assault rifles with barrel-mounted flashlights. With the lights shining in this direction, Mallory couldn't make out their faces. They were just silhouettes. Their poise and movements told him enough. They stood in a triangle formation, covering all angles leading off from the jetty, sweeping the beams of their flashlights around efficiently, looking for movement.

Further back, the other three were standing, along with Graves, in the halo of light cast by the lamps over the back porch. Mallory could see the spot he had sat shooting the shit with Graves just ten minutes before. His half-drunk bottle of beer was still on the table. It reminded Mallory how quickly everything had changed.

Graves was rubbing her upper arm with her free hand. She was talking to the man closest to her. He wore a black T-shirt under a Kevlar vest. It looked like he was wearing a headset, and he assumed the others would be, too. He looked around forty. By comparing him to Graves, Mallory judged he was about five-eight. He had short brown hair and glasses with black frames. Next to him was a taller man with hair so blond it was almost white. The guy Scott talked about, perhaps? The third man was black and heavily built. He was midway in height between the blond man and the one in glasses.

Graves's voice carried across on the night air. Mallory was just within range and could make out the words.

'Well maybe if you guys hadn't shown up with a fucking light show, I would have made a little more progress.'

'How far to the next house?' the blond man asked. American accent. This was Scott's interrogator. Willer, that was the name Graves had suggested.

'About twenty miles,' Graves said. 'You'll find him out there or you won't find him.'

'Take it easy, we'll find him. Six against one.' The shorter man spoke with a British accent. Hard to place regionally. Public school, probably. His confidence, and the fact Graves was addressing him, told Mallory he was in charge. He didn't have the same military bearing as the other two nearby, or from what he could see of the three silhouettes at the foot of the jetty. MI5 or MI6.

'Easy for you to say, Branagh,' Graves replied.

Branagh. Mallory wondered if that was his real name. Graves was speaking in a louder voice than her conversational tone from earlier. Was she feeling bad about this? Feeding him information? After all, her gun hadn't been loaded.

None of them spoke for a while, and the three at the front continued sweeping the swamp with the beams of their flashlights. Mallory shrank back behind the trunk as one of the beams moved slowly past. He steadied himself on a small stump of a branch that stuck out. It was about eight inches long, the width of a walking stick. Might be useful, if he could snap it off without making too much noise.

'He's close,' Branagh said.

'How do you know?' The third one in the light was speaking now, the black guy. Another American.

'Because the splashing stopped too quickly,' came the reply.

Mallory had hoped they wouldn't have twigged that.

Branagh took three steps forward, closing the distance between himself and the three men on the front line. His third step took him out of the area illuminated by the lights of the cabin. He stopped and then spoke again.

'Mr Mallory, we know you're out there, and we know you're close.'

He waited for a reply. Mallory kept still.

'It isn't pleasant out there. You can't be comfortable. Our mutual friend tells me there are alligators. Alligators like to feed at night.'

'He ain't there, mate.'

It was one of the three silhouettes who had spoken this time. He sounded like an Australian. This was shaping up to be a pretty international team.

'He's there,' Branagh said, then raised his voice again. 'Mallory, we don't want to have to come out there to get you, but we will. We're not going to hurt you.' He hesitated and glanced back at the blond American, then added, 'As long as you cooperate.'

Branagh waited again. He looked at Graves.

She spoke up. 'Come on, Mallory. This is nothing personal, but you're being a real pain in the ass. Grow up, tell these guys what they need to know and we can all go home. I know you're not stupid.'

Mallory gritted his teeth. There were a lot of things he wanted to say to Graves right now, none of them nice. But he wasn't about to give them what they wanted: a voice to home in on.

Instead, he looked over at the vine that was draped between the two trees closest to him. He pulled it free and looped it loosely around a rock he had retrieved from beneath the water.

He released the vine. It swung silently across twenty feet of darkness, and then the rock dropped into the water with a loud splash. Immediately, the flashlights changed to focus on the sound, lighting up the ripple of water and the movement of the swamp weeds. Timing it to coincide with the splash, Mallory snapped off the branch stub from the tree.

'Remember: alive,' Branagh called out. Unnecessarily, going by the fact none of them had started shooting. Mallory was impressed. He was also pleased, because their reluctance to shoot first would be one of the only advantages he had.

He slid smoothly back into the water and began moving quickly in the opposite direction as he heard Branagh's voice again.

'Bring him in.'

Mallory didn't bother to glance back to confirm that he was addressing the three men at the front. He heard heavy splashes as the three of them moved into the water. Without looking down, he ran his hand over the snapped branch. It was strong, far enough above the water not to be damp, and it had broken so that it was tapered off to a sharp point at one end.

He kept moving, forcing himself to go slower than he would like to minimise noise. He made good progress, covering a hundred yards or so relatively quickly. The first thing he had to do was put some distance between himself and the men. After that, he could consider his options.

His ears were attuned to the voices of the men behind him, so he flinched when he heard another sound up close.

His hand, reaching out to the dark form of a tree trunk, brushed something leathery – and alive.

He cursed as a flock of surprised bats took flight, the sound of their wings cutting through the other sounds of the night.

And then there were more sounds. The men changing course, splashing through the swamp. And then the bright beams of the flashlights turning this way.

47

'I got a visual, nine o'clock.'

Mallory had seen the beam of the flashlight sweep across his right arm and immediately ducked away. Damn it. They were close, and getting closer.

Plan B. He wasn't going to be able to outrun them, and hiding was a strategy that would only work for so long. Three men with automatic weapons who knew how to use them against one man with a sharp stick. He would have to even those odds, and the first step was to split them up.

Ahead of him, there was a short rise of solid ground with an old tree growing out at an angle. Mallory climbed up, slid behind cover and watched as the men approached, easily visible with their flashlights. They were talking to each other, their voices low enough that he couldn't make out individual words. And then the lights winked out, one by one. Shit. He knew what that meant. They had night vision. There was enough light from the moon that he could see them lower goggles over their eyes.

He didn't panic. Because he had taken the time to smear

mud over his face and arms, it would still be a challenge to see him, since his skin wouldn't be reflecting light. Unless they had heat vision as well, in which case he was really stuffed.

He hunched behind the tree and watched. He was starting to think they would stay in that tight formation when the one at the head of the triangle made two gestures and the other two peeled off at diagonals. The one on the right flank was now headed straight towards the area Mallory was in.

His path would take him right under the tree where Mallory was hiding. There was no chance he wouldn't stop to examine it. Mallory kept completely still and watched as the man approached. He kept his rifle moving, covering the immediate area around him. He knew what he was doing, which would make things difficult. But, Mallory reminded himself, the other guy had a job to do: capture the target alive. That would be more difficult than Mallory's job.

He could see more details now. The man was within fifteen feet. He was a stocky guy with cropped hair. He was carrying what looked like an M4. There was a pistol holstered on his belt, too, and a knife strapped to his thigh. Mallory could tell by the outline that he was wearing the same kind of Kevlar vest as his boss. That was good news for Mallory. It protected the upper body, but not the neck.

Mallory felt the blood begin to rush through his veins. He felt elated. That feeling of standing on the edge of the diving board again, knowing what was about to happen. In another second, there would be no turning back. This wasn't some pub fight, it wasn't even taking on Devos's men. This was as real as it gets. He welcomed the bloodlust as he felt it rise.

The man turned his head to look directly at him. Mallory

didn't flinch. He knew what the man would be seeing: a brightly lit collage of greens and whites. He would definitely be able to see Mallory at that moment. But it wasn't quite as simple as that. The night vision increased visibility by a thousand per cent, but it also increased visual noise, especially in an environment as visually busy as this one. It was like looking at a *Where's Wally* picture. The thing he was looking for was right there in plain sight, but it took a lot of looking to find it. If Mallory moved, or even flinched, he would draw attention to himself. Instead, he relied on the overdose of visual information and kept perfectly still.

Mallory gripped the broken branch he had snapped off.

Ten feet now. Eight. The field of vision was narrowing. Soon it would be clear where Mallory was.

He didn't move. Kept waiting. He tensed the muscles in his legs and arms, waiting for the signal to move. The signal would come from the man who was stalking him.

And then it came. The head raised a fraction and then stopped.

Mallory launched himself from his perch, coming down on top of the guy.

The Sentinel man yelled out and put his free hand up, but Mallory had swooped, plunging them both into the water.

Mallory ignored the rifle and went straight for the killing blow. Shifting his weight, he grabbed the top of the man's forehead with his left hand, yanking it up. In the same moment, he jammed the sharp end of the stick hard just beneath his jaw. He felt warm blood spurt from the wound and heard a rattling in the guy's throat. He kept the hand on the forehead for a few seconds, until he was sure the guy was bleeding out, ignoring the spasmodic jerks of his hands as he uselessly tried to push Mallory off. Then he let the body slide into the water.

The rifle was gone. Mallory spent a few moments trying to locate it with his foot and gave up.

Rapid splashing revealed that the next closest man had changed course and was heading this way. Mallory could tell exactly where he was from the sounds. He looked around and saw that the nearest cover was twenty feet away, across an open stretch of black water. He wouldn't have time to wade across before company arrived.

The approaching man had heard the struggle, was confident he could get here before the winner of the struggle had time to move away. Overconfident, in fact.

Mallory took a deep breath and slipped beneath the surface. The water was cold, but he had already got used to it. He reached up, felt for the dead man's body, and moved himself underneath it, slipping out the guy's sidearm from the holster as he did so.

Mallory kept his eyes closed and focused on the other sensory information – the dulled sounds of splashing, the water and mud moving around him as the second man approached. He felt the body above him lift as it was turned over.

Now was the moment, while he was distracted, looking everywhere but down.

Mallory reached up and his fingers closed around the strap of the rifle around the man's shoulder, yanking it down. With his other hand he jammed the pistol under the man's chin as he flailed, and pulled the trigger twice. The water muffled the sound to a couple of deep *whumps*.

Mallory released his grip and stood up.

Two down. Four to go.

He heard raised voices. More than one. Splashing. More of them had entered the water as backup. Was Graves among them? He doubted it. Tonight had demonstrated that he didn't know Graves as well as he thought he had, but he was pretty sure she wouldn't put her neck on the line. If she did, it was her funeral. If they kept coming, he wasn't going to stop.

They would expect him to flee further into the swamp, so he did the opposite.

He circled back around until he could see the lights of the cabin again. He leaned against the trunk of a thick tree that was jutting out of the water at an angle and watched for a minute. There was no one on the end of the jetty. He wasn't surprised. Anyone standing there would be a sitting duck, now that they knew he had taken a weapon. He moved closer.

Just then he heard a whisper of movement, close by. He froze and turned his eyes in the direction of the sound.

The blond man was there. Willer. The moonlight lit up his hair like it was shining on snow. He was moving slowly, passing by where Mallory was hiding. He stopped as he heard the cry of a nightbird close by, turning his head and his gun away from Mallory's direction. Mallory aimed for his head and then, with a force of will, stayed his hand. He made a quick decision. If he could take a hostage, he might be able to make them back off.

Silently, Mallory straightened up. He put the muzzle of the gun against the back of Willer's head as he spoke.

'Drop it,' Mallory said quietly.

Willer tensed, but didn't move.

'I mean it. You're getting a warning, the last two didn't. Makes no odds to me. You want to die, give me an excuse.'

Willer released both hands from his rifle, but it still hung around its neck by the strap.

Mallory told him to lift the strap over his head and then drop it. He told him to do it slowly and use his left hand.

'You're a dead man,' Willer said as the rifle dropped into the water. His voice had a gravelly tone. He sounded furious. Mallory suspected he was just as angry at himself for letting his opponent get the drop on him.

'Says the guy with the gun to his head,' Mallory said. 'I can save you some time. I don't know anything about any fucking code, and neither does Scott Nel.'

'But you know where Scott Nel is. Either way, you're coming in.'

'No, mate. We're going to walk back to the cabin, and you're going to tell your buddies to stand down.'

'They're not going to let you do that.'

'We'll see. Start walking.'

Willer hesitated until Mallory nudged the back of his head with the barrel of his gun again, and then he started moving towards the lights of the cabin. He started to lower his arms. It looked natural, like he was adjusting for balance, but Mallory had already clocked the hilt of a blade strapped to the upper thigh of his right leg, just above the water level.

'Keep 'em up.'

Willer grunted and raised his hands again. Mallory kept his eyes on him, ready to fire at the first sudden move. He listened out for anyone else moving through the water nearby.

They reached a patch of solid ground and stepped out of the water. Just then, a dazzling beam of light flashed in Mallory's eyes and there was a surprised yell. In a split second Willer ducked out of the way and dived back into the water. Mallory fired at the source of the light and then ducked and rolled as the return fire came.

The ground dropped away before another narrow channel of water, so he hunched down and fired another two shots towards the position of the shooter. Beyond the channel of water was more solid ground, retreating away from the cabin. That plan was out of the window now, and he didn't fancy trying to hold this position now that two of them knew where he was. He had fired five shots already, and he didn't fancy running out of ammunition with his enemies closing in. Firing another shot for cover, he slipped into the channel, climbed out on the other side at a spot where he was hidden by a low-hanging branch.

He was pretty sure the surprise had been luck on the part of the second shooter, rather than a planned act. Otherwise he would have had a bullet in his face rather than a bright light.

A moment later, Willer's voice, raised in anger, told him he was right. 'Hogan, I had him!'

'I'm sorry, I couldn't tell which—'

'He went that way. Go!'

Mallory had stepped out of a patch of water on to solid ground and started running. He ducked and wove between the trees, putting as much distance down as possible. Lights flashed around but not near him. He crossed another stretch of dank water, forcing himself to slow down and keep the splashing to a minimum. He reached the far side and looked back the way he had come.

He could still see lights and hear voices, but they were further away now. Neither of the two men had seen the direction he had taken off in. He kept running.

48

Mallory kept pushing ahead, making slow but steady progress through the swamp. He concentrated on striking out to the south and west first, putting maximum distance between himself and the cabin. Soon, he would turn north and hope to approach the road from at least a mile or two up from Graves's cabin. He knew that every minute expanded the search area, and took comfort from the fact that he hadn't seen any signs of life for a while.

When he had gone long enough without seeing or hearing any evidence that they had managed to pursue him, he stopped and looked back the way he had come. The closest trees were spaced widely enough apart that the moon and the stars provided enough light to see for a reasonable distance. He was grateful for the clear night; it would have been much trickier to orient himself without the night sky. The trees got thicker a little further back, fading into darkness.

A bird called out, closer than he had heard for a while, and saw some kind of heron flutter down from the treeline and alight on a gnarled root that curved up from the water.

Up past its bedtime. Mallory guessed his passage had disturbed it.

The mud was beginning to crack on his face as it dried in the night air. He reached up and scraped some of it away from his forehead. As he did so, he thought about a few hours earlier, when the thought of disappearing into the swamp had sounded like an attractive challenge. Be careful what you wish for.

Reaching into his hip pocket, he took out his phone. It was unresponsive after being submerged along with its owner in three feet of murky water. The screen remained stubbornly dark when he tried switching the power on again. He knew that there were ways to revive waterlogged electronics, but he reckoned he was a good fifty miles away from the nearest two-pound bag of rice.

There would be no signal out here anyway, but he needed to get to a phone soon. Thinking back over what he had said to Graves, he was confident he hadn't used Ivy's name, but he wanted to tell her to be careful, just in case. He had spoken about a former female colleague of Bartho. They might be able to narrow it down to her from that, but it would take time.

He also needed to check in with Scott and get hold of Susan. If he were in the shoes of his opponents, he would be chasing up the lead that he had unwittingly given them. They would make a play for Donno now that they knew he was conscious. At least he was an ocean away.

Mallory slipped the dead phone back into his pocket and turned his eyes to the stars. This was all back-of-an-envelope stuff, but based on his memory of the bird's-eye photograph of Graves's house, he estimated he could head for about a mile due north from here and find the road.

Hopefully, they wouldn't anticipate that direction of travel. He looked back the way he had come again. He hadn't seen any flashlight beams since a little while after he had slipped away from the American. It had been a while since he had heard anything bigger than a—

Somewhere in the darkness, Mallory heard something large brush through the undergrowth. He raised his gun, eyes wide open, on full alert again.

How the hell had they followed him here?

Whoever it was must have been on him all the way. Why had he waited until now? Mallory quickly moved to the thickest tree he could see, pressing himself against it, keeping his eyes on the source of the sound.

He waited, hearing the sound of his pulse thump in his ears. The bastard knew he had been spotted, was keeping still.

And then there was a soft lap of water as he shifted position. Mallory blinked, letting his eyes adjust to the dark. He could make out movement, maybe twenty yards away. Not far from the tree root where the heron had alighted. Moonlight glinted off the outer edge of a ripple as it travelled out from the source. Perhaps Mallory's adversary hadn't seen him at all.

He risked moving from the tree and slowly took three steps through the water to get a better angle, ready to fire.

Then he saw him.

Just behind a small patch of ground that broke the surface of the water like a mini-island. It looked like he was lying down, but facing the opposite way from Mallory.

Slowly, Mallory approached, calculating. Give him a chance to surrender, or play it safe?

And then the shape moved and light bounced off wet, scaly skin, and he realised he had spotted a different kind of killer. One far more at home in this part of the world.

Mallory smiled and stepped back, retreating on to the dry land. He lowered his gun and watched as the alligator leapt and swallowed the heron whole. There was a tumult of water and then it slid beneath the surface and a moment later there was nothing to see but ripples.

Mallory tapped his forehead in a little salute and turned north. He was keeping a closer eye on the water this time. That was as close as he wanted to get to one of those things.

49

Branagh raised his gun as he heard footsteps from the jetty outside the cabin. He moved to the door and relaxed as he saw Willer's frame come into view. Willer stopped at the doorway. His legs and his lower stomach were drenched and coated with dirt from wading around in the swamp water.

'Koncak and Mills are dead.'

Branagh looked back at Willer in disbelief. He had long since given up expecting good news. It had been too long since Mallory had fled into the swamp for him to expect an ideal outcome, but ...

'Dead?'

'That's what I said.'

Branagh looked from Willer to Graves, who was massaging her upper arm and glaring back at him.

'I told you,' she said. 'I *told* you not to underestimate him.'

'You told me you had it under control. That you could get him to cooperate.'

'He was cooperating, right up until you tipped him off.'

Branagh suppressed his irritation and turned back to Willer. 'What do we do about Mills and Koncak?'

'Nash is with the bodies. Repatriation could be complicated.'

Branagh hadn't even thought about that. Although it had always been a theoretical possibility, he had never had to deal with the logistics of losing a man. It was certainly nothing he had expected to deal with outside a war zone.

'Do they have family?'

'Koncak doesn't. Mills has an ex-wife and a kid.'

Branagh weighed it up. Coming up with a story. Bribing local law enforcement. Arranging for the bodies to be repatriated. In all, a complex and risky operation. All things considered, it would be far easier to come up with a story for the ex-Mrs Mills. The cash settlement would cushion the blow, if she even cared that much.

He sighed. 'Drag them out further, weigh them down.'

Willer nodded in approval, but hesitated before responding. 'Nash won't like it.'

'He's not paid to like it.'

Willer didn't move for a moment, and Branagh wondered if the American didn't like it, either, if he was going to refuse. He felt an unexpected stab of uneasiness at that prospect. But it turned out Willer wasn't thinking about that at all.

'When we find him, after we get what we need? He's mine.'

'No argument from me,' Branagh said, thinking that he wouldn't be in Mallory's shoes for all the money in the world.

When Willer had departed, Branagh looked back at Graves.

'Okay, here's what I think we should do. We pull the team from Joburg and go to the UK. If Mallory's right about this, we've been talking to the wrong son all along. There's a flight—'

He stopped when he saw Graves was shaking her head. 'I'm out.'

'What?'

'I should have been out when I found out Mallory was involved.'

'It was an unavoidable personal conflict,' Branagh said. 'But you can't walk away from this.'

'Nothing to do with it being a personal conflict. This gig isn't paying me enough to take these kinds of risks. Now I have to watch my back and wonder how pissed he is. Judging by what happened to Koncak and Mills, I'm guessing pretty pissed.'

Branagh thought about it. He didn't need Graves. She had been a peripheral consultant for Sentinel, and he had hopes they could work with her again, but this was turning out to be a costly job all round.

'Fine. I'll make sure you get the fifty per cent kill fee, as per your contract.'

She gave a humourless laugh. 'I got you better intel in a half-hour with Mallory than your boy managed in a week with Scott Nel. I should get a hundred per cent. But I'll take seventy-five in exchange for never having to hear from you again.'

'Done,' Branagh said immediately. He went back out on to the deck and radioed Willer.

'You almost done?'

'On our way back.'

'Good. Our plane leaves in ninety minutes.'

50

It was difficult to judge the passage of time, but Mallory kept moving. Perhaps a couple of hours after he had seen the alligator he stopped again and tensed when he heard another sound that didn't fit with the swamp. It was like a low rumble, growing louder. It took him a second to register what it was. An engine. He pushed forward until he found an embankment and crawled up until he reached a gap in the trees – just in time to see a grey Econoline truck blow by at sixty or seventy miles an hour.

The highway. He had made it. Now all he had to do was work out what the hell to do next.

He stepped on to even ground for the first time in hours and started to walk. After a few minutes, he saw another set of lights approaching. Not a truck this time, a car. He tucked the gun into his back pocket and stepped out on to the road, raising a hand. As the car got closer, it slowed down. He held up both hands and waved, wishing he had a sign or something. He could say he had broken down, needed a ride to the nearest gas station.

The driver, a young-looking woman wearing glasses, locked eye contact with him and then stared straight ahead. She quickly accelerated and blew past him.

Damn it. But understandable now that he thought about what he must look like: a guy who had just dragged himself through several miles of swamp. He reached a hand up to scrape some more of the dried mud from his face and saw that his hand was spattered with the blood of the first man he had killed. The submersion had washed some of it off, but not all. It was all over his shirt as well, mingling with the dirt. He had about as much chance of hitching a ride as he had of winning a beauty pageant.

It was ten minutes before another set of lights appeared, headed the other way. He thought quickly. There was no way of telling how far he was from the next town. He wasn't getting a ride looking like this. Unless the people at Graves's cabin worked out that he could have gone this way, in which case eventually a car would come along that was only too happy to pick him up. Maybe in an hour, maybe sooner than that. His only other option was hoping he could follow the road and make it on foot before they showed up.

No, there was no time for niceties.

He stepped into the shadows at the side of the road so that he could take a look at the car before the driver saw him. A red pickup truck. Safe enough to assume it wasn't the kind of vehicle the Sentinel people would rent. Mallory stepped out on to the road.

It was within two hundred yards now. The driver had seen him and was slowing, no doubt at the start of the same cycle of curiosity as the previous driver: close-up look, then rejection. Mallory drew his gun. He stepped out into the road ahead of the pickup and pointed it straight at the driver's head.

The driver slammed on the brakes the moment he saw Mallory in the road. By the time he realised there was a gun pointed at his head, it was too late to speed up again. At least, too late to be sure of not getting shot.

The pickup came to a stop and Mallory circled around to the passenger side, keeping the gun aimed between the driver's wide-open eyes.

He was a heavyset man in his thirties. He had reddish brown hair and a beard and the black ink of a tattoo peeked out from the sleeve of his white T-shirt. He had his hands up, shock in his eyes, which stayed on Mallory as he moved around.

'Open the door.'

The driver hesitated. Blinked.

'Open the door,' Mallory said again, not raising his voice.

The driver leaned over, shaking, and opened the passenger door carefully. It took him two tries to get the handle to open. Mallory stepped back as it swung out towards him.

'Hands on the wheel.'

'Don't kill me, man, you can take the car, I have money, I have ...'

'Hands on the wheel.'

The driver did as ordered. His knuckles gripped the wheel tight.

Mallory slid into the passenger seat, keeping the gun pointed at his head. As he settled in the seat, the driver noticed the blood on him and closed his eyes.

'Oh Jesus, oh Jesus ...'

He was starting to hyperventilate. He didn't look in the

best of shape. The last thing Mallory needed was him having a heart attack, particularly when he had no clue where the nearest emergency medical clinic was.

'I'm not going to hurt you,' Mallory said as he gave him a quick look over. No holsters, no bulges in his pockets that could conceivably be a weapon. But then, this was America. 'Do you have a gun? A knife?'

The driver shook his head quickly.

'Open the glove box,' he said. 'Left hand.'

The driver obliged and leaned over, his hand shaking. The glovebox was stuffed full of flyers and candy wrappers and loose change, but nothing more threatening than that. Mallory gestured for him to close it. After he had done that, he returned his left hand to the steering wheel without being asked.

'What's your name?'

'Haskins. Da— Dave Haskins.'

'Dave, I'm going to lower my weapon, because you're doing everything right, okay?'

Dave agreed hurriedly and Mallory lowered the gun.

'Okay. Take a couple of deep breaths. In through your nose, out through your mouth. I'm not going to hurt you.'

Dave made a stab at it. He was still sweating and shaking, but his breathing had slowed a little.

'I need you to take me somewhere.'

'Anything you want, sir.'

Mallory considered. He couldn't exactly have this guy drop him off at the airport. He needed new clothes first.

'Do you have a phone?'

Dave reached for his pocket. Mallory reminded him to reach with his left hand. He took out a phone and unlocked it, handed it to Mallory.

He brought up the map. The airport was on the west side of New Orleans. There was a Walmart three miles from the airport and it would be open by the time they got there. That would do. Google said it was a seventy-two-minute drive.

'Where do you want to go, sir?'

'Stop calling me sir.'

'Yes, sir, I mean, yes ... Where do you want to go?'

'Thanks for the lift, Dave. I think I'd like to go shopping.'

AFGHANISTAN

SIX MONTHS AGO
HELL HOUR

Mallory took the lead, advancing up the first flight of stairs. He didn't want to risk Yorkie blowing away any non-combatants without checking if they were armed first. Their footsteps echoed off the narrow walls in the darkness.

There was a half landing and a turn. The building was still in complete darkness. No movement, no sound, other than muted bursts of gunfire from elsewhere in the compound.

Mallory paused and then stepped on the first step, then the second. Donno was a step behind him. He ascended to the third, putting himself on eye level with the next floor.

There was an empty corridor. No windows. Mallory could see that three of the doors were tight shut. The fourth, at the far end, was all the way open.

Donno started to advance to the next stair. Mallory held up a hand. *Wait*.

A moment later, a man appeared at the door, crouched. He came out shooting.

Mallory and Donno ducked. Bullets smacked into the wall behind them.

There was a yell and the sound of running footsteps. Mallory didn't hesitate. He straightened up and sprayed the corridor with bullets. There was almost no need to aim in the tight space. In the moment he stood up, he saw that the man wasn't holding a gun, but there was a grenade in his hand. He was pulling back to throw it into the stairwell. In the confined space, there would be nowhere to run.

He jerked as Mallory's bullets hit him, the grenade dropping from his hand and rolling down the corridor. Mallory saw the gunman behind him dive back into the room.

Mallory put a hand on Donno's shoulder and pushed him down, then threw himself after him.

The grenade detonated, deafening in the close confines. Mallory jammed his eyes shut against the sudden glare in his goggles and felt the sharp edges of the stairs as he tumbled down after Donno.

He scrambled to his feet and looked up again. The wall of the stairwell was spattered with shrapnel. He climbed to the landing again. The body of the grenade man was lying where it'had fallen. His legs had been blown off by the blast. The floor was slick with blood and littered with debris. The blast had blown out all of the closed doors.

Mallory's ears were still ringing. As his hearing started to return, he became aware of the sound of his own pulse thudding in his head, and his own breathing. It sounded ragged, like he was wounded. He frowned and looked down at himself. He was unmarked. The breathing wasn't coming from him.

He made the top of the stairs and advanced towards the

first door, keeping an eye on the one at the end of the corridor, ready to fire as soon as the gunman appeared. He didn't want to be ambushed by someone who had been biding their time in one of the other rooms.

Donno followed, walking backwards slowly and covering the next flight of stairs in case anyone tried to come down. He heard the scuff of boots behind him as Yorkie followed.

Each door opened on to a small bedroom. None took more than a couple of seconds to clear: there was no one in sight.

Mallory drew level with the final door.

The raspy breathing was coming from the man who had fired on them. He had been hit by the blast, and was covered in blood. His gun had been blown out of his hand and was lying on the other side of the room.

Donno and Yorkie joined Mallory at the doorway. Donno lowered his weapon as he saw the condition of the man inside. Yorkie kept his gun on him.

'Cuff him,' Mallory said to Donno, while giving Yorkie a warning look. 'If he's still breathing in ten minutes, we'll take him with us.' He turned his attention back towards the final flight of stairs. At the half landing, the muted green shade of their surroundings turned into a dazzling emerald.

A light had been turned on.

Donno was already moving towards the stairs. Mallory followed. He was getting a feel for the layout now. The upper floor would be a truncated version of this floor. Perhaps only two doors, with space for the roof terrace.

Mallory put a hand on Donno's shoulder to stop him for a second and scanned the stairs ahead for tripwires. It looked clear.

Donno straightened and took the next two stairs quickly, before stopping and training his gun on a target.

Mallory saw in the next second there was a man at the end of the corridor, wearing sweatpants and a T-shirt. He was silhouetted in the light from the room at the far end, but Mallory knew who it was. Even in silhouette, he knew it was the man they had come here for. He could see Donno's laser sight on the HVT's chest. He was wearing an explosive vest. He had a gun in his hand, but it was pointed towards the ground.

'Down on the ground,' Donno yelled. Then he repeated it in Pashto. The figure didn't move.

'Wait a second,' Mallory said. He couldn't see much beyond the figure in the doorway, but he could see light glinting off monitor screens. He thought about the mission briefing. This had to be the treasure trove.

'Down on the fucking ground!' Donno yelled at the man. This time, the man in the vest dropped the weapon, but didn't move to get down. He was staring back at them, thinking.

Mallory examined the landing. He could see wires running from the room with the computers. He kept his gun on the man in the doorway but let his eyes follow the wires. They led to a small box on the wall, five feet from the man. The room was rigged to blow. If he detonated in the doorway, it would likely blow the explosives in the room. But they couldn't risk shooting him where he stood. They had to get him to surrender, or at least get him away from that room.

Mallory heard Westwick behind him in the stairwell. There was only space for two of them to stand abreast. Khan and McKenzie were behind. Yorkie another step down. Mallory was pleased that Yorkie was as far back as possible.

The gunfire from elsewhere seemed to have died away completely. There was no sound but the echoes of their breathing off the walls of the stairwell.

The figure shuffled slowly forward. It was difficult to read the movement. If he was complying, he was doing it slowly. Perhaps he didn't want to make any sudden moves.

'I'm going to put him down,' Donno said, adjusting his aim.

'Drop him,' Yorkie yelled. Mallory knew if he had been first to the top of the stairs he would have done it already.

Before he had thought about it, Mallory had put his hand on Donno's shoulder.

'Wait a second,' he said again. He wanted to let him get closer. Away from that room. More than that, he didn't want Donno turning into another Yorkie. Another bully with a weapon. He had seen it before, the blood lust becoming addictive after the first kill.

'I don't like this,' Westwick said, eyeing the same wiring Mallory had been looking at. 'He's not going anywhere. Let's hold off getting any closer.'

'We don't have the time' Mallory said. 'We need to get him the hell away from that—'

'Get down on the floor!' Donno yelled again, his voice cracking.

Mallory raised his voice. 'Donno, no.'

'I'm going to—'

'No,' Mallory said, the sharp tone stopping Donno mid-sentence. 'I can do this.'

Mallory stepped up to the top stair. His own red laser was on the HVT's chest. He could see his other hand now. He was holding a dead-man switch. If they shot him, the vest would blow. He felt the sweat break out on his forehead. They were standing in the middle of a death trap.

He heard Westwick's voice from behind him, sounding like it was coming through clenched teeth. 'We need to fall back.'

Mallory swallowed.

'Raise your hands.'

The HVT smiled.

He started running towards them. Mallory and Donno fired.

And then the world exploded in white light and fire.

51

JOHANNESBURG

Scott didn't recognise the security guard from his brief stint as an employee of MTC, and from the guard's expression, he knew that was mutual.

'Can I help you, sir?' he asked, looking at Scott with undisguised suspicion.

Scott affected a casual tone, looking beyond the guard to the elevator bank. 'Yeah, I have a meeting with Ivy Maritz. She works for MTC.'

'A meeting?' the guard repeated, openly giving Scott a look up and down. Scott knew it wasn't the way he was dressed. Shorts and T-shirt wouldn't be out of place in the office, although they looked cheaper than anything anyone in the building would be seen dead in. No, he knew it was the person, not the clothes. He had avoided looking at himself in the mirror after that first glimpse at the hotel. He had to have lost six or seven kilos. He was unshaven, his hair needed a trim, and his eyes were rimmed with red. He looked like a junkie, not to put too fine a point on it. The fact he was still wired from the narrow escape earlier this morning didn't help with that.

The guard finished evaluating him. He didn't move aside. 'Why don't you give me your name and I'll call upstairs?'

'Sure. My name is Scott Nel.'

'And she's expecting you, yes?' He made no effort to keep the scepticism out of his eyes.

'Scott?'

The two of them stopped and looked back towards the sound of the voice. The doors of one of the elevators had opened, and Ivy Maritz was standing there. She was wearing beige shorts and a tie-dyed vest top. She had a canvas backpack, one strap draped over her right shoulder. She hurried to the turnstile and tapped out with her security card.

The guard looked from Scott to Ivy with mild surprise. 'You're Ivy?'

'Yes,' she said offhandedly, before turning her attention to Scott. She gave him the same up and down appraisal as the guard, but her reaction was of concern, rather than disdain.

'Do you know this gentleman?' The guard still sounded sceptical.

'Uh, yes. Hi, Scott. What are you doing here?'

Scott cleared his throat. 'I ... I mean, we had a ... meeting. Remember?'

The guard raised an eyebrow.

Ivy cottoned on quickly. 'Of course. Sorry, completely forgot.'

'Would you like to sign your guest in?' the guard asked.

Ivy glanced back at the elevators. 'You know what? Let's go to a coffee shop instead.'

Ivy led the way. Scott glanced at the security guard and then quickly followed.

'Are you okay?' Ivy asked as soon as they were through

319

the main doors of MTC and outside on the pavement. 'You look ... you don't look great.'

'It's a long story,' Scott said. 'Listen, I know a guy came to see you about me a couple of—'

'Mallory.'

'Yeah, that's him.'

'I talked to him today,' Ivy said. 'He told me what happened to you. He thinks it's something to do with what your father was working on.'

'What?'

'Long story short, we were working on a program that Mallory thinks could have been valuable to someone. There's a missing section of program code that they need for it to work. He thinks that's why they kidnapped you.'

It took a minute to sink in. 'That's what they meant by "the code"?'

'We think so. Did Bartho ever say anything to you about it?'

'No,' Scott said. 'Never. If I had known that I could have told them. Wait.' He stopped and looked back at the MTC building. 'Can we get it? The thing they want?'

Ivy was already shaking her head. 'That's why I was there. I thought maybe I could find it if Bartho had left a copy in the office or in his file space, but there was nothing.'

Scott sighed. 'I knew that sounded too good to be true.'

They had reached the crossing and were waiting for the lights. Ivy was opening her mouth to say something when there was a squeal of tyres. Scott's head snapped around to look towards the source of the noise. A delivery van had run the red light and almost collided with a taxi. The taxi driver leaned on his horn and stuck his head out of the window to scream abuse at the van driver.

When he looked back at Ivy, she was staring at him again, the worried look back on her face. Instinctively, he had raised his hand in front of his face, like someone cowering from an attack.

'Scott, are you okay?'

He took a second to steady his voice before speaking. He hoped Ivy couldn't see that he was trembling. 'Too many people here. Can we go somewhere quiet, please?'

52

LOUISIANA

Dave was a reasonably fast driver, but he didn't take any risks. Mallory couldn't have asked for a better chauffeur. He kept his eyes on the road and his hands steady on the wheel as he guided the car along long stretches of unlit road. The trees and the swamp flashed by as a black blur. Mallory kept his eyes on the road too, looking out for police cars. He didn't think Dave would try anything rash, but he wanted to be ready just in case. Mallory had been awake since the flight from Dulles. He wasn't tired yet, but he knew the fatigue would hit him hard when he got to safety and allowed himself to switch off.

Dave broke the silence after they had been driving for about ten minutes.

'What, uh ... what are you going to do when we get there?'

Mallory looked over at him. The silence had suited him; both because he didn't want to give Dave anything else to tell the police beyond his description, and because he was thinking. About Graves and the people she was working with. About Scott and Ivy. About what had really happened to Bartho Nel. And about how they could all extricate themselves from this situation.

Dave glanced away from the road to look at him, uneasily, wondering if he had made a bad decision by breaking the silence. Mallory didn't want him to be any more scared than necessary.

'I'm going to let you go. Like I said I would.'

Dave was silent again, but Mallory knew there would be follow-up questions now. The seal had been broken. He shifted in his seat so he could look into the back and saw there was a discarded hoodie there. Dave was bigger than him, but not that much bigger. The hoodie would cover his muddy and bloodstained shirt long enough for him to get new clothes.

Dave cleared his throat and Mallory looked back at him.

'So uh ... what's your story?'

'My story?'

'Yeah, I mean with the ... with the blood and the, uh ...'

'The gun?'

'Yeah.' Throat clear again.

Mallory let out a long sigh. 'This isn't the best night of your life, am I right, Dave?'

Dave glanced at him before answering. 'Not really, no.'

'Well, believe it or not, it isn't mine, either. Some boys back there tried to make it a pretty shitty evening, and they did a good job of it.'

Dave's gaze darted to the blood, and then back to the road.

'You uh ... you okay there? Are you hurt?'

'I'm fine.'

Silence for another couple of miles.

'You're not from round here, are you?'

323

'Australian,' Mallory said, not caring whether Dave bought it or not, but deciding it wouldn't hurt to throw a little doubt on the description.

Every time they passed a gap in the trees that lined the road, he could see the sky had lightened a little more on the horizon.

They made it to the Walmart just after 5.30 in the morning. Mallory hoped that the men at Graves's cabin would still be tramping through the swamp looking for him. The sun would be up in an hour. Mallory pulled the hoodie from the back and put it on. He examined his face in the vanity mirror in the sunshade and rubbed off a line of dried blood he had missed. Presentable.

'Give me your wallet.'

Without hesitation, Dave shifted in his seat and took a battered canvas wallet from his back pocket. Mallory opened it. There were some bank cards and a driver's licence and two fifty-dollar bills. He used Dave's phone to snap a picture of the bank card.

'Is that ...' Dave gulped. 'Is that so you can ... you know, so I don't say anything?'

Mallory glanced over at him. He knew what he was thinking: that this was an 'I know where you live' thing.

'Dave, how much did your phone cost you?'

'I don't know, it's a contract.'

'Okay.' Mallory took one of the fifties and put it into the pocket of the hoodie with the phone. 'I'm going to ask you not to speak to the police about this. Not for, say twelve hours.'

Dave was already shaking his head. 'No sir, I won't say anything.'

'Relax. I'm not coming after you. You'll never see me again. But I would like a head start, you know what I mean?'

'A head start?'

'You give me twelve hours before you go the police, and I'll make it up to you. I have your bank account number. I'll send your fifty back, plus, say two hundred for the phone. I'll round it up to five hundred for the ride.'

Dave looked confused. Trying to work out what the catch was.

'You did me a favour, mate. I just needed the ride, and I'm sorry for putting you through this.'

'Why . . . why didn't you just ask?'

Mallory looked down at the gun. 'Would you have stopped?'

'I guess not.'

As Mallory turned to open the door, he was conscious that Dave was holding his hand out. He considered for a second and then took it, shaking.

'I hope your day gets better, sir.'

'You too, Dave. Thanks again.'

53

As the pickup drove off, Mallory took Dave's phone out and turned off location services. Next, he looked up Ivy's number on the MTC website and sent her a text, asking her to call him on this number.

The staff member welcoming customers at the entrance of the Walmart gave Mallory a suspicious look, but didn't stop him. He didn't look too different from the bums gathered in the parking lot outside, but the hoodie he had taken from Dave's pickup concealed the blood on his shirt. He bought new clothes and changed in a cubicle in the public restrooms, balled up his damp and bloody clothes, bagged them and dumped them along with the gun in the bottom of a waste bin.

Leaving the store by the entrance at the opposite end, he surveyed the parking lot for police cars. Nothing. He believed Dave would be as good as his word. Maybe he wouldn't even call the police at all, since Mallory hadn't hurt him. Other than some psychological damage, perhaps. Mallory still felt a little bad about it. Dave had been a good bloke. He hoped his reparations for the enhanced hitch-hiking would make amends.

Mallory considered his options. They were not numerous.

He couldn't go back to Graves's place, of course. Hertz would just have to come and fetch their rental car, assuming Graves didn't drive it out to the middle of nowhere and torch it. He was glad that he had, as always, packed light on this trip. All he was missing was a couple of changes of clothes and his toilet bag. Keeping his passport in his back pocket had turned out to be a good idea. The interior pages were a little damp from the swamp, but the laminated part with the important information on it was fine.

The phone buzzed. No name on the display, just a cell number that looked like it could be South Africa. He picked up the call.

'It's Ivy.'

'Ivy, great. Listen I need you to—'

'Scott Nel's with me.'

It took Mallory a second to adjust to the whiplash caused by Ivy's statement. 'What?'

'I think we might be in trouble.'

'Put him on.'

Scott's voice came on the phone. 'Hi, where are you?'

Mallory had to restrain himself from yelling and attracting the attention of the customers who were filing into the store. 'For Christ's sake, Scott, I told you to stay—'

'I know, but they found me somehow,' Scott said quickly.

'What? How?'

'I don't know. They showed up at the hotel. I only just got away.'

Almost immediately, Mallory knew what had happened.

He had told Graves the general area they were in. They must have gone door to door until they hit the right place. 'Okay. It's all right. You need to go somewhere safe.'

'Are you coming back here? Please tell me you're coming back.' Scott's voice was pleading.

'No, I have to go back home. I think they might try to get to Donno.' As he said it, he remembered that Scott didn't have the latest news yet.

'Donno, why would they—'

'He woke up, mate. Your mum called me last night.'

'He woke up? That's amazing, what did—'

'It is amazing and we can talk about it later, but right now, I need you to put Ivy back on.'

There was a pause, and then Ivy came back on the line.

'Hi.' Her voice was shaking slightly. Mallory felt a twinge of guilt.

'Is there anywhere you and Scott can go for a little while?'

'Yes. We're on the way to my place.'

'Probably best not. They know I was speaking to someone on Bartho's team. They don't know your name, but I wouldn't bet against them finding out.'

'Shit.' Ivy sounded scared. That was probably a good thing. 'Okay, let me think.'

'I'm sorry, this one is my fault,' Mallory said, 'but I'm going to see if I can fix it. You two should be safe if you stay away from your place until this is over.'

'What do you mean over?'

'I'm going to find a way to finish it.'

She sighed. 'I went to MTC. I went through all the stuff from Bartho's office.'

'Did you find anything?'

'No. I checked out his drawers, everywhere I could think of in his office.'

'What about somewhere else in the building?'

'No. If he hid it somewhere, it would have been in his office, so it would be in the stuff they packed up and put in storage. He had to know it would be close, and safe.'

Mallory closed his free hand into a fist in frustration. 'That's what I was worried about. These guys want something that we can't find. Something that may not even exist. If we can't find it, we have no leverage.'

'Then what do we do?'

'I don't know. I need to go home and make sure I can get to Donno before anyone else does. Maybe he'll be able to tell us what the hell his dad did with the code.'

54

Mallory got in a taxi outside Walmart. Twenty minutes later, he was at the airport – back where he had been less than twenty-four hours ago, and somehow feeling more awake and energised than he had when he had been there the first time.

He had been considering his options ever since he had got into Dave's pickup truck. First of all, he had to get the hell out of the country, for the second time in the past couple of days. This time, there wasn't the option of jumping the border and taking the long way home. But he hoped the fact the Sentinel men were still looking for him in the swamp would mean they couldn't spare any bodies to watch the airport. It felt like a gamble, but it was the only course of action open to him. Back in Joburg, the Sentinel guys had managed to get the police looking for him by setting him up. They wouldn't be able to do that here in the US.

Keeping his head down, Mallory moved through the terminal until he found a display board showing departures. There was a flight to Toronto leaving in a couple of hours.

Assuming that was on time, he could fly straight to Gatwick from there and be in London tomorrow morning GMT. In another two hours he could be in Birmingham. He wanted to leave it until the last moment before buying his ticket, so he found a small coffee shop in an out-of-the-way part of the terminal. There was a table at the side that let him watch the travellers passing in both directions and gave him multiple ways to leave. He bought a coffee and a sandwich and kept his eyes on the crowds.

He ran through his conversations with Graves again, kicking himself for not picking up on the fact that something was different about the way she was talking to him. But this was part of who Graves was. Getting information out of someone without them realising. She had been doing it since the first call, when she casually asked where in Joburg he had stashed Scott. Like she was just making conversation, wanted to make sure he had covered all bases. He hadn't been specific, thank God, and she hadn't risked making him suspicious by pushing it. But he had told her the general area. That was what had allowed them to narrow the search down and, eventually, find Scott's hotel.

Susan, though. He had told Graves that she was in the UK, that Donno was awake, and that there was a possibility he knew what had happened to the code. Whether they were able to get Scott or not, it was a definite that they would now try to get to Donno, particularly if they thought Mallory's theory was correct: that Donno might have been the son trusted to safeguard the code.

That had been when Graves, realising she was running out of time, had overplayed her hand. It was the first time he had been suspicious, when she started really pushing, asking which hospital Donno was in. He had recovered quickly enough to lie, and he thought he had been convincing about it. So Sentinel would check out Portsmouth first. But if they were as good at their jobs as he suspected, they would quickly establish Donno wasn't in Portsmouth. There were only seven MoD Hospital Units in the whole of the UK, and Birmingham was the biggest. It wouldn't take them long to narrow it down.

But they would have to move fast. Graves had spoken of Sentinel as a small, tight team. They were already spread thin, looking for him in Louisiana and Scott in Joburg. That evened up the race a little. One of them would get to Birmingham first. Mallory just had to hope it was him.

If he could get to Donno, maybe he could get to the code. If he had the code, he had leverage. He could work out a way to make sure they backed off.

Mallory sat back in the chair and rubbed his eyes. The adrenaline was wearing off. The best night's sleep he had had in the last three days had been on the bare floor of a makeshift cell, possibly with a mild concussion. Now he was facing another long journey and he needed to get his head back in the game. He thought again about his team. About the other people he had lost. What he wouldn't give to be able to pick Westwick's brains right now. Westwick had always been able to take a breath and think analytically, no matter how desperate the situation. He needed some of that cool-headedness right now.

Something was missing here. Mallory couldn't shake the feeling that there was another piece of the puzzle. He looked up at the departure screen on the wall of the coffee shop, wanting to make sure the gap between buying a ticket and boarding the plane was as short as possible. A line of text above the list of scheduled departures warned, *Gates close 30 minutes before departure.* Time to move. He got up and walked briskly back towards the ticket desk. A moment before he got there, a heavyset woman cut in line, shooting him a dirty look, and started berating the woman on the ticket desk.

Mallory stood behind her, watching the screen above on the United desk show his flight departing next. *Gate closes in ten minutes.* He hoped security would be quiet.

55

JOHANNESBURG

Given that Ivy had a whole lot less notice that she might be in danger than Scott, she seemed to be coping with it remarkably well. She told Scott what Mallory had said on the phone: chances were, they wouldn't easily be able to trace Ivy, but better safe than sorry. Scott couldn't argue with that.

Ivy seemed to take it in her stride. She was clearly a little scared, but didn't lose time panicking.

'Mallory said we can't go near your place, and it's best to avoid mine. What about a hotel?' she suggested.

'They found me at the last hotel. They were asking around. I don't know exactly how they found me, but what if they do again?'

Ivy bit her lip, thinking about something.

'What?'

She spoke grudgingly, as though she were hoping a better idea would occur even as she was speaking. 'I think I have somewhere.'

They got into a taxi and Ivy gave the driver an address in Westdene. They sat together in the back seat, Scott trying to cover his face with a hand every time the traffic slowed down. Logically, he knew the people who had arranged for his kidnapping couldn't be everywhere at once, but that wasn't how it felt. Mallory seemed to think they had police on their payroll. If that was true, they really couldn't trust anyone. Ivy looked out of the window, saying nothing. He didn't ask where they were going. She seemed preoccupied, probably thinking through some of the same concerns as him.

Twenty minutes later, they pulled up outside a two-storey apartment block. The building looked as though it had been built in the sixties, and it had seen better days. The render on the walls had fallen away in patches, exposing rough concrete, and there were bars on the windows of the ground-floor apartments.

'This place?' Scott asked.

'What's wrong with it?' she snapped.

He held his hands up in apology.

She paid the fare using her phone and they got out.

'Did you call ahead? Who lives here?' Scott asked.

'We'll talk about it later,' Ivy said.

Scott followed her up the bare concrete staircase at one end of the building to the open terrace that led along the fronts of the apartments on the upper floor.

She stopped in front of the second door from the end and looked around before knocking. There was no bell.

The door wasn't too sturdy. Scott found himself thinking about how easily it could be kicked down. He heard footsteps from within and then there was a pause. Someone was inspecting them through the peephole. The pause lasted longer than he expected, as though the person behind the door was thinking about whether to open it. He looked at Ivy. She was frowning.

Then he heard a rattle as an interior chain was removed, and the door opened five inches. Scott had been expecting someone older: a parent, or maybe a grandparent. The occupant of the apartment was a young woman, around the same age as him and Ivy. She had shoulder-length dark hair, with brown eyes and a lip piercing. Her eyes looked sleepy. She wore jean shorts and a white tank top.

She glanced at Scott and then stared at Ivy, waiting for her to speak first.

'Hi, Helen,' Ivy said. She said it like she was speaking while holding her breath.

Helen blinked once. 'What are you doing here?'

Ivy looked around. 'This is kind of an emergency.'

Helen nodded. 'It would have to be.'

'Can we come in?'

Helen held her gaze for a long moment. Then looked at Scott.

'Hi, I'm Scott.' He held out his hand to shake. Helen stared at him until he dropped the hand.

'Good for you.'

Helen looked back at Ivy. 'I'm on shift in an hour.' She sighed and opened the door wider. 'I suppose you better come in.'

56

LOUISIANA

The woman in front of Mallory in the line finally gave way. The attendant at the desk narrowed her eyes when Mallory told her what flight he wanted, but sold him the ticket anyway.

'You'll have to be fast, sir.'

He thanked her and ran for security. The fact he had left most of his stuff at Graves's place made it easy to make sure he wasn't detained unduly. The backpack he had bought at Walmart contained a couple of changes of clothes, and no liquids or electronics. He had bought it mostly because an international passenger with no baggage would raise red flags. He had nothing in his pockets besides his passport, his phone and his wallet. No loose change: he had spent every cent of Dave's fifty dollars at Walmart and the coffee shop. The officer at the metal detector looked suspiciously at the three basic items rattling around in the large rubber tray.

'No coins, no jewellery?' she asked.

Mallory forced himself to smile good-naturedly and not act in as much of a hurry as he was. Looking harassed was an invitation for a pat-down. 'No jewellery,' he said. 'I leave my tiara at home when I'm travelling.'

'Always wise,' she murmured, and Mallory guessed he wasn't the first traveller today or any day to come up with that witty response. Which was perfect, because it meant he didn't stand out.

Retrieving his stuff, he then ran hell for leather for the gate. Along the way he saw his flight listed on screens with the blinking red *Closing* tag. He willed it to stay that way for just another couple of minutes.

He made it to the gate as a cabin attendant was closing the security door. He held up his boarding pass, looking as apologetic as possible, and she took pity on him. He made his way through the link tunnel and on to the plane, drawing eyerolls from some of the seated passengers.

Mallory was in a middle seat. A thin, grey-haired man in a business suit looked up in irritation as he approached his row. He had already fastened his seatbelt and put his laptop on what he had thought was going to be a spare seat. He sighed and got up to let Mallory in. Mallory slid in beside him and heard the sound of the cabin door slamming shut.

'Just made it,' the elderly lady in the window seat said to him.

Mallory nodded. 'Better late than never.'

He sat back and closed his eyes as the captain started reading his spiel, telling them they would be leaving right on schedule, and that the flight time was a little under three hours. Weather in Toronto was overcast but warm for the time of year.

He had made it. Perhaps the Sentinel crew were still look-ing for him in the swamp, perhaps they had given up for now. Either way, he was leaving the country, and he would be back in the UK in a matter of hours.

He looked out of the window as he felt the plane push back from the gate. The stewardess picked up the baton from the captain and started her own spiel. All devices switched to flight safe mode, tables in the upright position and so on. Mallory reached into his pocket and took out his borrowed phone to turn it off.

Something was niggling at him. Something about the security officer at the metal detector. He couldn't work out what it was. Had she looked familiar? No, that wasn't it. It had been something she had said.

And then he had it.

Jewellery.

The trusted son.

He looked down at his phone. Went back into recent calls and tapped on Ivy's number. He heard the man in the busi-ness suit clear his throat loudly as one of the flight attendants approached. The call took an age to connect.

'Excuse me sir, all devices need to be turned to flight safe mode.' The flight attendant was small, but there was a steeliness beneath her southern accent that would rival some sergeant majors Mallory could think of.

Mallory held a hand up as the call connected and he heard the ringtone. 'I'm sorry, this'll just take a second, I promise.'

'Sir—'

The third ring cut off as it was picked up. Ivy's voice.

'Mallory? Is everything—'

'Are you still with Scott?'

'Sir, I'm going to have to ask you to hang up now.'

Mallory held up a finger – one minute.

'Yeah, he's here,' Ivy said. 'What is it?'

The flight attendant had turned away and was beckoning somebody over to join her. Backup was on its way. Mallory felt the businessman's hand on his wrist, trying to take the phone away from his ear. He ignored it and talked fast.

'Scott's pendant. Take a look at his pendant. I think that's it. That's what his dad gave to him.'

The man was actually trying to pull the phone away from his ear. Mallory reached up, not thinking about it, and squeezed the pressure points of the guy's wrist. He emitted a squeal that probably sounded a whole lot less manly than he would have liked and snatched his hand away from Mallory's.

Ivy was saying something. 'A pen?'

'No, pen*dant*, he was wearing it around his neck. Check it out, see if—'

'Sir, if you do not end the call immediately we will have to escort you off the flight.'

Ivy was still asking questions in his ear. The fierce southerner had returned with a solidly built male flight attendant, who was looking at Mallory nervously. The passenger beside him was massaging his wrist.

'Check it out,' Mallory said. 'I'll call as soon as we land.'

He cut the call off as Ivy was still talking and turned the phone off, turning it around to show the flight attendant that it was shutting down. 'I'm very sorry, that was kind of an emergency.'

The male attendant stepped back and took a sigh of relief. The female attendant didn't move an inch, kept glaring at

Mallory. She opened her mouth to say something and noticed the man beside him was rubbing his wrist, looking pained.

'Are you okay, sir?' she asked.

The man looked at Mallory. Mallory gave him a look that conveyed how displeased he would be if the man answered the question the wrong way. He blinked and Mallory could see him make a quick mental calculation. Best case: get the rude passenger thrown off the flight and cause a delayed flight. Worst case: fail to get the rude passenger thrown off the flight, and still have to sit next to him for several hours.

He cleared his throat. 'No, ma'am. Just a muscle spasm.'

The flight attendant held his gaze for a moment and then looked back at Mallory. She pointed at his phone. 'Keep that off.'

'No problem at all, ma'am,' Mallory said. 'I appreciate your understanding.'

She kept her eyes on him for another few seconds, then shot a look at the other guy as though expecting him to try something. With that, she turned and marched back down the aisle to join in with the pre-flight demonstration of the oxygen masks.

Ten minutes later, they were in the air. Mallory barely noticed take-off. He was too busy thinking about the pendant. The one Scott had been wearing that matched his brother's.

The matching pendants their father had given them days before he had been killed.

57

JOHANNESBURG

'A what?' Scott asked.

'He said you have a pendant,' Ivy said. 'Do you still have it?'

They were in the small living room of the apartment in Westdene. The mysterious Helen had left five minutes before, after changing into her uniform for work. Dark trousers and a light blue shirt. Scott guessed she was a nurse, or a dentist's assistant, but hadn't wanted to ask. The atmosphere seemed to be tense enough.

Ivy's eyes were searching Scott's neck. She spotted the thin black cord and reached for it. Instinctively, he pushed her hand away. His neck was still bruised from where the American had held it while pushing him against a wall. 'Whoa, easy now. What are you talking about?'

'Your pendant, Scott.'

He reached down the front of his T-shirt and pulled out the stone pendant. He lifted it from around his neck and held it out for Ivy in the palm of his hand. 'My dad gave it to me.

To tell you the truth, I don't even like this kind of thing. I wouldn't have worn it if he hadn't—'

He stopped as he saw some kind of realisation dawn in Ivy's blue eyes. She was working something out. 'If he hadn't what?' she said quietly. 'Scott, did your dad make you promise to wear it all the time, something like that?'

'How did you know that? Yeah, that's what he said. It wasn't like him. And honestly, I don't think I would have bothered if he hadn't ... well, if he hadn't died soon after. I guess I thought it was something I could do for him. I mean, he couldn't have known, but this was the last thing he gave me.'

Ivy took the pendant out of his hand and held it up to the window.

'What are you doing? It's worthless. No diamonds or anything like that.'

Ivy didn't answer. She was squinting at the smooth black stone, her brow furrowed. She stopped and went to her handbag, took out a small case and slid on her red-rimmed glasses, then examined the pendant again.

Ivy went over to the lamp that was perched on a bookcase in the corner of the living room and switched it on. Scott followed her, utterly bemused. What the hell had Mallory's call been about? And why was Ivy now staring at his pendant so intently? It was just a useless, smooth hunk of polished flint. Dad had joked that it would bring him luck – he knew it was a joke because his father was the least superstitious, least sentimental person he had ever known. He assumed the stone had some kind of significance for Dad. He had a love of geology, after all. Or perhaps it had been something to do with the rock climbing. Ironic, if so, given what had happened to him not long afterwards.

With a guilty feeling, Scott realised he had thought more about the pendant in the last thirty seconds than he had when his father had given it to him. What he had said to Ivy wasn't strictly true – he hadn't actually worn it every day, but he had kept it on him, in his jacket pocket. Maybe it was an act of remembrance, but if so, he had only kept it up because it was easy, because leaving it in there was a passive act.

'I don't get it. What did Mallory say?'

Ivy said nothing. She seemed to be trying to scrape the thinner edge of the flint with her thumb.

'Ivy?'

'Mallory didn't have time to finish. He got cut off. Do you have a screwdriver?'

'What? Why would I have a screwdriver? I don't just walk around carrying a full toolbox. I mean—'

'Shut up.' She raised her head and turned around in the chair, searching the room. Her eyes alighted on the kitchen doorway. 'Go get me a knife. A sharp one.'

'What are you going to do?'

'Just get me a knife.'

The urgency in her voice made Scott move faster. He went to the small galley kitchen and opened drawers until he found the cutlery. There were only table knives. He couldn't see a knife block anywhere. He held one of them up and turned around. 'Will this do?'

'Just give me it.'

He walked back into the living room and handed Ivy the knife. She took it without looking at him and seemed to be trying to scrape the pendant with it. No, not scraping, it was like she was trying to push the knife through it.

'It's rock, Ivy, you can't cut it with a—'

Suddenly Ivy let out a satisfied gasp and the flint pendant seemed to snap in half. Confused, Scott looked more closely. The top third had somehow been chipped off. He looked closer again. The edge was perfectly square, as though it had been machined. There was a small cavity in the dead centre of the part that was lying on the desk. Ivy was holding the bottom two-thirds of the flint, squinting at what Scott could see was another small cavity in the centre.

'What the ...' he began.

Ivy didn't respond. She held the truncated pendant in the palm of her hand, the cavity down, and tapped the top of it hard. She discarded the flint and held her hand out to Scott triumphantly.

There was a Micro SD card in her palm.

58

36,000 FEET

An hour into the flight, Mallory got up and went to one of the bathrooms. He took his phone out, made sure that sound and vibrate were switched to silent, then turned flight mode off. Of all the laws he had broken in the last few days, he decided a violation of Federal Communication Commission guidelines was a fairly minor one. He stared at his phone expectantly until the message from Ivy came through.

You were right. Call me soon as.

He tapped out a message.

In the air, can't talk. What did you find?

There was a wait of two minutes that felt like two hours and then the screen lit up with her reply.

Memory card, checking it out. Will text when I know more.

The flight was a little late getting into Toronto, and Mallory had to rush to make the connection. He called Ivy as he waited to board the flight to Gatwick, but she had nothing more to tell him. It would take some time to confirm whether this was what they were looking for.

Mallory kept his phone on. After take-off, they dimmed the lights in the cabin and the passengers were split between those trying to get some sleep and those watching movies. Mallory decided he should do the former. He couldn't do anything for the next few hours, and tomorrow was going to be a busy day.

He dozed restlessly as they crossed the Atlantic above a blanket of dark cloud. Every so often he would check the phone, but the hours passed with no update.

59

GATWICK AIRPORT

SATURDAY

The 737 touched down at Gatwick at 09:47 local time, ten minutes ahead of schedule. Mallory was on his feet with his phone in his hand as soon as the seatbelt lights winked out. He tapped out a message to Ivy.

Just landed. Anything?

He turned sound and vibrate back on and put the phone back in his pocket as he waited for the doors to open and the line to start shuffling forward. As he stepped through the cabin door, he felt the phone buzz. This time it was an email from Ivy's account, not a text message. There was a file attachment and a short message.

Can you call?

He quickened his pace and cleared the connection tunnel and exited out into the queue for immigration. As he walked, he downloaded the preview of the attachment. He didn't recognise the extension, and the file opened in some sort of default text-only format. It looked like a wall of gibberish. Was this it?

He stood to one side and called Ivy.

'Did you get it?' she asked as soon as she picked up.

'Yeah. Is it the code?' He gritted his teeth, braced for either answer.

There was a pause. 'Yes and no.'

'What do you mean, yes and no? It is or it isn't, right?'

Ivy gave a weary sigh. 'It took me hours to download it, check it and compare it against what I got from the MTC office. It's partial. It fills in a lot of the blanks, but not everything. There's enough to tell me that we were right – Bartho solved the problem and then he hid this deliberately. But it's not all of it.'

'There's something missing,' Mallory said. He was starting to understand what Bartho Nel had done.

'I got everything there was, but this is only half of the code.' Ivy's voice betrayed tired irritation.

'It was deliberate.'

'Yeah. He must have saved half the code on this, and half somewhere else, and I don't—'

'I do. Bartho sent both of his sons a pendant. Donno has the other one.'

'Of course,' Ivy said, the defeated tone suddenly evaporating. 'If you get the other pendant, I think we'll have the rest of it.'

Mallory couldn't help but smile. Ivy sounded as though she had solved a tortuous clue in a crossword puzzle. 'If we get that, do you think you can work out how to get the tech working?'

'Based on this? I think so, yes. I'm not a hundred per cent, and Bartho was way ahead of me, but I can see his working here. If we get the rest of the code, it'll work.'

'Then if we need it,' Mallory said, 'we have the best bargaining chip. We can give them what they want.'

Ivy was silent.

'What is it? Aren't you sure?'

'It's just . . . Bartho hid this for a reason. He didn't want it to be in their hands.'

Mallory opened his mouth and then stopped dead. She was right. In all of the excitement, he hadn't thought through what this meant. Bartho had wanted to safeguard the code, and had given two parts of it to his two sons. Without Scott's knowledge for sure, maybe without Donno's knowledge too. He had done that because he wanted to keep it away from the people he must have known wanted it. Did he know they would kill him? Maybe, or maybe he had planned to fool them somehow, and hadn't lived to retrieve the two halves of the code.

And yet, Bartho hadn't foreseen everything. He hadn't foreseen that they would work out what he had done, if not how he had done it. And now they knew the code still existed, his family was in danger.

Mallory sighed. 'You're right. But I'm not sure that makes any difference.'

'What do you mean?'

'I still don't know exactly why these arseholes want this, but I know it's something worth killing for. That alone tells me they shouldn't have it. But that's not the only consideration here. They have a good idea that the code exists now, and they think Scott and Donno know about it. Or at least, they're a way to get at it.'

'Sooner or later they'll give up, surely?'

'They ain't giving up,' Mallory said. 'If anything, the last couple of days will have made them more determined. And I'm afraid you're part of this, too.'

Ivy was quiet for a long moment. Mallory looked up and saw that the queue at the passport autoscanners had gone down. He moved forward and stood at the end of the queue, lowering his voice.

'Is Scott with you now?'

'He's asleep.'

Mallory shook his head. 'Typical.'

She snorted. 'It wasn't like he was going to be much good crunching code.'

'Still. He's napping while you're doing all the work.'

'You need to go easy on him,' she said, softening her voice. 'This has been tough for him. All of it. He didn't ask for this.'

'I know. And I agree with you, it's shit. Maybe there's a way to fix this without giving them the code. But if we need to, I'll do it without a second thought.'

'Don't tell me. Choose your battles, right?'

'Exactly. You pick the wrong battle, and you'll spend the rest of your life wishing you could go back and change it.'

'Okay,' she said. Perhaps she'd heard something in his voice that told her he knew what he was talking about. 'I just wish there was another way.'

Mallory said nothing. There *was* another way. Maybe the way that attracted him more. That way was to track down every last one of these bastards and take them out. Burn the whole house to the ground. And if Graves really wanted to, she could join them.

He felt the strong pull of that idea. The thrill of hunting them down, doing to each of them what they had tried to do to him in the swamp. It would be satisfying. It would be justice, white-hot and purifying.

But he knew that wasn't the answer. For practical reasons, if no other. Graves had told him a little about Sentinel, but she had given him no real idea of how big an operation it was, how many operatives they employed. Right now they were deployed on two continents. There would be no way to be sure he had cut all the heads off this snake.

Reluctantly, he withdrew from the idea. He didn't like it, but he had more people than himself to think about. The least-worst thing to do was to give Sentinel what they wanted and make sure they were dissuaded from any further contact. But that meant getting the other half of the code. He hoped to God Donno would have it.

'Let's cross that bridge when we come to it,' Mallory said. 'In the meantime, you and Scott should stay put.'

'Okay.'

'Listen, thank you, Ivy. We're a lot further forward than we were a few hours ago, thanks to you. Your expertise might be able to get us all out of this.'

'All right. When are you going to call again?'

'I need to get up to Birmingham and check on Donno. If I'm right, I've bought enough time. I should be ahead of them.'

'And if you're wrong?'

'Then it's time for my expertise.'

Ivy took an audible breath on the other end of the line. 'I'm scared.'

Mallory gripped the phone and tried, for once, to think of the least-damaging thing to say.

'You're right to be scared, Ivy. Scared is good. Scared people are careful. Scared people stay alive.'

She thought that over for a little while.

'Mallory?'

'Yeah?'

'If you manage to get the other part of the code, and if I can get it to work, and if you manage to make a deal . . . how do you know that they'll leave us alone?'

He didn't have an answer to that question.

Mallory called ahead to Susan. Her phone went straight to voicemail again. It could mean she was on the phone to someone else. He left a message and called the hospital and asked to speak to the duty nurse in ward 624. He said he was visiting a friend and wanted to check he had the right ward. They told him Donno was still there.

That was good to know. But the fact they had told him meant they might well tell anyone else who called. He asked if Dr Patel was on duty.

'I believe so. Can I take a message?'

'Yes. Ask him to call me back on this number. It's very important. Potentially life or death.'

The nurse sounded concerned and promised to do what she could.

Mallory emerged from the terminal building into the biting cold under a gloomy British sky and went straight to the car rental offices. He wasn't sure if Hertz kept an international register of customers, but he went to Enterprise just to be on the safe side. They rented him a blue Vauxhall Corsa, which he picked up at the garage a short walk from Arrivals.

He found the car in the car park and just as he was

unlocking the door, his phone buzzed. He took the phone out, hoping it was Ivy or Susan, but it was a Birmingham number.

'This is Doctor Patel.'

'Thanks for returning my call,' Mallory said. 'This is really important. I met you the other day, when I came to visit Donovan Nel.'

'Oh yes.' The doctor sounded less than pleased, which was good, because it meant he remembered him.

'You gave me a bit of a hard time about asking questions, which is why I'm calling you now.'

The doctor's voice was weary. 'If you have a complaint, I'm going to ask you to contact the—'

'It's not a complaint. I have reason to believe someone wants to harm Donovan. Is there any way you can limit visitors for the next couple of days?'

'He's on the ward. I can't keep tabs of everyone who comes in and out.'

'But you have the authority to do something. I can't explain right now, but I think he could be in danger.'

There was a long pause. 'Someone else called to ask about Mr Nel half an hour ago.'

'A man or a woman? Was it an American?'

'A man. I think he was an American.'

'Keep all visitors away from him,' Mallory said. 'I'm on my way.'

60

BIRMINGHAM

The timing of the flights worked out pretty well, all things considered. Foster and Booth had a head start, since Branagh had instructed them to get on the first flight out of Johannesburg as soon as Graves had told him about the probability that what they were looking for was in a British hospital. They had been able to get on a direct flight within two hours. What Mallory had told Graves didn't ring quite true, though. There were several MoD medical units in the UK, but Branagh didn't think Donovan Nel would be in Portsmouth.

Graves herself had pointed out that she thought Mallory suspected something by that point; that she had overplayed her hand a little. She left Branagh in no doubt that this had been his fault for rushing the capture. He supposed that was fair. But then it was also fair to say that Graves had ruined their chance of capturing him by insisting on ten more minutes to finesse the information out of him.

There had been no trace of Mallory in the swamp after a three-hour search that hadn't ended well for Koncak and Mills. Branagh knew the decision to cut and run had been the right one. It was possible Mallory was dead already, but either way, he couldn't get in their way now. And yet, there was that niggling seed of doubt in the back of Branagh's head. Mallory had already proved he was a dangerous adversary. If he had somehow managed to get past them and make it to the road, Branagh knew where he would go next. He had a contingency plan for that already.

No, Portsmouth wasn't quite right. It would be one of the bigger hospitals, probably the one at Birmingham. That was where the Royal Centre for Defence Medicine was based. He had no idea where Donovan Nel had lived in the UK before he had been injured, but he knew they specialised in battlefield brain injuries at Birmingham. Three phone calls confirmed the information via backchannels. Donovan Nel had been a patient at the Queen Elizabeth for several months.

Branagh hadn't told Maddie he was back in the UK yet. She would immediately want to know why he wasn't coming home. It was an unavoidable omission, the latest of many, but he had still felt a twinge of guilt when he passed within thirty miles of the house on his way to Birmingham. He made himself a promise. If he could just close out this job, he would take some real downtime. It would be feasible to do that, because the money that was coming would make the debt and the school fees and the basement extension easily solvable problems.

With that in mind, he forced himself to focus on the task in hand. If Donovan Nel was indeed conscious, as Mallory had told Graves, then the South African might be able to save them all a lot of time. If not, then Branagh thought they could use him as leverage if Mallory turned up again to cause more trouble.

Mallory was an enigma. Branagh thought that this time last year he would have welcomed the challenge. Right up until the recent Ukraine problems, if Branagh had one complaint about the private sector it would have been that everything was a little too easy. The money was great, the hours were your own to choose, the odds always stacked in your favour. He had forgotten what it was like to risk something on a job. The last few months had furnished him with an unwelcome reminder of what risk to his livelihood felt like, and the last few days were starting to remind him of what a risk to his life felt like.

Two good men were already dead, lying in shallow watery graves, thousands of miles from home. Branagh hadn't lost a single person from his team before now. The worst thing that had happened was Nash sustaining a minor gunshot wound to the shoulder during the operation to take delivery of some Ba'athist gold bullion in Mosul after the fall of ISIS.

Willer called him when he was ten minutes away from the hospital. Bad news. Not only was Mallory still alive, but he had managed to convince the hospital to lock down their patient. They had to assume he had made it back to the UK. If they had made the journey, Mallory could have as well.

Willer was waiting in the car park of the Queen Elizabeth. Branagh parked in the next space. Willer got out of his car and got into the passenger seat beside Branagh.

'He's definitely still in there?'

Willer nodded. 'They wouldn't move him from the building. My guess is they have him in a private room. They have that whole ward shut down to visitors, so Mallory must have been very convincing.'

'It's okay,' Branagh said. 'He's not going anywhere. We don't even know for sure that he's conscious.'

'Could be a long wait,' Willer said.

Branagh had been thinking about this. 'Let's go get some insurance.'

61

The mid-morning traffic on the M25 was crawling for the first twenty miles north of Gatwick, but Mallory made good time after that. The M40 was quieter by comparison. He kept in the fast lane, staying between seventy and eighty. He occasionally glanced at his phone on the passenger seat, but there were no messages. Nothing from Ivy or Scott, nothing from Susan Nel. That didn't mean anything was wrong, but he would check in with both as soon as he'd made sure Donno was okay.

Mallory made it to the Queen Elizabeth just after one o'clock, taking one of the few remaining spaces on top of the multistorey car park. He tried calling Susan again as he jogged towards the visitor entrance. Her number rang six times before going to voicemail. He left a message asking him to call her asap. If she didn't call back soon, he would have to check in on her at home. He was beginning to get a bad feeling.

Slowing as he approached the visitors' entrance, he saw that Dr Patel had taken him seriously. There were two police cars outside, a pair of uniformed officers watching the doors. Who else was watching?

He scanned the immediate surroundings. There were too many parked cars, too many pedestrians idly standing around or smoking outside the exits. Impossible to tell if any of them was working with Branagh.

Mallory skipped the visitors' entrance and went around the back, to a smaller door. He climbed the stairs to the floor ward 624 was on. There was a uniformed police officer on the other side of the fire door at the top of the stairs. Mallory took a sharp breath, then reminded himself that he hadn't done anything criminal in this country this week.

The officer held a hand up like he was stopping traffic. He had close-cropped blond hair under his hat. His eyes were deep blue, and when he spoke, his voice had a nasal quality. 'I'm sorry, sir, this floor is closed to visitors. You'll need to go down one floor and go around.'

'It's okay, I'm expected. Doctor Patel is—'

The cop took a step forward, clearly hearing something he didn't like in Mallory's tone.

'Did you hear what I said?'

'Yeah. Did you hear what *I* said?'

The officer put his hand on Mallory's chest. 'Take a step back, sir.'

Mallory opened his mouth to retort when he heard a voice from along the corridor. 'Just a second, officer.'

It was Dr Patel. He was wearing scrubs and pristine white trainers. He jogged along to the door. 'It's all right, this man can come in.'

The officer looked at Patel and then back at Mallory with distaste. 'I'm not supposed to let anyone in.'

'This is an exception. Call your boss.'

Mallory stood, fuming, while the officer called his boss, who asked to talk to Dr Patel, who explained that he could go in. He wasted about three minutes in all.

'Mind how you go now,' the officer said.

'Seriously?'

Patel escorted him down the corridor. 'Impressed?'

'With that tool?' Mallory asked. 'He'd be overpaid as a bouncer at my local kebab shop.'

'But they're making it pretty difficult for civilians to get in.'

Mallory conceded the point. 'It can't just be limited to civilians, though. If they're letting anyone through in a white coat . . .'

'They're not. Full ID checks on all staff, too. The others are a little more polite about it. And we are taking it seriously. Less than an hour after you called, somebody tried to bluff his way past the front desk.'

Shit. That meant they were here already. Were they still outside, biding their time? Mallory had managed to make Donno a hard target, but these men were patient.

Dr Patel stopped and turned to Mallory. 'Now, suppose you tell me what the hell is going on here?'

'Long story short, some very bad people want to get to my friend, and I don't think they should get anywhere near him. They probably have someone outside watching the place.'

'Are my staff in danger? Other patients?'

Mallory shook his head. 'I don't think so.'

'What is this? What do they have against my patient? Is it a terrorist thing?'

'No, the good news is this isn't personal. This is about cold, hard cash. Which means I don't think they'll do anything rash, and there might just be a way to get them to back off. Donno might be the one who can help with that.'

Patel led Mallory down a corridor. Mallory noted the CCTV cameras. The doctor scanned his pass at a security door at the far end and pushed it open.

'Does everyone's pass open this?'

'Senior staff for this ward only,' Patel said. 'And the pass won't get you through this one.' He gestured at another door on the inside that had a keypad lock.

'I set the code myself when we moved Mr Nel.' He tapped a six-digit code in. 'Which means it's in here and nowhere else,' he said, tapping his head.

The door opened on a private room with a single occupant.

Mallory stepped inside and the patient opened his eyes. It took Donno a moment for him to register who he was seeing, but when he did, he broke out into a grin.

Mallory approached the bed. Donno didn't look all that different from the way he had looked for the past few months, but it was difficult for Mallory to adjust to how it felt to see him awake, moving. He slowly raised his right hand. It still had a drip attached. Mallory gently put both of his hands around Donno's.

'How are you?' he asked, before he had a chance to think of anything more intelligent to say.

Donno grimaced. 'I've been better.' His voice sounded weak, hoarse. The vocal cords and the facial muscles out of practice.

Mallory glanced back at Dr Patel. 'He woke up on Thursday night?'

'Yes. He's been sleeping on and off.'

Mallory looked back at Donno. 'Napping on the job, huh?'

'They say I've been out for a while.'

Mallory looked back at the doctor for guidance. He had no idea what you were supposed to do in this situation. Could it be damaging to encourage him to remember too much of the trauma?

'How much does he know?'

The doctor shrugged. 'He knows what I've been able to tell him. He's been in a medically induced coma for the past six months while he recovers from brain injuries sustained on the battlefield.'

Mallory gave Donno's hand a squeeze and released it. 'Just a second, mate.'

He went over to the doctor.

'Does he know what happened to him?'

'I don't know the details. That's not my department. I know the injury and the treatment and the prognosis. Those details have all been communicated to the patient. Perhaps someone –' he paused and looked meaningfully at Mallory '– more familiar with the facts of what happened to him should talk to him about that.'

'Is there any danger I can ... ?'

'Do any damage to him?' Patel smiled thinly and looked over at Donno. 'He's taken a lot of damage already. I'm not a psychologist, but ... look, you're his friend. Talk to him. If it feels like you're pushing too hard, you probably are.'

Mallory nodded. All of a sudden, he remembered he had another purpose here, beside this reunion.

He went over to Donno.

'I know what you were talking about,' Donno said, his speech still a little slurred.

'Oh yeah?' Mallory examined the scar on the side of his

head. 'Then that knock on the head must have improved your hearing. What was I saying?'

'You were checking it was okay to bring flowers.'

'If it's okay with you, I'll leave that to your mum.'

Donno blinked. 'Here?'

'Of course. She's been here all the time, mate.' He looked back at Dr Patel.

'He was asleep again when she came in last night,' Patel said. 'We suggested she come back in the morning.'

'My father too?'

Mallory's smile faded, and he felt a sinking sensation in his gut. He glanced back at the doctor, who raised his eyebrows. He had no idea what the problem was.

Mallory cleared his throat. 'How much do you remember?'

Donno closed his eyes. 'Nothing. I mean, the doc told me what happened. IED on a raid. Were you there?'

'I was there.'

'Was everybody else okay?'

Mallory shook his head.

Donno's jaw clenched and he blinked twice. Steeling himself. 'Who?'

'Yorkie, Khan, McKenzie. Westwick, too. We didn't even get to bring him back.'

Donno closed his eyes. 'The last thing I remember was ... I don't know, it's all jumbled up. Last thing I remember is Wheeler breaking his leg on training.'

'That's right,' Mallory said. The incident he was remembering had been six weeks before the raid. If he really couldn't recall anything after that ... 'Do you remember the last time you saw your folks?'

'Back home, I think,' Donno said. 'Yeah. July, maybe? Is that right?' He searched Mallory's face for approval.

Mallory thought of something and brought up the picture of the pendant on his phone. Ivy had sent him two: one of the whole pendant, one of it split open. He showed Donno the picture of the full pendant.

'Does this look familiar?'

Donno stared at it, as though trying to decode a cryptic puzzle, and then it was like a light blinked on in his eyes. He reached for his chest. There was nothing around his neck.

'Dad gave it to me, I think. Yeah. It's from Dad.'

'He gave you this a couple of weeks before … what happened.'

'Oh, okay.'

'I think you were wearing it the night of the raid.'

Donno closed his eyes again. He patted the empty patch on his chest again a couple of times. He opened his eyes. 'Dad's dead,' he said.

Mallory nodded. 'I'm sorry, mate.'

'I remember the phone call, but … I don't remember who told me. It must have been Mum, right?'

'Probably. I would think so.'

'I don't remember what happened.'

'It was a …' Mallory stopped himself. He didn't believe it was an accident, not any more. 'He was rock climbing. He fell.'

'I remember now,' Donno said. 'I guess I'll be following him soon.'

'What do you mean?'

'You always told me to pay attention, boss. Use my eyes and ears. See what people aren't telling you. I'm in a private room. Either I'm a VIP, or I'll be checking out soon.'

'I told you not to jump to conclusions, too, didn't I? No, we just needed to take special care of you. You're going to be around for a long time.'

A soft ping sounded from behind Mallory and he looked around to see the doctor examining his pager. Mallory remembered that time was of the essence.

'We're going to catch up properly soon, but I need to ask you something right now. It's really important. Do you have any idea what happened to the pendant?'

Donno squinted, making an effort to remember. 'No idea, I'm sorry.'

Mallory gestured towards the bedside cabinet, wordlessly asking permission to have a look. Donno waved for him to go ahead.

It was practically empty. A sudoku book, half completed; a ballpoint pen; some lavender pillow spray. All no doubt left by Susan. The patient hadn't been awake long enough to gather any clutter.

'Okay. That's fine,' Mallory said. 'I'm going to leave you to get some sleep.'

Outside in the corridor, he spoke to Patel again, keeping his voice low so Donno wouldn't hear. 'You're doing a good job. Keep everyone away from him. Chances are they would just do what I've done: ask him some questions and realise he didn't have the answers, but I don't want them to have the chance.'

'It isn't the first time we've had to be careful with a patient.'

'Good. His mum – you said she was going to come back when he woke up again?'

Patel frowned. 'Yes, that's what we advised.'

'She hasn't been in? Does she know he's been moved to a private room?'

'She would have been informed, I imagine.'

'But she's not been in today? You said you were the only one with the code.'

Patel thought about it. Mallory suspected this kind of thing wasn't at the top of his list of concerns. 'You're right. She hasn't been in here.'

'Thank you, doctor.'

Mallory patted him on the shoulder and walked quickly for the exit, taking the phone out of his pocket. It was still on silent. There was still no word from Susan Nel, and he didn't think there was any way she would have failed to come back to the hospital to see her son.

He thought back to a few minutes ago, priding himself on making Donno a hard target. What if Branagh and his men didn't hang around? What if they chose a soft target instead?

62

'Hi, this is Susan, please leave a message.'

Mallory cursed out loud as he hung up. He pushed through the doors, passed the police officer from earlier, ignoring the dirty look, and descended the stairs. He called Scott on the way. Ivy answered his phone.

'He's still asleep on the couch.'

'Wake him the fuck up. I need his mum's address.'

Scott couldn't remember the address off the top of his head. The sleepiness disappeared from his voice as the urgency of the situation started to sink in. Mallory stayed on the phone while he jogged back to the car park, only half listening to Scott's mumbled attempts to talk through his actions as Mallory looked out for Branagh's men.

If they were there, he didn't see them, and no one approached him. Eventually, Scott managed to log into his webmail on Ivy's phone and found the email where Susan had given him her address details.

Mallory was in the car with the engine on as Scott read it out to him. Mallory tapped the address into the GPS. It was only six minutes away, but he had the sinking feeling he was already too late.

'Mallory? Why do you need the address? What's wrong?'

'I'll call you in ten,' he said, and hung up.

He floored it, taking the winding road that led out of the hospital grounds and speeding up when he hit the dual carriageway. The lights on Bristol Road changed to red as he approached the turn on to Bournbrook Road. He leaned on his horn and turned across the oncoming traffic, just making it. He found the street, wide and lined with oaks, and slowed enough to see street numbers. A minute later, he pulled up outside the address and got out. Susan's rented house was a big Victorian semi with red-brick walls and gothic arches above the windows. There was no car in the driveway. The street was empty. Aside from a jogger a few hundred yards away and a cat perched on the neighbour's wall, there wasn't a single sign of life.

Mallory approached the door, wishing he still had a gun.

There was a garage at the side of the house that looked as though it had been converted from a carriage house, and a narrow passageway leading around to the back garden. Mallory kept his eyes on the windows as he approached the property, then quickly took the passageway at the side. It opened out into a covered patio with a dining table and chairs. Stone steps wound down to the garden, which was on lower ground than the house and extended for fifty or sixty yards to the edge of a stream that passed between the back gardens on this street and a cricket ground.

There was a door leading into the back of the garage. It was open.

Mallory entered and found himself in an almost empty

garage with whitewashed brick walls. There was enough space for a vehicle, but he had no idea if the absence of one meant anything. He didn't know whether Susan Nel had a car over here, or even if she could drive. There was a battered wooden chair and a pile of empty plant pots and some gardening implements hanging from hooks on one wall. Below the tools was a steel toolbox. Halfway along the wall was a door into the house itself. This door was open too.

Mallory paused a second and opened the toolbox. He took a claw hammer and felt the reassuring weight of it in his hand. Good for up close, and it would make an effective throwing weapon if necessary.

Stepping through the doorway, he found himself in a narrow corridor with terracotta floor tiles. A blank wall on his left, a closed door on the right, what looked like the main hallway at the other end. He gripped the hammer and opened the door. There was a spacious kitchen with marble worktops and mahogany cupboards. A big window looked out on to the back garden and the cricket field across the stream. Mallory wasn't consciously thinking, letting the training take over. He was looking for a threat first; everything else was secondary. There was no one in the room. At first glance, it didn't look like there was anything out of place. And then he looked more closely.

Beyond the dining table in the centre of the room there was a splash of dark liquid on the deep-brown floorboards.

Mallory stepped into the kitchen. Obscured by the dining table had been the spot on where a china cup had smashed, splattering what looked like a full cup of coffee on the floor. The half-full cafetière was still resting precariously on the edge of the sink. Mallory moved around the splash and the fragments of the cup, being careful not to step in anything, and touched the back of his hand to the cafetière.

It was warm, but only just above room temperature. An hour or two, perhaps.

Mallory had only known Susan Nel for a week, but he was positive she wasn't the kind of person who would leave a smashed cup on the floor to go and attend to something else.

Mallory turned from the fragments and listened. The house was entirely quiet. Speed had now become more of a priority than stealth. He gripped the hammer and left the kitchen, turning right and then left into the main hallway. It was empty, but from here he could see he could have got in by the front door: the lock was splintered and the door had been pushed to.

The training again, room by room, ready to strike. The downstairs rooms were neat. No evidence of a struggle. Upstairs, the bedrooms were neat and made up. When he entered the third bedroom, he saw the first evidence of something untoward since the smashed cup. This room was set up as a home office. There was a chest of drawers, all pulled out. There was a monitor screen and a keyboard, but no tower unit. The desk had been moved aside. Somebody had taken the computer.

Probably at the same time as they had taken Susan Nel.

In the middle of the desk was a phone with a Post-it stuck to the screen. Mallory stepped closer to read the note: *Don't be a stranger.*

The screen woke as Mallory lifted the Post-it. No PIN. The phone was box-fresh; it still had the film over the screen. It was fully charged. He tapped on the phone icon to check recent calls and the phone book. There was one number, saved under the name *Call Me.*

He held the phone in his hand and looked around. If he wanted to take out an enemy, one he was reasonably sure would be in a particular place, but not at a particular time, he might do something like this. The phone signal could be used to trigger an IED. He didn't think that was the case here, but still.

He went out into the back garden. It was sheltered from the neighbouring houses by thick hedges. He descended the steps and turned to look back at the house as he hit the call button.

No explosion. Instead, there were three rings and the call was answered.

'You got there faster than I expected. Excellent work.'

The voice sounded familiar. It was the guy from Graves's place. The one Mallory had identified as the leader.

'Hello, Branagh,' he said, keeping his voice even with effort. 'Where is she?'

'You know what I want,' Branagh said immediately. His voice was all business.

'What makes you think I'm any more able than your men to get it? You've been looking for it a hell of a lot longer than I have.'

'Are you still in the house?'

'No. I decided to get some fresh air before I called.'

'Of course,' the voice said. 'Understandable caution, but why would I kill the person who can get me what I want?'

'I'll say it again. I can't help you.'

Mallory walked back inside. He could check each room again while he spoke to Branagh.

'I think you can, Mallory. Our mutual friend Graves spoke very highly of you.'

'Did she? I guess that's a guilty conscience speaking.'

'Not at all. What you told her in Louisiana: you had worked most of it out. Your friend at MTC – Ivy, wasn't it?'

Mallory said nothing.

'That's fine, you don't need to confirm it. But I think Ivy got the code. Or she's on the right track. And if she doesn't have it, then we already know Donovan can help you now that he's back in the land of the living.'

'Where is Susan?'

'That was a nice move, by the way: locking down the hospital. How did you convince them?'

'If you've harmed her—'

'Relax, she's fine for now,' Branagh said. 'I know she hired you to look for her son, but I can't imagine she's paying you well enough to justify the effort you've gone to. I'm impressed.'

'Well, that just gives me a warm feeling inside. How about saving me some more effort and letting her go?'

'Gladly. And you know what will make that happen.'

'I know you want the code to complete the program Bartho Nel was working on. This is all about oil, right?'

Branagh sounded amused. 'You're on the right track. Bartho Nel inadvertently found buried treasure. It's worth a lot to my clients to get that program code. It'll cost you nothing. But you'll get the woman back.'

Mallory was climbing the stairs again. He reached the landing and entered the office. Tried to think. There was no way Branagh would let Susan go if he explained that there was only half a code, and no guarantee the rest of it even still existed. Somehow, he didn't think that would cut it. But he had to play for time.

'And?'

Branagh sounded confused for a second. 'And what?'

'And, if I manage to do this, I want some guarantees.'

'Of course. You don't have to worry. This is purely business. If I get what I want, we'll never come near you or the Nel family again. We'll have no reason to.'

'And if I can't get the code?'

'We've already spent some time trying to discern whether Mrs Nel knows anything about it. Personally, I don't think she does. My colleague would like to try harder. Either way, it doesn't look good for her.'

Mallory gripped the phone so hard he thought it would shatter in his hands.

'Call me back in two hours, whatever happens. I know you can do this, Mallory. Impress me.'

The line went dead.

Mallory punched the wall and yelled out. His fist left a dent in the plasterboard. He wanted to trash furniture, throw a television against the wall. Anything to channel the white-hot rage that was coursing through him.

Instead, he forced himself to breathe deeply. To cool down. He would need that energy to get Susan back. He closed his eyes and forced himself to plan, rather than act on pure instinct. Now, more than ever, was the time for thinking before action.

AFGHANISTAN

SIX MONTHS AGO
HELL HOUR

Mallory couldn't see anything when he opened his eyes. Almost none of his senses were working. His body felt numb. His ears were ringing. His mouth and nostrils were packed with something. Taste was the only sense that still functioned. He could taste dirt. Dirt and blood.

He was trapped under something. He moved his arms and it gave a little. He pushed harder and felt something heavy lift off his back and shoulders. He had fallen face down. He managed to get to his knees, flailed out with his hand and found a vertical surface. A concrete wall, pitted with holes. He scrabbled for purchase and managed to stand. His ears were still ringing, but now he was out from under the rubble, he could hear noises. Shouts, male voices. He couldn't make out what language they were speaking.

He spat dirt from his mouth and carefully rubbed his eyes. His pack was still on his back. Keeping his eyes closed,

Mallory searched for his canteen with practised fingers, finding it in the side pocket. Cool water ran over his fingers as he pulled it free. It was punctured, but most of the water was still in it, judging by the weight. He turned his head up and rinsed his eyes out, blinking as his vision started to clear.

What the hell had happened?

The images came back to him. The HVT standing in the doorway. Donno's laser sight on his chest.

'Wait a second.'

And then the smile. And then a blinding explosion.

Shit. The others.

Now that he could see a little better, he was able to orient himself. He was standing knee deep in a pile of rubble. The night sky was above him. The remains of the walls of the building extended twenty-five feet up. No sign of a ceiling. He was on the ground floor again, somehow. The stairwell must have collapsed.

He examined his body and found the reason for the numbness in his shoulder. There was a three-inch shard of metal sticking out of it.

He heard a closer shout and saw flashlights playing over him. He looked around for his rifle. Shit, where was it?

'Mallory!'

He looked up and blinked again. It was Rankin, from Alpha.

'Are you okay?' Rankin yelled.

He didn't answer, not really listening to the question. He was just thinking about who else was under the rubble.

He looked around and saw that the building had not been completely demolished. The western-facing half was still standing, including the room with the treasure trove.

As his gaze travelled the height of what remained of the stairs, he saw a body lying face down. Yorkie. He could tell from his position that he was dead. A little further he saw McKenzie, the whole left side of his body a bloody mess, a major head injury.

Donno. Westwick. Where were they? Donno had been standing next to him. He had wanted to take the shot.

Mallory started rummaging in the rubble at his feet, arms pushing deep into the debris, ignoring the fact that his shoulder had stopped being numb and was now singing out in pain with every movement. Two other men came to help him. More were running to join the effort. Mallory stopped to direct some of them up the stairs, to confirm Yorkie and McKenzie were dead, but also to retrieve the computer equipment.

His fault. This was his fault.

He knew there was a ticking clock. This place would be swarming with insurgents in minutes. They had to take the injured and the dead, salvage any intelligence and get the hell out of there.

But he wasn't leaving without Donno. Dead or alive, he was going home.

Rankin stopped digging and put a hand to his ear.

'Mallory, we've got hostiles coming in. Multiple vehicles, five miles away and closing. We have to get to the evacuation point.'

'Keep fucking digging.'

And at that moment, his fingers touched something soft and yielding. He stopped and found it again. A body. The clothing was damp with blood.

'Down here,' he yelled to the other two who were helping.

They cleared some more concrete fragments and found a hand. They cleared more. Donno. He wasn't moving. His eyes were closed. He had a big gash in the side of his head and was bleeding badly from it. Mallory put pressure on it with his hand, thinking that as bad as it looked, it was a good sign. Bleeding meant a pumping heart.

They got Donno stable over the next couple of minutes, staunching the bleeding, uncovering the rest of him, checking for other wounds. As they worked, other men carried the bodies of McKenzie and Yorkie past.

Another man arrived, carrying a stretcher for Donno. Rogers. His name wasn't really Rogers; he was called that because he had ginger hair. Ginger Rogers. Mallory couldn't remember what the hell his real name was, and wondered why his brain was trying to focus on something so insignificant.

They strapped Donno on to the stretcher as Mallory heard the sound of the rotors of the second Chinook landing just outside the compound walls.

Rogers took the bottom end of the stretcher, Mallory grabbed the top. They picked their way out of the pile of rubble and started running when they cleared the demolition site and hit flat ground. Mallory could see the headlights of approaching vehicles as they reached the helicopter. The first Chinook was already in the air. They were the last to board. The men waiting at the tailgate grabbed Donno's stretcher. Mallory let go. He wanted to drop to his knees in the dirt. Neither of his arms felt like it was working any more. He turned and saw the pickup trucks had got within range now.

He saw the muzzle flash as one of the men riding in the back of the first truck started firing. Dust was kicked up around them as the shooter tried to find his range. Mallory raised his gun and returned fire. He took his time aiming, not bothering to move or try to take cover. He took the shooter out first and then fired a burst into the windscreen. The pickup swerved and slowed as the driver collapsed behind the wheel. The two other pickup trucks steered to avoid the first one, and the gunners on each started shooting too.

Mallory felt hands on his shoulders, dragging him aboard. A moment later, the pitch of the rotors stepped up a notch and they lifted off the ground. He heard bullets snap through the air, a couple of them impact on the shell of the Chinook. The man beside him fired back one handed while gripping the support strap at the side.

The pilot took them straight up, climbing fast. In seconds, they were out of range and the trucks below were shrinking to dots next to the conflagration in what remained of the compound.

Mallory staggered forward and collapsed beside the seat he had occupied only a few hours before. Out of the window, hundreds of feet below, the compound was burning. He looked away and saw somebody zipping up Yorkie's body bag. Another man was working on Donno. He didn't look confident. He saw Mallory watching and talked as he worked. 'You were with him?'

'Yes. Khan and Westwick were there too. Did either of them . . . ?'

The man looked up and shook his head. 'I'm sorry.'

Mallory put his head in his hands.

This was him. This was all on him. If he had only let Donno shoot that bastard when he had his sight on him. If only he had listened to Westwick.

'You all right, mate?'

He didn't look up at the sound of Rogers's voice.

'Jesus.'

He opened his eyes and saw that Rogers was looking at the shrapnel sticking out of his shoulder. He knelt beside him, opened up the med kit and started to examine the wound closer in the light.

'You carried one end of a stretcher with this sticking out of you?' He puffed out his cheeks in wonder and started to cut away the fabric of Mallory's sleeve. Mallory roughly pulled his arm away, ignoring the stab of pain.

'Leave it,' he snapped. He pointed over at Donno. 'Work on him.'

Rogers followed his gaze and he saw a solemn glance pass between the two men working on their injured comrades.

'Come on, mate, get this patched up and you can help us out.'

'My fault,' Mallory said quietly.

'What was that?'

'It's my fucking fault,' he shouted, pointing at Donno with his good arm, then at Yorkie's body bag. 'This is my fault. I told him to wait.'

Rogers took a moment to look at Donno again, then started to work on Mallory's arm, spraying iodine on the wound. Mallory ignored the sharp sting. It barely registered.

'I don't know what happened in there, but we all do what we think is best. You know what they say about plans?'

Mallory just stared back at him. Kevin, that was his name. Kevin 'Ginger Rogers' Bradley.

'Everybody has one until they get punched in the face.'

Mallory said nothing. He was replaying the last few

moments before the explosion again. The last seconds when all of them were alive, when it was still possible for all of them to walk out of there in one piece.

'I'll tell you one thing,' Rogers continued. 'We hauled a shitload of intel out of there. I haven't seen anything like it since Qara Bagh.'

Mallory glanced at him, then looked out of the window.

'They'll be able to use it,' Rogers continued. 'You heard the man at the briefing. This is going to save lives. Think about that. That's what counts.'

Mallory didn't answer. He rested his head against the window and stared out at the blackness. The orange glow from the burning compound had disappeared behind the mountain range.

Maybe Rogers was right. Maybe the intel they had captured would save lives. But that was in an unknowable future. All he knew now was that his decision had cost lives. That couldn't ever be taken back.

63

BIRMINGHAM

Mallory sat on the floor, staring at the hole he had punched in the wall of Susan Nel's bedroom office.

Past and present seemed to collide. Bad decisions. Events spiralling out of his control. From the moment Susan Nel had asked him to get involved, he had known this was inevitable. That he couldn't help her, he would only make things worse. And so it had proved. Sure, he had managed to find Scott and get him out, but now they had his mother instead. Branagh would kill her unless Mallory could give him something he knew he couldn't provide.

He forced himself to think. All he could do now was play for time. When Branagh's deadline expired, perhaps he could bluff him that he had the code. Set up an exchange and hope that he could find an advantage. But he knew that as soon as he showed up empty-handed, Branagh would kill Susan, and probably him as well. It was useless.

Head in his hands. Hell Hour came back to him. The

explosion, the aftermath. Sitting in the Chinook, head still reeling. Donno on the stretcher. Yorkie in the body bag in front of him. The two other men who had been killed had been taken on the other helicopter. At least their families had something to bury. Westwick's body hadn't been found before the evacuation. His grave was a pile of rubble in the mountains of Faryab Province.

And then Mallory was somewhere else. Sitting in the debriefing room two days after the raid, barely restraining himself from throttling Cartigan. The youthful spy massaging his throat, no fear in his eyes despite the fact Mallory could have and very nearly had killed him.

'You got the intelligence. It will save other lives, days and months from now. That's something.'

In the present, in Birmingham, Mallory opened his eyes. The red mist had cleared a little. He stood up and looked at the hole he had punched in the wall of Susan Nel's home office and wondered why it made him think of something.

Then he had it. Aside from the broken cup downstairs, most likely dropped in surprise by Susan, he had caused more damage to the house and the furniture than the men who had broken in here and abducted the owner. There were no broken windows, no ripped upholstery, no upturned drawers. It was familiar because it was exactly what he had found at Scott Nel's apartment in Johannesburg. They hadn't bothered to rip the place apart, but each time they had taken a computer. They thought the code was either stored on a specific computer, or accessible from one. They didn't yet know about the pendants.

Which meant they didn't know Bartho had split the code in half.

Which meant there was an information deficit, and it was in Mallory's favour.

'Ivy, can you send me what you've got?'

'What do you mean?' Ivy sounded confused on the other end of the call. She had been up for more than twenty-four hours, and Mallory realised he had probably woken her from a much-needed nap.

'The code, the half of it you've got so far.'

'Sure, but like I told you, it's no good by itself. We need to find the other half.'

'We're out of time to do that,' Mallory said. 'I don't even know if it exists any more. But I need you to send it to me. Can you do that by email, or is it too big?'

'I'll send it via an encrypted file transfer service. More secure that way, anyway. Just give me the address.'

A minute later, there was a notification on Mallory's phone. An email had arrived with a link to download a document with an extension Mallory didn't recognise.

'Got it, thanks. Will this open on a normal computer?'

'As long as they have the software. These guys should have it.'

'Okay. How long did it take you to identify it as the code?'

Ivy thought about it. 'Pretty much immediately. It took a lot longer to confirm everything for sure.'

'Is that because you worked on it?'

'Yes, but anyone familiar with the program could do it.'

'Okay, good. Next question: how soon did you realise there was only half of it there?'

'Almost immediately.'

'Almost?'

'Two minutes.'

Mallory grimaced. He was hoping she was going to say half an hour or something. 'Somebody who wasn't you – it would take them longer, right?'

Ivy sighed. 'I ... I don't know.'

'Not the time for modesty, Ivy. If you worked it out in two minutes then that's a baseline, right? It'll take somebody else longer.'

'Probably. Yeah, you could say five minutes or longer.'

'Okay.'

'What are you going to do?'

'I'm going to walk into the lion's den.'

64

Branagh was used to finding secure safehouses in all kinds of countries at short notice. Doing it in Birmingham hadn't been too much of a challenge. He paid cash for the temporary use of a storage unit beneath the railway arches at Locke Place.

All being well, Mallory would come through. He thought there was a good chance of that. Branagh was gambling that the threat of killing Susan Nel would concentrate Mallory's mind, and that of Scott Nel. If there was any way at all Mallory could find the code, this would force him to do it, or to exert pressure on anyone else necessary, like the girl from MTC. They had nothing to gain from keeping the code, and everything to lose. They weren't the only ones with everything to lose, now he thought about it. He certainly had a pressing motivation to close this deal.

There were half a dozen messages on his phone from Maddie. He hadn't read them, but had sent one back promising to call her later.

His other phone rang five minutes before the deadline.

Mallory was using the burner they had left at Susan Nel's house.

'You're early.'

Mallory lost no time with niceties before getting straight to the point. 'I want to see proof of life before I say another word.'

'I'll put her on the phone.'

'No. I want to see her.'

'Of course.' Branagh nodded to Willer, who stood up and walked over to the locked store cupboard at the back. 'I'll video call you in a second.'

Willer brought Susan Nel out. She looked pale, seemed to have aged ten years over the afternoon, but she walked unaided, her eyes contemptuously fixed on Branagh's. She was wearing the same light blouse and jeans she had been dressed in when they went into the house. If Branagh had been there, he would have suggested taking a coat. The storage unit didn't seem to have any heating. When she got within a few paces, Branagh held his hand up. She stopped. He gestured over at a patch of bare whitewashed wall which would give nothing away about their location. Susan Nel hesitated, then walked to the spot he had indicated.

'Stop there. Turn around.'

She did as he asked.

'Chin up.'

'You're telling me to chin up? I've—'

'No, seriously,' he said, and then pointed up at the lamp that was the only source of light. 'Your face is in shadow.'

He called Mallory back. Video this time. He stood with his back to Susan, framing the picture so the two of them were in shot and nothing else was but the blank wall.

Mallory hadn't activated his camera, so he was represented by a black screen and the number of the phone.

'Mallory, can you see me?'

'Yes.'

'Can you see her?'

'Susan, are you okay?'

'They haven't hurt me,' she said, and then took a sharp breath, as though worried she would give them ideas.

'Don't worry, I'm going to get you out of there,' Mallory said.

'Okay, that's it.' Branagh tapped the camera off and put the phone to his ear again. 'I take it that's good enough?'

'Yes.'

'Your turn. What do you have for me?'

Mallory drew the silence out. He was doing it deliberately, perhaps enjoying having this small measure of power over his opponent. 'It wasn't easy, but I did it.'

'Really?'

'Yes.'

'You have it? The missing section of code?'

'Yes.'

Branagh's turn to pause. 'How?'

'Does it matter?'

'Humour me.'

'Bartho Nel did just what you thought he did. He stashed the code on a flash drive so that you wouldn't get your hands on it. He kept it entirely offline.'

'And where exactly did he hide it?'

'That's not your concern.'

'I see. With the girl, perhaps. Ivy, wasn't it? We knew he had been in touch with his sons, but we didn't know about his relationship with his young co-worker.' He shot Susan Nel a glance. 'Perhaps we weren't the only ones.'

'So how do we do this?' Mallory said, not taking the bait.

'Not so fast. I'm going to need more than your say so.'

'Check your messages.'

Branagh took the phone from his ear. There was a new text. He opened it. It was a screenshot of a page of code.

'You see it?'

'Yes.'

'That's one screen. There are a lot more. I expect you'll have someone who can verify this.'

'You expect right. Give me ten minutes to check it out. In the meantime, we can get the ball rolling. If you give me the full code and it checks out, you get the woman back. Deal?'

'Deal. Tell me where and when. Make it somewhere quiet.'

Branagh was about to remind him he was in no position to give instructions, but stopped himself. Instead, he simply said: 'Keep the phone on. I'll call you back.'

'How about I call you instead?'

'Have it your way.' Branagh considered. He would need a little time to set things up, to take proper precautions. It would be stupid to rush into anything at this stage. 'Let's say two hours. Nine o'clock.'

Branagh hung up without waiting for an acknowledgement and tossed the phone to Foster so he could look at the screenshot. He took a moment to check his personal phone. A message from Maddie, asking him to call. That could wait. After this was all done and dusted, he could give her the good news that he was coming home. All being well, he could spend a lot more time at home after tonight.

He looked over at Foster, who was tapping away at

the laptop in the corner, glancing from the laptop to the phone screen that showed the first page of code. 'How does that look?'

Foster looked up. 'Impossible to tell until we get the whole thing, but it looks solid.'

'Excellent. Let's get moving.'

65

Mallory had only been resident in the city for the past few months, but he knew half a dozen ways to lay his hands on an untraceable firearm in a hurry. He didn't waste time pursuing any of them. If this was going to work, he would have to get close to Branagh and his people. They would search him thoroughly. There was no way he would be able to walk into the situation carrying anything more lethal than a toothpick.

But he reminded himself that he had an advantage. He knew exactly what was going to happen. Branagh and his men did not.

It was Afghanistan all over again, only this time he was on the other side.

It was thinking about Hell Hour that had made him realise that he still had a card left to play. Back at the compound, he and his team had their eyes on the prize. They didn't want to risk the HVT destroying a treasure trove of intelligence secrets. And so they had let him get too close. *Mallory* had let him get too close. If he had let Donno shoot, he would have detonated closer to the computer room, and the booby traps protecting the computers would likely have gone off. Instead, he had gambled with his and his team's lives, and had paid the price.

Branagh and his team were now in the same position. They didn't know for sure that Mallory had the code, but the fact he had been able to send them a screenshot had reassured them. They knew it was still possible they would all walk away from this with a nice pay packet. But to find out for sure, they had to be prepared to give him what he wanted: to release Susan in exchange for the code. And to make sure they could convince him to hand the code over, they had to have Susan with them.

And they had to let Mallory get in close.

He didn't know where Branagh was going to tell him to go. Maybe a deserted warehouse, or underneath a motorway flyover. Or perhaps he would go the other way and make sure the handover was in a public place, where Mallory would find it more difficult to spot anyone watching.

He didn't have any idea which point on the compass Branagh would send him to, but he assumed it would be somewhere in or around the city, so he went to the place he knew best. Standing at the edge of the parapet on the roof of his tower block, he looked out at the night sky, the city glow dyeing the clouds a dirty yellow.

He took out the fresh burner phone he had taken from the shoebox under his bed and switched it on. He dialled Branagh's number. Branagh answered on the first ring.

'I'm going to send you on a little trip, Mallory. Do you know where Clayton Road is?'

'I can find it.'

392

'There's a business park there. Go to unit B12 and wait for me to call. No need to change your phone this time. It'll all be over soon.'

Mallory hung up and descended the stairs of his tower block as he looked up the address on his phone. He knew exactly why Branagh had picked a place like that. It would allow someone to check he was unarmed from a distance. He got behind the wheel of the rented Corsa and drove to the industrial estate. The B units were at the far end, in front of a chain-link fence that divided the industrial estate from a thin strip of woodland beyond. There was a yellow grit bin in front of the fence. Mallory got out of the car. The place was deserted.

He looked around for a sign of the watcher he knew was there. If Branagh was completely confident that he had the code on his person, then the easiest and safest thing to do would be to take him out then and there. A sniper could do the job from a mile away. He would never know what had hit him. He remembered his thoughts a few days ago in Joburg. Not the worst way to go, if you had to.

But Branagh couldn't do that, because he couldn't be sure he had the code with him.

So there would definitely be a watcher, to confirm that Mallory was in position and that he was unarmed and alone. Branagh would make absolutely sure of all these things before he appeared.

Mallory identified three viable positions from which he could be observed, deciding that the most likely was a bridge over the railway line half a mile away.

Mallory walked around the bonnet and stood so that the Corsa was between him and the bridge. He waited.

A minute later, his phone buzzed.

'Move five paces to your left.' A familiar voice, but it wasn't Branagh's. This was one of the men from the cabin, the Australian. His instructions confirmed that he was watching from the bridge.

Mallory took the five paces, not hurrying. When he was clear of the bonnet, the Australian spoke again. 'Stop.'

Mallory stopped.

'Strip down.'

Mallory glared in the direction of the bridge. 'Are you fucking kidding me? It's February.'

'I thought you special forces guys could handle the cold. Do it.'

Mallory crouched to unlace his boots and stepped out of them. Luckily it hadn't rained in a day or so, so the pitted concrete of the car park was dry. He took his jacket off and folded it. Then his T-shirt, then his jeans. He took the car keys and the flash drive from his jeans pocket, then tossed the clothes into the back seat of the car and closed the door.

The night air was just above freezing. He gritted his teeth, but he wasn't going to give the Australian the satisfaction of shivering. He had experienced much worse discomfort than this.

'Hands in the air. Turn around three hundred and sixty degrees.'

Mallory did as instructed.

'Good enough, or do you want me to bend over and cough?'

'You see the grit bin? Walk over to it.'

Mallory walked across to it in his socks, weaving to avoid a puddle and a patch of broken glass. He got to the bin and waited for instructions. The Australian told him to open the lid. Inside the bin was a Sainsbury's bag for life containing a pair of grey sweat pants, a matching sweater, a pair of white Nike trainers. Smart. He would find it difficult to conceal anything dangerous in this outfit.

'Get dressed.'

Mallory quickly pulled on the clothes and laced up the trainers. There was something thin and plastic in the pocket of the sweatpants. He took it out. It was a contactless travel card. Interesting.

'What now?'

The call ended.

Mallory tensed and waited.

66

A moment later, another call came in. A different number. Branagh's voice this time. He said Mallory's name.

'I'm here. Thanks for the new wardrobe,' Mallory said.

'Leave the car. You can take the keys, your phone and – I'm hoping – whatever the code is saved on. We're watching you, so don't try to put anything else in your pockets.'

'Where am I going?'

'Leave the business park by the main entrance and turn left.'

'Then what?'

'Then keep walking.'

The call cut out. Mallory understood exactly why they were doing this. First they had established he was alone and unarmed and not wearing a wire. Now they could watch him all the way, make sure he didn't make any detours or talk to anyone on the phone. This was just the staging area. The exchange would take place elsewhere.

He put the keys and the flash drive and his phone in the

loose pockets of the sweatpants and started walking. He passed by the closed-up industrial units. Only one still had a light burning. A black Audi was parked outside. The boss working late.

There was sparse, late-evening traffic on the main road. Mallory wasn't familiar with this part of the city, but up ahead he could see a McDonald's and some assorted warehouse stores lining the road. He didn't think they were going to close this deal over a McFlurry, but stranger things had happened.

He kept walking. A moment before the phone buzzed with a text message, he saw the familiar red and white British Rail symbol and knew it was his next destination. Snow Hill Station. He took his phone out and read the text.

> Go into the station. Platform 3. Use the card.
> You have 2 minutes.

Mallory had never been through this station before. It was far from rush hour, but there were still passengers around, moving to and fro. He kept his eyes on them. None of them looked as though they were watching him, but he knew somebody was. He looked around for a sign directing him to the platform. He found it and tapped the travel card on the ticket gate. As it processed, he wondered what he was expected to do if the card failed. But the light flashed green and the gate sprang open. He moved through and towards the stairs down to Platform 3.

There was a train pulling in as he reached the bottom of the stairs and stepped on to the platform. There were only two people waiting: a woman with a pram and a guy in a suit. He was pacing, his phone held in front of his face as he had a video conversation.

The phone buzzed again.

Get on the train

He glanced at the destination board as he moved towards the nearest set of doors. This was the 22:28 for Stratford-upon-Avon. There was a list of more than a dozen stations. He wondered how far along the line they would send him.

The woman with the pram stepped on to the train without difficulty two carriages up. The man with the phone continued his conversation and stayed on the platform. Mallory waited until the door alarms started beeping to board.

The doors closed and he surveyed the other occupants of the carriage. It was barely a quarter full. No one looked up when Mallory stepped on board. He stayed on his feet and gripped the handrail as the train moved off.

So far, this was all pretty much as Mallory had expected. Forcing him to move on foot. Putting him on a train so he couldn't be followed by vehicle, and picking a quiet train so an accomplice tailing him could be seen.

Mallory stood in the corner between the door and the partition so that he could observe every occupant of the carriage. A young, fit-looking man looked up from his Kindle as he felt Mallory's eyes on him. He was dressed in comfortable, loose clothes. Could he be the watcher?

Mallory met his gaze and the man immediately looked back down at his Kindle.

The train slowed and the phone buzzed once more.

Get off

Already?

They pulled into Moor Street. The doors opened. Mallory watched the other passengers. Two older women got off, chatting to each other. No one else moved. The man with the Kindle glanced up. Again, the door alarms sounded and Mallory stepped out. Even quieter than the last station: no one on the platform at all.

Here?

As the Stratford train pulled off, he saw another approaching on the parallel tracks going in the opposite direction. Another text arrived. He knew what it would say before he read it.

Get on.

A hairpin turn, sending him back the way he had come. He thought he knew where the final destination was now.

He sprinted over the footbridge across the tracks, arriving on the opposite platform just as the train pulled to a stop.

The doors opened. Mallory stepped on and took the same position as he had on the last train, standing in the corner between the door and the partition. There were a few more passengers on this train, but it wasn't close to full. Plenty of unoccupied seats.

This time, one of the passengers was paying attention to him.

He was sitting in an aisle seat in the middle of the carriage. He was mid-forties, short, dark hair, a tanned complexion. He had glasses. He was wearing a dark suit and a blue, open-necked shirt. And he was staring right at Mallory.

67

The man in the dark suit got up and walked along the aisle towards Mallory. He swayed with the motion of the train, keeping his balance like a dancer. His eyes never moved from Mallory's.

He drew level and stood on the opposite side of the partitioned section around the door, holding the support post. Up close, Mallory was sure of it. This was the man he had seen at Graves's place.

'Not delegating this part, then?' Mallory asked.

Branagh smiled. 'I like to be hands-on.' He broke eye contact to give Mallory a quick appraisal, scanning his body for any sign of a weapon. The sound of the wheels on the tracks became louder as they passed beneath St Martin's Queensway.

'Do you have it?'

Mallory reached into his pocket and produced the flash drive. He half-expected Branagh to make a grab for it.

'Password protected, and it'll wipe if you try to crack it.'

'Naturally,' Branagh said. 'But how do I know it has anything on it at all?'

'You get the password when I see Susan Nel.'

Branagh nodded. 'Fine.'

'Do we have far to go?' Mallory asked, though he was pretty sure where they were going.

Branagh didn't answer. The train pulled to a stop at Birmingham New Street. Branagh held his hand out in an 'after you' gesture.

Mallory stepped out on to the platform.

'Straight ahead.'

Mallory walked, with Branagh following a couple of paces behind. Branagh would be armed, that was for sure. New Street was quiet this late at night, only a handful of passengers moving around, almost lost in the space. They emerged out on to the concourse beneath the arched glass ceiling.

Mallory stopped and looked back for direction. Branagh gestured towards the escalator leading up to the mezzanine that wrapped around the concourse.

They rode up, Branagh a couple of steps behind Mallory. Mallory looked around him as he was lifted slowly up to the upper level. A decent location for the handover. In plain sight. Not too many customers around at this time of night, but an entirely random selection of people. No one would ask questions about why they were waiting around in a station. An unexpected melodic sound drew Mallory's attention and he looked down to see a young guy wearing a backpack playing an overly familiar tune on the piano on the far side of the concourse.

'"Imagine",' Branagh commented approvingly. 'One of my favourites.'

'Always been more of a Stones man, myself,' Mallory said. As the escalator brought Mallory to eye level with the upper floor, he saw them immediately: a group of four. He recognised the American, Simon Willer. There were two other men: a tall, wide-built man wearing a jacket that looked like it was struggling to contain his upper arms, and a rangy figure in a grey suit with a ponytail and a greying beard carrying a laptop case. And there was Susan Nel.

It took her a moment to spot him, and then their eyes met. Mallory gave her a brief smile. She looked okay, at least from a distance. The escalator delivered Mallory to the end of its run and he stepped off and stood aside, waiting for Branagh to join him.

It was even quieter up here than on the concourse below. The shutters were down at the entrance to the John Lewis that adjoined the station. The tables and chairs in front of the food courts had a handful of customers killing time before the last train.

Mallory and Branagh approached the group of four.

When they were close enough to speak without raised voices, Mallory stopped. He looked at each of the three men in turn. He was pretty sure all of them were armed. The big guy and the one with the ponytail were both tensed, watching him carefully, as though a threatening-looking dog was approaching. Willer stood to one side of the others, his eyes narrowed. A study in body language: the others wanted this to go smoothly; Willer wanted Mallory to give him an excuse. Mallory suspected he would be obliging him. He turned to look at Susan.

'Are you all right?'

'I'm okay. Is Donovan all right?'

'He's fine,' Branagh answered before Mallory could say

anything. 'If your friend here has indeed come up with the goods, we won't need to bother any of you again.'

'Amen to that,' the big guy said, his voice marking him out as the Australian who had given him instructions back at the business park. 'This has been a bloody nightmare.'

Mallory looked around. They had picked a spot away from the open food places. They had done well getting him into this position while making sure he was unarmed and alone. There were no clear routes of escape. There was a door marked FIRE EXIT, but the Australian was standing between the rest of the group and the door. Lots of space.

There was a security guard positioned on the lower floor, diagonally across from them. Could he do something with that? Make a scene? He discarded the thought. What would that accomplish? They could bundle Susan away by whatever exit they had planned in advance. And besides, the guard would be unarmed.

The Australian looked around too, then put his hands on his hips. For a second, his thumb drew the side of his jacket back, just enough time for Mallory to see that he had a gun in a shoulder holster. The message: *Don't even think about it.*

'Okay,' Branagh said. 'Well, it was a long way round, but here we are.' He looked at Mallory, then at Susan Nel. 'She's fine, as you can see. All you have to do is hand over the code. We'll confirm it's what we're looking for, and we can all go our separate ways.'

Mallory looked back at Susan. She was barely fifteen feet away from him, but she might as well have been on the other side of the planet.

Mallory reached into his pocket and took out the flash drive. 'You really want this thing, don't you?'

403

Branagh looked back at him, straight-faced. 'What gave us away? Personally, I don't want it. I'm just completing a contract.'

'I know the feeling,' Mallory said. 'So who are you working for?'

'Does it matter?'

'Just curiosity, really. This tech was developed to find water for drought relief. I'm guessing your backers have a less high-minded use for it. I think Bartho found a big oil deposit in Anambra. Probably worth a fair bit to the right company.'

'Close, but not quite,' Branagh said.

'Can we get this over with?' Willer was glaring at Mallory. He didn't like this small talk. Mallory was glad to see that it was putting him on edge. Below them, the piano player got bored with 'Imagine' and started on 'Hey Jude'. Willer shot an irritated glance in the direction of the music.

'It's all right, Simon. We'll get there,' Branagh said.

'It's not oil?'

Branagh shook his head. 'As it happens, no. Fossil fuels are so twentieth century. You've been carrying the answer in your pocket this whole time.'

Mallory was confused for a second. Was he talking about the flash drive? And then he realised what Branagh meant. He reached into his pocket and took out the burner phone.

'That's right. Practically every citizen over the age of twelve in every developed country is walking around with one of those in their pockets. And do you know what they rely on?'

'Lithium,' Mallory said. 'It wasn't oil Bartho found, it was lithium deposits.'

'Got it in one. It's in your phone, your laptop, your smart watch. It's in e-cigarettes. It's in electric cars. We're hooked on it. It's what makes the modern world go round.'

'And Bartho didn't want anyone to know about what he had found.'

'That's right. He was concerned for the population there. He thought exploitation of the lithium deposits would have a catastrophic impact on the local population and environment.' Branagh shrugged. 'I don't think he was wrong.'

'So that was why he resisted your attempts to buy him off.'

Branagh nodded. 'None of this had to happen. He could have sold the tech to my client and made a handsome profit. He could have told his employers about it and they would have done the same thing. Or he could have just stepped back and let nature take its course.'

'Nature?'

Branagh smiled. 'Well, human nature.'

He walked around Mallory and behind Susan Nel. He put his hands on her shoulders. She flinched.

'But he didn't do that. He actively obstructed us. We knew he had taken out the code and we thought we knew who he had given it to. That meant he was disposable. Unfortunately, once he had been disposed of, we found out the code wasn't where we thought it was. A few months later, we discovered he had met with his son right before we killed him. We had to assume he had given the code to his son.'

'That's why you had Scott kidnapped.'

'Exactly. And now you've found the code. You did what we weren't able to.'

Mallory said nothing.

'I have to admit,' Branagh continued, 'you've caused me a lot of trouble, but I think we might be alike in some ways. If this evening works out okay, I might have a job opportunity for you.'

Mallory just stared back at him in response.

Branagh shot a glance at Willer, who was glaring back at Mallory. 'Perhaps a good thing from a team chemistry point of view.'

He stepped away from Susan.

'All right, enough chit-chat.' He walked around to Mallory and held his hand out to receive the flash drive. Mallory paused. He glanced from Branagh to the security guard downstairs and, this time, Branagh caught him looking. He dropped his hand. He walked to the barrier in front of the drop and waved. As Mallory watched, the security guard glanced up at him. Branagh pointed to a spot across the floor. The guard walked straight to the spot Branagh had indicated.

Damn. Either the guard was one of them, or they had paid him off. Perhaps they had paid off more than one. It didn't matter. He would be able to make sure his co-workers didn't interrupt them.

Branagh turned back to Mallory, an almost apologetic look on his face. He held his hand out once again.

Mallory hesitated. As soon as he handed it over, the train would be set in motion. The man with the ponytail would check the flash drive on his computer and within minutes he would realise that half the code was missing. Unless he didn't know quite what he was looking for. Best-case scenario, they would see enough to release Susan. Mallory wasn't counting on best-case scenario.

Willer was still glaring at him. Maybe the two of them weren't so different. Maybe there was a part of both of them that wanted this to go south.

'Mallory?'

He handed Branagh the flash drive. Branagh gave it to the guy with the ponytail.

'Foster, do the honours?'

There was a bench over by the wall. Foster took the drive over there and sat down. Willer moved position to stand behind them, the Australian stayed between the rest of them and the fire exit. Foster took the laptop out of its case and opened it up. He held up the flash drive and examined it. Satisfied, he plugged it into the machine.

'Password?' Foster asked, without looking up.

'*qarabagh*,' Mallory said, and spelled it out. 'All lower case.'

Mallory held his breath. The file opened and Foster stared at the screen for a moment. The light was reflected in the lenses of his glasses. After a moment he looked up at Branagh.

'Check everything is there,' Branagh said.

Foster stuck a thumb up. 'Looks good so far. Give me a couple of minutes.'

Branagh turned back to Mallory. He looked pleased. More than pleased, actually. He seemed relieved. Mallory wondered how much was riding on this for him.

'You did well. And with a pretty aggressive deadline.'

'You can put a gold star on my report card.'

'Indeed. Maybe I should have come to you first.'

Mallory kept his eyes on Foster, tapping away at the laptop. Perhaps Foster wouldn't be as painstaking as Ivy had been. Perhaps the bluff would be all he would need.

'That's your whole thing, isn't it?' Mallory said. 'You just get other people to do your dirty work.'

Branagh's eyes were on Foster too, but at that he looked at Mallory. 'You say that like it's a criticism. That's absolutely what I do. That's what Her Majesty's Government paid me to do for twenty-two years.'

'And now you've got what you want. Can I go now? I want to change out of this polyester.'

'Just another minute. Foster?'

Foster was still focused on the screen. Any hope Mallory had that he would be slipshod in his approach to confirmation was fast evaporating.

Willer was looking around uneasily. They had been chasing this code across three continents, and it was all coming down to this.

'All right, I think we're good here,' Foster said.

Immediately, Mallory moved. He took Susan Nel's hand and started to move away towards the escalator.

'Wait a second.'

Foster had spoken again. Willer stepped into Mallory's way, and he stopped.

'We're missing some of it.' He tapped the keys and checked again, his lips moving soundlessly. Then he looked up again. 'There's only half of it here.'

Branagh looked at Mallory. The Australian moved forward and took Susan's arm.

Mallory frowned. 'There were two files on there.' He moved over to where Foster was sitting, holding his hand out. 'Give me it a second.'

Foster looked up at Branagh for confirmation. He hesitated and then nodded. Foster handed Mallory the laptop.

As he did so, his jacket moved so that Mallory could see the grip of his gun in its holster. There was nothing to unbutton, ready for quick draw.

Mallory sat down and adjusted the screen of the laptop, angling his body so it looked like he was reading what was on screen. What he was actually doing was checking out the relative positions of the other three men and Susan. He needed a snapshot to block out each move in his head before he made it. Foster beside him. The Australian close by, holding on to Susan Nel's arm. Branagh and Willer a couple of steps further away.

'Got it,' Mallory said. 'It's there, see?' He indicated a random point on the screen.

Foster leaned forward.

In the instant before he acted, Mallory thought about what Branagh had just said. About how they were alike. He was about to show him exactly how different they really were.

As Foster reached forward to take the laptop, Mallory snapped it closed and slammed the hard edge of it into Foster's face. Foster's hands jerked up instinctively, even though he was way too late to protect himself. Blood exploded from his nose. Before anyone could react, Mallory launched the laptop over the glass barrier guarding the drop to the concourse. It sailed up and over. The other three men had frozen, just as he had expected. Mallory was already moving. He reached into Foster's jacket for the gun, sliding it out of the holster and feeling the grip in his hand. His thumb clicked the safety off as he heard the laptop smash on to the concourse below.

He shot the Australian first: two in the chest, then turned and put one in Foster's face. Then he was spinning and firing at Willer's position, but Willer had reacted faster than he expected, ducking behind cover. He thought he might have hit him, but he couldn't be sure.

Branagh didn't hesitate – he was running for the escalator. The piano playing had stopped, replaced by yells and screams.

Mallory grabbed Susan's arm. 'Move it.'

He was practically dragging her at first, but she soon started running, keeping pace with Mallory as he headed towards the fire exit. He could hear sounds of panic from the few passengers on the concourse below. Mallory slammed into the push bar of the fire exit, sending the door swinging. It opened on a narrow breeze block corridor leading to a flight of stairs going down. He hoped it would take them outside.

He pointed at the stairs. 'Get out of the building and find a cop. It shouldn't be difficult.'

'What about you?'

'I don't fancy looking over my shoulder for these guys. I'm going to finish this.'

Susan opened her mouth, but Mallory wasn't interested in whatever she had to say. He pushed her in the direction of the end of the corridor. 'Go!'

He turned and saw Simon Willer standing in the doorway, his gun gripped in both hands, pointed at Mallory's head. There was a bloodstain on the edge of Willer's right shoulder where Mallory's earlier bullet must have grazed him. The wound certainly wasn't doing anything to stop him holding that gun straight.

Willer was twenty feet away. There was no way Mallory could raise his gun before Willer shot him.

'Toss it.'

Mallory dropped the gun.

'Kick it to me.'

Mallory kicked the gun. It skated over the tiled floor towards Willer.

Willer kept the gun on him. 'Where is the fucking code?'

'There is no code. The part I gave you is all that's left. Nothing for you to do here but get the hell out before the police arrive.'

Willer stared. Mallory realised that he believed him. He knew he was telling the truth. But the code wasn't the only reason he wanted to track down Mallory. He wanted to settle a score. Mallory tensed. No way out. This was it.

And then Willer lowered his gun and put it back in his holster. He shed his jacket, unbuttoned his shirtsleeves and put his fists up.

Mallory felt himself smile.

68

Branagh reached the concourse and ran towards the spot where the laptop had come to rest. A terrified-looking woman with pink hair ran across his path, looking up at the top level. Screams and shouts echoed over the calm automated voice announcing that the 23.10 to London Euston was boarding at Platform 2. He reached the laptop and found it was still in one piece, but the screen was shattered. The flash drive had popped out on impact and was lying twenty feet away. He picked it up and put it in his pocket.

He looked up and saw Mallory and Susan Nel running along the top level. None of his men were still standing. That was a bad sign. And then he saw a blond-haired head and a torso rise above the barrier as Willer stood up.

The concourse was clearing before his eyes. People running in panic from the gunshots. They thought it was a terrorist attack. On one level, perhaps they were right. Mallory was a bloody terrorist. He had walked unbidden into the middle of a perfectly lucrative job and set off a bomb.

Branagh turned towards one of the backup exits he had

scouted out earlier in the day: a café with a fire exit that would take him straight outside. But someone was blocking his path. A security guard was approaching. Not the guard he had paid off; *he* was nowhere to be seen. This guard was approaching Branagh because he had come from the direction of the shots. He was holding a bright yellow taser, but looked unsure about what he was going to do with it.

'Sir, please don't move.'

Branagh transferred the laptop to his left hand.

'Somebody *shot* at me up there, you've got to help!' he cried out, injecting his voice with just the right whine. The guard glanced up to the top level. Branagh drew his gun and shot him twice in the chest.

The concourse had emptied out completely in under a minute. He could hear sirens in the distance already. Armed response would be here in minutes, seconds perhaps. He avoided the front entrance and ran for the café.

Damn it. He was rueing the day he had agreed to take this job. It had already hit a stumbling block when Scott Nel either didn't know where the code was, or was proving unusually resistant to interrogation. But it had really gone off the rails when Mallory had got involved. He wished he could have cut his losses at that point; found some other way to pay off his debt. Perhaps all wasn't lost yet. Perhaps there would be enough on the flash drive for his clients to fill in the blanks. He doubted it, but it was better than nothing.

Branagh couldn't understand why Mallory had held back the rest of the code. Why would he endanger the woman like that, if he was willing to risk his life to get her back?

All of those were questions for another day. Branagh had one goal: to get the hell away before the police set up a hard perimeter. As soon as he was clear of the station he would get rid of the gun. No one would have had time to view the CCTV yet, so he was confident he would be able to talk his way past any police officers. Just another terrified civilian fleeing the scene. He didn't fit the profile the police would be looking for.

He had planned out every exit from New Street as a matter of course. This one led to a loading dock that opened out on to the back of the Bullring. In less than a minute, he would be outside.

And then he turned a corner and saw a familiar figure fifty yards along the corridor, heading for the street.

69

They had traded some good blows. The two of them were evenly matched.

Mallory realised that he had been right about the rest of Branagh's crew: they didn't like getting their hands dirty. Willer was different. Willer was much more Mallory's kind of animal. Willing to do whatever it took. Mallory had taken a few solid hits and given a few in return. It felt like a couple of his ribs were cracked from the last blow. Willer, for his part, was favouring his right side. Mallory had taken full advantage of the wound to his left shoulder. He had only got one good punch on that side, and it had almost been enough to put him over the top, but Willer had rallied and had been able to shield his weak spot for the last couple of punches.

They separated for a moment, both breathing heavily.

Mallory spat dark blood on to the white tiled floor. 'You should run. Police are coming.'

Willer shook his head slowly, his eyes burning into Mallory's. This was utterly personal. Willer no longer cared about the code, or avoiding arrest, or anything but beating

Mallory to a pulp with his bare hands. And he had a pretty good chance of getting his wish.

He ran at Mallory again. Close-quarters corridor fighting. Mallory blocked his first strike, then his second. Willer had left his left side open. Mallory risked going for it, putting all he had into it. But he had fallen into a trap. Willer sidestepped at the last second and got his arm around Mallory's neck, shifting his weight around until he had him in a headlock.

Mallory felt the arms curl around his neck, finding purchase. And then the pressure began. He gritted his teeth as the edges of his vision began to darken. In another few seconds, he would lose consciousness. But the blond giant wouldn't stop then. He would keep squeezing until Mallory was dead.

Mallory's fingers grabbed at the forearms. He tried the pressure points, but he was in the wrong position to get any purchase. He tried clawing at the face, but Willer just adjusted his position without loosening an ounce of pressure.

And then Mallory heard the fire door behind them slam open. Willer looked around. The pressure lessened and his grip shifted for a split second, putting his bare wrist under Mallory's mouth.

Mallory didn't pause for thought. He bit down hard, trying to take Willer's fucking hand off, or at least tear away a good chunk of it.

Willer grunted in pain and his grip loosened again. Mallory spat a chunk of flesh out as he pushed away from him and dived for the gun on the floor. From the corner of his eye, Mallory saw a woman in a red coat standing in the open doorway, hand to her mouth.

Mallory gripped the gun and raised it as Willer was

charging for him. His finger was tightening on the trigger, but he wasn't quite fast enough. Willer kicked it out of his hand.

Mallory rolled and grabbed Willer's foot before it came down. He twisted and sent him tumbling. Willer banged his head on the wall, enough to daze him for a second.

And then Mallory was on top of him. Positions reversed, headlock. Willer grabbed at Mallory's arms, just as Mallory had his. But he gave up faster. Why? Mallory realised what he was doing – reaching to the knife that was strapped to his belt. Mallory beat him to it. Pulled out the knife. Willer grabbed for it, the blade first, cutting himself and not caring, and then his hand was around Mallory's. They didn't move. Every ounce of strength was going into trying to pry the knife away from the other. After everything, it was coming down to an arm wrestle.

But Willer's fingers were slippery from his own blood. Slowly, painfully, Mallory was winning.

The knife came away with a sound like a champagne cork popping. Willer gave up and tried to twist away, but Mallory was too fast. He brought it up, under Willer's jaw and through the roof of his mouth.

Willer gagged on the blade and Mallory twisted it, feeling the body quiver beneath him. Then he took it out, pulled it back, and slammed it through Willer's right ear.

The blond man dropped, a pool of arterial blood already spreading out on the floor, running into the channels between the tiles.

Mallory looked up at the doorway to see if the terrified passenger who had saved his life was still there, but it was empty. He scrambled to his feet, trying to stay clear of the fast-spreading puddle of blood, and ran for the stairs.

As he descended to ground level, he was focused on how he was going to get out of here without being stopped by the police. He could hear more sirens, seemingly coming from all points of the compass. Maybe it was already too late to make it out. Maybe Willer had doomed both of them. At least Susan was safe, though. That was the main thing.

As he opened the door and stepped into the alley running along the exterior of the station, all of those thoughts melted away.

Susan Nel was there. Branagh was standing behind her, one arm around her neck, the other hand holding his gun to her temple.

70

Mallory stopped in his tracks. Branagh's eyes were already looking beyond him. It took Mallory a second to realise who he was looking for.

'Willer's dead,' he said. 'They're all dead.'

'Give me the code!' Branagh yelled. Not so smooth now. He looked like a man facing down a wild animal. A man who was armed, but wasn't quite certain that would be enough. He was right.

'I don't have it,' Mallory said quietly. 'You have all there is.'

'You can find it,' Branagh said urgently. 'You know where it is. Or you can get it.'

Mallory felt strangely relaxed. The police were coming. Maybe he and Branagh were both going down. Maybe they were both leaving here in body bags, but it didn't matter. Scott was safe. Donno was safe. And if he had anything to do with it, Susan would be safe, too.

Mallory just shook his head. 'I'll give you one chance. Walk away.'

Branagh gripped Susan's arm more firmly. She took a sharp breath.

'In case you hadn't noticed, I'm the one with the gun here.'

Mallory said nothing. He took one step forward, then another. He was within five feet of Branagh now.

'That's far enough. I'm going to count to three.'

'You're not going to count to anything,' Mallory said. He spoke in a hush. An icy calm had descended over him. 'You're not going to pull that trigger, because you know what will happen.'

'Don't test me.'

'I can't give you the code because it doesn't exist any more. What I gave you on that flash drive? That's all there is. Bartho Nel split the code. He gave it to his two sons, only he didn't tell them what he had given them.'

Branagh's eyes narrowed. He was conflicted. Wasn't sure whether to believe Mallory. But part of him already did.

'Then Scott still has it. We can—'

'You've got Scott's half. Donno had his on him when he was blown up. You want to know where the other half of the code is? It's in pieces, scattered halfway across Afghanistan.'

'Then . . .'

'Yeah. All of this was for nothing. You were never getting that final payment on delivery.'

Branagh shook his head. 'You're lying.'

'No, Branagh, I'm not. I don't give a shit about it. All I wanted was for you and your friends to lay off this lady and her family.'

Branagh tightened his grip on Susan again. She didn't scream, but took a sharp breath. Her eyes were on

Mallory's. He got the message: she hoped he knew what the hell he was doing.

'Cut your losses, mate,' Mallory said, softening his tone. 'The code's gone. You wait here much longer and the police will be along to take care of us both.'

Branagh swallowed and adjusted his grip on Susan Nel. He didn't look as though he was about to release her, instead pushing the muzzle of his gun against the side of her head. This time, she let out a whimper.

For the first time since he had stepped outside, Mallory was truly worried.

Branagh didn't look like he was playing with the full deck any more. Up until this moment, his behaviour, if not his precise tactics, had been predictable. Not now.

Mallory had seen that look in a man's eyes before, on the battlefield. He was on the edge. He was panicking, and panicked men make bad decisions. Something had snapped within him. Branagh was a man used to having everything go to plan. Used to a world where things went his way. Now he was in over his head.

He was in Hell Hour.

'If you pull that trigger, you know what I'll do. You know what will happen next.'

'I still have the gun, remember?'

'It won't make any difference. You won't have time for a second shot. And even if you did, it wouldn't matter.' Mallory opened his hands, presenting his centre mass as an open target. 'You might even be able to hit me once. You think that's going to stop me ripping your throat out with my teeth?'

Branagh swallowed. Blinked. But he didn't loosen his grip.

He was looking at the blood on Mallory's mouth from when he had bitten a chunk out of Willer's hand.

'I'll give you one chance. Walk away now. You can keep the gun. I'll let you go.'

The silence seemed to draw out for a hundred years. And then it was broken by a soft buzzing noise.

Branagh's phone.

Who the hell was calling him? All of his people were dead.

And then Branagh nodded. The interruption seemed to have made his mind up. He loosened his grip on Susan Nel's throat. She slipped free and ran towards Mallory. Branagh held the gun on them both.

'What a bloody mess.'

'Welcome to my world,' Mallory said.

Branagh opened his mouth to give a rejoinder and then changed his mind. He turned and started to run towards the street. He did what Mallory had suggested. He kept the gun.

Susan threw her arms around Mallory. He flinched at first, and then allowed it, patting her gently on the back of her neck.

'Thank you,' she breathed. 'I was sure he was going to kill me then.'

He had been. Mallory hadn't been at all sure whether his strategy would work or push Branagh over the edge. It had been fifty-fifty.

'What if he comes back?'

Mallory was watching Branagh as he ran full pelt for the end of the alley and towards the Bullring. He was really sprinting, not thinking, just trying to put as much distance between himself and this clusterfuck as possible.

He hadn't even thought to throw his gun away when he had made it a safe distance from Mallory.

'He's not coming back.'

Branagh reached the mouth of the alley and then froze, looking at something, or someone, out of Mallory's line of sight.

He heard yells from the main road. Authoritative voices telling him to get down on the ground.

Branagh turned slightly. Mallory wasn't sure what he was trying to do. Maybe he was trying to do as he had been ordered, maybe he was considering running back the way he had come, into cover. Either way, he made a sudden movement at the very moment he should have done no such thing.

Mallory felt Susan Nel flinch in his arms as they heard the staccato crack of gunshots echoing off the walls of the alley. It was a familiar sound to Mallory, but it was alien to hear it in an environment like this.

Branagh's body jerked and he fell to the pavement, unmoving.

Two armed response officers came into view, clad in tactical gear, MP5s trained on Branagh's body. They kept their distance from him.

Mallory's hand was still on the back of Susan's neck. He realised his fingers were touching the back of her necklace. He narrowed his eyes and gently moved her aside.

'Is he dead?' she asked, keeping her eyes resolutely focused ahead.

When Mallory didn't answer, she looked up at him. His eyes were on the slender necklace that disappeared beneath the collar of Susan's blouse.

'What ... what's wrong?' she asked.

Mallory didn't answer. There would be time for that later. He glanced back to see if they were boxed in and saw there was another narrow alley running away from this one. The cops hadn't spotted the two of them yet, but they would in a moment. Mallory didn't want to be there when they did.

'Put up your hands before they see you,' he whispered. Susan did as she was told.

Mallory stepped away and ducked into the smaller alley. From all around he could hear more sirens approaching the area.

It would be a challenge to get out of here without being seen, but compared to what he had already been through tonight, it would be a breeze.

71

SIX WEEKS LATER

Mallory stood in the shade of the awning at the back of the house in Selly Park and gazed down the slope to the bottom of the garden. Sixty yards or so away, Susan Nel and her two sons sat around a table in the afternoon sun. Beyond them, some cricketers were setting up for an early spring match on the other side of the stream that marked the edge of the property. Scott was pouring champagne into the flutes on the table. There were four flutes, but he had only filled three.

They had a lot to celebrate. Even from this distance, Mallory could see that Donno was looking great compared to the last time he had seen him. He had put on weight, his hair had grown out, and his colour was a lot healthier.

Mallory thought about that phone call to Susan, a day after what had happened at New Street. He hadn't known what Susan would do with the information he had to give her, but as it turned out, she had found the perfect thing to do.

The second pendant had been hidden in plain sight all the

time. Without knowing it, Branagh and his men had had it for the ten hours they'd held Susan Nel prisoner. It had been around her neck all along, from the first time Mallory had met her in Donno's ward.

The pendant was in Donno's box of personal effects, returned to his family after his injury. Susan hadn't recognised it, but she knew her son had been wearing it when he was injured, and so she wore it every day.

As soon as Mallory and Susan had confirmed that the second pendant contained an SD card with the rest of the code, they had a decision to make: what to do with it. Mallory pointed out that it could make Susan and her family rich, potentially. But, on the other hand, if Branagh's backers knew it existed, they would send more people after it. The only thing to do was make sure they wouldn't be able to use it.

In the end, the decision was unanimous. Ivy was able to complete the work Bartho had started, and MTC launched the new programme with great fanfare. A small village in Anambra was tipped off that they were sitting on top of a sizeable lithium reserve, and they were able to come to a brokered agreement that would be very lucrative for them and the whole area, while safeguarding the environment. The companies mining the lithium wouldn't make quite so much money out of it, but such is life.

Money isn't everything. That was what Susan had said when Mallory told her about the value of Bartho Nel's code on the open market. Looking at the three of them now in the garden, he knew exactly what she had meant.

A loud peal of laughter sounded across the distance as Scott cracked a joke. Susan gave him a disapproving slap on the forearm. Donno smiled and then turned to look in the direction of the house. He spotted Mallory. He opened his mouth to say something to the other two and Mallory shook his head. Scott was pointing at something on the cricket field and speaking to his mum. Donno put his hand on Susan's shoulder and said something, then started walking back up to the house. The other two didn't seem to notice him leave.

Donno was limping a little. It took him a while to get to the top of the garden. He grinned as he approached.

'It's great to see you.' He glanced back at the family gathering at the bottom of the garden. 'You're going to join us, right?'

Mallory looked past him at the other two, who were deep in conversation. 'No, mate. I just wanted to check in on the three of you before I go.'

'You're leaving?'

'Already left. It was a bit dicey around here after what happened.'

'Mum didn't tell the police who you were. I know they're still looking for the fifth man from New Street, but I'm sure if we talked to them ...'

'Best not to, mate. I don't mind staying under the radar. Easiest place to be.'

Donno considered for a minute. Mallory could tell by the look in his eyes that he understood in a way that his brother and his mother might not be able to.

'You have a place here when you need it. We owe you.'

'No, I owe you. All of you. I've been in a pretty dark place since we got back.' As Mallory said it, he thought about the people who hadn't made it back. Westwick, Khan, McKenzie. Even Yorkie. 'Helping your mum and your brother ... I don't know how to explain it, but I think it helped me. I think I need to do more of that, if I can.'

'Where will you go?'

'Somewhere else,' Mallory said. In truth, he wasn't sure himself.

'You sure you won't join us? They would love to see you.'

He shook his head. 'Tell them I was asking after them. And take good care of them. That brother of yours needs a full-time nanny.'

'You know it.' Donno held his hand out and they shook, finishing with a tight hug.

Mallory watched as Donno made his way back to the bottom of the garden, and then he started moving towards the side passage that led out to the street. At the last moment, he turned and looked back. His last sight before he left the garden was of Susan Nel and her sons, laughing in the spring sunshine.

Mallory walked out on to the quiet road and turned west. He had everything he needed in his backpack. It was a beautiful April day and the closest station was only a mile away on foot.

He could decide where he was going when he got there.

72

NEW ORLEANS, LOUISIANA

Evangeline Graves removed her sunglasses as she stepped out of the bright noon sunshine at the far end of Bourbon Street and entered the comfortingly familiar darkness and clutter of Fritzel's bar. A four-piece band was set up at the far end, playing something she vaguely recognised as a John Coltrane piece.

The place was about half full, the clientele at this hour mostly tourists. She took her usual seat in the corner near the window, positioning herself so that she had an equally good view of the interior of the bar and the street outside just by moving her head in one direction or the other. As a rule, she didn't like meetings in person, but this particular person had managed to grab her attention.

A waiter in a short-sleeved black shirt saw her sit down and started to walk over, swaying a little in time with the music. Graves hadn't seen him before, but they had a pretty high turnover in here. She ordered an old-fashioned.

Woodford Reserve bourbon instead of Scotch. Lemon twist instead of orange.

'Does that still count as an old-fashioned?' the waiter asked, giving her a mischievous look.

Graves answered with a lift of her eyebrows that she hoped conveyed how little she cared about that, and turned her eyes to the street outside the window. The waiter got the message and retreated to the bar. Her drink arrived a couple of minutes later and she sipped it. They had done a good job, despite any reservations about the authenticity of her modifications.

She spotted the man she was here to meet as she was putting her glass down on the coaster.

Up until this moment, he had been text in an email, and then a voice on the phone, but looking at the tall, slightly pale man striding along the covered sidewalk with a brisk, confident gait, she knew her lunch date had arrived. He had that military look that is impossible to shake entirely, no matter how long you've been out. As he got closer, she saw that there was a thin red scar on the left side of his face, running from beneath his sunglasses all the way down to his jawline.

He removed the glasses as he paused in the doorway and looked around, taking in the bar and the band and then seeing Graves in the corner. She was the only lone female in the place. He approached and stopped when he got to her table.

'Thanks for meeting me.' He had one of those British accents that's so neutral it doesn't even count as an accent.

Graves didn't respond verbally, but gestured at the seat across from her. The man hesitated for a moment, and she recognised his disquiet at sitting with his back to the room, but he sat down anyway. The black-shirted waiter material-ised and took an order for a gin and tonic.

'Which gin would you prefer, sir?'

The man with the scar didn't take his eyes from Graves as he answered. 'I don't mind, as long as it isn't too expensive and isn't paint stripper.'

'So,' Graves began, when the waiter was out of earshot again. 'We're talking about Mallory.'

'Everybody's talking about Mallory,' the man agreed. 'He seems to have caused quite a stir. And some problems for you, I hear.'

Graves nodded and swirled her drink in the glass before taking another sip.

'You know, if we're going to be working together, it would be good to have a name.'

For the first time, the man smiled. The left side of the smile didn't go all the way up because of the scar.

'Where are my manners?' He offered a hand across the table. 'I'm Jonathan. Jonathan Westwick.'

ACKNOWLEDGEMENTS

This book has been a true labour of love for me. I am so proud of the story it tells and the character it brings to life: Mallory.

I couldn't have embarked on such an exciting project without the help of a truly awesome team. My mantra is 'always surround yourself with positive people'. I couldn't have wished for a more positive and creative group to help Mallory into the world.

Thank you to Gavin Bell who has taught me so much about writing fiction. Thank you to everyone on the *Cold Justice* team at Little, Brown/Sphere for believing in me as a thriller writer and most particularly to: Charlie King, Catherine Burke, Lucy Malagoni, Gemma Shelley, Kirsteen Astor, Thalia Proctor, Tom Webster, Sean Garrehy, Sarah Shrubb, Hannah Methuen, Tamsin Kitson, Charlotte Chapman and Oliver Cotton.

Special thanks must go to my editor Ed Wood. From our first meeting, I knew our ambitions were the same and vision aligned. Above and beyond, mate, thank you.

Thank you, as always, to my agents at YMU. Jordan Johnson, you are my man. Thank you to Mary Bekhait, Holly Bott and Lizzie Barroll-Brown. To my literary agent, Amanda Harris, let's keep the bestsellers coming hard and fast. GUYS you are my TEAM!!!

Family is everything: thanks to Terry Batt, my Uncle Tony and Oakley, Shyla, Gabriel, Priseïs and Bligh. And to my beautiful, awesome wife Emelie – you keep the show on the road and allow me realise my ambitions.

And finally, to my readers and listeners. Your support inspires me and drives me on to deliver the very best books I can. I never take your loyalty for granted and am humbled by it every day. Thank you.

Now read on for a sneak peek at
the next action-packed Mallory thriller ...

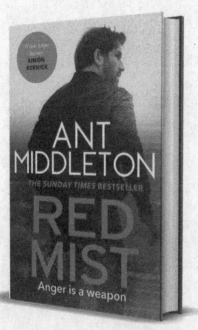

Coming Autumn 2022

1

ST-JEAN-DES-PERTES, NORMANDY

Up until the moment the two guys pulled up in the shiny red Renault Alaskan, shattering the tranquillity with aggressive revs and a radio turned up too way loud, it had been a very pleasant afternoon.

It was a proper French village tavern: white stone walls, a thatched roof, exposed oak beams inside. Mallory was sitting at the table farthest from the bar, by the window that overlooked the Vire as it flowed endlessly by. The place was sublimely quiet. No conversation, no music. If he closed his eyes, he could hear nothing but the flow of water and occasional birdsong.

The job was complete, and today had seen an early finish after four days of back-breaking work. Mallory could barely feel the chill of his beer glass through the new calluses on his hands. He was tired, but it wasn't an unpleasant feeling. He had worked hard, bonded with the rest of the crew, and they had finished the task more quickly than the stony-eyed foreman Philippe had predicted. The Corsican, usually so sour-faced, had even cracked the first smile Mallory had seen on him.

Mallory had tried his hand at a lot of jobs for the first time over the last year, since he'd stepped out of the passenger seat of the long-haul lorry that had carried him from Caen. He had done his share of digging while in the military, but this was the first time he had dug a well. It had been tough work, but he had enjoyed it. It was soothing to clear his mind and focus on nothing but the spade. Dig, shovel, toss, repeat, with the hole growing deeper imperceptibly. The repetition of work that kept the thoughts away.

In the age of peace and quiet before the red truck showed up, Mallory had been wondering what the old man in the corner was upset about.

He looked to be in his seventies or eighties. He was solidly built, wide across the shoulders, with a thick bushy beard that was mostly grey with traces of red. He was dressed like most of the men of his vintage Mallory had encountered in this part of France: dark trousers and a loose cotton shirt. The top two buttons were open, showing a thatch of grey chest hair. He wasn't demonstratively upset. He wasn't sobbing uncontrollably, or rending his garments, or even knocking back that wine he was nursing, but still, Mallory could tell something was wrong. It was a faraway stare that he recognised.

Mallory made a point of minding his own business, as far as was possible, but something about the old man made him curious. He was of half a mind to walk over and strike up a conversation. They were the only two customers. Or rather, the only two drinkers. A young mother wearing pink and black jogging clothes was spooning mush from a Tupperware container into her baby's mouth at a table at the other end of the bar.

All of that went out of Mallory's mind when the red truck rolled to a stop, some kind of raucous French rock band blaring out of the radio.

The old man didn't react. His thousand-yard stare didn't waver, even as the baby spat a mouthful of its food out to wail in displeasure, and the young mum shot an infuriated look in the direction of the car park. Mallory shifted in his seat a little so he could see past the brick pillar in the middle of the room and watch as two men got out.

They were both young, late twenties, perhaps. The driver was over six feet tall and the August sunshine glinted off his shaved head. He stepped out of the truck unhurriedly. He was dressed in camouflage trousers and a white sleeveless T-shirt with the logo of a beer company on it. The passenger seemed in more of a hurry, skirting around the bonnet of the truck like he was worried he might be left behind. He was four or five inches shorter and quite a bit skinnier than his friend, and wore a faded denim baseball cap. They looked similar enough to be brothers, but maybe that was more about their dress and demeanour than anything else. The passenger caught up with the driver and matched his pace as they entered the bar.

Mallory picked his glass up and swirled the remnants of his beer as he watched them approach. The driver raised a hand in greeting to the bartender, who was polishing glasses. He acknowledged the two of them with a wary nod. They stopped halfway across the floor and looked at the old man. If he noticed them, he did not react. Then, as one, they turned the other way and looked at the woman and the baby. She definitely noticed them, but avoided their gaze. The driver kept looking at her while the passenger turned his head to inspect the bottles on the shelf behind the bar. So far, they had taken the time to look at everything and everyone in the place except Mallory.

That was how he knew there was about to be trouble.

They reached the bar, both of them still studiously avoiding Mallory's gaze. The passenger in the truck, the one wearing the denim cap, jutted his chin in the direction of the bartender. 'Laurent. L'habituel, eh?'

The usual.

Mallory's French wasn't anywhere close to fluent yet, but it had come a long way over the long, hot summer.

The bartender muttered something that was a little too fast for Mallory to catch, but he was pretty sure it didn't translate as 'Right away, sir.'

The driver came up with a rejoinder, then smiled and pulled a roll of euros out of his pocket, waving them to show the bartender he was good for a round.

Mallory rolled his shoulders and put his hands on his thighs. He wanted to be ready for the fight he knew was coming. He reminded himself he wasn't looking for trouble. A familiar tingle at the back of his neck suggested that wasn't the whole truth.

The bartender started pouring a couple of beers. Finally, the two men looked over at Mallory. They did it simultaneously, as though responding to a wordless signal.

Mallory felt his pulse slow a little as they approached his table, an almost relaxed feeling. That worried him, because it meant something else was about to take over. As soon as the first punch was thrown, his body would react, and for the duration, proportionality and morality and consequences would cease to be factors. He hoped the two of them would go down easy. It wouldn't do any of them any good to prolong the fight.

The shaved-headed driver broke into a grin as he reached him. He reached a beefy hand out for the chair opposite Mallory and pulled it out, twisting it around so that the back was facing the table, straddled the chair and sat down heavily, resting his forearms on the chair back.

'Bonjour.'

Mallory didn't reply right away. He just stared back at the driver, keeping his own face impassive in contrast to the belligerent grin on the other man's face. The second man had stayed on his feet. He stood a couple of feet back from the table, between Mallory and the door, his hands clasped behind his back like a weekend yacht captain.

After leaving a pause long enough for the grin to start fading, Mallory returned the greeting.

'Bonjour.'